Praise for #1 *New York Times* bestselling author
KRESLEY COLE
and the **IMMORTALS AFTER DARK** series

"When it comes to creating adversarial protagonists who must overcome enormous emotional and deadly obstacles to get their HEA, no one does it better than Cole!"

—*RT Book Reviews*

"Sexy, funny, twisted, and all the wonderful things that make this series a favorite amongst readers."

—*Harlequin Junkie*

"Emotionally compelling . . . equally adventuresome and romantic."

—*Single Titles*

"Packed full of dry, sarcastic humor, crazy violent scenes and super-sexy times . . . there is a reason Kresley Cole is one of my favorite authors."

—*Parajunkee*

Praise for *New York Times* bestselling author
LARISSA IONE
and the MOONBOUND CLAN VAMPIRE series

"Exceptionally entertaining. . . . Ione kicks off a new vampire series [and] does what she does best: paranormal romance with a sexy and dangerous bite!"

—*RT Book Reviews*

"A great series by a fantastic author."

—*Heroes and Heartbreakers*

"Larissa Ione never fails to deliver solid and engaging storytelling, transporting the reader into a world of action-packed dark and gritty goodness. . . . Readers who enjoy escaping into a captivating and seductive PNR world will definitely enjoy the MoonBound Clan Vampire series."

—*Fiction Vixen*

"Absolutely spellbinding in every way possible."

—*Single Titles*

BOOKS BY KRESLEY COLE

The Immortals After Dark Series

The Game Maker Series

The Arcana Chronicles

The MacCarrick Brothers Series

The Sutherland Series

Blood Red Kiss

KRESLEY COLE
LARISSA IONE
GENA SHOWALTER

POCKET BOOKS

New York • London • Toronto • Sydney • New Delhi

Pocket Books
An Imprint of Simon & Schuster, Inc.
1230 Avenue of the Americas
New York, NY 10020

This book is a work of fiction. Any references to historical events, real people, or real places are used fictitiously. Other names, characters, places, and events are products of the author's imagination, and any resemblance to actual events or places or persons, living or dead, is entirely coincidental.

"The Warlord Wants Forever" copyright © 2006 by Kresley Cole
"Forsaken by Night" copyright © 2016 by Larissa Ione
"Dark Swan" copyright © 2016 by Gena Showalter
"The Warlord Wants Forever" was previously published in the anthology
Playing Easy to Get

First Pocket Books paperback edition October 2016

POCKET and colophon are registered trademarks of Simon & Schuster, Inc.

For information about special discounts for bulk purchases, please contact Simon & Schuster Special Sales at 1-866-506-1949 or business@simonandschuster.com.

The Simon & Schuster Speakers Bureau can bring authors to your live event. For more information or to book an event, contact the Simon & Schuster Speakers Bureau at 1-866-248-3049 or visit our website at www.simonspeakers.com.

Interior design by Devan Norman

Manufactured in the United States of America

10 9 8 7 6 5 4 3 2 1

ISBN 978-1-5011-4258-1
ISBN 978-1-5011-4259-8 (ebook)

CONTENTS

THE WARLORD
WANTS FOREVER

Kresley Cole

"I want to know the rules of the game. So I can dominate it."

—NIKOLAI WROTH, VAMPIRE GENERAL,
FORMER HUMAN WARLORD

"No one possesses me, except in their fantasies. I'll kill you as easily as kiss you."

—MYST THE COVETED, CONSIDERED
THE WORLD'S MOST BEAUTIFUL VALKYRIE

Excerpted from
The Living Book of Lore

The Lore
". . . non-human sentient creatures united in one stratum, secret from man's."
- Most are immortal and can regenerate from injuries, killed only by mystical fire or beheading.
- Their eyes change with intense emotion to a breed-specific color.

The Valkyries
"When a maiden warrior screams for courage as she dies in battle, Wóden and Freya heed her call. The two gods strike her with lightning, rescuing her to their hall and preserving her courage forever in the form of the maiden's immortal Valkyrie daughter."
- They take sustenance from the electrical energy of the earth. Their emotions can spark lightning.
- They possess supernatural strength, speed, and senses.

The Vampires
- Two warring factions, the Horde and the Forbearer Army.
- Each adult male seeks his *Bride*, his eternal wife, and walks as the living dead until he finds her.
- A Bride will render his body fully alive, giving him breath and making his heart beat, a process known as *blooding*.
- *Tracing* is teleporting, the vampires' means of travel. A vampire can only trace to destinations he's previously been or to those he can see.

- *The Fallen* are vampires who have killed by drinking a victim to death. Distinguished by their red eyes.

The Horde

"In the first chaos of the Lore, a brotherhood of vampires relied on their cold nature, worship of logic, and absence of mercy to rule. They sprang from the harsh steppes of Dacia and migrated to Russia, though some say a secret enclave, the Daci, live in Dacia still."

- The Fallen comprise their ranks.

The Forbearers

" . . . his crown stolen, Kristoff, the rightful Horde king, stalked the battlefields of antiquity seeking the strongest, most valiant human warriors as they died, earning him the name of Gravewalker. He offered eternal life in exchange for eternal fealty to him and his growing army."

- An army of vampires consisting of turned humans, who do not drink blood directly from the flesh.

The Accession

"And a time shall come when all immortal beings in the Lore, from the Valkyries, vampire, Lykae, and demon factions to the witches, shifters, fey, and sirens . . . must fight and destroy each other."

- A kind of mystical checks-and-balances system for an ever-growing population of immortals.
- Occurs every five hundred years. Or right now . . .

1

*I*f the overgrown vampire didn't stop staring at her, even his talent with a sword wouldn't keep his head upon his shoulders.

The thought made Myst, an immortal known as the Coveted One, grin as she watched two vampire armies battle from her cell window. She leapt up to the sill, curling up and resting her forehead against the reinforced bars.

The poor warlord with his broad shoulders and jet-black hair was about to join a legion of other males—the ones whose last sight had been her smiling face.

She tilted her head when he ducked and ran through an enemy. He was a big male, at least six and a half feet tall, but surprisingly fast.

She knew fighting and liked his style. *Dirty.* He'd cut with his sword then strike out with his fist, or dodge a thrust then throw an elbow.

What she wouldn't give to be down there fighting. In the middle. Against both sides. Against *him.*

She fought dirtier.

His attention continued to stray toward her; once he'd even killed while his gaze was still on her. She'd blown him a kiss, sincerely, choosing to see it as a tribute.

He found time to glance back even as he thundered orders to the army of rebel vampires. His strategy was brilliant, she grudgingly admitted, even though some of his men used firearms.

Loreans scorned human weapons like these. Guns could only kill humans, which was beyond unsporting.

Yet pesky bullets—aside from ruining couture—*hurt*. They could immobilize an immortal for precious seconds, long enough for a dirty fighter to take a foe's head. Used enough times, they could help take an "untakable" castle like Ivo the Cruel's.

Ivo. Her jailer and tormentor.

Myst hardly cared that he was about to have his ass handed to him. Her situation wouldn't change, because these rebels, turned humans known as the Forbearers, were still vampires.

A blood foe is a blood foe is a blood foe. . . .

An explosion rocked the castle, then another. And another. Debris rained from the dungeon ceiling. In neighboring cells, low beings—those who made up the creature-feature underbelly of the Lore—howled.

With each blast, their wails increased in volume, until . . . the battle was over.

Silence. An aftershock here and there. A muted whimper.

The defense of this castle was no more.

Invading rebels searched for enemies, but Ivo and his men weren't fight-to-the-death sorts. They'd probably teleported. *He who fights and runs away, lives to run away another day.* Ha.

The sound of heavy footsteps echoed inside the dungeon. Someone was making his way down the corridor, directly to her cell. . . .

The warlord appeared on the other side of the bars.

From her perch in the window, she examined him. He had thick, straight black hair that hung over his face in careless sections, as if he'd sheared them off with a blade. Some hanks were kept from his field of vision with those small ravel plaits like the berserkers used to wear. His body was powerful, his muscles swollen from use.

She wanted to purr—central casting had just sent her a fierce warlord!

"Come down from there, woman." Deep voice. Russian accent, moneyed, aristocratic.

"Or what? You'll lock me away in a dungeon?"

"I might free you."

She was at the bars before he'd had time to lower his gaze from the window. Had his squared jaw slackened a touch? She listened for a quickening of his heart, but he had no heartbeat whatsoever.

So the vampire was single?

His eyes were clear of the red haze that marked bloodlust, which meant he had never drunk a being to death. But then a Forbearer never took blood straight from the flesh.

Even after beholding her face up close, he didn't

immediately shove the key into the lock to free her. Yet his lips parted, exposing his fangs for her to see. His were kind of sexy—not too prominent or even much longer than a human's canines.

When she saw the short, splendid scar that passed down both of his lips, her lightning struck just outside. Scars, any external evidence of pain, attracted Myst. Pain forged strength. Strength begat electricity. This one could give it to her.

He might even be missing an eye under a thick hank of hair.

She stifled a throaty moan as her hand shot out to brush his hair back. But he was quick, catching her wrist. When she curled one finger in a beckoning gesture, he released her, allowing her to reach forward. She brushed his hair back, revealing a hard-planed, masculine face covered with grit and ash from the battle.

He was still in possession of both of his eyes, and they were *intense*. Flinty gray.

She dropped her hand and gripped the bars, lazily stroking them as her gaze dipped to his mouth again. She was surprised by how carnal she found it, especially since the vampire could use it to hurt her.

The gold chain she'd worn around her waist for millennia now felt heavy on her.

"What are you?" he asked in his pleasingly low voice.

She realized his accent was actually Estonian, not Russian. The general was from neighboring Estonia, which made him a kind of Nordic Russian (though she doubted he would appreciate that description).

She frowned at his question and pulled back her hair to reveal her pointed ear. "Nothing?" She parted her lips and tapped her tongue against her small, dormant fangs. No recognition.

Rumors in the Lore held that King Kristoff and his Forbearers knew little of their fellow immortals. The male before her was an army leader, a general most likely, and he hadn't a clue she was a Valkyrie.

An enemy.

Killing these Forbearers would be easy for her and her sisters. Too easy. Like being your own secret Santa.

Myst had just confirmed rumors of asses and elbows—and this army's inability to differentiate between the two.

"What are you?" Nikolai demanded again, surprised his voice was steady.

When he'd seen this female in the light, he'd felt like exhaling a stunned breath—if his kind respired.

Flawless skin, coral lips, flame-red hair. The eyes that flickered over him were an impossible green.

She was strikingly lovely, with a beauty only hinted at from a distance. On the battlefield, he'd been recklessly drawn to her.

Though she clearly expected him to recognize her kind, he could determine only that she wasn't human. Her ears said fey, but she also had the smallest fangs.

"Free me," the creature said.

"Swear fealty to my king, and I will."

The way she held the bars was suggestive; everything about her was . . . suggestive. "I can't do that, but you've no right to keep me here."

His brother Murdoch passed by, raised his eyebrows at Nikolai's discovery, and muttered in Estonian, "Sweet Christ." Then he walked on.

Why was Nikolai unable to do the same? "What are you?" He wasn't used to his questions going unanswered. "And what's your name?"

Another stroke of the bars. "What do you want it to be?"

He scowled. "Are you a vampire?"

"Not the last time I checked." Her voice was sensual. He couldn't place her drawling accent.

"Are you innocent of malice against us?"

She gave a dismissive wave. "Oh, good gods, no. I love to kill leeches."

"Then rot in here." As if she could kill a vampire. She was scarcely over five feet tall and delicately built—aside from the generous breasts showcased in her tight shirt.

When he turned to go, she called after him, "I smell smoke. Ivo the Cruel burned his records before he fled, didn't he?"

Nikolai stilled, clenching his fists because he'd have to return. "Correct," he grated at the cell once more.

"And this new king's army is full of Forbearers—turned humans?" she asked. "I'll bet you chose to attack this particular Horde stronghold—over the four others, including the royal seat—because you needed Oblak's records."

How did she know their agenda so well?

Nikolai could plan battles and sieges—he'd earned his rank by this victory alone—but he knew nothing of this new world that would help to advance the army. Unfortunately, he wasn't the only one.

"The blind leading the blind," King Kristoff had muttered when they'd found the records reduced to a smoldering heap of ash.

"You think to bargain for your freedom?" Nikolai said. "If you do happen to have information, I can torture you for it."

"I wouldn't recommend that," she said with a laugh. "I dislike torture and grow sulky under pincers."

The *things* in the other cells, many of which he never could have imagined, howled at that.

"Now, let's not quarrel, vampire. Free me, and we'll go to your room and talk." She offered her graceful hand to him. A smudge of ash was stark against her alabaster skin.

"I don't think so."

"You'll call for me. You'll be lonely in your new quarters and will feel out of sorts. I could let you pet my hair until you fall asleep."

He drew in closer to ask in all seriousness, "You're mad, aren't you?"

"As—a—hatter," she murmured back.

He felt a hint of sympathy for the creature. "How long have you been in here?"

"For four long . . . interminable . . . days."

He glowered.

"Which is why I want you to take me with you. I don't eat much."

The dungeon erupted with laughter again.

"Don't hold your breath, female."

"Certainly not like you, Forbearer."

"How did you know what I am? And who we are?"

"I know everything."

If true, she had a wealth they lacked.

"Leave her," Murdoch called at the gateway of the dungeon. His brows were drawn, no doubt in puzzlement at his brother's interest.

Nikolai had never pursued women. When he'd been human, they'd either come to him or he'd gone without. He'd had no time during the war. As a vampire, he had no such need. Not until he could find his Bride.

He shook his head at the insane, fey *creature*, then forced himself to walk on. But he thought he heard her whisper, *"Call for me, General,"* making the hair on the back of his neck stand up.

He followed his brother to Kristoff's new suite. Their king was gazing out into the night from a generous window—one that would be shuttered at dawn. When he turned to them, his gaunt face looked weary.

Kristoff was the sole natural-born vampire among them. Killing his own kind must have been difficult for him, no matter how crazed the Horde had become—and no matter that they followed his uncle Demestriu, who'd stolen his crown centuries ago.

Nikolai had no such hesitation. He was weary, but only because hacking through the Horde had overworked his sword arm. "Were any of the records salvageable?" he asked with little hope.

If the vampires of this castle had spent as much energy fighting as burning, they might have kept Oblak. To Wroth's disgust, they'd fled. He didn't understand it. When defending your home, you fought to the death.

He had.

Kristoff answered, "None."

The rules of this new world were complex and often counterintuitive. Without those records, their own ignorance would defeat them.

Kristoff, the rightful Horde king, had been raised by humans far from Demestriu's reach. For centuries he had lived among mortals, hiding his true nature and discovering little of the Lore. His army consisted of human warriors he'd turned as they died on the battlefield, so they knew nothing more than he did.

Nikolai had thought vampires were mere myths until Kristoff had stood over him like an angel of death, offering eternal life in exchange for eternal fealty.

The Forbearers were trapped in a kind of twilight—no longer human and yet universally shunned by all the factions of the Lore. Those beings hid in the shadows, fleeing from whatever land Kristoff's army occupied, working together to be one step ahead.

Loreans had kept themselves hidden from humanity for ages. That same effort went into keeping Kristoff's soldiers in the dark.

"Any sign of Conrad or Sebastian?" Kristoff asked.

Nikolai shook his head. He hadn't seen his two

other brothers since shortly after they'd been turned. But natural-born vampires often clashed with turned humans, so he and Murdoch had distantly hoped the pair might be in the dungeon of this castle.

"Perhaps the next Horde stronghold."

Nikolai nodded, though he doubted it. He feared his brother Bastian was dead and believed the mind of the youngest, Conrad, was unreachable even if he could be found. The two had not appreciated the eternal life Nikolai and Murdoch had forced on them.

Murdoch seemed unconcerned that they hadn't located their brothers, but then he generally seemed unconcerned about everything.

Though they shared similar looks, he and Nikolai couldn't have been more different in personality. Nikolai believed in Kristoff's cause, seeing many parallels to his own past, and wanted to continue to fight. Murdoch didn't particularly care. Nikolai suspected his brother fought only as a favor to him—or because they had nothing else now.

"Nikolai found a being in the dungeon," Murdoch said. "She seems to have extensive knowledge of the Lore."

"What kind of being?"

Nikolai answered, "I have no idea. She appears fey, with pointed ears. But she also has small fangs, and her fingernails are more like . . . claws. She's not a vampire."

Kristoff frowned at that. "Perhaps she's born of more than one species?"

"Possibly." More speculation. Nikolai was sick of it. He wanted to know the rules of the game.

So he could *dominate* it.

"Find out everything you can from her."

"She won't talk," Nikolai said. "I've interrogated enough to predict that. And she hates vampires."

Kristoff's eyes narrowed. "Then we'll treat her as the Horde would. If we haven't extracted information from the rest of the prisoners by tomorrow night, torture her for it."

Nikolai nodded, but the idea sat ill with him. As a human, he'd been merciless to his enemies, but he'd never tortured a woman.

She isn't truly a woman, he reminded himself. She was a Lore female, and their army's survival could depend on the knowledge she held.

Perhaps he'd never tortured a woman because he'd never needed to.

As he made his way to his new chambers, Nikolai realized the creature had been right. He *was* going to call her up to him.

To do what with her, he didn't know.

2

"*D*id you miss me? Because *I* missed *you*," the female said when a guard escorted her inside his new bedroom and withdrew.

Out of habit, Nikolai stood—his ingrained habit when a lady entered—and she flashed him a brilliant smile. "A gentleman warrior. Who cleans up very well." She fanned herself with her hand. "I think I'm in love."

He didn't answer, and she didn't seem to mind as she surveyed the room. "Retro Nosferatu. Not what I would have done, but then I'm not married to sunproof shutters like you must be." With a shrug, she headed for the bathroom. "Taking a shower," she said airily over her shoulder.

He raised his brows in surprise. Not knowing what else to do, he said, "Very well," and sat once more.

At the doorway, she removed her tight blouse, leaving only a lacy black bra. She turned to him, revealing her scantily clad breasts. When she bent to remove her boots, creamy flesh almost spilled free.

Why give him this show? He was usually quick to determine people's motives. Yes, she wanted her freedom, but he didn't believe she'd sleep with him for it.

Perhaps she was truly mad? Most maddened people didn't think they were, but she seemed to be proud of it.

Maybe she simply didn't view stripping in front of him and making herself at home in a stranger's bedroom as odd. In fact, he suspected she didn't see them as strangers at all.

She untied the fastening of her silky skirt, and it too fell to the ground, leaving her in only that bra and an intricate pair of wispy black underwear. They were like a work of art—or a ribbon decorating one.

A fine gold chain around her tiny waist caught his attention. The unusual design appeared very old, but the metal gleamed like new when she moved.

She gave him a teasing smile. "Vampire like?"

He scowled because he did like. Very much.

She unfastened the front of her bra. Would she remove—

Off went her bra.

He ran a hand over his mouth at the sight of those high, plump breasts. Could they be any more beautiful? He could spend hours tonguing those coral-pink nipples and fondling her pale flesh.

He began to speak, then had to cough into his fist to continue. "You'll strip in front of a vampire when you don't even know his name?"

She gasped with mock horror and covered her breasts with her hands. "You're right! So what's your name?"

"My answer will be as forthcoming as yours. What do you want it to be?"

She smiled at that, then replied, "Some kind of

name befitting a battle-scarred, overgrown vampire warlord."

Battle-scarred? Overgrown? Why in the hell should he care how she saw him? She was divinely wrought, but mad. He'd take his scars with his sanity. "Nikolai Wroth," he grated.

For a second, he thought recognition flickered in her eyes.

But then she breathed, "Oh, you are good. Wroth, the old word for rage? That's a bingo idea for a warlord name." Her hands dropped. "I'll just call you by that." She shook her head with a rueful smile, as if she couldn't believe he was so clever.

. . . as a hatter.

Then she leaned back against the doorway, raising her arms above her head and grasping her elbows. Displaying her mouthwatering breasts and flashing a flirtatious smile that would've dropped most men to their knees, she asked in that whiskey voice, "Care to join me, *Wroth*?" She winked when she said his name and rolled her hips.

"No," he bit out. He didn't want her to know his body didn't respond to hers. His mind did, his vague memories of being human did. But not his body.

He was the walking dead. No respiration, no heartbeat, no sexual need—or ability. Not until he found his predestined Bride and she blooded him fully.

With his blooding, something inside him— maybe even his soul—would recognize her as *his*, the woman he could love without measure (if one believed in love). And his body would wake for her.

In the past, he'd yearned for his Bride because she would bring him power—he would become as strong as blooded vampires, his senses as acute as theirs—but he'd never missed sex before this.

And Nikolai knew she was not his. This display should've blooded any vampire.

She shrugged, the movement a sight to behold, then entered the bathroom. Ten minutes later, she emerged with a towel wrapped around her.

He suspected she'd used his toothbrush, which charmed him for some reason.

She traipsed to his closet and dropped the towel, leaving her with only her chain.

At the sight of her exquisite ass, he swallowed. "Have you no modesty?" Never in his life had he encountered a female so quick to be naked. Of course, he'd never encountered a female who should so utterly be naked at any chance.

"Not at my age," she said. He frowned. She looked young, maybe early twenties.

When she began exploring his recently unpacked clothing, he found his head tilting as she moved. The chain swayed at her waist, and her long, damp hair cascaded over her breasts. She turned, giving him a particularly rewarding glimpse.

He stifled a groan. A true redhead. And he couldn't have her. "How old are you?" he rasped.

"Physiologically, I'm twenty-five. Chronologically, I'm . . . not."

"So you are an immortal?"

An amused smile played about her lips. "I am." She pulled on one of his shirts. It swallowed her, the collar baring one shoulder, the hem hitting her knees.

"Why did you stop aging at twenty-five?"

"When I was strongest. Not for the same reason you were frozen at"—she eyed him—"thirty-four?"

"Thirty-five. And why do you think I stopped aging then?"

She ignored him to continue digging. After a few moments, she plucked an antique bejeweled cross from his bag. She held the relic away from her, keeping her gaze from it. "You're Catholic?"

"Yes. It was a gift from my father." To help keep him alive in wartime. Nikolai shook his head at the irony of just how well it had worked. "I thought I was the one who should be repelled by a cross."

"Only a turned human would say that. Besides, I'm in no way repelled. With jewels like that? If I look at it, I'll want it."

"So you wouldn't want it because you're Catholic?"

"My family was orthodox pagan. Can I have it? Can I, can I, Wroth?"

"Put it back," he said, fighting the unfamiliar urge to grin.

With a pouty expression, she returned it, mumbling something about tightfisted vampires. Then she dipped her feet into his boots and turned to him with her hands on her hips.

His lips almost curled at the sight of her, a mad pagan immortal trying on his boots.

"What did your mother feed you?" she teased. "Renaissance anabolics?"

His urge to smile faded. "My mother died young."

"So did mine." He thought he heard her murmur, *"The first time."*

"And I was born after the Renaissance."

She withdrew her feet from his boots and sauntered past him. "But not by much."

"That's true. And why do you think I stopped aging at thirty-five?" he asked again.

She frowned as if she didn't know where his question had come from, then said, "Because naughty Kristoff found you dying on a battlefield, decided you'd make a fine recruit, then made you drink his blood. Bit a wrist open, perhaps? Then with his vampiric hoodoo blood in your veins, he let you die. Unless he was in a hurry, in which case he would've killed you. A couple of nights later, you rose from the dead—probably with a frown on your face as you thought, *Holy shit, it worked!*"

He ignored the last and asked, "How do you know the blood ritual?" He'd thought only vampires knew the true way to turn a human. In books, the change always came as a result of a vampire's bite, when in fact a human had more chance of turning if *he* bit a vampire.

"Like I said, I know everything."

Yes, but he was learning. She was an immortal who'd been frozen physiologically at twenty-five. If a pagan, she was at least several hundred years old. She knew of the blood ritual, and that Kristoff "recruited" his soldiers straight from the battlefield.

She scooped up her clothes, marched to his door, and yanked it open, then snapped her fingers for a guard. Nikolai merely watched like a bystander.

"Psst, minion. I need these laundered. Very little starch. Don't just stand there gawking, or you'll anger my good frenemy General Wroth. We're like *this*." She twined two fingers together.

Once she'd foisted her laundry on the guard, she closed the door and dramatically leaned back against it—as if to say, *You can't get away from me now.* Then she glided over to him.

As a rule, he observed, he calculated, and he waited for his move, but he'd never enjoyed watching events unfurl this much. Unpredictable didn't begin to describe—

She clutched his shoulders and straddled him.

Nothing between them but his pants and a few inches. He could *feel* her heat.

She was definitely not his Bride or he would've ripped through his zipper to get inside her. His heart would've started to beat, his lungs drawing their first breath. In the space of one of those breaths, he would've been buried so deep in her tightness, wrenching her down on him. . . .

"Now, Wroth, we need to work out some logistics. When I'm kept as a pet, my care is very involved."

His brows drew together. "I have no wish to keep you as a pet."

"You hold me prisoner. You think to order me. How does this differ?"

"You're not a pet," he insisted. He couldn't think—her eyes were mesmerizing, and her sex remained so close to his. That heat . . .

She leaned in to murmur at his ear, "What if I want to be your pet? Would you like that, vampire?"

She grasped his wrists and moved his arms to the chair's armrests. She gave both of his hands a squeeze—to tell him she wanted them to stay there?

He wasn't about to move, couldn't imagine what she'd do next.

Her fingers brushed their way over his chest, unbuttoning his shirt. "If I was your pet, you could keep me for your pleasure, and I would serve you in every way you desire." She pulled his shirt open, clearly admiring his chest. "Hard." Her voice was breathy. "Scars." She moistened her lips. "At sunrise, you would fall asleep still deep inside my body. I'd wake you at sunset with my lips wrapped around your shaft. You could break your fast with a drink— from one of my thighs."

God almighty.

Her hand trailed down, her eyes raptly following the jagged scar that had been his deathblow. "I am here for the taking and ache for your touch." Before he could grip her wrist, she'd reached down and cupped him.

His lack of an erection didn't seem to surprise her.

Her seductive look vanished as she felt his cock. "Well, my word, Wroth." She arched an eyebrow. "If you were hard, I wouldn't know whether to be tantalized or terrified."

Then with blurring speed she was off him and on the bed, lying on her stomach, chin propped on her hands. She was unaffected by what had just occurred, while he was angered and . . . shamed. He wanted to show her *hard.*

"How do you plan to keep me here during the

day?" she asked. "An unblooded Forbearer shouldn't be so difficult to vanquish."

Vanquished by her? Amusing. "I'll send you back to the cell. You want to be my pet? I'll take you out of your cage and put you back in at my pleasure."

She blinked at him. "You don't want to send me back. Who will entertain you? I can deal poker *and* make shadow animals."

He shook himself. This was just another instance of the Lore playing with them. She was not *normal*.

If she could be unaffected, he could pretend it. "I want you to answer some questions. I need to know what you are and what your name is."

"I might tell you if you answer some of my own questions."

"Done," he said quickly. "Ask."

"Were you afraid when Kristoff stood over you?"

Strange question. "I was . . . tired."

"Most mortals would have been terrified to see the Gravewalker."

"Is that what he's called?" Kristoff would find that amusing. At her nod, he said, "Well, I'd seen a lot by then."

"What's his agenda? Does he want to replace Demestriu?"

Nikolai hesitated, then answered honestly, hoping she would do the same. "He wants his crown back, but he doesn't want to rule over any faction except our own."

"Uh-huh." She raised an eyebrow as if she didn't believe him, then asked, "That was your brother in the dungeon?"

"Murdoch, yes."

"Turned vampires don't usually have *family*."

"Murdoch died in the same battle. I've two other brothers turned later as well."

"You're young. Yet you're a general. How'd you swing that?"

He was more than three hundred years old. Young compared to her? "I refused to accept the dark gift unless certain conditions were met."

Her eyes grew bright with new interest, and she patted the bed for him to come sit with her. He felt as if he was on the verge of learning something, so he complied, resting against the headboard to face her, stretching his legs out.

He almost laughed. The first time he'd been in bed with a woman in centuries—and she was easily the most beautiful of any before—yet he could do nothing with her. He couldn't even drink her, though his fangs ached to pierce the pale column of her neck. Thank God he'd fed before he'd sent for her.

"Wroth, you *bartered* with Kristoff as you lay dying?"

When put like that, his negotiation sounded more reckless than it'd been. As Nikolai had lain in his own cooling blood, nearly freed of the constant struggle, of the never-ending war, of starvation and disease, he'd told Kristoff, "You need me more than I need to live."

Kristoff had seen him in many battles and agreed.

"I did," Nikolai said. "I was used to giving orders and would take them from no one but a powerful king. I wanted my brother turned if he was dying, and trusted compatriots as well. Kristoff complied."

That wasn't all. Nikolai had asked for sixty years so he and Murdoch could watch over the rest of their living family—their father, four sisters, and two other brothers.

Already too late to save them. . . .

"You know, I'd heard of you when you were a human," she said. "Weren't you called the Overlord?"

This surprised him. "By kinder tongues. How could you have heard of me? Your accent isn't from the northlands."

She sighed. "Not anymore. I'd heard of you because I'm interested in all things martial. You were quite the vicious leader."

His voice grew cold. "We were defending. I was anything I needed to be to see it done."

Her lips parted. As if she couldn't help herself, she sidled closer to him on the bed.

She'd clearly liked his answer.

More gently, she said, "But in the end, you lost."

He stared past her. "Everything." The enemy had already scorched and salted their lands. Famine and plague had followed. Nikolai's country had been like a dying man, that last battle the final blow.

"Wroth," she said softly. He turned his gaze to her. "Let's make a pact, you and I." Her eyes were so captivating in her ethereal face. "Let's vow we won't harm each other in this room."

When he nodded, she flashed him a warm smile that made him feel praised. She guided him to lie back, and he complied. What would she do next?

She eased open his legs and knelt between them. With the back of her hand, she smoothed her damp hair to one side, baring her tantalizing neck.

A rush of her intoxicating scent swept him up, like a drug. If she smelled like this, what would she taste like? Heaven?

He wished she'd bared her supple flesh in offer to him. He imagined her cry as he pierced her for the first time. . . .

"Wroth, this is embarrassing," she murmured in a sensual voice, "but I think I've caught you staring at my neck. Hungrily."

"You did," he admitted. She'd caught him contemplating his order's most reviled crime, and yet he felt no shame. Odd.

She brushed her fingertips over her skin. "Are you tempted to take a drink from me?"

In the worst way.

He wondered how many times Ivo had sampled her and felt some unfamiliar feeling claw in his gut. "We don't drink from living beings. It's how we got our name." Forbearing was his order's pledge, their pact. Nikolai had never tasted flesh as he drank.

But then, he'd had no inclination to before her. "Why?"

"So we are never lured to kill," he said, giving her the official line, which was true, but the whole truth was more complicated. And they kept the details they'd managed to learn secret.

When a vampire drank living blood, blood not separated from its source, he would harvest his victim's memories. Kristoff believed these memories drove natural-born vampires insane and turned their eyes permanently red.

As far as the Forbearers could determine, the only way to avoid this was to drink blood that had died, avoiding the evils—and the benefits.

"What if you drank from an immortal who couldn't be killed from that?" she asked, her words lulling. He couldn't seem to take his eyes from hers.

An immortal would have far too many plaguing memories, vastly more than a mortal. He answered her question with one of his own. "Do you want me to take your flesh, creature?" The mere idea made his words rough, his fangs ache.

At her titillated look, he feared she'd say yes, calling his bluff. What would he do then?

"Rain check," she answered brightly. Then, to his shock, she curled up between his legs. Nuzzling her face against his uncovered torso, she wrapped her pale arms around his thigh.

"I never asked my questions," he said, staring at the ceiling, trying to sound casual. He'd seen a great many things in his life, but this female was throwing him.

"We have all the time in the world for that, do we not?" She kissed the scar on his lower stomach—and gave it a slow little lick.

He lay tensed, rasping, "At least tell me your name."

"Myst," she whispered, then fell asleep.

Myst. How fitting that she was named after something intangible and capricious.

In sleep, his little pagan clutched his leg with her pink claws. And they *were* claws, sharp and curling, though somehow elegant. Imagining that she clutched him for comfort, he ignored the pain, for it was little compared to his sense of satisfaction.

For hundreds of years, their army had been constantly on the move, hiding in the shadows of the northlands in grueling conditions, keeping their growing numbers secret. Everything had been about the war, all adding up to this attack.

Now he savored merely *resting* with her, doing nothing but watching as her hair dried into glossy red curls.

He brought a lock to his face and brushed it over his lips. So soft, like her flawless skin. Tomorrow night, if she hadn't given him information, could he lash her skin to get at her secrets? After Myst had clung to him so trustingly?

Could he break her bones and bear seeing pain in those green eyes?

If she were his Bride, he would have been forbidden from ever harming her—his life given over to protecting hers.

He ran the backs of his fingers down her silken cheek as her light, quick breaths warmed his stomach. He had never truly felt the sting of jealousy in his life, had never envied other men—except those who enjoyed peace in their land.

Nikolai had been born affluent, his family aristocratic, and fortune had followed him until the latter years of his mortality. To envy was to lack.

So why did he want to destroy any vampire who might be blooded by her?

3

Where the hell is my warlord?

Myst jerked upright, waking from her first real sleep since she'd been taken by the Horde. She was alone in Wroth's bed, her laundered clothes folded at the foot. He'd even drawn a blanket over her. *Awww.*

She needed to keep up with him until her sisters broke her out of this pokey. According to plan, they would extract her from Oblak at dawn tomorrow.

Once more Myst swore that she would never again be bait—and this time she meant it.

Rumor was rife in the Lore, but tales of Ivo the Cruel making dark alliances had proved worrisome enough for the Valkyries to investigate.

Operation: Myst Gets Nabbed.

She'd learned little about Ivo for her troubles—the acting, the letting herself get caught, etc.—only that he was definitely planning something major.

She chuckled. Well, at least until General Wroth had punked his ass out of a castle.

No, she hadn't learned much about Ivo, but Kristoff and the general would make good dish. What if this king wanted to kill Demestriu—only to rule over his own kind? Was it possible not all leeches had a predisposition toward sociopathic evil?

What if the Valkyries didn't have to war with these Forbearers?

Doubtful. Her sisters wouldn't discriminate between the two vampire factions. They'd behead first and then say, "Fuckity, were you good? Oops!" Vampires were too powerful a species to go unchecked.

Demestriu and his Horde had been brutal to all the Lore, but especially the Valkyries. Fifty years ago, Furie, their queen, the strongest and fiercest of them all, had tried to assassinate him. She'd never returned.

Tales abounded that Demestriu had chained Furie to the bottom of the sea—a never-ending torture for an immortal. If true, Furie had been drowning again and again only to have her immortality revive her.

Once the Valkyrie covens found and freed her at last, their queen would be as none other on earth, awash in rage. Furie wouldn't check for vampire affiliation before she slaughtered, and she would expect her sisters to follow her example.

So until the Valkyries decided on their plan of action with the Forbearers, Myst would go about business as usual. Which meant she needed to find Wroth.

Before he'd come, she'd been powerless here. She could handle weapons as well as most of her kind, but a sword and bow were not her strengths.

Her preferred weapon was men.

She manipulated them, played them, made them believe she lived for them alone—in order to have them do her bidding. That was her m.o.

Furie had once asked her, "Why would you ever send a man to do a woman's job?"

Confused, she'd answered, "Because. I. Can."

And now Myst had one in her clutches—a big, scarred one with skin she wanted to lick until her tongue got tired.

Or she'd had him. *Where is he?*

The problem with Ivo's vampires: they'd had no appreciation for her whatsoever. At least Wroth liked to look at her.

For the Horde, blood was all-important, and she could neither withhold it nor capitalize on it.

Their eyes were red from sucking the life from their victims to the very marrow—not from merely drinking from the flesh, as these Forbearers feared. One kill while feeding put a vampire in a downward spiral, because bloodlust compelled him to do it over and over.

The buildup of their victims' memories over the years drove many of them mad.

Yet for the last four nights, Ivo and his men had never tried to drink from her, vacillating, examining her as she yawned with boredom.

Finally, she'd snapped, "Get dental with me or don't, but make a damned decision." Ivo's eyes had slitted with menace, his red gaze a contrast to his pale face and shaven head. In the end, he'd decided not to drink from her, thinking her too old, her blood brimming with too many memories.

Worked for her. In fact, she'd never been bitten.

She wondered what it would have been like for Wroth to take her neck when his irises had flickered black with want.

She was an awful person, weak and perverted even to entertain these thoughts. Probably the only

Valkyrie on earth who'd ever fantasized about a vampire. She frowned. No. There'd been one other. . . .

Myst tapped her chin, wondering if she should tell the Forbearers they forwent for really no reason.

Neh.

Maybe if the scrumptious general continued to be nice to her, she'd hint a little. She actually had heard of him back in the day. Most Valkyries had.

Naturally, they'd sent a correspondent into the field to cover that northlands war, and she'd reported that Wroth had been cunning, brave, and deliciously ruthless to his enemies. Though the Overlord had lost in the end against a much larger force, he'd bought his people at least a decade of protection.

Myst and her sisters had sat by the hearth, sighing over tales of his deeds. She remembered feeling loss at the news of his defeat, because a great man like him would've fought to the death.

But he'd made a comeback, and in person, he hadn't disappointed. Except for the fact that he was now a mortal enemy—or rather, an immortal mortal enemy. Oh, and a leech.

She tried the door to his room, in case he'd decided to trust her. Locked. But not mystically reinforced the way her cell was.

She could have broken out with ease, but she didn't have to be back in the dungeon until dawn. So she dressed and piled her hair up in a way she thought he'd like, and still had time to root through his things again. She averted her eyes from the jeweled cross, lest she get sticky-fingered with it.

She investigated his clothes—his style was

modern but still aristocratic somehow—and inhaled his scent. She rolled in the bed with one of his big cable-knit sweaters, her face buried in it, uncaring if he returned and found her like that.

But he never showed.

In time, two guards arrived to escort her back to the dungeon, as per his orders. Wroth wasn't keeping her? The vampires wouldn't meet her eyes as they ushered her down to her cell.

Once they'd locked her in, she paced the area. She was in trouble, and she knew why. His words echoed in her memory: "If you do happen to have information, I can torture you for it."

The dungeon was eerily quiet, all the other cells emptied. The low creatures had been taken away already, no doubt tortured and killed.

None of them would've talked. Before Wroth had summoned her, she'd given her fellow prisoners some friendly advice: "Say nothing to these rebel vampires. Or else my sisters and I will peel you and your families. Good talk, buddies."

No vampire threat could trump Myst's.

The leeches might come and take one's village, but Valkyries would creep in, hiding under a bed to take one's head from one's pillow. *And may you never feel a Valkyrie's breath at your back* was a drinking toast among the Lore. Their word was law.

Which left only her. . . .

She looked up when she heard the warlord's footsteps echoing over stone.

A guard opened the cell for him, then left them alone in the dungeon.

"Listen carefully, Myst," Wroth said. "I'm going to ask you questions about your kind and the different factions in the Lore. You must answer them. Or else I've been ordered to get the information from you by force."

"Torture, then? You can't disobey Kristoff for me?"

"You know I'd be dead if not for him. My brothers and friends as well. My life has not been my own since that night." He was actually serious about this.

But then, Myst hadn't been kidding about torture; it really did piss her off.

She'd given Wroth preferential treatment because he was, like, a *celebrity* in martial circles. But now she needed to accept his descent into vampirism. She'd push and cajole to the end, but after that . . . *Bring it, leech.* "You could help me escape."

He narrowed those gray eyes. "I swore my fealty, and I'll see my vow through. Answer or face the consequences," he said. "I'll begin with the most basic. What are you?"

"Pussycat Doll?" she asked, immediately doing a slow headshake. "Judge, jury, and executioner." He scowled. Her eyes lit up. "Transient! What? Really. No? Babe in Toyland?"

"Damn it, just answer the questions. Then you can come back up to my room." He lowered his voice and curled his finger under her chin. "We can sleep together again as we did today."

"Enduring torture would be easier than going back to the Lore as an informant." She'd no longer be an A-lister, an avoid-at-all-costs enemy. She'd lose her status as a creature with which one did not fuck.

"We've tried to get information from the others—"

"But they didn't talk either, huh?" Had she sounded smug?

He seemed to shake himself, hardening his resolve. "You're leaving me little choice."

Well. She was about to experience firsthand the Overlord's ruthlessness she'd admired. Apparently he'd decided she was an enemy, just when she'd thought they were getting kinda cozy.

Way to hurt my feelings, Wroth. She sniffled. *Now I'll really have to kill you.*

With his thoughts constantly on her throughout the night, Nikolai had stalled for hours. He'd interrogated the other creatures till nearly dawn; at least her questioning would be brief.

"You're truly going to do this?" she asked as she turned from him, moving into the back corner. Her shoulders began shaking. Was she laughing?

He crossed to her, taking her arm and turning her. Genuine tears streamed down her heartbreakingly beautiful face.

"Wroth, I thought we had an arrangement." She cast him a brows-drawn look of betrayal.

She wasn't feigning this. In her wild, mixed-up mind, she had thought they were . . . friends?

The cell wobbled, and he braced himself, but she seemed not to notice. Probably just aftershocks from last night.

He didn't want her to hurt. But her eyes blazed with it, raw and true and bare. He was actually seeing *her*—without her false swagger and play. Suddenly he found it unbearable as each tear fell. When one dropped to her cheek, he flinched as if he'd been hit.

The cell shook again.

She lowered her face and wiped her tears away. When she gazed up, her expression was blatantly sexual. Yet another mask.

"Myst, I don't want to hurt you, but you must answer my questions. This isn't a game."

"Oh, but it is," she murmured. "You want to know about the Lore? Learn this lesson well—we are all pawns."

The castle quaked once more. Explosions? He glanced around wildly, but she didn't even blink. "What are you?" he demanded again. No, his surroundings weren't shaking.

The sound booming in his ears like an earthquake was coming from . . . within him.

Myst pressed her hand against his chest—to feel his heart stutter to life. Because he'd finally recognized her for what she was. . . .

"Apparently, I'm your Bride."

4

"I was wondering if I could get this to beat for me," Myst purred to Wroth, as he struggled to hide his shock.

She'd heard that a blooded vampire's new heartbeat was deafening, the rush of sexual desire overwhelming.

With soft touches, she coaxed him to lean against the wall. She rubbed his chest as he took his first unpracticed breath. "How does the air in your lungs feel?"

He inhaled deeply. "Cold. Pressure, but it feels good." He looked at her with such gratitude for blooding him.

They always did.

Her hand dipped. "How does your blood feel, heating and moving?"

His eyes went heavy-lidded. "Stronger. It's . . . searing."

When she palmed his erection through his pants, he threw back his head to bellow.

My gods. She'd known Wroth was well endowed, but hard, he was like a demon or a Lykae.

He curved her fingers around his thick shaft and slowly thrust against her palm.

In a sensual whisper, she asked, "How does this feel when it swells and distends?" She stroked his length, relieved she'd never have to take his uncomfortable size within her.

"So damned good," he grated with a shudder.

"It's been three centuries?" When she imagined the onslaught of lust clawing at him, her body softened. Could she still desire him—even after he'd planned to torture her? "Well, you are due, I suppose," she said, unzipping his pants and reaching inside. She thumbed the slick tip of his penis.

His eyes rolled back in his head, and he groaned, "*Yes*, touch me." He thrust again. "Take me in hand."

But she only continued her light teasing. "Does your shaft ache to be stroked? Does it throb from that hot, undeniable pressure to come? Your cock's so heavy and tight—you must be close to exploding."

Brows drawn, he stared at her. "Why are you tormenting me?"

Because I can.

His eyes were growing black. Soon he would attack.

Five, four, three, two . . .

Wroth snatched her wrists in a viselike grip, securing them behind her back. Then he slanted his mouth over hers, seeming to brand her with his lips and tongue. He took her mouth deeply, *possessively*.

She found herself responding. When her tongue met his, he groaned into their kiss. Sharing breaths, tongues twining . . .

He left her panting when he bent down to lick her nipples, sucking at them through her blouse. His other hand cupped her sex, fingers rubbing a moan out of her.

Yet he abruptly drew back from her. "Come with me."

Damn it, dawn neared. Where were her sisters? She had to keep him here. She cried, "But I can't wait!"

"Won't claim my Bride in a dungeon."

"Wroth"—she gripped his cock hard while whispering in his ear—"my body weeps for this coming inside me."

With a growl, he tore open her blouse and bra. He stared at her naked breasts and licked his sexy lips. Then he set in, suckling her stiff nipples.

Her back arched, pressing her breasts to his gorgeous mouth. To his wicked tongue. When had she begun undulating her hips for him?

"I've waited for you," he rasped against her breast. "So long I've waited."

One hand pinned her wrists above her; the other shot up her skirt and ripped her panties away. His fingers roved between her thighs, hot and slow. "As soon as I saw you, I wanted it to be you." Using her moisture, he thumbed her clitoris in slick, mindnumbing circles.

Unable to control herself, she rocked to his fingers. Myst made a decision then. There was simply no way she could miss out on this. She gave an abandoned moan, and her sharp emotions triggered lightning outside.

"My Bride's so wet." He sucked a hardened nipple till it throbbed, then turned to the other one for the same attention.

She arched her back more, offering up her breasts. "Yes, yes, it feels so *good*." She yearned to stroke his shaft, but her hands were trapped.

He sank one finger into her sheath, withdrew, then returned with two. He slid them into her unhurriedly, but with enough force that she was rocked to her toes each time.

She widened her legs, about to come around his fingers. "Don't stop." She panted, so close.

"Never." He thrust harder, until she didn't know if her toes even touched the ground.

When he spread his fingers inside her, she whimpered at the overwhelming fullness. She hooked her leg over his bent knee, opening herself even more to him.

At her ear, he rumbled the words, "Come for me, *milaya*."

"Ah, yes . . . *Wroth*," she moaned again, about to succumb to his stroking. "So close! So—" She gave a strangled scream. Pleasure seized her as she toppled over the brink. *"Yes! Yes!"* Rolling her hips to his masterful touch, she orgasmed for the vampire, squeezing his fingers with a fiery, wet pulsing.

"I can *feel* you, feel you coming!" he grated. Even when she was too sensitive, he didn't stop until she helplessly cried his name.

Her release had staggered her—and made him groan as if he'd come as well.

Spent, she sagged against him, still weakly undulating for him. Her nipples were damp and achy from his tongue.

He cupped the back of her neck and yanked her

up to face him. Lust made his voice harsh as he said, "I will be good to you, Myst. I will protect you. *You are mine*." When he fumbled with his pants to free himself, her heavy-lidded eyes widened.

He'd said those things because he planned to shove that huge shaft inside her. To *claim* her. A true vampire's Bride.

Alarm made her heart race. Yet then, she heard a whisper at the dungeon entrance.

Before Nikolai could react, Myst flung herself away. Why would she do that? He reached to pull her back, but she shrank from him.

Why wasn't he inside her right now? He'd made sure she was wet, ready to receive him—

He heard movement inside the dungeon and jerked his head around, fangs sharpening in fury.

"Look at the lovebirds." A creature similar to Myst was standing at the cell door, a bow at the ready.

A second female with glowing skin joined the first, chewing gum and flipping a dagger in the air. "Don't make me look—I think I'll be sick. Myst, cavorting with a vampire is a new low even for you."

"What is this?" Nikolai demanded, stalking toward them.

With supernatural speed, the archer nocked an arrow and let it sing. He traced to dodge it; she'd anticipated his move, and the arrow pinned him to the wall. A second arrow took his other shoulder, drilling its tip half a foot into the stone.

Casting her a killing look, he lunged forward to

let the arrows tear through him—but the shafts were ringed like shank nails.

When he realized he wouldn't be moving, he bellowed with rage.

Myst had pulled her clothing together and turned toward the door.

"Don't you walk away from me!"

"So sorry to interrupt your plans." She cast him that hurt look. "You almost made me forget you'd come down here to torture me. You want to learn? Know that we *hate* torture. It starts to add up over the years."

"That was before I knew you were my Bride."

Her face went cold. "Before you knew you could screw me? Now that your body's in working order, you won't flay the skin from mine?"

"You're my Bride. *Mine.* You belong *to me.*"

She flew back at him, enraged. The bright one tossed her the dagger, and Myst caught it behind her without looking.

What the hell is she?

She pressed the blade to his jugular. Her pupils had turned *silver.* "If I *belonged* to every man who wanted it so—or to every vampire I've blooded—there'd be nothing left of me."

"You've not blooded others! They would be here protecting you, fighting for you."

"Not"—she leaned in closer, tilting her head like an animal—"if I killed them all." She grabbed the back of his head and pressed her lips against his, kissing him hard.

He tasted . . . her blood. Unimaginably warm and

rich, it was as exquisite as everything else about her. He shuddered in ecstasy at the luscious taste.

She drew back with an inscrutable expression on her face.

"You know I'll want nothing else now," he rasped.

She snapped her teeth at him, then exited the cell.

"Don't walk away from me!"

Myst commanded the others, "Leave him."

As he strained to free himself, the other two Valkyries exchanged a confused glance.

The archer said, "And by 'leave him,' you clearly mean leave him beheaded, disemboweled, and chock-full of quills like a pincushion."

"You heard him—I'm his Bride."

"Ohhh," the bright one said, blowing a bubble. "You mean he hasn't released the first time since his blooding?" With a quick glance at his crotch, she said, "And he stays like that without you, right?" She chuckled. "I'm cool with the plan."

The archer wasn't convinced. "Don't get me wrong, I enjoy condemning vampires to unending sexual torture as much as the next fabulously talented huntress—" A guard charged in, and she leisurely shot an arrow in that direction. Tilting her head at the result, she sighed. "—but *Vampire Bride* sounds so B-movie. He just dragged you down to B-moviedom."

The bright one made her voice overly dramatic: "For that alone . . . *he must die*. Seriously, Myst. Your 'husband' has damaged your street cred beyond repair. Unless you kill him like the others."

They were all mad.

Yet still he was hard, aching for her, for the blood she'd given him just to torture him. "You evil, teasing witch. Kill me then."

He might have imagined a flicker of compassion in her eyes, but then she shrugged.

His hazy mind grasped his future. She was going to abandon him with a body knotted from lust and a taste of blood he would go to his knees for. "You're the most malicious bitch I've ever known."

"Flatterer," she chirped. Across the corridor, she leapt dozens of feet to a barred window. She plucked the metal grid free, as she might a piece of lint.

"I will find you," he bit out. "I will find you and make you pay for this a thousand times."

She offered a hand for the others; the bright one bounded up and caught Myst's forefinger with her own. "Sounds like he's setting up a date," she said as she dangled.

"Oooom," Myst purred, her gaze flickering over him. "Dress casual."

5

Never-ending sexual desire that could never be slaked.

Five years ago, his Bride had knowingly—delightedly—damned Nikolai to this torment. She'd blooded him, giving him his first carnal need as a vampire, then stoked it to a fever pitch.

Yet he couldn't lose his seed the first time without his Bride.

His cock hard and aching, Nikolai tossed in his bed at Oblak. His length throbbed so painfully, sleep was forever elusive. He'd gone weeks without.

If only she had stayed long enough for him to claim her, or merely to touch her skin as he'd taken his own ease. She could've spared him. But she'd *wanted* him to suffer.

Why else would she have given him her blood? The minuscule drop taken directly from her flesh had cursed him in two ways. It'd made any other blood taste like tar to him. And it'd transferred her memories to him—just as the Forbearers feared.

With her living blood came dreams where her memories unfolded. They were so realistic that he experienced scents she'd smelled and textures she'd touched. Sometimes he could even feel her hands clench in anger.

But he'd told no one, because he didn't want to lose power within their army—or be executed.

Each sunset, he checked his eyes for the telltale red. Any day he actually managed to sleep, the same series of dreams/memories plagued him, subtly growing in detail. . . .

Finally he stopped tossing, and the oblivion of sleep overtook him.

His first dream found her atop a hill, the sun shining bright, snow still on the ground. He perceived her every sensation—the sway of the chain around her waist, the smell of the nearby sea, brine on a cold day.

She spoke an ancient language Nikolai shouldn't understand, but he did. "I've cursed you to your hell," Myst hissed at the sight of a gravestone. She roiled with so much hostility, she must have murdered whatever being lay there.

Another dream revealed a drunken Roman senator kneeling at her feet. "At long last, I'm about to have Myst the Coveted," he slurred. "And you'll no longer be coveted, you'll be possessed." He gave a broken laugh. "You'll make me twist on your little hook no longer."

Myst the Coveted. The full name of Nikolai's tormenter.

She would have to be well over a thousand years old. Maybe two millennia.

The Roman took Myst's dainty foot in his mouth. As she slowly lifted her skirt for him, he sucked her toes and masturbated.

The first time Nikolai had experienced that dream, he'd dreaded its sick conclusion. When another scene interrupted it, he'd felt relief. But never again . . .

Myst was running past a Viking raiding party on the coast of some northern land. Purposely. She wanted them to hunt her. To catch her and throw her to the ground in the hard snow.

What kind of twisted need did she have? She was excited, her blood pumping. Her skin sizzled with electricity. When the men yelled and gave chase, she stifled a smile.

As ever, Nikolai forced his mind away before a dozen Vikings rutted on his Bride. To her delight. . . .

At last, a new dream arose. Myst sat with a group of females—all half sisters—around a great hearth in some residence. Their clothing indicated early twentieth century. The snow outside was packed so high it covered half of the window.

Nikolai knew their faces as well as Myst did. He recognized the archer as Lucia, the bright one as Regin the Radiant. The vacant-eyed Nïx was the oldest, believed to be a soothsayer. One named Daniela the Ice Maiden was part ice fey, with freezing skin that burned when touched by anyone not of her kind. Their leader, a somber creature named Annika, rocked a motherless baby girl.

They were meeting about the baby's fate—a niece to them all. Annika wished to keep her. . . .

Myst frowned at the little girl, confused by the stirring of some feeling.

"How are we to care for her, Annika?" Lucia asked.

"That doesn't matter!" Regin snapped. "How can you

bring a vampire among us when they slaughtered my people?"

A vampire child?

Daniela knelt beside Annika and touched her arm with a pale, icy hand. Myst shivered to think of Danii's pain from that rare contact. "Sister, the babe needs to be with her own people. I know this well."

Annika shook her head determinedly. "Her ears. Her eyes. Emmaline is Valkyrie as much as vampire."

Valkyrie? Impossible.

"She'll grow to be evil," Regin insisted. "She's already snapped at me with her baby fangs. By Freya, she drinks blood!"

"Trifling," Myst interjected in a casual tone. "We eat electricity."

Nix laughed. "Two of Emma's three grandparents on the Valkyrie side were gods. Perhaps she's more divine than Valkyrie or vampire?"

Three grandparents? Was Myst descended from gods as well? How could she feed off electricity? Nikolai's heart was racing.

Annika said, "I will keep Emma safe from the Horde and guide her to be all that was good and honorable about the Valkyries before the ages took their toll on us." Her words were laced with sadness and triggered a memory Myst hated.

Nikolai wanted to see it but couldn't. Instead, he had vague impressions of Myst's parents: a fierce Pictish princess—who'd plunged a dagger into her own heart rather than be taken alive by an enemy—and, yes, gods.

Annika rubbed noses with the baby and asked her, "Now, where's the best place to hide the most beautiful little vampire in the world?"

Nix laughed delightedly. "Laissez les bons temps rouler. . . ."

New Orleans.

Nikolai shot up in bed, body drenched with sweat.

My Bride's a Valkyrie? he thought with a choking cough. His mind couldn't wrap around the idea.

He hadn't known they even existed. A being from legends told around campfires was linked to him for eternity.

She didn't eat because she took electrical energy from the earth and gave it back with her emotions in the form of lightning. She was a killer and had been a Roman senator's whore. She despised men and enjoyed tormenting them, just as she'd done with Nikolai.

She might be divine.

He glanced down at his straining erection. Even his hatred couldn't quell his relentless need for her. He fought the impulse to take his shaft into his fist, knowing he could never bring himself to come, knowing it would only increase his pain.

She'd sentenced him to this for five years. Before he'd learned there was no relief, he would futilely stroke himself and thrust against the bed, always imagining Myst beneath him.

Other females repelled him—because they weren't *her*. He'd felt his Bride's incredible softness, her wet desire for him. He'd felt her sheath squeezing his fingers as she'd climaxed from his touch.

He shuddered, and his cock pulsed hungrily.

Linked for eternity to Myst the Coveted, a mythological being who despised him. The only way he'd keep her forever would be to punish her for that long.

He knew he coveted her as no other had. And now he knew where to find her.

6

The fumes of steamed hot dogs and soured beer wafted up to Myst and her sisters as they perched on a roof above Bourbon Street.

There were rumors of vampires running about in New Orleans.

Vampires in Louisiana? Unheard of.

But a demon friend had sworn he'd seen one, and a phantom had whispered that not just one faction of vampires had arrived, but *two*.

If for some reason leeches had come to the New World—which the Horde historically found vulgar and beneath them—that still didn't mean *him*.

Wroth. One of her true regrets.

Myst shouldn't have left that vampire to suffer; she should have killed him.

She shook her head, needing to stay focused and keep watch. Annika and Daniela were down there somewhere.

Myst surveyed the Quarter, but couldn't help sighing at the couples grinding against each other in dark alleys. If Daniela were here, she would blow them a kiss and cool the mortals off, freezing hands to asses and making her sisters chortle.

Myst supposed the Valkyries were easily amused.

"Not that I believe actual vampires are here," Regin said, "but if they were, they should know New Orleans is our turf." She tossed her blade up, caught the point in her claw, then flicked it up once more.

"Should we ask them to rumble? Or monster mash?" Nïx asked as she braided her waist-length black hair. Even sporting the old-fashioned hairstyle and an often confused glance—she saw the future more clearly than the present—Nïx still looked like a supermodel.

"I'm serious," Regin said. "New Orleans may once have been the mystical melting pot of the world, but we control this place now."

"We can always send Mysty the Vampire Layer to battle them," Nïx said thoughtfully. "Oh, wait—she'd run off with them."

Regin added, "Or use her famed tongue assault to flay their skin—as they line up to sacrifice themselves."

"Har-de-har-har," Myst mumbled. She'd been razzed about this nonstop since the episode at Oblak. And she deserved it. She might as well have been caught freebasing with the ghost of Bundy.

Others had overheard the jokes in the coven, and the word had spread. Other factions of the Lore—even the nymphs, for fuck's sake—now whispered about Myst's seedy penchant for vampires. But it wasn't vampires plural—it was only one.

Nikolai Wroth. She shivered. With his slow, hot fingers . . .

Whenever she touched herself, she fantasized about him, remembering his hard chest and harder shaft. She imagined his ferocity if he ever found her again.

Truthfully, she'd thought he might have by now. She'd given him her blood—and possibly her memories—which could lead him straight here.

She often pondered that reckless kiss. Though she hadn't decided to give him blood, in the back of her mind she must've known his fangs would be razor-sharp.

Had she *wanted* him to find her?

"Lookit." Regin pointed to the street. "Men that big shouldn't get schnockered."

Myst turned her attention to a tall, stumbling man. He reminded her of Wroth from the back—why couldn't she get that vampire out of her brain?—though this guy had a rangier build.

He leaned against another massive male, hanging on for balance.

Regin glanced at Myst's curling claws. "Can't you control that?"

"I can't help it. I like big males with broad shoulders. And I bet that trench coat is concealing an ass that begs to be clutched."

Nïx offered, "It's not like she can put Band-Aids over them—"

"Holy shit," Regin exclaimed. "I see a glow. Ghouls, down by Ursulines Avenue."

"Damn it," Myst muttered. "In public again? They are hard-up recruiting, then." Ghouls were maniacal fighters bent on increasing their numbers with their contagious bites and scratches. They had thick green blood; every time the coven fought them, the parish of Orleans went gooey.

"Again." Nïx sighed. "And there's only so many

times we can convince drunken tourists they're extras in a zombie flick."

Regin slid her blade into her forearm sheath and rose. "Nïx and I'll go mix it up with the ghouls. You keep a watch out for *vampires*." She made a ghostly *wooo-wooo* sound. "And try not to lift tail for any of them, 'kay?"

As Myst rolled her eyes, her sisters linked arms and leapt down, moving so quickly they were a blur. As usual, no mortals saw. Even if they did, no one registered any weirdness in this Lore-rich city.

Myst surveyed the glow. Not that extensive. Her two sisters could handle it. As eldest, Nïx was strong, and Regin was wily.

Besides, Myst had new boots on, and she'd be damned if she'd lose another pair to the epic battle between buttery-soft Italian leather and goo. Too many casualties already. It was terribly saddening. Really.

Her attention fell once more on the man below. If his front matched his back, she'd be tempted. Literal ages had passed since she'd had a little some-some, and she deserved—

He turned to peer down an alley, and she sucked in a breath. The drunk was no drunk at all! She recognized that profile—it belonged to her "estranged husband," as the coven liked to tease.

She'd been ogling Wroth's body!

He stumbled not from drink but from weakness, his build different because he'd lost weight. And that was his brother Murdoch helping him—helping Wroth *find her*.

Time for a retreat. Shaking, she crept along the roof, pressing herself around the dormers.

Wroth lifted his head above the milling crowd, then swung around in her direction. His gaze locked on her. His crazed eyes were black—and riveted to her with a look of utter possession.

When Murdoch's gaze followed his brother's, the male gave her an almost pitying look; then he slapped Wroth on the back and traced away.

Wroth tensed, about to pursue.

She leapt to the roof of the adjoining building, gaining speed for the next—

She screamed when Wroth traced in front of her. She sprinted in the other direction, but he seized her, pinning her body to his, making her feel his straining erection.

She elbowed his throat, dropped from his arms, then dove over the edge of the roof. Tumbling into a high-walled courtyard, she landed on hands and feet.

Her speed was no match for his tracing. Before she could leap from the darkened area, he caught her again, yanking her back against his front.

She fought, but even in his condition he was stronger—maybe *because* of his condition. With his free hand, he snatched up her miniskirt.

"Don't do this, vampire!"

"Five years of hell," he sneered, groping her ass. "You deserve to be fucked till you can't walk."

She gasped. "So the warlord claims his prize? It figures you'd take your Bride whether she wants you or not. You'd force me?"

After a hesitation, he bit out, "No. God, no."

She heard him freeing himself. *"Myst,"* he groaned, "just feel me." He took her hand and made her cup his heavy sac, then grip his shaft. Never had she felt such hardness. At her ear, he rasped, "Rub the head." Beads of precum made her shiver. "That's as close as I can get without you. I need to fuck you so bad I'm sick with it."

"Wroth, don't. . . ."

With a bitter curse, he lowered his head, forehead against her neck, but he only ground against her ass. "Can't stop," he grated. He wasn't going to shove inside her? Why would he restrain himself?

When his fingers strummed her nipple, lightning flashed. No, she couldn't *crave* this.

The strength in his racked body . . . his desperate touch . . .

She *could* crave it, just as she did every night in her lonely bed.

This jasmine-scented courtyard was dark. No one was around. He wouldn't fuck her, so why not enjoy him for a time?

She went soft in his grasp. Raising her arms, she locked her hands behind his head.

With a growl of approval, he kicked her feet apart. He thrust violently against her ass. Once, twice . . . He threw back his head and yelled.

Just before he came, he turned to spill his seed on the ground.

Low, guttural sounds erupted from his chest. As he clenched her, his shudders of pleasure went on and on. . . . Each moment reminded her how badly he'd needed this.

When she thought he'd finished, he clutched her ass even harder. Was he stroking himself anew? To come again? How many nights he must have envisioned this!

The second time he ejaculated seemed even more powerful. He roughly squeezed one breast, then the other, reminding her of that night in the dungeon when he'd made her orgasm.

She wanted to now—wanted him to work those fingers on her next. . . .

Once he was sated at last, he lifted her hair and brushed his lips against her neck, fanning his hot breaths over her sensitive skin. Her eyes closed with bliss. She was just about to say, "My turn," when he released her.

He pulled down her skirt and smoothed it into place, then arranged his own clothing. Turning her to face him, he cupped her nape and stared down into her eyes.

Instead of drinking her or hitting her, he squeezed her against his broad chest with those muscular arms.

Which was disconcertingly pleasant.

Curious, she let him embrace her, relaxing a fraction. In return, he lowered his head to kiss her hair.

Finally he drew back. His expression was not as wild, but grim. "I've searched for you, Bride."

"Been right here."

"You've treated me ill, leaving me in that state."

"My sisters were going to kill you, but I saved your life. And you were about to treat me far worse."

"And licking my fang?"

That had been an accident! Still, she raised her chin and said, "The least I could do since you were about to torture me. Consider it a memento."

His face hardened at that, but then he seemed to regain control of his temper. "For five years, I've plotted my revenge, constantly imagining how I'd make you pay." He exhaled a long breath. "But I'm weary of this, Myst. I want to look forward and get on with our life."

Our life?

"I'm willing to start with a clean slate. We are even for our misdeeds against each other, and I will move past any of your . . . indiscretions that happened before we met."

How magnanimous of the vampire to give her an empty scorecard. To fill back up. "Indiscretions?"

"Your blood gave me more than a mere taste. How do you think I found you?"

"So you collected my memories?" Lovely. Did he now know she'd been infatuated with him? Had he harvested all her knowledge about the Lore? "Did you enjoy telling your brother and your friends all about my life—my private thoughts and private . . . deeds?"

"I have never told anyone anything I've seen. Believe me," he added in an odd tone. "That is between us."

"Can you vow you'll never use information about my family to harm them?"

He scowled.

"Forget it, then. Doesn't matter anyway," she said, trying to wrench away from him. "There's no starting *our life*—even if you hadn't been about to interrogate

THE WARLORD WANTS FOREVER 61

me that night. Would you have broken my fingers? My legs?"

He didn't deny these things. "That is in the past. You've paid me in kind. If it is consolation you want, I've suffered far worse than I could ever have dreamed of hurting you. For these years, I couldn't sleep, I couldn't drink. The only thing I could do was fantasize about fucking you, with no relief."

Warmth bloomed in her belly. But then she frowned. "It doesn't console me. I just want you to let go of my arms and allow me to walk away. My kind detests yours. Even if I liked you and you were decent to me, my sisters would kill you, and I'd be ostracized by the Lore. There's no way I'd choose pariah-hood over my current life—which I happen to enjoy the hell out of—so back off. I don't want to have to hurt you again."

He raised a patronizing eyebrow, which made her bristle, then said, "I can't let you go. I'll never do that. Not until I die."

"I've given you fair warning. I'll say this only once more—release me."

"It will never happen. So what will make you accept this? A vow? Done. I vow to you I will never use what I've learned to harm your family. As your husband, I could never hurt them anyway because the end would be hurting you."

He was dead serious about this. Playing with him was over. He planned to force her to live with him. Because he felt that was his right over hers.

No different from all the others. Her name should be Myst the Possession.

She wondered if she'd keel over if someone finally *asked* her to be with him.

"Wroth," she whispered, snaking her arms up his chest to twine her fingers behind his neck. "Do you know what it would take to make me your Bride in truth?"

"Tell me," he said quickly.

"The life leaving my cold, dead body." She kneed him, deciding at the last second not to break his tailbone with her blow. When he fell to his knees, she backhanded him, sending him flying twenty feet into the courtyard wall.

As she sprinted down a breezeway, he bellowed with fury.

She closed in on a pair of wrought iron gates that led to a street, but he traced forward, lunging at her. His fingertips brushed down her back, hooking the chain.

She screamed in pain when it broke from her. *Great Freya, not the chain.*

If he figured out its power, her Valkyrie strength and centuries of training wouldn't matter.

She ran for her life, busting through the locked gates, blowing them off their hinges to clatter and spark across the pavement. For two thousand years, the chain had been unbreakable.

Don't hear, don't hear, run, escape from his voice. . . .

Nikolai had snatched only the fine gold strand from her waist. Nearly choking with frustration, he roared, "Myst, stop!"

She froze, her feet planting so quickly she almost toppled forward. Then she turned toward him, sauntering back. Smoothing her hair, she said, "That chain is mine." She reached for it.

He held the strand of gold high above her. He was in no way magically inclined, but even he felt the power in this chain. The power of what? "How badly do you want it?"

Lightning streaked the sky behind her. *Ah, very badly indeed.*

"Would you steal from me?" she asked.

"You've stolen from me. You've taken *years*."

"I thought we were even."

"Until you tried to unman me."

"I will be kinder to you if you give it back." Her green eyes were mesmerizing. They were the color of an emerald, and just as luminous. . . .

He had to shake himself. "We're past that point. I wanted only to make my life with you, and you left me in pain. Again." When he'd finally been released from his torture, he'd felt overwhelming gratitude to her. Which was irrational, since she was the one who'd cursed him.

Still, he'd been satisfied for the first time in years. Then she'd lashed out again. "After tonight, I understand you'll never be brought to heel," he continued. He clutched the chain, recalling how she'd stopped so suddenly. "Unless . . ." He gazed down at her. "Kneel."

Her knees met the stone as if she'd been shoved.

Shock hammered at him. Not quite believing, he commanded, "Shiver."

She did, her skin pricking as if with cold. Her nipples hardened, and she hugged her arms around herself.

He knew his grin was wicked. Five years imagining his revenge had never prepared him for this. "Grasp my belt."

Her pale fingers curled around the leather. She was staring into his eyes, her expression pleading, when he said, "Come."

7

As soon as Myst's mind registered the command, her body obeyed with a swift, searing climax.

Screaming with pleasure, she swayed on her knees and frantically brushed her breasts against his legs. Her grasp on Wroth's belt was the only thing that kept her from collapsing on the pavement.

Once the bliss faded and she could catch her breath, she raised her face, parting her lips to ask—

"Again."

Her second orgasm wrenched a ragged cry from her lips. Her sheath clenched, squeezing only emptiness. She rubbed her face against his huge shaft, needing it. "Please, no more. . . ." Even as she begged, she ran her mouth over his length.

Though she'd hurt him, he was recovering right beneath her lips.

"Come harder."

To her shame, she did, arching her back and screaming. Opening her knees, she rocked her hips for him to come fill her.

As her waves of pleasure faded, he scooped her up into his arms. She was limp, yet every nerve was on fire. There was blackness, dizziness. . . .

Suddenly she was in a new place, a paneled study.

He set her on her feet, but she'd gone boneless from his orders and from . . . tracing?

In a tremulous voice, she asked, "Where am I?"

He steadied her. "You're at Blachmount, my manor in Estonia. This, Myst, is your new home."

Her eyes widened. "You can't just keep me here!"

"Apparently, I can do anything I want to you. This is where I'm going to show you all the mercy you showed me." He crossed to a small wall safe. As he locked the chain inside, he said, "Listen carefully. The metal of this safe is indestructible. Still, you will never attempt to break into it. You will never touch the lock or try to figure out the combination. Do you understand? Answer me."

"Y-yes."

He clutched her arm and traced them into what looked like a bedroom—with the bed on the floor, as vampires preferred.

She shivered, knowing she was well and truly screwed in every possible sense.

"Undress," Nikolai ordered her from the steam-filled shower.

In the short while since they'd arrived at Blach-mount, her anger had replaced shock. She glared at his order. But she obeyed it.

Watching her disrobe was like witnessing a gift being unwrapped.

He stood under the pounding water, healing at a rate he'd never imagined. He'd taken a blow from her that should have crippled him for days, yet he was already hard for her again.

In fact, his pain had been the only reason he hadn't claimed her in the courtyard as she'd writhed from her orgasm.

Once she was completely naked, he stared at the creamy breasts that had haunted him, his mouth watering at the thatch of auburn curls between her legs.

After years of agony, to have this chain . . . the possibilities were endless. If Nikolai had had a sense of humor, he might have laughed.

Though he didn't understand the chain's power, he wasn't one to speculate about its origin. If he'd spent time questioning every new development in his life over the last centuries, he would have gone mad.

The chain was a tool he needed. Simple enough.

His decision to bury the past had been short-lived—just as his dreams had shown, she was too vicious to accept him—but could he use this mysterious chain to make her a biddable wife?

When she'd come earlier, she'd rubbed her face against his cock, wanting it. In an alley, with his clothes on, having just had his manhood battered, he hadn't been able to capitalize on her need. But now . . . ? "Join me, Bride."

Though compelled to enter the shower, she wore an expression of disgust. "You keep calling me that, but you don't have the right to."

"Fate says I do." He grasped her tiny waist and pulled her under the water with him. "You are my fated wife. And I'm from a time when a husband had certain freedoms with his wife."

"Was I wife to every vampire I blooded? Then I'm a widow several times over. I'd almost forgotten what it was like having to kill all you pesky leeches when your pesky little hearts would beat for me." She cast him a look of pure venom. "But it's coming back to me."

When she bent down to wash off her knees, he sat on the shower's marble bench and watched her move. "If I weren't a vampire and we had no history, would your body be aroused by mine?"

She'd just straightened to lift her face to the water. At his words, she clenched her jaw.

"Answer me."

"Yes," she grated.

"Good. Come here. Closer." When she sidled over, he commanded, "Kneel once more."

"You can't make me do this," she hissed even as she obeyed.

"I'm not going to make you do anything. Despite how badly you've treated me, I will never force you to touch me or force myself upon you. In fact, to make this more difficult for you, I will never touch or kiss you unless you *ask* me for it. This will be even sweeter when you beg me to fuck you."

"*Never.*"

He ignored her protest. "However, if at any time you want to touch me, I give you leave."

"Are you off your meds?" she snapped, but she was clearly nervous.

He cradled her face with both hands, thumbing her plump bottom lip. "Touch yourself."

She gasped, her hand flying to her skin as though

magnetized. She caressed up and down between her breasts.

"Lower," he commanded. *"Lower."*

Though she resisted, twitching from the fight, her delicate fingers snaked down her flat stomach.

"Open your knees wide, and pleasure yourself as if I weren't here."

She whispered, "Don't," even as she spread her knees to pet her sex.

When her eyes fired silver, his cock pulsed, the head growing slick. After long moments of simply staring in awe, he rasped, "Are you wet?"

"Yes," she moaned.

Electricity rolled from her, pricking at his skin, quickening his own need. "Inside, Myst. Put your finger inside."

She cried out when she slipped her finger into her sheath.

"Two fingers. Deeper." He clenched the edge of the bench, and the marble cracked under his grip. "Harder."

As she obeyed, she bowed her head above his lap, her hair cascading over him. She panted against his sensitive cockhead, and her tongue flicked out.

"Ah! Fingers deeper. Faster. . . ."

She took the crown between her soft lips, behaving just as he'd suspected. Her mouth was so hungry as she started to suck.

"Woman! Feels so fucking good."

Her lips glided lower down his shaft, her cheeks hollowing. Fingers dipping in and out of her heat, she used her other hand to explore him, wickedly seeking.

His Bride was on her knees, masturbating at his command and greedily devouring his cock. A dream. "Do you want me to touch your breasts?"

When she nodded eagerly, he grated, "You have to ask me for it."

Her fingers slowed, and she released him from her mouth.

He'd pushed too far. "I want to, Myst. I want to have my hands on your beautiful breasts. I've dreamed of this for so long," he admitted.

She hesitated, her body quivering. "Will you touch them?" she breathed, kissing his cock again.

"God, yes!" He covered her breasts with his hands, closing his eyes as he fondled her.

She moaned around his shaft, sucking it deeper. And deeper. She kissed with such abandon she must be on the verge again.

"Ah, yes, suck me, Myst! Your mouth . . . heaven." He groaned and tugged on her nipples.

How did I live so long without this?

The pressure built inside him; his sac tightened. He widened his knees and planted his heels on the floor as he tensed to spend. *"Watch me come,"* he growled. He didn't want her to watch him spill seed; he wanted her to meet his gaze as pleasure overwhelmed him.

Somehow she knew. She raised her head. Silvery eyes riveted to his, she worked her fist on his engorged cock. She pumped it in time with her thrusting fingers—as if she yearned for him to fill her.

That thought sent him over the edge. He cupped her beautiful face when the unbearable pressure exploded. He bellowed, *"Myst!"* and began to ejaculate. Mindlessly, he bucked his hips, fucking her fist. Anything to lose his seed. Ropes of it arced across his torso.

"Oh, my gods!" Her eyes grew wide before fluttering shut. "Wroth, I'm coming!" she cried, jerking against her busy fingers as she orgasmed all on her own. . . .

Once she'd wrung pleasure out of both of them, she collapsed against his knees. Still shuddering, she clutched his leg as she had that night in Oblak.

Before she left me in agony. Now that he'd taken the edge off his lusts, his familiar resentment returned.

He coldly brushed her aside and stood. As he rinsed his seed away, he stared at the ravishing, evil creature. She remained on her knees, hands on her thighs. Her wet hair splayed all along her slim back. The sight of her perfect ass aroused him yet again.

But she was breathing hard. For their first night together, he'd worked her pitilessly. "Rise and come to me."

Her pupils flickered as she stumbled to obey.

Guilt flared, but he made himself remember all his grueling pain. The hunger and exhaustion.

He recalled days he'd spent in his bed, drenched in sweat as he'd desperately fucked the very sheets for relief. She'd reduced him to that.

With a curse, he snatched a towel from the rack, running it over his damp skin. She wisely said nothing when he dried her stunning body as well.

Standing before her, he murmured, "Sleep." He

caught her as she fell limp, then traced her to his room, to the bed in the darkened corner.

This should have been a time of satisfaction—he had a living, breathing Valkyrie for a Bride—yet there was little. She was under his control, but he wished she didn't *have* to be.

Like a natural-born vampire, he hunched over her, dragging the beauty into the shadows with him.

8

*R*ise.

Myst hazily heard the command. She must still be dreaming because her skin was touching another's, and she hadn't slept with a lover in memory.

She frowned at how pliant her body felt. Where was the tension she normally carried? And why was her face pressed against the naked, broad chest of a man?

His delicious scent surrounded her, made her go warm and liquid. Snuggling closer, she pulled her leg up over his.

She heard a rumbling sound of male pleasure, and her eyes went wide. She shot up, drawing the sheet to her neck. Dread settled over her as the events of the night caught up with her. She was in a vampire's bed, here as a slave to his every whim. Or as she figured it, she was in hell.

"Were you dreaming about last night?" His voice was husky, his eyes steely gray.

"No," she answered honestly. She'd been thinking about licking every inch of the hard male beneath her.

"How do you feel about what we did?"

"We? What *you* did."

"I only commanded you to take your pleasure. Of

your own volition, you sucked me into your mouth."
He raised an eyebrow. "Greedily."

"Then I feel shame."

"And?" When she frowned at him, he said,
"There's rarely an instance when emotions do not
conflict. What else do you feel when you think of
last night?"

She recalled being mindless with lust as she had
never been before. In the heat of the moment, she'd
considered straddling him and slowly fitting his huge
shaft inside her. Shivering at the delicious image, she
said, "A-aroused."

"Are you aroused now?"

Her cheeks heated. Why? Myst *never* blushed.
"Yes."

"Do you need to come?"

"Yes." She turned from him, bringing her knees to
her chest. "But I won't ask you."

"Even when I can give you what you need?"

"The only thing I'll ask you for is my chain."

"You'll get it back when I am convinced you will
stay with me," he said. "Explain to me what it is."
When she didn't reply, he grated, "Answer me."

"It's called the Brisingamen."

"Why do you wear it?"

She shrugged her pale shoulders. "As punishment,
and to protect it."

"Punishment? For what exactly?"

Myst turned back to him, her green eyes taunting.
"When I was seventeen, I was caught in a compro-

mising position with a demigod of no importance—other than his mind-shattering talent at kissing. My family was unamused."

He felt a muscle tick in his jaw. Demigod? Nikolai was a battle-scarred vampire who would never walk in the sun with her.

She studied his expression. "Jealous, vampire? Or do you realize I'm out of your league?"

He ignored her words. "So your family punished you with a vulnerability that gave men control of your body? How many have had it, commanding you to fuck them for your very life?" When she glared at him, he said, "Answer. Fully."

"There was no vulnerability. It's never been broken. I've been tossed by it, caught by it, even held above a pit of boiling tar by it. In the olden days I tried to have it smelted from me, and then lasered recently. Nothing could touch the integrity of the chain before—"

"Before I pulled it free like a thread? So I'm the first." He exhaled in relief. Then his eyes narrowed. "Over all females in any time and place, you are my Bride. And I've freed you from something no man has before. You think this is merely coincidence?"

She clenched her jaw.

"How do you find those facts? Answer honestly. Now."

"I find them . . . they might be . . . it might be fated," she bit out.

"*We* might be fated." He already knew this without a doubt. He couldn't believe his heart would beat for a woman who could never want him back. But then, she'd spoken of blooding other vampires.

"Maybe fate's got a sick sense of humor. Who knows? But that doesn't mean my feelings about you will change. Are you going to keep me prisoner for eternity?"

"Before I let you go philander with your demi-gods? Yes."

With a roll of her eyes, she stood. The ends of her wild red hair brushed her waist as she sauntered around the room, exploring her new surroundings.

He lay back, proudly ogling his Bride's ass. Myst didn't merely *walk*; her every movement was the stuff of fantasy, her every touch as well. He gave his hardened cock a stroke. He hadn't gotten the chance to claim her—in the shower, he'd been too excited by her wanton sucking—but he would remedy that soon.

She ran her hand along an old papered wall. "I'm surprised a run-down heap like this even has modern plumbing." She opened a rusted shutter and gazed out into the night. He knew she'd see neglected grounds.

Heap? He had a sudden urge to explain the condition of his home.

"You're actually going to keep me *here*?" she asked. "Your torture is fiendish and boundless, Wroth."

Christ, she got his back up. "As I told you, *here* is called Blachmount. It used to be awing and will be so again, but the estate's been abandoned for many years. I only come here on occasion." Whenever he missed his family.

As soon as he'd determined Myst's location, he'd left Oblak. He could have traced from the castle to search, but the distance was demanding, and he'd been weak. So Murdoch had purchased a renovated mill on the outskirts of New Orleans for them to live in as they combed the city for her.

With a sigh, she meandered to the pile of her clothes. She blinked up at Nikolai, clearly wondering what his next move would be.

Comprehension hit him full force: no matter how he felt about her, taking care of his wife was his responsibility. He'd best get this ancient keep back to its former glory to give her a home that befitted her.

In the meantime, she would require things he couldn't anticipate, because he was clueless about female needs. Did he dare take her to get her belongings?

He needed to return to the mill anyway for the supply of blood there. He was thirstier than usual, his appetite reawakened, and claiming her in this condition would not be wise.

As they'd slept, he'd dreamed of drinking from her white thighs.

He could check in with Murdoch, send word to Kristoff that he'd found his Bride, and drink in preparation for claiming her. While in New Orleans, he might as well visit a Valkyrie den. "We go for your belongings tonight."

9

*H*ow?" Myst asked. "You can only trace to places you've previously been."

"But I can drive anywhere," Wroth replied casually, every inch a modern warlord.

So she was to return home in torn clothing, with her skin flushed and her body still singing for a vampire's touch.

Lovely.

She would never live this down. And for an immortal, *never* was particularly bad.

When he rose and strode to his closet, she studied his ripped, naked body. So strong. *Too* strong. Going to Val Hall might give her a chance to escape, but he could kill one of her sisters if they tried to free her.

He caught her gaze just as it drifted south to his hard shaft. She almost missed the shirt he tossed her.

He smirked. "Come here," he ordered, and she dragged her feet over. He piled her hair atop her head and leaned down to nuzzle her neck. At her ear, he murmured, "Bride, this is embarrassing. I think I've caught you staring at my cock. Hungrily."

She shivered. Years ago, she'd teased him the same way when he'd stared at her neck.

In a sensual rumble, he added, "You like it, don't you?"

Once the question sank in, her eyes went wide. She would be forced to answer!

His lips hovered over her shoulder. "Answer me honestly."

I want to curl up between your legs and suck on it for hours. She quelled the thought and came up with another honest answer: "It's too big."

He dropped her hair, smirking again. "So my size terrifies you more than tantalizes?" he asked, using the words she remembered well. Little by little, he was getting his revenge.

She gritted her teeth against her answer. "Both."

He chucked her under the chin. "I'll be sure to break you in slowly, ride you easy the first few times."

Myst—usually quick with the witty banter and dripping sexual innuendo—was speechless. Break her in? Arrogant male!

When he turned toward the shower, she told herself not to stare at his muscled back. Not to notice how it tapered to his narrow hips. Not to gawk at his chiseled ass with the hard hollows on the sides. She'd been right, it did beg to be clutched.

Damn her claws for curling—

"I believe you like everything about me," he rumbled from inside the bathroom.

She gazed at the ceiling, cheeks heating again. Of course he'd realized she was staring—her eyes had probably burned holes into his skin.

As she dressed in his shirt, she admitted he was right; she *did* like everything about him physically. Considering her attraction to him and the way he'd made her feel last night . . .

Soon she'd be asking—no, begging—for him inside her.

She had to escape before then, before he "claimed" her. He hadn't drunk from her, and they hadn't had sex. As long as those two things stayed sacred, she could get past this rocky patch in her life.

She'd just dragged on her boots when he returned, looking like a male dream. Though his outfit was casual—low-waisted jeans, a leather belt, and a thin, black V-neck sweater—his expensive clothes accentuated his powerful physique.

She shuffled her feet, embarrassed by her ridiculous getup: his billowing shirt and her knee-high boots.

He put his hands on her waist. "Are you ready?" Ready? To kiss him, hug him, go to her knees? He pulled her against him, wrapping his arms around her. "Close your eyes," he commanded. She did. "Open them."

Suddenly, they were in a modern and stylish kitchen. This was the first time she'd had the luxury to think about the process as they traced. She'd dropped an intoxispell or two in her day and found tracing on par with that.

"What is this place?" She drew back to look around.

Wroth traced to a refrigerator and retrieved a bag of blood. "A restored mill outside of the city." He poured the cold bag into a mug. "This is where I stayed while scouring the streets for you—for as long as I could manage every night . . . before succumbing to agony and exhaustion."

Feeling guilty, she didn't even comment when he downed the mug. *At least warm it up, leech.*

Whatever he saw in her expression made him say, "You should get accustomed to seeing me drink." He set aside his cup.

Should I?

He took her arm again and traced her into a garage with several sports cars. She tried to be cool, but of course Wroth caught her eyeing them with appreciation. Especially the Maserati Spyder.

Valkyries prized fine things, and they were acquisitive to a fault. Myst's first word had been, roughly translated, "Gimme."

He opened the passenger door of the Spyder for her. Inside, she savored the upscale leather, lids gone heavy.

Sliding behind the wheel, he cast her an inscrutable expression. "We are fortunate, Myst. You'll want for nothing as my wife."

She was already fortunate. She already wanted for nothing. The coven divvied their collective earnings from investments, and the take was always generous. She had enough money to buy anything that struck her fancy, from video games to her own sports cars. Last week she'd spent two grand on hand-painted underwear to placate her lingerie obsession. "Oh, joy. I'm rich."

He started the engine and pulled down the drive. On the road, he commanded her, "Direct me to your home."

Muttering, "Your funeral," she did.

Half an hour later, they closed in on Val Hall. Myst and her sisters didn't hide their address the way Batman did the Bat Cave, yet they didn't often have trespassers. When his breath hissed in at the sight of the manor, she was reminded why.

"*This* is where you live?" he bit out, forearms resting on the steering wheel.

She tried to see it from his eyes. Fog shrouded the cavernous thirty-room mansion, and lightning struck all around. Even at this distance, shrieks could be heard coming from within. The Valkyries often screamed. If Annika got angry enough, car alarms in three parishes would blare.

Copper rods dotted the grounds, but sometimes they didn't catch all the bolts. Smoke wafted from many of the charred oaks in the yard.

The wood nymphs were way behind on repairing the trees. If Myst heard them whine, "But, Mysty baby, there was this orgy . . ." as an excuse one more time—

"Hellish," Wroth said.

She tilted her head. In the olden days, they used to mark a grave with a sword, and she'd always fancied that the rods made Val Hall look like a mass burial site.

Okay, it might be a *bit* hellish.

"It's time someone took you from here," he said as he drove closer.

She frowned at him. "This is where I belong. I'm as much a monster as what lies within."

"You're a lot of things, Bride. But you're not a monster."

"You're right." She'd play along. "I'm what monsters like you fear beneath their beds."

He flashed her a heated look. "But now you're *in* my bed where you belong."

"So in this life of ours—the one that your crazed mind envisions—I'm not going to fight?"

"No." He parked some distance from the manor. "I know you're deceptively strong and that other beings would rather die than risk your wrath. But I won't ever allow you to put yourself in danger again."

She batted her eyelashes at him. "Because I'm just so darn precious to you?"

"Yes," he answered simply, making her roll her eyes. As he got out of the car, she opened her door—

Instantly he traced to assist her, looking almost offended that she hadn't waited for him.

Perfect. A gentleman warrior. Which she was discovering she might have a weakness for.

As they walked along the drive, he said, "Hold my hand."

"Big vampire scared the wittle Valkyrie will get away?" Her hand slipped into his big, rough one.

He gazed down at her with his brows drawn. "I just want to hold your hand."

What was that flutter in her stomach?

As they neared the manor, he grew tense, ready to trace them away in a split second. She almost felt sorry for him. He was of the Lore, yet he'd never seen anything like her home. In so many ways, he was as human as he'd once been.

He made her point out the window to her room. With a destination in sight, he was able to trace them inside.

Those discerning eyes of his scanned the ultrafeminine space. She was the girlie-girl of the coven, with her silk sheets, ornate jewelry armoire, large wardrobe cabinet, and gilded vanity. The walls were cream, the accents soft pink.

The next room over, belonging to Kaderin the Coldhearted, housed only a spartan sleeping mat, an armory, and the string of vampire fangs Kad had taken as trophies. Across the gallery was the room of timid Emmaline, who was half vampire, half Valkyrie. She made her little vampire nest *under* her bed.

One could argue that Emma proved not all vampires were evil—and that the coven could coexist with one. Yet Emma was the daughter of a beloved sister; her Valkyrie half was believed to "temper" the other.

An exception had been made for her. Still, did anyone besides Myst notice Emma's big blue eyes glinting whenever the coven railed about killing leeches?

Wroth crossed his arms over his chest and said, "Start packing."

"What do you want me to bring?"

He raised an eyebrow. "You should be used to this. Choose clothes as if you were going away with one of your lovers."

She traipsed to the lingerie dresser that contained her Agent Provocateur, Strumpet and Pink, and Jillian Sherry collections. Opening a drawer, she said, "Depends on which lover." With one hand, she held up a quarter-cup bra of red leather; with the other, a translucent baby-doll teddy.

"Both," he rasped, his expression pained. He was getting hard again. He noticed her noticing, and his eyes darkened.

Assuming a brisk manner, she pulled a weekender bag from her closet.

"Ah-ah." He picked her up and moved her aside to drag out a four-foot-long trunk. "Use this, because you're never coming back to this place."

Myst sighed at him as if he'd uttered nonsense.

If Nikolai had to battle against her for the rest of their lives, he would. "Pack. Now."

With a defiant look, she swept dozens of fingernail-polish bottles over the edge of her vanity into the trunk.

Nail polish was out of his realm of understanding. He shrugged.

She began combing through her wardrobe with a leisurely air. They'd be here all night at this pace.

"Faster."

"Dick." She dumped an armful of hanging garments into the trunk.

He crossed to her copious film collection. Movies must be important to her. He was unfamiliar with the titles, but then he wasn't versed in *any* leisure activities. "Which of these do you prefer?"

She hated having to answer his questions, struggled against it every time. "I like romance and horror."

"A bit disparate."

She pinned his gaze with her own. "Funny, I used to think so."

Ignoring that, he tossed a few DVDs into the trunk. As she packed another load of clothes, he turned to her dressers.

Every drawer was filled with lingerie: thongs, hose, lace, and silk nightgowns that made his blood pound. It would take him months to bite all of these off her body.

The woman had a drawer for nothing but garters!

He frowned. Females wore clothes like these for a lover. How many did she currently have? When he imagined that gold chain slapping her body as she writhed on another male, Nikolai crumpled one of the bed's iron posts.

Reading him so clearly, she said, "Wroth, if you can't control your jealousy, we're heading straight for divorce." She tapped her finger on her chin. "Make a note that I'll expect the house, the jewels, and the hellhound. Actually, you can keep the house."

With a scowl, he tossed handfuls of her under-clothing into the trunk. Tracing to her bathroom, he searched the cabinets. "There are no medicines," he called. "No things . . . females need."

"I don't get ill, and I don't have bodily functions. Just like you, vampire."

He traced back to her. "None at all?" Perhaps she couldn't get pregnant. He might not have to be as careful as he'd planned.

"None. Why, you can force me to have sex with you nonstop all month!"

"Why would I force you when I can barely keep your hands—and mouth—off me now?"

"Wroth, darling," she purred, smiling so sweetly,

"I can't wait to get my mouth on you again." She snapped her teeth and yanked her head back as if she were chewing something free.

He inwardly cringed at the visual. "If you've packed enough clothes, get changed." He fastened down the top of the trunk.

"Fine." She removed his borrowed shirt.

"Indeed." At the sight of her body, his cock shot hard as steel. His fangs sharpened, though he'd downed blood at the mill.

With sensual movements, she slid a tight red thong up her shapely legs, wriggling her taut ass as she pulled it into place.

His breath left him when she bent over in just that thong to step into a skirt. The urge to feed his length into her from behind was undeniable—

Shrieks erupted from downstairs.

Inhaling for control, he crept to the landing outside her room and peered down. Ten or so Valkyries had gathered below. Some lounged in front of a TV with bowls of popcorn—which they didn't eat. Two practiced swordplay. When the pair blocked the television, the others screeched and threw popcorn at them.

Another Valkyrie stalked inside. She was covered in blood.

"Cara!" they shouted in greeting, unsurprised by her appearance.

"What'd you get into tonight?" one of them asked.

Cara unbuckled her sword sheath. "My human unknowingly went into a demon bar. A demoness

thought to use *my* mortal to make her lover jealous."
She shook her head. "That demon was about to rip
Michael's throat out with his teeth."

"How'd you stop him?"

Without blinking an eye, she said, "I ripped the
demon's throat out with my teeth."

When they all laughed, Nikolai vowed Myst would
never see these malicious creatures again. Never!
Without their influence, she would be kinder, gentler.

She sure as hell couldn't get worse.

"Has Myst or Daniela returned?" Cara asked.

"No. We'd expect this from Myst—"

Because she often ran off with men?

"—but certainly not from Daniela. She never
came back from the Quarter."

"Well, the hits keep coming," Cara said. "I just
saw Ivo the Cruel—in the Quarter."

When they laughed again, she added, "You should
know by now that I don't jest about vampires unless
they're dead."

They sobered, and one asked, "Has Ivo returned
for Myst? Somebody needs to warn her."

Nikolai turned back to Myst's room; she was gone.

At her opened bedroom window, he caught sight
of her across a field, sprinting away. He yelled for her
to stop, but somehow she kept running.

She was fast and might have outrun him with
her unnatural speed as she covered miles, but she
couldn't outpace teleporting. He traced for her,
lunging from his momentum to snag her ankle. She
tripped forward, landing in the grass.

His eyes narrowed. She wore plugs in her ears

from a music player! Some song blared, blocking out his commands. Enraged, he yanked the plugs from her, and threw the contraption far away.

She'd almost escaped him. *Before I claimed her.* A red haze descended over his vision. Thoughts grew distant. He tossed up her skirt, ripping the silk thong from between her legs, glorying in that feeling. He was finally going to take his Bride!

Was she struggling against his hold?

"Wroth, you want it?" Her words echoed inside him. "I'll fight you for it."

He would always fight for her, *always*. Would he fight her for the right to her body? "Then you're *mine*."

10

A nightmare was about to take Myst.

Wroth's fingers dug into her skin as he dragged her beneath him. His eyes were black, his fangs sharpening.

She slammed her forehead against his. He bellowed with rage, and she twisted around and drove her elbow into his throat. As he fought for breath, she scrambled away to mule-kick his chest.

His big body went reeling.

Why hadn't she broken his neck with her elbow? Or shattered his breastbone with that kick? No longer would she hesitate to hurt him.

She leapt on top of him, drilling her fist into his face repeatedly. Lightning came down like a hail of bullets, as quick as her punches.

His lip split. Another two hits in rapid succession. She thought she cracked his cheekbone.

"You'll get no mercy now," he bit out, his gravelly voice unrecognizable. He caught her fist and squeezed.

Hissing in fury, she swiped the claws of her other hand down his chest, tearing his shirt and flesh open.

He seized both her wrists and forced her onto her back. Pinning her hands above her head, he gave a brutal growl . . . and sank his fangs into her neck.

She cried out, going limp beneath him. Her eyes widened in shock as she watched her lightning fork across the sky. This wasn't pain he was giving her.

His bite was ecstasy.

Mindless, he withdrew, and pierced her neck lower. Then again. Each time his fangs entered her was like the thrust of a man. Each time he released her skin was like a slow, measured withdrawal.

Dizzying pleasure. Scorching agony. Her claws curled for his body.

Myst had a primal need deep inside her: to be dominated by a powerful male. Yet she'd never been defeated in a contest of two—no male had ever been strong enough.

Wroth was more powerful than any before.

Her mind rebelled. He was a vampire! She'd killed the last three she'd blooded. Why not Wroth? He'd planned to torture her in that horrid dungeon, planned to control her with the chain.

But his bite . . . She moaned, her aching sex getting wetter and wetter. She needed his shaft to fill it.

Please be strong enough. Please . . . For once in her life, would a man take control?

So she could finally lose it.

Snarling against her neck, he ripped open her shirt and bra, baring her breasts. His big hands kneaded her flesh till she arched her back in delight. He released his bite and bent to her breasts. His lips closed around one nipple, sucking her hard. Then the other.

She rocked her hips; signaling him for more?

He must have thought so. He yanked open his pants, shoving them down his thighs. He rose above her. His torn shirt gaped, revealing his clawed chest. His eyes were full black, and blood dripped from his fangs and one corner of his lips.

A vampire from legend.

As his menacing gaze feasted on her body, his huge cock pulsed between them, straining toward her sex.

Her eyes widened. Too large for her! She dug her heels into the ground to scuttle back. Break her in slowly! That's what he'd said.

His palms landed with a slap on her upper thighs, lifting her pelvis. He used his thumbs to spread her folds, then wrenched her down on his thick shaft.

He gave an inhuman yell; she cried out from his size. He'd buried himself deep in her core. She grimaced in pain as it throbbed inside her.

He'd bested her. *Myst will want the first man who can defeat her.* The Lore had always whispered that about her. She'd challenged Wroth, and he'd won. In her mind, he deserved to claim his prize.

No matter the consequences.

His hips remained still. How was he resisting his instinct to thrust? His skin sheened with sweat, his muscles rigid from his effort. Somewhere in his crazed mind, he must want her to have pleasure—he leaned down to drag his tongue over one nipple, then the other.

As if to soothe her.

Then he pierced and sucked her neck again, the bite turning pain to pleasure. Her sex slickened once more, trying to accept the invasion.

Slowly withdrawing his fangs—and his hips—he groaned, "So wet." He plunged his cock back inside her.

She hissed in a breath, eyes watering. "Wroth, it h-hurts."

Seeming to come out of a daze, he bit out, "Can't stop." Sweat dripped from his forehead.

"Tell me not to feel pain." She gripped his damp hips, her claws sinking in.

"Don't hurt." His words were ragged. "No pain."

Suddenly all she felt was . . . fullness.

When he tentatively rocked inside her, she cried out again. He tensed.

"No, Wroth . . . it's good! Keep *going*."

He did, adding another bite to the mix. He timed each draw from her neck with a surge of his hips. His cock was so swollen, he could barely move within her, was already hitting the end of her sheath.

She gave herself up to the pleasure, arching her back. The lightning whipped up the wind, and it rushed over her heated skin, over her stiff nipples.

Never slowing, he positioned himself on his knees and maneuvered her to straddle him.

His body was so big compared to hers, making her feel truly vulnerable. As if he'd read her mind, he tightened his arms around her, trapping hers at her sides.

Completely captured. This position allowed no evasion. So she relaxed in the crushing vise of his arms; her breasts swelled against his heaving chest.

He bucked his hips up. And again. Keeping her body immobile, he started to fuck like a piston.

Her head fell back, and she watched the sky in a daze of pleasure, seeing her lightning thrashing the earth.

Bliss welling up, strengthening. "Ah, gods, Wroth! I'm so close. . . ."

"*Myst!*"

Would he order her to come? He tightened his arms even more—as if to threaten her not to disobey. But no order came.

He met her gaze and rasped, "*Milaya*, I want you so much."

Milaya. That endearment from years ago sent her over the edge. Her orgasm seized her like a shock wave. "Wroth, *YES!*" She screamed from the shattering pleasure.

But it only built as he wrenched her up and down on his shaft in a frenzy. Growling, snarling, he tensed to come.

A savage bite made her scream again, her body hurtling into a second release. Her core clenched him, milking his cock.

She was still coming when he released his bite. He threw his head back, cords of muscles in his neck and chest strained. The force of his ejaculation tore a bellow from his lungs.

She felt him shooting hot semen inside her, endless jets. He yelled to the sky as he pumped and pumped his release. . . .

Then after-shudders. He loosened his hold on her, though she didn't want him to. She didn't want this to end.

When his breaths had calmed somewhat, he drew her back to search her face. His eyes had cleared, his fangs receding. "I didn't want to hurt you." His gaze dipped, and he winced. "Ah, God, your neck." He tenderly brushed his fingertips over the bite marks.

"It didn't hurt. Even before you . . . we . . . uh,

worked it out." They would be healed by tomorrow. "You've really never seen this before?"

"Never."

"I was your first bitee?" Why should that please her so much? She should be leaping away from him in disgust. She was just so overwhelmed with everything. And she felt . . . tenderness toward him.

Yes, Myst had always been the girlie-girl of the coven, but she'd never in her long, long life felt truly feminine—until this male had squeezed her in his arms and *taken charge*.

Myst had never experienced that much pleasure.

"You were the first." He rested his forehead against hers. "My eyes will go red from this. I will turn."

He looked so horrified, she found herself saying, "Your eyes will go red only if you kill as you drink living blood. Red-eyed vampires drink to the marrow of their victims, sucking from the pit of the soul. They take all the bad, all the madness, all the sin."

His jaw slackened. "Is that why pure-blooded vampires go mad?"

"It's more than that. They grow addicted to killing, which means they can never drink from the same source. After years and years of different victims, the memories add up."

He cupped her head. "Every sunset I checked my eyes, unsure whether I would turn from your blood. Not knowing if my brother would have to kill me."

His tone wasn't reproachful, but hell, could she feel more guilty? This male was still inside her body—which was thrumming as never before—and she'd tortured him. "Wroth, you're a vampire. Others might not agree, but I believe you're meant to drink from another—to connect, to live. But never to kill like that. And it takes decades of killing every night for the memories to reach critical mass."

In a stunned voice, he said, "I won't turn. I'm meant to drink." His lips curled. His arm was still coiled around her—as if he'd never let her go.

He's bested me. She shivered.

"And you found pleasure in it."

Not a question, but she answered, "Your bite was the only thing that saved you from a stiff-legged kick to your groin." When he grinned, she added softly, "It was intense pleasure."

He groaned in approval and thrust into her, still semihard.

She moaned, desire stoking again.

"Did I take too much?" He gripped her ass, working her along his length.

Her eyes fluttered closed, and she answered without thought, "Immortal here. Remember?"

He stopped suddenly, clasping her against his chest, protective once more. "I heard something."

"It's nothing." Frustrated, she spurred him with her heels, rocking on him.

He stifled a groan but didn't move. She opened her eyes to find his enraged gaze focused on . . . the sword point tucked under his chin. Blood trickled down his neck.

Regin wielded the blade; Lucia stood beside her with an arrow nocked. Both stared in disbelief.

"No!" Myst said, her voice hoarse from screaming. "Don't."

Regin snapped, "This *thing* just violated you." Her entire race had been destroyed by the Horde; she'd learned to count by her mother's bite scars.

"We followed the lightning here," Lucia said quietly. "She allowed whatever he did to her."

Myst could imagine what she and Wroth looked like. They'd fought wildly in this field. They were bruised, bloody, their clothing in shreds.

Why hadn't he thrown her out of the way and attacked Regin? Or traced Myst away? She suspected he wanted them to see her like this. Their relationship couldn't be made more brutally clear.

Myst pulled away from him, though his arms tightened around her to prevent it. "Please, Wroth," she whispered in his ear, "let me face them." He finally released her.

But jealous Myst didn't want her sisters to see Wroth, all hard and magnificent. As she rose, she yanked his shirttail down. *That's mine*, she thought irrationally.

She'd been acquisitive all her life—but never with men.

11

When Myst stumbled away, Nikolai reached for her, but Regin's sword pierced his chest muscle. He had vowed not to harm her family, so he didn't fight back.

Besides, he could hardly feel the pain. He was euphoric. There stood his Bride, her chin raised as she adjusted her clothes.

Claimed. He stifled an evil grin. With witnesses. She could never go back now. She was his.

His heart pumped madly for her, his blood rushing inside him—and her luscious blood as well. She'd enjoyed his bite. Lightning had streaked the sky each time she came.

He'd *seen* her pleasure.

He could give her lightning whenever he drank, without fear of turning, without fear of hurting her. No more checking his eyes at sunset.

They could sustain each other. He'd never known greater satisfaction.

Now if he could get her witch of a sister to cease stabbing him.

"You just had sex with a vampire," Lucia said to Myst. "Where is your mind? You know the repercussions. You'll be shunned by the Lore, mistrusted."

Regin added, "And when Furie rises . . ."

At that, Myst's face paled. Why? She appeared shocked by everything, as if her sisters' arrival had splashed ice water over her, waking her from a dream.

He needed to get her home, away from them.

Suddenly Regin gasped. She stared at Myst in horror. "Oh, fuck," she whispered, "where's your chain?"

Before Myst could answer, Nikolai ordered her, "Come to me quickly!" She obeyed, diving forward to grab his outstretched hand. He traced her away just as Regin leapt for Myst's legs and an arrow sang for him, plugging his chest.

Back at Blachmount, he set Myst on the bed. He tore the arrow free and fastened his jeans. "Stay here," he commanded her. He would return for the goddamned trunk he'd gone to get in the first place. He traced back to her room, snaring it—just as Regin and Lucia bolted up the stairs. "Give her the chain back, leech!"

"I've claimed her. She's my wife now," he said simply, then traced with an ease he'd never known. Back home, he tossed Myst's things to the side. "Rest, *milaya*." He clasped her shoulders. "Take a hot bath and relax here until I return."

She didn't respond, still in a daze.

He didn't want to leave her like this—unsteady from tracing and reeling from the events of the night. But he had to let Kristoff know Ivo was in the New World, so they could hunt that vampire down and destroy him.

As Nikolai gazed down at his Bride, he wondered how Ivo could *not* be searching for her.

He brushed her shining hair from her face. "Make yourself comfortable here. Your clothes are here. This is your home now."

She nodded absently, her pupils blown.

He couldn't leave her in this state. He would warm her with a bath, then put her in bed. He ran water, undressed her, then carried her in and set her in the steaming water.

She sat silently as he scrubbed the dirt and grass from her alabaster skin. She barely seemed to feel it when he held a cloth against that line of bite marks.

She turned to him suddenly, cupping his face. "You vowed never to hurt my family?"

"Yes. I make it again."

"I believe you. You could've traced and attacked Regin and Lucia tonight. But if you take more memories from my blood, please don't reveal our weaknesses. Don't allow others to hurt them either."

He stared into her spellbinding eyes. Was his first loyalty to his king or to her? She was his Bride—that meant she was his family. Nikolai's family had always come first; nothing had changed except that he'd added to it. "If I learn of other factions, I will relate that information. But never about your kind."

She pulled him to her and kissed him with trembling lips. Drawing back, she whispered, "Thank you." Her soft smile made his heart do things he didn't remember from being a human before.

Her shoulders tensed just as he heard voices downstairs.

Trespassers. His fangs sharpened. That someone would dare enter his home when he had his Bride within it . . . "Myst, finish up, then go to the bedroom and wait for me. If anyone but me comes in, run faster than you've ever run and escape them."

Her immortal blood taken directly from her flesh gave him power. He would use it to protect her. He traced downstairs to the great room, his muscles swelling, his fists clenched. His fangs were like razors—

"Wroth, I pity the being who wishes to harm your Bride," Kristoff intoned from his seat at the long table. Murdoch and a few Russian elders sat with him. All showed surprise at Nikolai's appearance.

As he struggled for control, he imagined how they saw him. He was filthy, his skin clawed—and, God help him, Myst's delicious blood marked his shirt. He was fairly certain she'd gotten in a few hits to his face as well. "I would not wish to attend you in such a condition," he said. "I'll go wash and change." Would they suspect he'd drunk from Myst's neck?

"No, we know you are eager to get back to her for the remainder of the night." Kristoff appeared proud. "Congratulations, Wroth. You've now been blooded *and* claimed your Bride. Though it appears she didn't acquiesce to you."

Guilt welled. Then he recalled her spurring him like a horse when he'd stopped.

"I'd like to meet her," Kristoff said.

"She is resting."

"I suppose she would be." The king was amused? "In fact, we'd wonder if she wasn't."

A couple of snickers from the Russians. Nikolai cast them a look of warning, and they quieted.

"And you drank her blood this night? Did you take her flesh as you did so?"

Why did I think my crime would escape Kristoff's notice? Nikolai had no choice but to confess to the most heinous act among their order. Shoulders back, he said, "I did."

Kristoff commanded, "Take off your shirt."

Murdoch caught Nikolai's glance, ready to fight their way free—

"Stand down, Murdoch," Kristoff said. "No one's dying tonight."

Perhaps my king will only flay the skin from my back. Nikolai removed the shirt, hoping. For the first time in his life, he had his wife waiting for him. For the first time, he truly cared whether he lived or died.

"Toss it on the table."

When he did, the others' eyes widened, their fangs sharpening. Kristoff had scented Myst's blood, and now the rest did as well.

"And what was it like?" Murdoch asked, his voice rough.

Nikolai hesitated to answer, but Kristoff raised his brows in a silent command.

"There is no description strong enough."

"And how did she feel about your bite?" Kristoff asked.

Nikolai didn't want them to know she'd climaxed with an intensity that had staggered him.

"You resist answering your king on the heels of confessing to our most reviled crime?"

This was Nikolai's Bride they spoke of. He wanted to lie, to say he wasn't sure, but he couldn't. Answering wouldn't break his vow to her—and if Kristoff ordered him killed for disobeying, Nikolai couldn't protect Myst from Ivo. Though it disgusted him, he grated, "She found it extremely pleasurable."

Kristoff appeared pleased. Or even relieved. He asked the others, "Do you think I should forgive Wroth his transgression? For which one of us could have resisted the temptation of our Bride's exquisite blood?"

Normally the king would've sentenced any transgressor who drank from the flesh to be chained in an open field until the sun burned him to ash.

Still staring at the tattered shirt stained with a Valkyrie's blood, Kristoff said, "Continue as you were—but if your eyes turn red, know that we will destroy you."

Nikolai masked his shocked expression. "I was coming to Mount Oblak tonight to tell you that Ivo was spotted in New Orleans. He's looking for someone, and I suspect it could be Myst. I need to—"

"*We* will hunt Ivo," Murdoch said. "For God's sake, you stay here and . . . enjoy . . . everything."

"Find out as much as you can from her." Kristoff eyed Nikolai intently as he rose to leave. "And you will tell us if the memories follow the blood."

As Nikolai left the room, dumbfounded by this turn of events, he heard Kristoff say, "Now, which one of you will accompany Murdoch to New Orleans, where this coven full of Valkyries is located?"

Nikolai heard every chair scrape the floor as they shot to their feet.

～

Like a cat licking her wounds, Myst sat in the bath, replaying the fight.

She'd pulled her punches, so had she truly been bested? Then she flexed her hand—the one he'd caught. It was sore, but not broken.

Wroth had held back as well.

She sighed, unable to work up outrage over what had happened in the field—or even concern over the possible threat downstairs. Wroth would take care of it. He was strong.

Her mind easily returned to tonight's developments. Her sisters knew her chain was gone, knew she'd been claimed by an enemy.

They could never guess how much she'd loved it. With a *vampire*, for fuck's sake. Something must be seriously wrong with her, because Wroth's bite alone had turned her inside out. She yearned for him to do it to her again. And again.

On top of that, he'd used his body in a way that was nothing short of divine, taking her as no other had before.

Though most assumed she'd taken tons of lovers, she'd had only three steady partners. For centuries, she'd dated a handsome warlock. Their relationship had been long-distance—in those days, reaching each other took half a year—and they'd parted ways amicably. Her other two lovers had both been long-term, the sex fun and enjoyable.

But Wroth . . . *divine*. And she believed their sex life would only get better. She shivered. Could she possibly feel more pleasure without dying?

Then there was a very compelling fact. He'd unchained her when no other could.

As she rose from the bath and dried off, she wondered—did that mean he was *supposed* to have the chain? To have her? Maybe he was supposed to command her like a genie from a bottle?

She'd always pitied the plight of genies until she'd freed one from a young berserker. Instead of saying thanks, the chit had laid into her, screaming, "To each her own, lightning whore!"

Myst dressed in an understated emerald-green nightgown that said neither "do me" nor "don't do me." She lay back in his bed, wondering how she could be so relaxed about everything. And how could she feel so at home in this cold, bare mansion?

Wroth returned and strode into the bathroom; she heard the shower start. There'd been no threat? Probably his brother visiting. Would Murdoch remark on Wroth's injuries? He should see when she *didn't* pull her punches.

Not long after, Wroth traced into the bed. Was he going to take her again? She was sore, but if he commanded her not to hurt . . .

Yet he only clasped her in his arms, pressing her head against his chest. His steady heartbeat drummed in her ear. He was hard, but he made no advance.

He brushed her hair from her neck, uncovering

his bites. He muttered something that sounded like a curse.

"Wroth?"

He curled a finger under her chin and raised her face to his. "I regret hurting you. The number of bites, the lack of care before . . ."

Lack of care? Ah, he regretted not preparing her body for his size. Who'd taught him to do that? When was the first time he'd realized he would *need* to? Jealousy flared.

"I can't believe I lost control like that," he rasped. "I am unused to being blooded. I am unused to being a husband. But I vow to you things will be different—I will be gentler."

She didn't want their sex to be different. Their sex—great Freya, was she thinking about keeping him? She would get used to his size, and then she would demand anything but gentle. She couldn't have ordered up a better match for her in bed, and she'd be damned if he held back all that magnificent strength.

He was everything she could ever dream of physically. His scars alone . . . She stifled a moan, but her claws were curling. He was a warrior, with a warrior's mentality, which she appreciated.

None of her lovers before had been warriors. No, they'd been the warlock, an immortal sultan, and an architect. Perhaps that was why she was so attracted to Wroth.

She and Wroth were kindred.

He murmured, "Speak to me." Then he amended: "Will you not speak to me?"

"I want my chain back. I want to choose." If he

gave it to her, she would stay awhile. Her sisters had already seen her screwing a vampire—Myst might as well enjoy the pleasure for a time.

He moved to his side, pressing her to hers as well. There they lay, gazes locked. Dawn was nearing, and she didn't want this to end.

He rubbed her shoulder, his palm rough from the grip of his sword.

Warrior. She relished the feel of it.

"I can't lose you," he said. "The very thought makes me crazed. I can't even imagine you leaving me." His hand tightened on her.

"Are you so certain I would?"

"Yes," he rasped. "I am."

She didn't deny it, because he was probably right. He called himself her husband, but she didn't recognize him as such.

She didn't recognize him as the one whose arms she would forever run to. She might stay for a time, but in the end, she would always go.

12

The harsh light of day. *Or night,* Myst mused. The harsh light of waking was upon her.

She should be feeling shame; instead, she was treated to big, warm hands massaging her back until she was a boneless heap of bliss.

She moaned. Maybe vampire lovers were misunderstood. Perhaps she was in the know and enjoying early adapter status.

"I have to go meet with my brother for a couple of hours," Wroth told her. "Can you content yourself here?"

"Uh-huh," she mumbled.

"Don't leave."

Huh? She wasn't going anywhere. She was too at home and relaxed here.

He bent down to murmur in her ear, "I've laid clothes out. Will you dress for me, *milaya*?" Then he disappeared.

Strangely lazy, she took another hour before getting out of bed. She raised an eyebrow at what he'd selected for her—a satin bustier fringed with transparent lace to cover her nipples, lacy garters, fishnet hose, and a thong—all in jet black.

She shivered. General Wroth had a wicked streak.

He wanted her to dress for him, and she didn't have a problem with that; finally someone—besides herself—would enjoy her fabulous lingerie. And it made a huge difference that he'd asked when he could have commanded.

But would he always? As she soaked in a bath, she realized her precarious position: she was dependent on his goodwill.

Which was intolerable for a creature like her.

Damn it, where were her sisters? She'd half-expected them to show by now—Nïx could often find her. With no sign of them, Myst decided she'd use her own tools and talents to win her freedom.

Wroth had said he'd return the chain when he was confident she'd never leave. Acting as if she wanted to stay forever wouldn't be that difficult.

After drying off, she surveyed the lingerie. Why not seduce him into thinking she desired him above all others? Play at love, and act at surrender. As she smoothed the hose up her legs, she wondered if deception had ever sounded so delicious.

She trembled when she donned the bustier, the fringe skimming her stiff nipples so sweetly. She was already wet with anticipation.

Dressed, she lay on the bed and fantasized about him. She pictured him railing her as his big hands kneaded her breasts. Would he drink her? She imagined him driving into her from behind, the length of his body stretched over hers to take her neck.

Her fingers found their way down her belly and into her panties. Wroth was supposed to be back soon, but did she care if he caught her masturbating? She'd already done it for his pleasure.

A stroke on her clitoris made her eyes slide closed. Had she ever been so slick? No, not until she'd fingered herself in a vampire's lair, waiting to seduce a warlord.

Her legs fell wide as she ran her finger lower. When she opened her heavy-lidded eyes, she found Wroth staring at her from the foot of the bed.

"Couldn't wait, then?"

Nikolai had known his Myst was a pagan, but she'd never truly looked it—until he'd found her pleasuring herself with her legs spread in abandon.

Her glorious red hair fanned out over his pillow, and her delicate hand was in her panties, stroking.

She hadn't stopped at his arrival.

"I couldn't have dreamed you'd be like this, Myst." The lush scent of her arousal made his head swim. "I believe I'm dreaming now."

She arched her back.

"Were you fantasizing about me?" *Say yes.* . . . He didn't think he'd ever wanted to hear anything so badly.

"Yes, Wroth."

He groaned. "What were you imagining?"

"You drinking my blood while you *fucked me hard*," she said, moaning the last.

Craving his bite too? "A dream."

She licked her lips. "In your dream, do you make me wait much longer?" Her whiskey voice dripped with need.

"You want this freely?" He fumbled with his belt buckle, then simply tore the leather apart.

Her hips rolled in reaction. "Yes."

"No games?"

"No," she panted, "just need you inside me."

"Your body wants to be fucked?"

Her fingers moved faster. "Yes!"

"By me?"

"Yes," she moaned.

He'd anticipated months of wearing her down until she truly wanted him—until they wouldn't have to play at commands and power.

Yet here she was, fingering herself in his bed. Waiting for him to return. He grew suspicious. "Convince me."

She sensuously drew her fingers from her panties. Rising from the bed, she sauntered to face the closest wall.

What would she do?

She dragged her flimsy thong down to her garters. Without a word, she spread her legs and leaned forward to rest her forearms against the wall.

When the position raised her ass and parted her glistening lips, he rasped, "You make a compelling argument." He kicked off his boots, ripped his clothing away, then traced behind her. He slipped his thumb into her tightness, briefly closing his eyes to find her so slick. Her body trembled with need, which affected him so much.

He replaced his thumb with one, then two fingers. Thrusting them, he said, "In my dream, I do fuck you. But I start slowly, feeding my cock into you inch by inch. When you're dripping wet and ready, I fuck you with all the strength in my body."

She raised her ass even higher. "What do I do?" she breathed.

"You come again and again from no command, just from pleasure." With a last plunge of his fingers, he withdrew them.

He grasped himself, aiming for her entrance. When his cockhead kissed her wet heat, he fought not to shove into her. *Easy, Nikolai! Inch by inch* . . . He shuddered violently from the battle, but he wouldn't repay this gift from her by hurting her tight little sheath.

Yet the crown was barely inside her when lightning exploded outside—because she was already coming. "Wroth!" She clawed furrows into the wall. "Now!"

"I am . . ." he groaned, straining his every muscle to enter her slowly, to make this good for her—

His eyes widened when her claws sank into his ass to yank him into her.

"Hard!" she demanded in a throaty voice.

He choked out, "Don't hurt." He forced his cock through the squeezing spasms of her climax—as if through a clenched fist. "Ah, God, Myst!" Even when he was seated deeply, she continued to come around him. He could have stilled and let her body milk him.

But he wanted to *fuck* her. To brand her as his own. To take her so fiercely she would forget other men. He palmed the curves of her ass, withdrew, then surged into her, hitting the end of her sex.

"More!" she cried.

"Can you know what this does to me?" he rasped,

grinding his hips, stirring her. She moaned, hanging on to the wall. "To see you finger yourself to thoughts of me?" He pulled out completely, then impaled her with another brutal thrust.

"Drink!" She was panting. "Please, please drink from me."

"You truly crave my bite?" He ripped the bustier clean from her body, then pulled her back against him. His hands covered her bare breasts, his grip possessive. He almost came just from fondling her plump flesh.

"Yes!"

He pinched and tugged her nipples. "As much as you crave my cock?" His voice was ragged with lust.

"Put *everything* in me, *yes, yes, yes*." She shoved her hips back, circling them.

"Uhn! Myst!" He lowered his head to her neck. His aching fangs pierced her luscious skin just as he thrust.

"Ah, Wroth . . . *YES!*" She came again, lightning shaking the manor.

He *felt* her screams as he drank, felt her sheath pulsating around his swollen cock. His balls tightened. *Can't hold back!*

Squeezing her heavy breasts, he mindlessly fucked.

When he began to ejaculate, he snarled against her skin. While her blood scorched his veins, he flooded her with his hot seed.

Wave after wave after wave of it . . .

Thought gradually returned. He released his bite and kissed her neck in thanks. As he slowly withdrew, he clutched her close. She was unsteady, but then so was he.

When he scooped her into his arms, her eyes were silver, her lips curling. He stared, still disbelieving. "Liked that, did you?"

She nodded.

"Want more?" He tossed her on the bed.

In answer, she went to her knees and pulled aside her hair, offering him the unbitten side of her neck.

He sucked in a breath. "That wasn't quite what I meant, but we can work something out. . . ."

In the hours toward dawn, they exchanged mind-boggling pleasure, licking, fucking, and both of them biting. He marveled that his Bride was happily—no, aggressively—partaking.

At the end of the night, he gazed down at her in puzzlement. He didn't know which facet of her he liked better.

The siren in black satin who made his cock and fangs ache.

Or this angel with her bright red hair spread across his pillow—who made his chest ache.

She brushed the backs of her fingers along his jawline. "I want you to let this grow naturally between us, without using the chain. If you vow you'll return it in two weeks' time, I vow to give *us* a fair chance."

He wanted to believe in her—and in himself, that he could convince her to stay. In fourteen nights, he would command her to close her eyes and raise her cupped palms. He wanted to see her face when he poured the chain into them.

Two weeks to win her. "Yes, *milaya*, I vow it."

13

Nothing in Nikolai's human life or his vampire existence had prepared him for living with a Valkyrie.

Myst had boundless energy and strength, and she exuded an otherworldly sensuality that set his blood on fire.

Each night, he traced her to different locations to make love to her. He'd taken her against the foot of a pyramid. He'd gazed in awe as she rode him on a moonlit beach in Greece. He'd licked her sex beneath a redwood until she'd begged for mercy. . . .

Once he and Myst had worked the edge off their need, they'd talked for hours. Little by little, he was learning more about her and her kind.

When he'd made a surprise gift of his jeweled cross, she'd seemed to go into a trance. Once she'd shaken herself, she'd admitted, "We all inherited Freya's acquisitiveness. Shining things, jewels and gems . . . we can't tear our gaze away without training for years, and sudden glittering is sometimes irresistible."

Nikolai had inwardly cursed this vulnerability. While her immortal species had distinct advantages—no need to eat, strengthening with age—he'd learned they were one of the few species in the Lore that could die of sorrow. And if one Valkyrie was weakened, the others suffered, because they were all connected through a collective power.

He couldn't always be there to protect her. Though he'd tried to use the chain as little as possible, he'd whispered to her as she slept that she would no longer have these weaknesses. . . .

In their talks, she'd been surprisingly curious about him and his past. He'd found himself revealing things he never had to anyone and feeling unburdened.

He'd told her of the night he and Murdoch returned home to find their six other siblings and their father on the verge of death. Myst's eyes had watered as he'd spoken of the gut-wrenching decision to make them drink. Then had come the agonizing vigil as he'd wondered if his family would be reborn, any of them. In the end, he'd lost his father and sisters, but regained two brothers.

The night he himself had "died" fascinated her, especially since he'd made demands of Kristoff.

She'd told Nikolai how proud she was of him— which made him uneasy. These days, he didn't have much to be proud about.

Though he traced to Oblak for duty, he avoided his brother and his king, telling Kristoff little when they did meet. Worse, Nikolai was coercing his Bride to stay. And if she chose to leave him at the end of the two weeks, he suspected he'd break his vow to her in a heartbeat's time.

What would she decide? He constantly searched for clues. At times, he was optimistic. When they fought mock battles with a game based on military strategy, she seemed to enjoy herself with him—and to like the fact that he always beat her. She wasn't a strategist, she'd explained. She was "frontline bad-assness," but she appreciated his talent.

One night, she'd sidled over to straddle him, placing his hands on her breasts. As she slid down his shaft, she'd whispered in his ear, "My wise warlord. You make my toes curl, you're so good." He'd struggled not to come instantly.

In fact, she seemed to delight in every reminder that he'd warred. Her eyes had widened when she hefted the considerable weight of his sword, only to narrow on him and grow silver with want. If her eyes even flickered silver, he went as hard as that sword.

And last night, as they lay spent in bed, he'd asked her, "What do you find attractive about me?" That could possibly compete against a demigod with a "mind-shattering" kiss.

Without hesitation, she'd answered, "Your scars."

He'd frowned. "Why?"

"They're evidence of the pain you've survived. Pain survived builds strength." She'd traced down his stomach. "This is the one that killed you?"

"Yes."

"Then I admire this one the most." She'd brushed her lips so tenderly over it. "It brought you to me. . . ."

But his contentment was never complete—because his dreams reminded him of her sordid past. He'd never been in love—didn't believe he'd even slept with the same woman twice—yet now he craved everything from this pagan immortal, was sick with wanting her.

He needed to strip her soul bare and make her give all of herself—all of what she'd been in the beginning before time twisted her.

Though he'd never actually seen her bedding another in those dreams, thank God, he drove himself mad with the mere idea of her past lovers. How did he compare to them?

Whenever she did some wicked thing to him, he'd stare at the ceiling in an agony of pleasure and shock—and later, wonder where she'd learned it.

How many had she been with? She was nearly two thousand years old. One bedmate a year? Two a year? One lover a month . . . ?

And how could he compete with gods for her? She was so beautiful, she'd clearly been made to be loved by them alone.

The dreams kept him from falling into the life they could share—the life he would gladly do murder for.

Though her blood built his muscle, making him physically stronger than he'd ever imagined, he dreaded sleep and took no comfort from it. His exhaustion mounted. Each time they awakened, he treated her coldly, so she asked about his dreams.

But he lied.

She would accept his reassurance, smiling over at him from her window seat. Her smile could bring down an army. Probably had.

How had he thought he was a match for it?

My apologies, Myst thought as she gazed down at Wroth, *but I'm enjoying the hell out of this vampire.*

His gray eyes were so fierce, his gorgeous body taut beneath her claws as she rolled her hips on him. They were both on the verge of orgasm, had been edging themselves for an hour.

His sweating muscles quaked; she'd never been wetter.

Panting, she leaned forward to cup her breast to his mouth. He suckled with a desperate groan, tension stealing over him as his release passed the point of no return.

"Wroth . . . I'm about—"

He bit her nipple, wrenching a scream from her lips and an orgasm from her body. Her sheath demanded his hot come; he was helpless not to give it. . . .

When she fell limp on top of him, he clenched her against his heaving chest, holding her through his after-shudders.

Eventually, they disentangled themselves, and he rose to shower.

She frowned when he returned dressed for work. Heading off to Oblak again? "I'm down with being your dirty little secret out here—for now," she told him. "But I can't just sit in this room with nothing to do while you're gone."

He sat beside her. "What do you need, love?" he asked, piling her curls atop her head. He seemed fascinated by her hair, always touching it.

Wait, he'd called her *love*? Cool. "Do you know what video-gaming is? No? Well, your Bride has a teeny little addiction to it."

"Write down whatever you need."

She jotted a note with the model of the console

and the games she wanted. Just before he traced, she took his hands and gazed up at him solemnly. "Bring this back and you might as well have slayed a dragon for me."

"I'll return directly."

She painted her toenails as she waited—Valkyries loved painting their nails, since most aspects of their appearance were unchanging—and reflected on how easily she'd settled in here.

In fact, only three things prevented her from being truly comfortable. The first? Though they traveled most nights, Wroth wouldn't take her to meet his friends and family—or let her see hers either. He'd explained that he wanted her undivided attention for these two weeks.

She suspected he was waiting until their relationship was cemented, which he believed would be in three days—the end of her two-week vampire demo. Had it resulted in a sale?

Accepting him as her husband would mean pariah-hood in the Lore and having to give up her family. She could just imagine bringing Wroth to the coven. Her sisters would thank her for the surprise, then pounce on him with swords and claws bared.

As twin sister to Furie, Cara for one would fight him to the death simply for what he was. Part fury, she had thousands of years more fighting experience—and the boiling hatred of a separated twin.

Wroth versus Cara would be like Godzilla versus Mothra, or some serious epic shit.

Myst's second concern was her worry for him. Each time he was out in the world, she feared he would face some Lore faction bent on killing all vampires. Because he knew so little about immortals, he'd always be at a disadvantage.

She believed Kristoff's agenda—and saw no conflict of interest with her coven—so she'd turned informant, teaching Wroth how to protect himself.

Her third beef? Each sunset when they woke, he was surly and curt with her. She suspected he was seeing her memories of flirting, or even making love. But Nïx had once told her that recipients of visions usually witnessed only major, life-changing events. And Wroth had assured her again and again it was nothing. . . .

Yet she could tolerate his moods because he spent the rest of the night treating her like a queen.

As promised, Wroth returned directly, with . . .

The slain dragon and its attendant games.

He looked at her with his brows drawn as if he'd missed her, and her heart did twisty things in her chest. The impulse came to jump him, so she did.

Only after he'd squeezed her up in his arms did she realize she'd run to get within them.

14

Nikolai shot up in bed, nauseated from his nightmares. He pinched his forehead, sorting through the chaotic scenes.

He'd been lashed by the usual dreams of Myst gloating at a grave site, then the Roman stroking himself: "I'm about to have Myst the Coveted . . . you'll be possessed."

But details of the memories continued to emerge. This time he'd heard Myst's amused thoughts: *No one possesses me except in their fantasies. I'll kill you as easily as kiss you.* "And I'll be yours, only yours," she purred, though she detested him.

He'd also witnessed a new memory of hers, a recent one.

Here in this room, Myst was smoothing on hose as she made a decision to . . . trick him? To act as though she'd accepted him—in order to get her chain back! *Play at love, and act at surrender.*

His grip on his forehead tightened. Irrationally, he waited for the soft touch of his wife's hand on his back. But she could never comfort him after a nightmare—even if she'd had that urge—because he was still secretly commanding her to sleep throughout the day.

So she wouldn't run away from him and leave him in torment again.

Play at love . . .

He'd thought they had a foundation to build on, but he'd been fooled by her beauty and abandon. She'd seduced him that night, had made sure he'd "caught" her touching herself, knowing he would lose his mind at the sight.

He was as much a besotted fool as the Roman. Worse. At least that man had suffered no delusions she could care for him. The Roman had known she was incapable of feeling and had wanted possession only.

Nikolai? He'd bought her a goddamned *wedding ring*.

He'd been falling for a fantasy, one that had easily manipulated him.

She desired her freedom and would use whatever means she had available to get it, leaving him as soon as she'd succeeded.

Fool.

~~~

When Myst woke, she burrowed down into the covers, feeling relaxed and content to her toes.

Today was delivery day for the chain—the end of the demo that *had* resulted in a sale.

She feared that life as she'd known it had ended when he'd vowed to give her the Brisingamen back. It was a leap of faith on his part, and she'd responded.

Smoothing things over with her family might take a while, but she would figure out a way. Somehow.

Eventually she would convince them that Wroth was different from other vampires.

She snuggled into his pillow, loving his scent, and considered her new feelings. Though she'd smugly planned to punk him, she'd been snared in her own machinations. Her femme fatale plans had resulted in the oh-so-nefarious leap into his arms.

She grinned. She'd take back her chain, but just because it looked so damned sassy on her.

When she rose and stretched, she found him watching her. Her grin widened, but he didn't return her smile.

In fact, he scowled at her bare breasts.

She drew her head back. "Are you angry with me?" He was usually brusque, but she could tell this was much worse. What could have happened since she'd gone to sleep, tucked against his chest?

His eyes were somehow crazed and bleak at the same time, his face exhausted. Alarm began to build inside her. Exhausted immortals weren't known for good judgment.

"We have a lot to discuss." He tossed her a robe. "Put this on."

She had no choice but to comply. He traced away, returning with the chain in his fist. "Tonight we're going to make some adjustments between us—or more accurately, *in* you."

Her eyes widened. "What are you doing? You vowed to give it back today."

"A woman like you should understand broken vows."

"What are you talking about? How can you do this to me now?" Right when she'd decided to stay.

His face was crueler than she'd ever seen it. "You mean after the last two weeks? Just because you've wanted to be fucked and I complied doesn't mean I won't treat you as you deserve."

She put the back of her hand to her face as if she'd been struck. "As I deserve," she repeated dumbly. He might as well have said, "treat you like a whore."

He grasped her arm, squeezing it hard. "I can't live like this, Myst. *With* this." At her confused expression, he said, "I've seen your past. I know what you were."

"I don't understand you!" She hadn't lived her life perfectly—there'd been missteps and misjudgments—but she'd done little to be ashamed of. Was the killing too much for him to handle? He'd been a fucking warlord! "If you find me lacking, know that I regret very few of my actions over my long life."

That seemed to enrage him. "No? What about playing at love and acting at surrender?"

Her gaze widened. "Wroth, that was—"

"Silence." He kissed her harshly. She shoved against him before he pulled back. "I've realized you are heartless. But what if I ordered you to be kinder? What if I made you forget your vicious sisters who kill without remorse?" He seemed out of his mind with rage, his eyes tortured. "Made you forget all the men who came before me?"

She gasped, tears welling, but she couldn't speak after his command. Her hands clenched, claws digging into her palms. Never in her life had she wanted more to scream, yet her lips parted silently when he said, "I should order you to want me so fiercely you can't think of anything or anyone else—"

A voice interrupted from downstairs. "General Wroth, you're needed at Oblak immediately."

"*Why?*" he bellowed.

She felt his gaze on her as she staggered to the window seat, tears beginning to fall. She curled up, leaning her forehead against the glass.

"Your brother's been badly injured, sir."

"Stay here until I return, Myst," Wroth bit out. "Do you understand?"

She looked at him mutely.

"Speak."

"I-I understand."

He disappeared.

She choked back a sob when she heard him downstairs, locking away her freedom. Then he was gone.

Stay here? In the room or the manor? He'd been so thrown by the news that he hadn't elaborated.

Stumbling, clutching at the wall as energy funneled out of her, she made her way to his study. She opened the cabinet, revealing the safe. When she reached for the lock, her hand veered off course as though pushed by an unseen force. She bit her lip and tried again.

Impossible. Because he'd commanded her not to touch it. Just as he would command her to forget who she was, that she even had a family! Lightning crackled outside in time with a sob. He'd been about to do it.

It was true then—vampires couldn't be trusted. Why had she gone against all she'd ever learned to be with him?

The years had been weighing on her, and she'd yearned to lean on someone, to have a partner watch her back and hold her when she needed it. She must have convinced herself to accept him because he was strong—and she had grown so weak.

No longer.

There were ways she could get around his order not to touch the safe—nimble thinking, creative reasoning.

But how?

If she could reach her chain before he returned, she could feign sleep. Once he drifted off, she'd have the entire day to get far away. . . .

The solution hit her. As tears poured from her eyes and the lightning grew continuous, she clawed the wall, tearing at the very stone surrounding the safe.

So he would use her? Like a toy. A mindless slave. *Adjustments?*

Toy, bait, whore. *Just because you wanted to be fucked,* he'd sneered.

She'd endured two millennia of people thinking they could use her. Always using her.

She'd take this safe with her teeth if she had to.

15

Nikolai traced into Murdoch's room, finding his brother's face torn, his limbs broken.

"You should see the other guy," Murdoch grated from his bed.

Short of a beheading or sunlight, nothing could kill them; still, Nikolai shuddered to see Murdoch like this. "What happened to you?"

"I was about to ask you the same. My God, you look worse than I do."

Nikolai pictured Myst crying at the window, staring out at the lightning storm that came from within her. The idea of her hurting all alone pained him so much. "We'll talk of my problems later. Who has done this to you?"

"Ivo has demons. Demons turned vampires. You can't imagine how strong they are. He is looking for someone, but I don't think it's your Bride. They mentioned something about a 'halfling.'"

"How many?"

"There were three demonic vampires in his party—other vampires as well. We took down two of the demons but one remains." He peered past Nikolai. "Where's your Bride?"

Nikolai hesitated—but after all, this was his brother,

THE WARLORD WANTS FOREVER   129

and the weight of the situation suddenly seemed unbearable. So, haltingly at first, he explained everything,
seeking the same unburdening he felt when he spoke
with Myst.

His brother's expression grew stark. "You took
away the free will of a creature who has had it for
upward of two thousand years," Murdoch said in-
credulously. "A good wager says she's going to want
it back."

"No, you don't understand. She's callous. Incapable of love. Her deception eats at me, because it's the
only thing that makes sense." He absently muttered,
"Why else would she want me?"

Murdoch reached for Nikolai's wrist. "All these
years I've seen you choose the most rational
course, even if it's the most difficult. I've been
proud to follow your leadership because you've
acted with courage and always—always—with
rationality. I never thought I would have to inform
you that your reason and judgment have failed you,
Nikolai. If she's as bad as you say, then you have
to . . . I don't know, just *help* her change, but you
can't order it. Get back to her. Explain your fears
to her."

"You saw her. Why else would she so quickly acquiesce?"

"Why don't you just ask her?"

*Because I don't want to demonstrate again how obsessed
I've become with her.*

"And about the other men," Murdoch continued.
"This isn't the seventeen hundreds anymore. This
isn't even the same world. She's an immortal, not an

eighteen-year-old blushing bride straight from a convent. She can't change her past, so if you want her, you'll have to adjust."

Nikolai scrubbed a palm down his face. "When did you get so bloody understanding?"

Murdoch shrugged with difficulty. "Someone explained a few rules of the Lore to me, and I learned we can't apply our human expectations to the beings within it."

"Who told you this?" When his brother didn't answer, Nikolai didn't push, not with all the secrets he'd been keeping.

"Get back to her, Nikolai. *Begin*."

"Will you be all right?"

"That's the thing about being immortal," Murdoch said. "It'll always look worse than it is."

Nikolai attempted a grin but didn't manage it.

"Good luck, brother."

Outside the room, Nikolai spoke with those in charge of Murdoch's care, explaining what would happen should his brother's condition worsen.

He was almost glad when Kristoff called a meeting about this newest threat, grateful for the time to cool off before he faced Myst again.

But as the meeting ground on, impatience to return to her hammered at Nikolai. . . .

Heading into the second hour, Kristoff asked him, "Why would your Bride not tell you about the turned demons?"

"I don't know. I will ask her." He wondered as well. Had she known? No, she'd been teaching him everything she knew—teaching him constantly.

Wait—why would she do so, if she only planned to leave him? His gut tightened.

"Something to add?" Kristoff was studying him.

Nikolai owed Kristoff his life, the lives of his brothers, and even for Myst herself. He would withhold information on her kind, but divulge the rest. "I have much to discuss with you, but I left my wife feeling poorly. I'd like to get back to her."

"By all means." Kristoff's face was unreadable. "But tomorrow we'll talk."

With a nod, Nikolai traced back to Myst, frowning as a hazy idea surfaced in his chaotic thoughts. Had his brother's heart been beating earlier?

Before he could contemplate this further, his attention was distracted by Myst's sleeping form. He gazed down at her, chest aching as usual. Sometimes he damned his beating heart because of the pain that seemed to follow it.

Murdoch was right. She couldn't change what she was, and he'd wronged her today. If only he could *think* more clearly where she was concerned—instead of reacting viscerally.

In the past, he'd never understood why men talked of madness and love in the same breath. Now he did.

He only hoped that when he asked her to forgive his weakness, she could.

Joining her in bed, he pulled her close. He buried his face in her hair and inhaled her soft, sweet scent.

At dawn, his exhaustion caught up with him, and he passed out. When he began to dream, he opened his mind to her memories, to what had become his nightmares. They overran all his other memories of battle and death, because these hurt him the most. *See her in a sordid light. Punish yourself.*

See them all.

16

*T*he dream of the Roman came first. Nikolai impatiently waded through the usual scene, seeking more.

Did he truly want to see this? Could he turn back?

Too late. He felt as if he'd opened the floodgates; these dreams were going to play out, each spinning to its gruesome, twisted ending.

Myst slowly lifted her skirt for the man. Yet then Nikolai felt something new. Chills crawled up her spine as she peered down at the Roman, with his wet lips and furious stroking.

She was ashamed at her disgust and closed her mind off to it. She was the bait. She'd be whatever it took to free her sister.

"I'm about to have Myst the Coveted . . . you'll be possessed."

No one possesses me except in their fantasies. I'll kill you as easily as kiss you. The Roman sought to make her his plaything, just as he had used Daniela for weeks.

Myst glanced up, and Nikolai saw through her eyes. Across the room, Lucia had Daniela's limp body in her covered arms. Most of their sister's icy skin had been burned. Daniela had been tortured by this animal at her feet, by his very touch.

The familiar rage erupted within her. *Control it*, she thought. Just a moment longer. "And I'll be yours, only yours," she somehow purred.

When Lucia signaled, Myst nodded. As she extracted her foot, his lips produced a loud sucking sound that made her grimace. She tapped the man's bulbous nose with her big toe. In a tone laden with sexuality, she said, "You probably won't live through what I'm about to do, but if you survive, learn and tell others you should never"—a tap with her toe—"ever"—tap—"harm a Valkyrie."

She kicked his head, punting his body across the room.

Myst had been . . . *rescuing her sister?*

Too quickly, another scene began, the one with the raiding party, the one Nikolai always most dreaded seeing. When the men neared, she pretended to be out of breath; she forced herself to stumble. All a part of the game.

One tackled her hard into the snow. Others snared her arms. She feigned fear, weakly struggling. Amid cheers, a burly Viking knelt between her legs and told her, "I hope you live longer than the last ones did."

Lightning streaked behind the man's head, and the wind seemed to follow. A few glanced around uneasily. Nervous laughter.

Myst informed him, "The last ones had names. Angritte and her daughter Carin." Young and simple, Carin had somehow recognized Myst as a Valkyrie. "Swan maiden," the girl had whispered, uttering one of the Valkyries' more beautiful names.

Both the careless mother and her innocent

daughter had been killed, brutalized by these men. Myst had loved Carin for her very innocence and joy; the girl had been stolen from Myst and from the world—which was poorer for the loss.

"I will live longer than them," Myst said. "And *you*."

The frown on her attacker's face was the last expression he'd ever make. A change came over her. Bloodlust welling. Thoughts turned feral. The rage . . .

She rose up, effortlessly shaking off the men. As lightning painted the sky, she slashed her way through them. When all but one had been felled, she told the sole survivor, "Anytime you think to hunt down a woman, wonder if she's not like me. I've spared you, but my sisters would unman you with a flick of their claws, their wrath unimaginable." She wiped her arm over her face, found it wet.

She crouched over the man and saw her grisly reflection in his gaze. Her eyes were silver, and blood spattered her face. "There are thousands of us lining these coasts, *waiting*." He was frozen in terror. "And I'm the gentle one."

She turned from him, dusting off her hands, and muttered to herself, "This is how rumors get started." But her swagger disappeared as she climbed the hilltop by the sea, where two recent graves had been dug.

"You stupid human," she hissed at Angritte's gravestone. "I've cursed you to your hell. Why did you disobey me? I told you to take Carin inland in the spring when the marauders come. Stay far from the coasts." Myst's voice broke on a sob as she ran to the girl's tombstone. She curled up against it, her cheek resting against the runes.

Choking with frustration, she hit the stone, her blood trickling along the new fracture.

For days, she stayed like that. Villagers held a vigil at the base of the hill, offering up tributes for Myst's protection and benevolence.

Nikolai shuddered at the physical pain Myst didn't seem to feel—her hand frozen in blood to the stone, her muscles knotted, her skin raw from cold. On the fourth day, her sister Nïx found her and lifted her from the snow as easily as a pillow. Tears were ice on Myst's face.

"Shhh, sister," Nïx said. "We've already heard the tales of your revenge. That league of men will never harm another maid. In fact, I doubt they will ever trouble this coast again."

"But the girl," Myst whispered, awash in confusion, tears streaming anew, "is simply *gone*." The last word was a sob.

"Yes, dearling," Nïx said. "Never to return."

Myst wept. "But . . . but it *hurts* when they die."

Nïx pressed her lips to Myst's forehead, murmuring, *"And they always do. . . ."*

Myst's sorrow pained Nikolai more than any physical wound he'd ever suffered, even his death-blow. She'd run from those men to test them; the ones who chased a "defenseless" maiden were the ones who would die.

He wanted to stay with that memory, but another familiar dream began. The meeting around the hearth. ". . . guide her to be all that was good and honorable about the Valkyries . . ." Snow outside, packed so high it covered half of the window.

As her sister spoke, Myst closed her eyes at a memory, the one Nikolai had struggled to see. Vowing again that she would be worthy, Myst remembered standing in the middle of a battlefield where one hundred thousand corpses lay hacked to pieces.

Barely fifteen, she'd been sent young as a *chooser of the slain*—because her mother had been a brave Pict who'd plunged a dagger into her own heart. Myst was supposed to be like that.

But she wasn't. Not yet. She was sick with terror. Nikolai wanted to be there to protect her, comfort her.

"They were all brave." She frantically turned in circles as electricity rolled from her in waves. A river of blood sloshed around her ankles. Sounding lost, she whispered, "How am I to choose? A beggar handing out coins . . ." She began trembling uncontrollably, and it shamed her.

Never be unworthy again. And she hadn't been, for two millennia.

Until she'd met a male from an enemy army . . .

A new memory arose. Could Nikolai withstand another?

Myst ran to him when he returned to Blachmount from an errand. As he squeezed her against his chest and kissed her, she thought, *I just ran to get in his arms. I just . . . Whoa. Whoa. Uhn-uh.*

Nikolai remembered she'd clambered down from him, looking flushed and panicky.

Now he knew why. Myst, along with all her sisters, believed she would recognize her true partner when he opened his arms and she realized she'd forever run to him—

Nikolai woke to his own yell. Everything he'd thought about her was wrong. His chest hurt with the loss and anguish she'd experienced. He reached for her. "You're free, Myst. . . ."

The bed was empty. Dread settled over him.

He shot to his feet, scanning the room. On a table, he saw the cross, with a bloody note beneath it. He read:

A heart for a heart

Even though falling for a vampire would make her unworthy in the eyes of her sisters and the Lore, she'd been losing her heart—to him.

Panic stabbed at his body like a blade. He half-staggered, half-traced into the study.

The safe was gone.

To his horror, blood coated the stone that had housed it. She'd dug through it to get to her chain, to her freedom.

Nikolai fell to his knees, head bowed as a guttural sound of pain erupted from his chest. At the first opportunity, he'd offered her torture. Once he'd found her again, he'd stolen her freedom.

And then . . .

A heart for a heart. She'd made his beat. Had he broken hers?

He'd lost her. And he deserved to.

17

Five days after Myst's escape to Val Hall, the coven met around the vampire's safe. The metal might be mojo-protected, but Regin wielded the Sword of Wóden, which cut through anything.

Well, anything but the chain, as Myst and Regin had discovered—after one scary experiment nearly made Myst a good deal shorter.

The sisters were still debating who would accept the responsibility of the chain. As long as Wroth lived, Myst wasn't allowed to wear it. Since no one wanted the thing, killing that vampire seemed a bingo solution to them.

Regin raised the sword above her. Even the wraiths flying outside slowed to catch a window. The Valkyries had recently hired those ghostly creatures to guard Val Hall against intruders—after a demon turned vampire had attacked.

With a dramatic breath, Regin swung the sword down and sliced through the safe. Sparks flew and smoke billowed.

When all was clear, Myst wearily reached forward to collect the chain. Beside it was a small wooden box, about the size of one of those velvet jewelry boxes.

Her sisters must have concluded the same; they dove for it as if it were a wedding bouquet. "Shiny, in the box, shiny," one of the youngest whimpered.

Myst snagged it first. Even if she hadn't, she would've clotheslined anyone who made a run with it.

"Open it, then," Regin cried, out of breath.

Myst did.

Light blazed from it.

"Great Freya," someone breathed. "Diamond. Big. Glittery."

Another said, "That's not a rock; that's real estate. When did vampires start ponying up rocks? No, really."

Myst closed her fingers over what had to be a ten-carat diamond, so she could look at the actual ring. Her name had been engraved on the inside of the band.

Suddenly exhausted, she rose, dragging her feet up the stairs. The others booed her for taking away "my precious." The chain was heavy and cold in Myst's other hand.

Nïx followed her up to her room.

"You didn't look surprised about this," Myst said, holding up the ring.

Nïx's pupils enlarged. "Surprise!"

Myst stowed it and the chain in her jewelry armoire. "You knew what was in the safe?"

"I'm not called the Ever-Knowing for nothing." Nïx dug two bottles of fingernail polish and some cotton from her pocket. She hopped on the bed and set them up to paint each other's toenails.

Myst had missed this little ritual, but she had no

interest right now. She crossed to the window and asked, "Why didn't you come for me? You knew how to find me."

"You were fated to spend that time with Wroth."

Wroth. Who had deemed her so lacking he'd decided to *adjust* her.

What had he seen that disgusted him so much? For the last five days, she'd racked her brain, but found nothing she'd be truly ashamed of—certainly nothing that would make a vampire *lose his freaking mind*. "He's probably out there." Myst stared out at the fog-shrouded yard. "Watching this house, waiting for a chance to take me again. But if I stay behind the wraiths, then I'm just as trapped here as I was there."

"Without the weakness of the chain, couldn't you fight him?" Nïx asked. "I'd bet kicking some vampire ass might be good for you."

Regin popped her head in. "Cara and I are going out to mix it up with some ghouls. You in?"

Myst turned to Nïx. "Any reason I shouldn't?"

Her sister bit her lip, staring at the ceiling as if recalling a memory—when she was doing just the opposite. "Hmmm. Kicking vampire ass or ghoul ass? I think either would be just the thing."

Myst nodded slowly. "Yeah. I could use a little goo."

Regin's glowing skin brightened, and she bounded across the landing to scream downstairs, "Myst is back online!"

Ready to fight, *needing* it, she dressed while Nïx did a buff job on Myst's neglected sword.

Myst had no doubt Wroth was out there watching her. How long would he follow his "heartless" Bride?

But she knew the answer, had felt the wild emotion roiling within him.

He'd follow forever.

⸺

Nikolai crept among the shadows of the sprawling cemetery as Myst split up from Regin and Cara.

This was the first time he'd seen her in days.

Sword sheath at her back, she vaulted to the top of a mausoleum. He was spellbound as she stalked her prey, perched on the edge of the roof, her claws curled into the clay tile. Her eyes swirled silver as she surveyed a large gathering of ghouls below her.

The unsuspecting creatures snapped fangs at each other or lazed in the dampness of the night.

She'd taught him about that species, warning him how dangerous they were. Ghoul bites and scratches were contagious—even to some immortals.

Clearly eager for the kill, she must be waiting for her sisters to return so they could attack as one.

He didn't want to spoil her hunt, but he burned to speak to her now that she'd finally left her home.

After she'd escaped from Blachmount, he'd traced to Val Hall, finding it even eerier than before. Ghostly, howling creatures clad in ragged red cloth circled the manor like a tornado.

He'd shrugged and traced to her room—but the things had intercepted and thrown him. When he'd eventually landed, his lesson had been learned.

Those sentinels would protect Myst from threats like Ivo, but they kept Nikolai from her as well.

No longer. Dawn was coming soon, and he needed to—

She drew her sword from its sheath and dropped into the middle of the ghouls. There were at least fifty of them!

He traced to her side. "What the fuck are you doing?" he bellowed, freeing his own sword.

"This isn't happening," she muttered to herself.

"In the middle of them, Myst?"

"I'm enraged enough to do this. You have no idea"—she struck out, slicing a ghoul from crotch to neck—"how much I need this."

"I do have an idea." A perfect one. He'd *felt* her rage and her need to fight; yet he'd arrogantly informed her she never would again.

"You'd better leave. Once I finish with them, I won't stop there."

"I deserve your anger. I've wronged you and seek to make amends." He wasn't optimistic about his chances. She couldn't be all things to him, and then forgiving on top of that.

"You think?"

One ghoul's claw whistled close to his neck; he leapt back just in in time.

She snapped, "Don't let them scratch you!"

"Concerned for me, wife?" He didn't dare hope.

"Of course I don't want you to get scratched. Leeches are easier to kill."

"If I help you, will you speak with me?"

"Don't need your assistance." She was merrily

felling them, one after another, with a skill that awed him. Her sword flew so fast, it was barely visible.

"Then you'll have to listen here," he grated, digging into the fight with her. "I'd had five years of torment. I'd had a hell of wanting you and feared you would leave me at the first opportunity. Then I experienced dreams of your memories."

These ghouls irritated him, especially when they got between him and Myst while he tried to convince her about something so critical. He increased his pace, killing them more quickly. "In each one you were evil . . . a seductress."

"Still am, Wroth." She kicked a ghoul in the belly, freeing her sword from the thing's chest.

"No, you're not—"

"Duck!" Her blade sliced over his head to decapitate a ghoul behind him. "As I recall, I asked you about your dreams every sunset, but you brushed away my concerns."

He slew two with one swing of his sword. "I should have talked to you, because those excruciating scenes of you . . . doing things were all out of context." When the largest ghoul howled and attacked, Nikolai stabbed the creature in the face, dropping it.

She raised her eyebrows as if impressed, then scowled, remembering herself.

"Myst, even then I was still falling for you."

That at least got her to pause. She blew a curl out of her eyes.

A ghoul behind her! Without turning, she thrust her sword backward, skewering its neck.

Now he raised his eyebrows. *Focus, Nikolai.* "I was angry when I saw your plan to trick me," he continued, "but I understand you rightly wanted your freedom back. I know what and who you are now. I saw all the memories clearly at last. Not out of context." Goddamn it, more ghouls? "Can we not just speak about this? Away from here? Dawn nears, and all I ask is a chance to—"

"I gave you a chance. Freely. And you threw it away. You were about to brainwash me."

"I never would've gone through with that, couldn't have lived with myself." With one hand, he carved up a ghoul. "I was wrong in many ways. I took your freedom when you needed it, and I hurt you just when you'd given yourself to me." Never had he regretted his actions so much.

He could have won her. *A heart for a heart.* "I wanted you so badly I resorted to any tactic and treated you ill when you didn't deserve it." He looked around. He'd been so intent on her, he'd scarcely noticed they'd cut such a swath the other ghouls had run. "If you give me a chance, I will make it up to you."

She cast him a killing look. "Just let me go giftwrap my chain for you."

18

Wroth's eyes flickered black, and his voice went low. "I'd destroy the goddamned thing if I saw it."

His reaction surprised her. "You'll certainly never get within arm's reach of it."

"Myst, I felt your feelings for me, felt you struggling against them. I know you care for me." Long moments passed as they stared into each other's eyes.

She was weak. When she'd first seen him here, she'd felt a flare of excitement. *Weak.* She shook her head. "I can't. It's just too late. I have a lot to lose from this. I won't hurt my family by accepting you."

"Kristoff seeks peace with the Valkyries. There would be no conflict. He wishes to fight the Horde together. And I would make an effort with your sisters. I know now how important they are to you. Believe me, I know."

She tapped her chin. "So you can see why the idea of being forced to forget them made me cranky? Huh? And what if you saw more out of context? This would just happen again and again."

"I would not drink from you."

She rolled her eyes. "Yeah, just like I'm going to finally beat my video game addiction."

"I would vow to tell you everything I saw, everything I was thinking, as if you could read my mind as well." With his brows drawn, he stepped closer. "We are wed. We should know each other's secrets. Myst, we are kindred."

She'd felt that way too. *Kindred.*

Wait. What the hell was she thinking? He'd been about to mind-erase her. Making her voice firm, she said, "Wroth, I could never trust you—"

Her words were cut off by a massive arm, squeezing the breath from her throat. Not a ghoul. A demon?

Wroth raised his sword, a savage look in his eyes; the arm tightened, and he froze.

"I wouldn't do that if I were you," Ivo said as he sauntered to the front of his gang. "He's a hybrid. He'll snap her head right from her neck."

She struggled to breathe. The male must be a *turned* demon. She'd thought that was an actual myth until one had attacked Val Hall, hence the wraiths. The Horde had upped their game. She'd known Ivo was planning something. . . .

His red gaze flickered over her. "Now, Myst, I thought I told you to wait in my dungeon." To the demon, Ivo said, "She's not the one."

Then he narrowed his eyes at Wroth. "So you're the former human who took my castle from me. You used guns? I'll kill you just for bastardizing our war." He glanced from Wroth to Myst, then back again. Anyone could see Wroth's body seeming to vibrate, his muscles knotted with tension. "I believe I have something the Forbearer wants very badly. His Bride. I'll take his life in exchange."

Wroth could trace away in a heartbeat—but he didn't move.

"If you walk into the sun," Ivo told him, "I'll vow to the Lore I'll free her. I'll hunt her again, but for this dawn she will live. If you trace instead, I'll dine on her perfect flesh every night for eternity."

"Fight me, coward," Wroth grated, his eyes black with rage.

"Fight you for the cards I already hold?" Ivo sounded confused.

Wroth was so strong, and yet he could do nothing. Frustration radiated from him.

"You know we've got the power here," Ivo said. "And you know a vow to the Lore will compel me to release her."

Wroth's eyes were assessing, his sharp mind studying the situation. She knew the exact moment he'd decided. A calm seemed to wash over him.

Ivo demanded, "Her life or yours, Forbearer."

One tight nod. "Done." No hesitation. "It is done."

Ivo and his gang traced her into the shade to ready for the dawn. Birdsong had begun.

"Catch and release?" Myst sneered. "Are you kidding me?" To Wroth, she said, "Are you eager to be ash?"

The sunlight hit the tops of the trees, descending inch by torturing inch. He stood sure and so brave, as if proud to give his life for hers.

The morning breeze blew his black hair from his face. His eyes were riveted to hers.

Rays were inches from him, almost reaching the moss of the great oaks. Now *she* felt frustration as she'd never known. "Don't be stupid!"

In a low, steady tone, he said, "I love you, Myst."

Feeling erupted in her chest. Yes, he'd wronged her, and yes, he was a vampire, but . . .

The light hit him. He did not close his eyes to the extreme brightness—and she knew it was because he wanted to see her longer.

Soon the intensity of the sun grew too great; he fell to his knees, his hands curling in agonizing pain.

He was going to die. Gone forever.

Wroth opened his eyes once more. Glowing, bare. A last look.

He's going to die.

They always do.

Just . . . gone.

"No." Saying the word out loud was like blasting a snowcapped mountain to free an avalanche. An immortal like him didn't have to die. He could stay with her. "No, no, *no!*"

"*Milaya*, don't fight," he bit out. "It is done."

The demon holding her smelled of rotting flesh. The cowardly gang of vampires smirked at Wroth's death when he was so much greater than they.

She'd waited millennia to love—she'd waited for *him*—and they dared take him from her. From Myst the Coveted.

She unleashed a shriek, the kind Valkyries were known for. The kind that preceded death. The demon fought to snap her neck, but her muscles lay in perfect alignment to prevent it.

Wroth struggled to get to her even as he burned. Battling to save her as he died.

He was hers. That they would *dare* . . .

She freed and raised her arms. Lightning struck her, a bolt from the gods.

Thunder hammered the two holding her. Her hand shot down to snatch one's sword just as he was cast into the sunlight.

With lightning-fueled strength, she slashed and clawed at the gang. She barely flinched when one broke her arm and the butt of a sword cracked her cheekbone. *Don't look through that eye, switch hands.* She cut a swath to Ivo, who alone remained.

"And here I thought you were merely the pretty one." With a mock bow, the coward traced.

Arm shattered, face beaten to a pulp, she flew to Wroth. With one arm, she started dragging him into the cool shade, biting her wrist open for him to drink.

He was unconscious, twisting in pain. His skin looked like lava burned within him.

"Seems like we missed the party," Regin said as she and Cara strolled over. "Why does Myst get to kill all the vampires? No, really. This was just supposed to be ghouls."

"What are you doing?" Cara demanded. "We heard your scream and thought it was something *important.*" She waved a dismissive hand at Wroth's writhing form. "The being dies. Leave him." She clearly couldn't fathom why Myst was frantically dragging his big body while shoving her gashed wrist to his lips.

"Oh, for fuck's sake," Regin said. "He's a leech. Let him fricassee."

Myst snapped her teeth at her sisters. Then she screamed two words she'd never uttered in her entire life: *"Help me!"*

19

Nikolai woke to wetness on his chest. He was in bed? With Myst's silky red hair tumbling over his arm?

When he opened his eyes, he realized she was crying over him. Impossible. "Myst?" he rasped.

Her head shot up, and she gave him a watery smile that quickly faded. She slapped him, a hard, cracking blow across his cheek. Then she leapt atop him, squeezing him as if she couldn't get close enough.

"Don't you ever do anything so stupid again!" Another slap struck his chest.

His healed chest? He flexed his muscles throughout his body. He was bandaged in places, but he had all his limbs. This was good. Now if he could just get his wife to cease slapping him. "If you do not stop, *milaya*, we will have words."

She turned to kissing him, with tears dropping to his face, each one like a gift. "You've been out for three nights. And you wouldn't wake the hell up."

"Where are we?"

"In Val Hall."

He stiffened.

"No, you're safe." She leaned back and raised an

eyebrow. "Do you think I would just let my sisters fall on you like a carcass?"

He winced at the image. "Can't wait to meet them all. How did you get away?"

"Ivo traced, but Cara and Regin are on his trail."

"I'm just glad I was there to save you," Nikolai said solemnly, making her grin. "Did you kill the turned demon?"

"The lightning and I did."

He remembered then. She'd been hit by a bolt, her hair whipping, eyes silver, the most awing sight he'd ever witnessed. "I saw you get struck." His voice went low. "You smiled."

"It feels good. Getting a direct hit is very rare—"

Outside, some male howled with fury.

Nikolai tensed to trace her away, but she waved away his concern. "Oh, don't worry. Just another crazy day at the manor. A Lykae nabbed little Emmaline and took her back to Scotland—thinks she's his werewolf queen."

"Werewolf queen?"

"Uh-huh. So Lucia trapped the Lykae's brother for leverage, but apparently he's proving uncooperative. Anyway, if you knew Em, you'd see how ridiculous the idea is. She's terrified of her own shadow, much less a Lykae's unique . . . appetites."

Nikolai would have to ask her about that later. "She's the halfling—the one who's part vampire." When Myst frowned, he rushed to assure her, "I will never tell Kristoff about her, but I suspect Ivo's searching for her."

"We know. We're sending a retrieval party for her.

Once they bring her back, she'll be safe here. The wraiths will shut out any threat." One flew by the window, cackling to punctuate her statement.

He raised his brows, but she merely grinned. With a bandaged hand, he cupped her face. "I love you."

"I know."

"Could you . . . could you feel the same way? Before you answer, I want you to know I meant what I said. I am sorry for forcing you to stay with me and for losing my head. I will always be shamed by my actions."

"Wroth, I wanted to stay with you after about a day! I'd planned to play you, but realized I was falling in love with you."

He hadn't heard her correctly. Yes, she'd been upset over his injuries, but . . . "You're saying you love me too?"

She nibbled her lip and nodded. "I'd always had a crush on you, you know. I used to adore hearing tales about you when you were human and was saddened when you died. Then to meet you in person?" She blushed a little. "I found that you more than lived up to my fantasy."

He was bewildered to hear this from his fierce, stunningly beautiful wife. "That gives my ego a bit of a boost, coming from you."

Her lips curled. "Several things have convinced me we should be together: the uncommon gift of a direct strike of lightning, *and* the fact that you freed me from my chain, *and* the fact that I made your heart beat, *and* the fact that you were so sodding eager to give up your life for mine—though mind you, if you try that again, I'm going to kill you."

"Always, Myst. I'd do it easily." When she was about to protest, he asked, "What about your family? I will try if they will."

"For all the reasons I just listed, a couple of my sisters have decided they'll attempt to overcome their repugnance toward you."

He scowled. "Big-minded of them."

"Yet they want nothing to do with Kristoff or any among your order. You're the exception, because they feel like they knew you as a human and because of what has happened between us. But if, say, your brother showed up here, they'd . . . it would be . . . bad."

"I understand."

"If you can make a genuine effort, I believe they will all come to accept you in time."

He wanted to be clear on this. "Accept you as my wife and me as your husband?" He wanted everything from her. Not just a few decades. He wanted forever. And as long as she was in a giving mood . . .

She nodded, a smile playing about her lips. "We still have a lot to muddle through, mind you. Our families and our factions, who controls the remote, and living logistics—because Blachmount needs TLC and lightning rods in a bad way. But I suppose I have to take possession of you, since I've already taken possession of this." She raised her hand and displayed the wedding ring he'd bought her.

He grinned. "You liked that, did you?"

"I couldn't take my eyes off it," she said with a saucy smile.

He pulled her to him and clasped her close,

knowing she craved being wrapped securely in his arms, as much as he needed her soft and trusting within them. "I can't quite believe this. Even after everything?" If she could give him another chance, Nikolai thought they could do anything together.

"Yes. But . . ." She stroked the smooth backs of her claws down his arm. "You'll have to spend eternity making it up to me."

He levered himself above her, cupping the back of her neck. His gaze flickered over her face, then met the eyes of his wife as she smiled up at him. Feeling love for her so strong it hurt him, his voice ragged with it, he rasped, "*Milaya*, it is done."

THE ORIGIN OF THE VALKYRIES

*J*n the blood-splattered snow, the lone warrior fell to one knee and shuddered with weakness. Still, an arm shot out to raise a sword against the on-coming legion.

Her dented breastplate swallowed her small form.

Though the winds howled, whipping her hair, she heard the twang of a bowstring. She screamed in fury when an arrow punctured the center of her armor, the force sending her flying back.

The arrowhead had pierced through metal, then barely through her breastbone, just enough that her heart met the point with each beat. The beating of her own brave heart was killing her.

But her scream had awakened two gods who'd been sleeping through a wintry decade. They stirred and looked down upon the maiden, seeing courage burning bright in her eyes. Bravery and will had marked her entire life, but the light ebbed with death, and they mourned it.

Freya, the female god, whispered that they should preserve her courage for eternity because it was so precious.

Wóden agreed, and together they gave up lightning to tear through the ether and strike the dying maiden.

The flash was violent and slow to fade and made the army tremble.

When blackness descended once more, the healed maiden woke in a strange place. She was untouched, her human mortality unchanged. But soon she would bear an immortal daughter who possessed her courage, Wóden's wily brilliance, and Freya's mirth and fey beauty. Though this daughter enjoyed the power of lightning for sustenance, she also inherited Wóden's arrogance and Freya's acquisitiveness, which merely endeared her to them more.

The gods were content and the maiden adoring of her new baby. Yet after an age had flickered past, the gods heard another female call out for courage when she fell in battle against a dark enemy. She wasn't a human, but a fury, one among the Lore—those clever beings who have convinced humans that they exist only in imagination.

Scarce moments had the creature; her breaths were no longer visible in the freezing night.

"Our halls are great, yet our family is small," Freya said, her eyes sparkling so brightly that a mariner in the north was briefly blinded by the stars and almost lost his way.

Grim Wóden took her hand, unable to deny her. Those surrounding the dying fury saw lightning tear through the sky once more.

In the coming years, it would strike again and again, until female warriors—be they human, demoness, siren, changeling, or any brave creature from the Lore—knew to pray for it as they died.

Thus the Valkyries were born.

Dear Reader,

I hope you enjoyed the revised edition of The Warlord Wants Forever, *the first entry in the Immortals After Dark series!*

To celebrate the tenth anniversary of the IAD, I've put together some bonus material: FAQs; the evolution of the A Hunger Like No Other *cover (the first cover imagined specifically for the series), from initial sketch to final product; and some fun stuff with fellow authors Gena Showalter and Larissa Ione, two incredible writers and friends.*

With your support, we can keep the Immortals After Dark *going for another ten years!*

Thank you so much for your readership!

Warmest wishes,
Kresley

AN IMMORTALS AFTER DARK (IAD) Q&A

I polled readers for questions, and you guys delivered!
I answered the ones that won't get me into too much
trouble, make me break blood vows, or get me arrested.

I love Robert Petkoff! How did he get to be your audio-book narrator?

—Paige

I was sipping a Sazerac in a sultry jazz joint down in the Vieux Carré when I heard his rich, deep voice across the room. I got shivers (the good kind), and I *knew*. He was the one who would deliver my series to a new medium. Our gazes met in the mirror behind the bar, and I mouthed: *Let's make an audiobook baby together.* He comprehended me perfectly.

↑ lies ↑

Okay, I *wish* I'd had something to do with hooking up the brilliant Robert Petkoff and the IAD series. That was all Simon & Schuster Audio (I'll take this opportunity to say thank you yet again).

How many IAD books will there be?

—Corinna

After 2016, there will be at least three more full-length novels. I have a dozen plotted out, so I'm ready for more if you are. (LET'S DO THIS, MOTHERFLECKERS!)

Can I read the books out of order? Or will I miss a bunch of stuff?

—Shelley

I've put a lot of work into making all the books stand-alone. Folks tell me they get more enjoyment reading them sequentially, but you could skip an installment here or there.

For instance, if werewolves aren't your thing or if demons don't do it for you, ~~get help~~ I get it. Bottom line: if you miss a book, I'll have you caught up with the next.

For those who'd like to read them in order, the series installments are:

If you didn't write romance, what would you do?

—Trilby

I'd be an investigator of "world's coldest beer" claims, committed to the pursuit of finding the world's truly coldest brew. I would be the most dedicated worker ever.

Will there ever be more Dacian installments? What do I have to do to get you to turn one in?

—Your editor

As a matter of fact, good editor, we'll have a Dacian

novella—*Shadow's Seduction*—in the spring of 2017 and a full-length book later that fall. Lothaire the Enemy of Old will make cameos in both!

How much research do you put into the IAD series? Are the books difficult for you to write or do they fly out of your head and onto the page?

—Meghan

I do a metric ass-ton of research for this series (measured and verified). I use any medium available to me, and I also travel to many of the settings in the books.

Unfortunately, nothing flies out of my head, except for little poofs of my sanity. True story.

Writing the IAD is freaking *hard*. The seventeen installments build on and refer to each other, so getting even the tiniest detail correct is critical.

Plus I'm so emotionally invested in this series—more than *a decade of my life* has been dedicated to writing them—that I want each book to be perfect.

What was the hardest IAD book to write? What was the easiest?

—Bernetta

Dark Skye was both the hardest *and* the easiest.

The easy part: I was excited about the settings, the characters wrote themselves (I love it when they play ball with me!), the conflict was strong and had been set up years before, and I got to show Nïx in her element.

But, I felt like the Pandemonia scenes could be better—more mystical, visceral, sensual. I'd turned in the book—had already been paid, no less—but I asked my editor for another go. (I like pain. Vacations are for suckers.) She played ball too, re-editing those pages.

The hard part: I gutted that section of the book, rewriting it so many times that I have a hundred extra pages that will never see the light of day. My editor and I joke that she made me rewrite those time-loop scenes over and over until I began to feel *I* was in a time loop.

Still, I can't regret it, because *Dark Skye* is in my top three favorites of the IAD.

How did you develop your interpretation of the Valkyries?
—Petra

I had to improvise most of their characteristics. There's very little research available on them compared to other mythical/legendary beings—a fact that was both problematic and freeing.

I read everything I could, even researched in Scandinavia, but in the end I needed to invent many of their traits—their acquisitiveness, their fascination with shiny objects, their love of fighting and all things modern (video games!), and their delicate, elven appearance. Also imaginary: the Valkyrie origin myth and their consumption of lightning.

This series has been going on for years and years. How do you keep the stories fresh?

—Katy

Taking IAD "breathers" and working on other series—like my Game Makers (erotica with Russian alpha-heroes) and the Arcana Chronicles (Tarot card characters come to life)—helps. And I think having numerous *types* of immortals adds unique layers. Each separate faction in the Lore has its own world of issues and conflicts.

For instance, the concerns, hopes, and goals of a Forbearer are very distinct from those of a Lykae, so their stories will be varied. Then when you have the hero and heroine from two different worlds, there's such a shakeup that I think it would be hard to write the same kind of scenario.

How did you come up with the idea for *The Living Book of Lore*? Why do the entries change with each installment of the series?

—Oni

A buyer for a retail book chain thought some explanations in the beginning of the books could help readers dive right into the world of the Lore. I thought this was a fantastic idea, so I started noodling how I wanted to provide that information.

In college, I'd studied grimoires and old texts written to classify evil spirits, such as demons. Often these books had encyclopedic definitions of the various entities, detailing their appearance, powers, weaknesses, and invocations. I pictured these ancient and eerie grimoires when coming up with the *Book of Lore*.

In each Immortals After Dark installment, I'll include only the entries relevant to that particular story. The entries themselves change because the *Book of Lore* is *living*. I imagine it as a crowd-sourced compendium; Loreans can edit and add as new information becomes known (e.g., a previously undiscovered realm, recent heroic feats, overthrown rulers, etc.). Whenever an edit is made, each *Book of Lore* in existence updates magically/mystically.

How do you pronounce Nïx, Annika, and Regin?

—Wilka

Technically, Nïx is supposed to be pronounced along the lines of *Neeks*. The *ï* sounds like a long *e* (as in *naïve*). But I think over the years the pronunciation could have been transmuted to sound more like *Nicks*. She would answer to both.

Officially, Annika should be pronounced *AH-nik-uh*, because that's how my Swedish husband pronounces it. Sometimes my southern twang kicks in, and I say it *ANN-ee-ka*. I think she'd answer to both, too.

Regin could be *Ree-gin* or *RAY-gin*. She answers to her superhero identity: the Fellatrix.

What are some typical compliments and complaints you receive about the Immortals After Dark series?
—Alexis

I'm very complimented when readers say the series is continuing to improve with each book. I know I work harder and harder on each installment (where will it end?? I just want to put thermometers in mugs of beer, for fuck's sake).

I'd say the biggest complaint I receive is that I don't write fast enough. But if I tried to avert that complaint, I might end up averting that compliment!

Some readers wish I'd concentrate solely on the IAD and leave off writing other series, but that would be impossible. I can only write so many of those complicated, maddening, hair-pulling IAD books a year, or I'd risk burning out.

What's up with the character quotes at the beginning of the books? Most authors quote *famous* people.
—Pauline

Well, I started doing it in *If You Dare*, my 2005 historical romance. I'd heard some writers say you have to be able to sum up your story in two or three lines, so I decided I'd sum up my characters the same way.

But then the quotes were kind of *fun*, and I wanted to share them. I thought I'd fudge the rules a bit and have my heroes and heroines *be* the legendary folks quoted at the beginning of the books.

My editor said, "I don't know if we can use these. It's not something I've seen before." I replied, "Then that's exactly why we should use them. Besides, it's not like it matters—no one reads my books anyway!"

Some of my favorite quotes:

"Women are like bottles of liquor. They should be sampled, savored, then discarded. Matrimony is for men who can't handle their liquor."

—MURDOCH WROTH, EIGHTEENTH-CENTURY
WARLORD, MODERN VAMPIRE SOLDIER

"Witches are good for one thing and only one thing. Tinder."

—BOWEN GRAEME MACRIEVE,
THIRD IN LINE FOR THE LYKAE THRONE

"A femme fatale? With a history of burlesque dancing? You must have the wrong girl. I'm naught but a humble ballet dancer, a mere delicate sparrow."

—NÉOMI LARESS, PRIMA BALLERINA,
FORMER FEMME FATALE AND BURLESQUE DANCER

"That sorceress might be an evil bitch, but she's my *evil bitch. And I'll have no other."*

—RYDSTROM WOEDE,
FALLEN KING OF THE RAGE DEMONARCHY

"When in doubt, squeeze till something breaks."

—JOSEPHINE DOE (A.K.A. LADY SHADY)

"Me, a steel magnolia? Steel, my ass! [Laughing, then abruptly serious.] Try titanium.*"*

—ELIZABETH "ELLIE" PEIRCE, EXPERT IN BOYS,
REVERSE PSYCHOLOGY, AND LAW-ENFORCEMENT EVASION

"The first rule of being a mercenary? Find out what the client wants, then convince him that, a) you can get it for him, and, b) you're the only one who can get it for him. Second rule? Lie. Often. The truth rarely serves you well in this business."

—CADEON WOEDE, MERCENARY,
SECOND IN LINE TO THE RAGE DEMONARCHY THRONE,
A.K.A. CADE THE KINGMAKER

"They say I'm as fickle as winter, as shy as frost, and as indifferent as a blizzard. It's rumored my body is pure as driven snow. Nobody imagines that I might be full of fire."

—DANIELA THE ICE MAIDEN,
VALKYRIE AND RIGHTFUL QUEEN OF THE ICERE,
THE FEY OF THE FROZEN NORTH

A lot of writers get inspired by other books. Do you? Where do your ideas come from?

—Dettie

I don't get to read novels as often as I used to, and when I do, I feel guilty because if I'm lucid and awake enough to be *reading*, then I should be *writing*.

I've had ideas come from anywhere and everywhere, from poems to bars to music videos. . . .

Poems

Lachlain, a werewolf king bent on vengeance, came about when I read *Beowulf*:

> *Then the sun was gone,*
> *And its heart was glad; glowing with rage*
> *. . . impatient to repay*
> *Its enemies.*

I dreamed up Mariketa the Awaited, heroine of *Wicked Deeds*, when I read "The Witch in the Glass," a poem by Sarah Morgan Bryan Piatt. The first stanza:

> "My mother says I must not pass
> Too near that glass;
> She is afraid that I will see
> A little witch that looks like me,
> With a red, red mouth to whisper low
> The very thing I should not know!"

TV

The Talisman's Hie is an immortal (read: bloody, gruesome, lethal) equivalent of *The Amazing Race*.

Néomi Laress, the heroine of *Dark Needs*, was born when I first saw the music video for My Chemical Romance's song "Helena." My takeaway: "A dead dancer with joy on her face." I must've watched the video a hundred times that night.

Films

Alien and ***Aliens***. I sneaked in to watch *Alien* when I was really young. My folks feared I would be scarred by the "chest bursting" scenes, but I was more thrown by Ellen Ripley's character. She was an action hero—and a woman! I believe I'd be a different person today if I'd missed out on Ripley.

In *Demon from the Dark*, she's the role model of Carrow the Incarcerated. Carrow constantly asks herself, "WWRD?" (What would Ripley do?)

Pride and Prejudice. The version with Keira Knightley and Matthew Macfadyen. One of my favorites scenes is when Darcy and Lizzie meet at dawn, and he declares his feelings. He's so overcome with emotion, he stutters and says "I love" three times. *Thud.*

That Darcy—his mannerisms, his deep voice, his intensity, his shyness—was the inspiration for Sebastian Wroth.

Let the Right One In. This movie is chilling, but it's also a kind of love story. (Spoiler: The Morse code tapped in the end is translated as K-I-S-S.) After watching this, I wanted to create a "bad" hero who did unheroic things. Lothaire's book came not long after.

Location inspirations

Bars

One of my first book signings was in a New Orleans bar called Loa's. I loved the name. When I discovered the definition—a voodoo spirit—the character of Loa the Commercenary started to come to life.

I conjured up Orion the Undoing with my editor during a plot session in a Bourbon Street dive bar. (We believe the location adds flavor. The things we do for our art!)

Travel

The rune stones in *Dreams of a Dark Warrior* are based on the Rök Rune Stone in Sweden, which is considered the country's oldest piece of written literature. *Rök* means *smoke*.

The demon Rök got his name from the same. In fact, that rune stone inspired the idea of the Smoke Demonarchy.

Galway Bay oysters, mentioned in *Dreams of a Dark Warrior*, are seriously the best oysters on earth or any dimension.

The shark farm in *No Rest* is based on a rumor I heard years ago in Jaco Beach, Costa Rica.

I've never been to Yélsérk, Hungary (home of the Fyre Dragán in *No Rest*), and I doubt anyone else has either. Yélsérk is "Kresley" spelled backward. (Just to prove I'm a one-trick pony: Erol's—the bayou tavern frequented by Loreans—is, you guessed it, "Lore" spelled backward.)

Who's your favorite character in all of the Lore?
—Pennyroyal

Nucking Futs Nïx. Apparently, readers enjoy her antics. Co-incidentally, I *adore* writing them. See, readers? This is why we're so right for each other.

What made you decide to dress Nïx in slogan T-shirts?
—Hannah

I love sucker-punch characters, the ones that masquerade as one thing, but are actually something else entirely. Nïx's nickname (Nucking Futs) and her T-shirts make her seem lighthearted and jovial—and she can be—but she's also a ruthless and powerful immortal. During this Accession, she's the wild-card game changer, yet most don't take her seriously. Just how she likes it.

Should we be pulling for the Møriør in the Accession? How did they come into being? Can you spill any secrets about them?

—Cal

Depends on if you like to pull for a winner. Just kidding, just kidding! (Or *am* I?)

The Møriør came into being because, as many of you know, I like to go back to a scene I wrote and show it from a different point of view. I'd always wanted to show *the entire Accession* from a differing perspective, so I thought, what if we pitted a small but powerful force of primordials against Nïx and her army?

Diabolical Nïx has done some shady things to her *allies*. When you see her in action against her *enemies*, you have to wonder, *What if I've been pulling for the wrong side?*

Hmmm, secrets. Orion, the Møriør leader, will play an unexpected role in Nïx's future. Rune is going to get closer to his goal of wiping out Magh's fey line sooner than he anticipated. Sian, the new—and newly returned—ruler of

Pandemonia, will receive a huge surprise from Lanthe and Sabine (you didn't think those two Sorceri would settle down just 'cause they got hitched, did you?).

**Do you put any autobiographical tidbits in the series?
—Gail**

Oh, yeah. For instance, the Valkyries' addiction to video games is based on personal experience. Lemme tell you a little story. . . .

So I'm in college, rooming with Swede, my husband-to-be. We get a Super Nintendo Entertainment System with a few cartridges, including *Donkey Kong Country*.

Now, I have tunnel vision, so when I start a quest, I need to finish it before I do anything else. Like sleep or eat. This is a problem with video games, because finishing an entire one could take weeks! Worse? I had a crew of very supportive friends.

My first indication that something was wrong? When Swede patiently explained to me and my friends that for the last two weeks he'd been going to sleep with the *Donkey Kong* soundtrack playing—and waking up to the same. Without glancing away from the screen, I told him, "Yeah, baby, I hear you, I *do*, but I'm closing in on King K. Rool and I'm up to my ass in Kremlings." My friends rolled their eyes at him: "Hellooo? Kremlings."

High on high scores, I grew totally addicted, turning grungy and vampire-pale. That time was all a blur: School? Classes, schmasses. *Must—get—to—next . . . LEVEL.*

I would even dial Nintendo 1-900 help lines for hints. I remember telling some kid (who sounded fifteen), "No, no, that can't be right. I've already sacrificed three Kongs doing that!" Fifteen-year-old's reply: "Lady, don't you have a job to be at or something?" *Humiliation.*

Then came the 3:00 a.m. intervention. Swede threw the

cartridge on our neighbor's roof! My only thought: *Where to find a freaking ladder at three in the morning? Aha, the other neighbor's backyard!* My friends were the lookouts, cheering in hushed tones as I dodged a dog and continued my mission.

Must hurry, dew might damage cartridge. As I scrambled across the roof, reaching for my precious, an idea started setting in that I might have a problem. I snagged the cartridge. *Triumphant!*

I got back inside with my precious. Wait . . . Swede had destroyed the console? *Scuttled???* Copious weeping. *Acceptance.*

But the Valkyries' video-game addiction wasn't the only idea I got out of that dark time. When I look back, I'm reminded that every heroine needs goals (however misguided), a hero who can be understanding if she's gone crazycakes, and a crew that supports her *in anything*, even going cold turkey with *Donkey Kong*.

For years afterward, I never touched another game . . . until Wii. I convinced Swede that my body would tire out before I could get as bad as before. And what great exercise! Until it too became all a blur: *Dance Dance Revolution! Love this song! Won't stop till I get an A. I can't feel my ankles! So thirsty. . . .*

Oh, and don't even get me started on the autobiographicalness of trash-talking, bowling witches.

Turn the page for an in-depth look at the
evolution of the cover for

A HUNGER
LIKE NO OTHER

Summer 2005. The original design sketch by artist
Vince Natale, with editorial feedback in the margins.

KRESLEY COLE

A HUNGER LIKE
NO OTHER

The draft that my editor originally sent to me.
I was in love!

KRESLEY COLE

Author of *If You Dare*

*Desire like theirs
is insatiable.*

*A Hunger
Like No Other*

Color! The art department ("Art") adjusted hues and
fonts, while editorial and marketing considered a tagline.
A Louisiana-esque wrought iron fence replaced the
Eiffel Tower in the background.

KRESLEY COLE

Desire like theirs is insatiable.

A Hunger Like No Other

Art made the colors crisper and removed all the
background elements to highlight the moon.
(This version really popped for me!)

KRESLEY COLE

A HUNGER LIKE
NO OTHER

Official cover, 2006: For a cleaner look, Art returned the
title to the earliest font and removed the tagline.

Rerelease of official cover, 2016: For the tenth anniversary
of the IAD, S&S updated all the series covers. Note the
glowing eyes (it's like they plucked Lachlain from my head!).

These new IAD covers would have one unifying theme.
As my editor described it to me: "Each immortal will be
gazing out from behind a specific design element, because
they secretly exist beside us, hidden in the shadows."

As a pingback to these early *A Hunger Like No Other*
versions, this revised cover depicts Lachlain
gazing out from behind wrought iron.

A Day in the Life of *Blood Red Kiss*

(Private text thread among the authors as they furiously work on their deadlines and hide out from their editor, Lauren McKenna, a.k.a. McKraken)

Morning:

KCOLE [Khaleesi]: Do you think Simon & Schuster would give us a tour bus for the release of BRK? I'm not saying we deserve one, but I'm not NOT saying that either. Wouldn't it be great if we could score 1. A bus 2. Fine-ass handlers 3. Snickers Minis and Absolut Vodka as sponsors?

GYNA [DogMom]: I hope you weren't actually asking a question, because YES. The answer is YES.

KCOLE [Khaleesi]: Hmm, how should we let S&S know?? If only there was a clever way of communicating our supersecret desires to them. . . .

GYNA [DogMom]: I'll be bringing only 9 of my dogs on the bus tour that will totally be happening. Wearing shedded fur is SO popular right now.

KCOLE [Khaleesi]: May it be forever! ::plucking at my befurred shirt::

LARISSA [loneUrSoul]: I don't have 9 dogs, but I have a very, very friendly hellhound. Okay, not that friendly, but she can be in charge of security. (We don't want the Snickers Minis or Absolut to be stolen. Priorities, obviously.)

KCOLE [Khaleesi]: I like where your head's at, lone.

Writing ensues for 1.25 minutes

KCOLE [Khaleesi]: I can't wait for BRK to release. Really excited about Warlord coming out in mass-market paperback for the first time. Been waiting a decade for this. I re-edited the shit out of that story!

GYNA [DogMom]: It's the ten-year anniversary of the IAD! This calls for an interpretive dance, Cowalter!

KCOLE [Khaleesi]: Damn, this author is freaking old. Kidding. I started writing as a zygote.

LARISSA [IoneUrSoul]: Valkyries are still kicking it old school! Like you! What? You said it first. . . .

KCOLE [Khaleesi]: That's fair, Ione. You know, I started writing the IAD back then because I couldn't find Valkyries in modern fiction. I wrote them to fill a need. Plus they get hot-as-lava heroes.

LARISSA [IoneUrSoul]: I still can't believe we've had ten years of dark, edgy IAD boys. Keep 'em coming (heh)!

KCOLE [Khaleesi]: More heroes will be coming (heh heh) soon.

GYNA [DogMom]: You give good "fill a need," KC! I've been drooling over your IAD men the entire decade. (Should seek medical help?)

KCOLE [Khaleesi]: Never! Speaking of drooling, y'all's (it's a word) next vampires and alien assassins need to get here now! G, readers have been DYING for Dallas's story (and by "readers" I mean "me, Larissa, and everyone on earth").

GYNA [DogMom]: What can I say—Otherworld Assassins needed another alpha man on his knees. Gotta keep those heroines happy :) And Larissa! MoonBound Clan vampire knocks it out of the freaking park. How do you keep things so fresh? (read: delicious?)

LARISSA [IoneUrSoul]: Mmm . . . fresh vampires. You know, I'm convinced that vampires are always fresh. Even when vamps are traditional, there's still something yummy about them—

KCOLE [Khaleesi]: Preach! Sorry, pls continue. . . .

LARISSA [IoneUrSoul]: ☺ For fun, I liked tossing mine into a world where they, the most powerful predators on the planet, have to fight for their existence. Who doesn't love a good vamp fight? Mmm . . . fresh vamp fights . . .

KCOLE [Khaleesi]: The only thing that could make fresh vamp fights better is fresh vamp Jell-O fights with one of Gyna's sexy aliens thrown in the mix. Hey, this should be a bonus scene! Lauren McKraken would be all over it!

LARISSA [IoneUrSoul]: I love Jell-O! Did you know they have pina colada and strawberry daiquiri flavors? I think either of those would make for a rather, um, delicious vampire/alien Jell-O fight. Ahem. Speaking of aliens, Gyna, as a megafan of sci-fi, I gotta bow down to your alien awesomeness. No one does hot alien romance like you do. Write more. And faster. I'm greedy.

GYNA [DogMom]: Dang. I just fell deeper in love with you, L. And your books!

KCOLE [Khaleesi]: I know, right? There went the last little piece of my heart, Larissa Ione. ♥

LARISSA [IoneUrSoul]: Group hug!

Writing ensues for 7.5 minutes . . .

GYNA [DogMom]: So how did y'all's (yep, it's a word) editing process go? I don't know how many times McKraken has asked me if I 1) wrote while on crack and 2) should just start over. JK! I know how many times. Every time. All the books. (What I reeeally hate to admit? She was right. About #2! Only #2!)

LARISSA [IoneUrSoul]: Poor Lauren. When she gets my manuscripts, they're full of comments like "Don't worry, I'll fix this!" I basically send an editorial letter along with the story . . . she has got to wonder if Gyna is sharing her crack with me. (She's not. I have to make do with coffee. Ooh, we need a coffee sponsor on the tour bus. I'll make a formal request.)

KCOLE [Khaleesi]: Larissa, you told me about that reverse editorial letter at the RT convention—I love it! I'm doing it on my next book. I won't tell Lauren where I got the idea, though. She'll never find out from me.

GYNA [DogMom]: How'd you handle editing for a reissue, K?

KCOLE [Khaleesi]: Just between us . . . I made more than twelve thousand tweaks to the story since the first time it was released in trade paperback. The story is the same, but I think the delivery is much smoother now.

LARISSA [IoneUrSoul]: Holy crap, KC! We'll have to honor your hard work somehow. I'm sure we can do that with alcohol. And chocolate. Hot dudes. The possibilities are endless!

KCOLE [Khaleesi]: How about hot dudes covered in alcohol and chocolate? I predict a new trend!

Writing for 15 minutes . . .

GYNA [DogMom]: So, I was recently asked to describe Dark Swan/Otherworld Assassins series in three words or less. I'm thinking: Aliens Get Freaky. But really, I'd rather describe the story in six words: Bring Your Climax to Work Day. How would you guys describe your story in BRK?

LARISSA [loneUrSoul]: Do Wolves Sh*t in the Woods? Okay, wait. There are vampires in this story too. How about: A Hot Vampire Meets Furry Wolf. Hmm, nope. I think I'm conveying the wrong message here. Third try's a charm. Shape-Shifter Vampires: Always Sexy, Sometimes Inappropriate.

KCOLE [Khaleesi]: My series in six words: Immortals doing dirty deeds after dark. For The Warlord: Sexy Alpha Vampire Learns His Lesson. Or Gorgeous Valkyrie Gets Her World Rocked. This is fun—like freeballing haiku. One more about The Warlord: The Love Scenes Are Beyond Dirty.

Writing for several hours . . .

KCOLE [Khaleesi]: Arghhhh. It's the middle of the night here. You guys up? Pretty sure my ass fell asleep in the writing chair. Taking a coffee break, gearing up for an all-nighter. What's your hardest deadline ever?

GYNA [DogMom]: I once had 2½ weeks to rewrite an entire book (read: weave my "written on crack?" crapperpiece into solid gold). After vomiting blood, I got that baby done!

LARISSA [loneUrSoul]: My answer is similar to Gyna's. I once had to rewrite an entire book (and I mean, the ENTIRE book—I only saved the prologue) in three weeks . . . while in the middle of a cross-country move. My husband drove, so I spent the drive with my computer in my lap and my fingers typing like mad for the entire trip. Then I sat on boxes and wrote while the movers unpacked. What's yours?

KCOLE [Khaleesi]: They're all pretty bad. Hee, funny story . . . My agent once called after I'd been awake for two days, carefully measuring my coffee intake against my Pepto-Bismol/Zantac consumption (balancing this potion is a science AND an art). I was fried. She asked me how I stay up so long. I answered, "I. AM. A. SORCERESS!" She said, "Well. Um, okay, so what are you working on now?" My reply: "SORCERY!"

—Radio silence—

KCOLE [Khaleesi]: Hellooooo? TMI?

GYNA [DogMom]: Uh, no, that sounds totally normal. I tend to call my fur family—and everyone around me—by character names. "Dallas! Lilica! Stop licking Mommy's leg!"

LARISSA [loneUrSoul]: Scratching coffee sponsor off bus tour.

An hour later . . .

KCOLE [Khaleesi]: I just got through writing a love scene and the characters shocked even me with their wanton demonic sex. What's the naughtiest thing your current hero does?

LARISSA [loneUrSoul]: The naughtiest thing? Ah . . . well . . . remember the furry wolf thing above? I might have been conveying the right message after all. . . .

GYNA [DogMom]: I think my hero's middle name is Naughty. He does this thing with his mouth . . . and he's really good at dishing punishment. You know, his method of choice is that tongue-lashing EVERY WOMAN fears. Tell me your favorite line for your BRK novella.

KCOLE [Khaleesi]: The dreaded, dreaded tongue-lashing. Fav line? When Nikolai and Myst (pet name *Milaya*) consummate their relationship, and she thinks he's about to order her to [expletive deleted]. Instead he simply says, "*Milaya* . . . I want you so much."

LARISSA [loneUrSoul]: From Forsaken by Night: "I'm not leaving you." Tehya's hot breath whispered across his ear, and his groin tightened. "I'd rather die with you than die alone." What's yours, Gyna?

GYNA [DogMom]: From Dark Swan: His smile bloomed, slow and deliberate. "I may not have something you want, sweetness, but I have something you need."

KCOLE [Khaleesi]: ::WANT&NEED:: What's your favorite line from your upcoming or current book? Mine is from The Player: He leveled his spellbinding gaze on my face. "When you've been in the dark as long as I have, *moy ángel*, there is no mistaking the light."

LARISSA [loneUrSoul]: *Thud.* From Rising Storm: Season 2, Episode 2: Ian's gaze locked on her, and his voice went low, vibrating her in places that hadn't been vibrated in a long time.

"What about you, Marisol? Would you like to see what Montana has to offer?"

KCOLE [Khaleesi]: Can we just talk about the verb *to vibrate*? I'm officially a fan. Give us a line, Gyna!

GYNA [DogMom]: ::Vibrating:: From The Darkest Promise (Cameo's story): "I will find you," he said, as much a sensual promise as a brutal warning. "I will always find you."

GYNA [DogMom]: Okay, now for the most important question of all: What's your favorite Gena Showalter novel, besides all of them?

–Simultaneous– **KCOLE [Khaleesi]:** All of them. **LARISSA [IoneUrSoul]:** All of them.

Next morning before writing . . .

KCOLE [Khaleesi]: Grunt. Bleary. Grunt. Okay, just between us, tell me a secret nobody knows about your series and when you do, that will mean we're married.

GYNA [DogMom]: Aren't you adorable? We've been married for years, KC. Years! Ever since I first hid in the bushes outside your window with my Nikon. (Larissa–any interest in being my sisterwife?)

KCOLE [Khaleesi]: Years and years, my lovely Gyna. As soon as I hit send on that previous text, I was embarrassed. The union between Gyna Cowalter and KresLAY Cowalter is etched in stone. And we're totally open, Ione. We could be the Conewalters! (But you're not getting out of secret, G!)

GYNA [DogMom]: An Otherworld Assassins secret . . . I recently sat down and interviewed character John No Last Name. I asked him if he wanted to kill me for not giving him a definite happy ending. His reply? "I've finally found someone I want. You will live, and you will give her to me." Uh, demanding much?

LARISSA [IoneUrSoul]: ::shivers:: John No Last Name sounds . . . intriguing. So about this marriage proposal thing. Do we have three rings? One to rule them all? (OMG, I'm such a nerd.)

KCOLE [Khaleesi]: Yes and yes! G, officially calling John No Last Name as my book boyfriend for all time. Ione, you're so not getting out of your secret either.

LARISSA [loneUrSoul]: Well, there's a spy inside my series, but I can't reveal that secret yet. I just get to tease you with it for another book or two! What's yours, KC?

KCOLE [Khaleesi]: Hmm. Most folks think Myst and Nikolai were the first characters I came up with for the IAD. Actually, Regin was the first IAD character I ever invented. I also added secrets in a Q&A after my story. . . . Sigh. Do you think we should go write now? Or something? It's all fun and games until Bowen loses an eye.

GYNA [DogMom]: No! Stay here and cuddle me! Fine. (grumble, grumble) I'm writing the next Lords of the Underworld novel, and I left Cameo in a very . . . sweaty situation. She's going to spontaneously combust if I don't return.

LARISSA [loneUrSoul]: We have to write now? Well, I suppose I should do something about that spy secret I mentioned. They don't just "out" themselves, you know.

One minute later . . .

KCOLE [Khaleesi]: OMG, my cat did the funniest thing . . .

FORSAKEN BY NIGHT

Larissa Ione

1

Somewhere outside Lobo's cabin, a lone shot rang out.

A hunter, probably. Or a poacher. Either way, he was going to check it out. He investigated all gunshots, a habit left over from his life at MoonBound clan, when he'd been part of the security detail.

Now, as an outcast, he still patrolled Washington's damp state forests, avoiding MoonBound warriors as best he could. For the most part, they avoided him too. And who could blame them? He was damaged goods and, as far as their chief, Hunter, was concerned, a traitor as well.

Hunter was also a huge asshole.

Lobo looked over at the sleek silver wolf lying on the rug in front of the woodstove. She wagged her tail, her ears perking when, in the distance, wolves howled into the twilight, their songs joining a symphony of hooting owls, screeching jays, and chittering squirrels that didn't seem to be bothered by the gunfire at all.

"You wanna go see what's out there, Tehya?"

She jumped up and rushed to the door, nearly knocking him over in her excitement. Once outside, she slipped away into the brush, disappearing like a ghost as he started jogging in the direction the shot had come from. He didn't worry about her; she'd catch up eventually.

He stopped atop a rocky ridge to search for signs of human activity in the thousands of acres of Pacific Northwest forest he called home. A welcome breeze blew in from the north and he lifted his face into it, letting it chase away the day's spring heat like a cougar sprinting after a herd of elk.

As a vampire, Lobo didn't feel heat and cold the way humans did. His body was designed to tolerate temperature extremes that would kill wimpy-ass humans. Not that the weather was a concern at this time of year. No, the concern, as always, was that humans were hunting the creatures that lived in the forest.

And that included vampires.

And wolves.

Reaching out with his mind—a talent forbidden by most vampire clans—he located the closest pack. As far as he knew, the wolves couldn't feel him the same way he felt them, and unless they were within a hundred yards or so, he couldn't communicate with them either. But once he connected with a wolf face-to-face, he could locate it with his mind in a matter of seconds no matter how far away it was.

He mentally counted the members of what he knew as the Sequoia pack; satisfied that they were all accounted for and hadn't been poached, he let them go and started off again.

He hadn't gone more than a couple of hundred yards when Tehya's presence prickled his skin and whispered through his mind like the soft rustle of leaves on the ground.

She was unique, this wolf, an individual the likes of which he'd never encountered in his nearly hundred and twenty years of life. He pivoted as she stepped out of the brush.

The instant her intense yellow eyes met his, an image flashed in his head, something that had happened once or twice a day for the last twelve years. The image was always the same: a tall, willowy vampire with dark shoulder-length hair and yellow-amber eyes. She was beautiful. Mysterious. And always naked.

"You know," he said softly, "I really wish you could tell me about this woman you keep projecting into my brain."

Tehya stepped closer, her huge paws landing silently on the soft ground, her powerful shoulders rolling. Another image of the woman popped into his head. She was walking toward him, her gemstone eyes holding him captive as her long, bare legs covered the distance between them.

Perspiration coated his palms, and he found himself actually reaching for her, curious to learn if that skin was as soft as it looked.

Then the image was gone, and Tehya's tail was wagging, her tongue lolling out of her mouth as she bounded toward him in big, goofy hops, wanting to run and play. Mystery woman forgotten, he braced himself for impact, and a heartbeat later, wolf paws the size of his hands slammed into his chest as Tehya bathed his face with her tongue.

Laughing, he ruffled his fingers through her fur and scritched behind her big ears. Sweet Maker, he loved this girl. She'd come to him at the lowest point of his life, when he'd realized he had nothing to live for.

Nearly dead when he found her, she was so weak from starvation that she couldn't stand. She'd been covered in ice and wounds, likely from other wolves or coyotes, and for days he'd wondered whether it would have been kinder to put her out of her misery instead of nurse her back to health.

But she'd survived, and it hadn't taken him long to figure out that she wasn't . . . normal. For a while he thought she might be a skinwalker like himself, able to shift form into that of an animal.

It would explain why, even though she was at least twelve years old, she possessed the physique and energy of a yearling wolf. The problem with that particular theory was that, as far as he knew, skinwalkers couldn't remain in animal form for more than a few hours. Not even Lobo, who was an extremely powerful skinwalker, perhaps the most powerful ever to have existed, could maintain a morph for more than a day, and even then the form he chose had a lot to do with how long he could remain in the transformed body.

There was, he supposed, another explanation for Tehya's uniqueness and the image of the woman. Within the dank underground walls of MoonBound headquarters, he'd been an orphan raised on tales of vampires whose totem animals could take physical form, and it was said that the vampire who was linked to the animal could communicate through it. If so, and Tehya was one of these physical totem animals, her vampire counterpart could be anywhere in the world.

She might even be a slave in some human's household.

The idea that the female Tehya projected into his mind was a slave made him snarl viciously enough for Tehya to back away, her ears drooping.

"That wasn't for you," he said, giving her another ruffle on the head.

Transgression forgiven, she wagged her tail and bowed playfully, doing her best to entice him into a run.

What the hell. They could run while he searched for whoever had fired the weapon.

Grinning, he closed his eyes and concentrated, and a moment later the familiar burn of his muscles stretching and contracting began. Pain racked him and blackness stole his vision as his bones broke and reformed and his skin sprouted fur. Gradually the pain faded, and he opened his canine eyes to find a different view of the world.

Tehya nipped his furry shoulder and took off at full speed, ears pinned to her skull, tail streaming behind her. Reveling in his black-furred wolf body, he chased after her, his tail high, his giant paws digging into the soft, moist earth.

Elation sang through him. This was what he lived for. The sheer joy of the wind in his face and a friend to keep him company.

It would be even better if I had a female two-legged friend too.

He stumbled like a cub learning to use its legs, and he swore Tehya laughed. As she should. He wasn't cut out to be with other people, and he had no business having those kinds of thoughts. He was too dangerous, and no one let him forget that.

Tehya slowed to snatch up a stick to tease him with, and after a few playful attempts to take the stick from her, he let go of his regrets and surrendered to the simple life he'd learned to love since Tehya entered his world as an emaciated, half-frozen wretch more than a decade ago.

They ran for miles, chasing deer and rabbits along the way to find the shooter, and once he had to plunge into a river to avoid a grumpy black bear sow with cubs. Tehya went in the opposite direction, and as he pulled himself out of the stream, her howl, maybe half a mile away, rose up into the darkening sky.

He shook the water out of his fur and started trotting in her direction, but as he cut through a valley that had recently been the site of a massive battle among three vampire clans and humans, another gunshot shattered the air. A gut-wrenching howl of pain cut through the forest, freezing him in his tracks.

Tehya.

Terror turned Lobo's marrow to jelly as he morphed back into his vampire form and sprinted in a mad rush through the trees, smashing through branches and leaping fallen logs and low-lying gullies. The sickening, metallic tang of wolf blood hit him even before the stench of the human who had fired the gun.

He burst over a ridge, and there, writhing in a rapidly expanding pool of blood, was Tehya, her hip blown open, bone and flesh spilling out through the ragged wound. And standing a few feet away, a man was taking a picture of his handiwork as the wolf flailed in agony.

A fucking *picture*.

What kind of sick asshole allowed an animal to suffer? And took photos of it?

With a roar of white-hot rage, Lobo slammed into the poacher, knocking him into a tree with so much force that he heard the crack of both wood and bone before the guy crumpled, unconscious, to the ground.

Unwilling to waste even the fraction of a second it would take to kill the scumbag, Lobo rushed over to Tehya. His heart clenched at the fear and pain swimming in her soulful eyes. Her chest rose and fell with her uneven, shallow breaths, and blood bubbled from her mouth.

"No," he whispered. "Sweet Maker, no."

She'd been the light in his life for the last twelve years, the reason he'd gone from merely existing to living. The reason loneliness hadn't been the catalyst for a swan dive off the nearest cliff. He had to save her.

But it wasn't as if there was a veterinarian hanging out over the next hill. The nearest town between here and Seattle was still at least an hour away at top speed. Carrying Tehya's hundred pounds of dead weight would slow him considerably, and he didn't think she'd survive the trip even if he could fly. And even if by some miracle a veterinarian could save her, he had little money. He got his food, clothing, and other necessities by trading venison, fish, or hand-made bows and arrows.

His mind spun with alternatives, but it always came back to one option. The only option.

The vampire clan that had banished him decades ago had a doctor.

Very gently, he gathered Tehya in his arms. She didn't protest or even whimper in pain, which wasn't a good sign. As quickly as he could, he tore through the forest until he reached the hidden MoonBound entrance carved into the side of a stone mountain face.

Memories assailed him, both good and bad but mostly the latter, as his time as a MoonBound member came back to him. He no longer possessed the mark that would allow him entrance, and he knew no one would let him inside. But there was a way around that.

A dangerous way. A forbidden way.

In his arms, Tehya took a deep, shuddering breath. The sound of her blood dripping onto his boot was louder than it should be, and his gut wrenched in anguish as her life drained from her body.

Screw the danger. Fuck the forbidden.

He had to do this.

Closing his eyes, he summoned the image of MoonBound's chief, a powerful vampire descended from the original twelve who, centuries ago, had spread the vampirism virus through North American native tribes. The familiar pain washed over Lobo as his body morphed, but unlike earlier when he'd shifted into a wolf, the pain was mild. He and Hunter were similar in size, weight, and, most likely, heritage, lessening the discomfort of his bones breaking and reforming, his joints popping and contorting.

When it was over, he was, theoretically, the spitting image of the black-haired, sharp-featured clan leader—right down to the MoonBound symbol that would allow him to enter the clan's residence.

He didn't waste another heartbeat standing around, but as he stepped across the threshold, he wondered how much longer he had to live. Merely impersonating another vampire had been bad enough to get him banished from MoonBound seventy years ago. But impersonating a *clan chief*?

That was a death sentence.

2

*L*obo jogged down the maze of tunnels as if he owned them—just the way Hunter would do. At first the hard-packed dirt hallways were empty and dark, but the closer he got to the living quarters, the more finished and bright the tunnels became, and the more people he encountered.

They stared, but then, Lobo doubted that Hunter often ran through the compound with a dying wolf in his arms.

Dying. She's dying.

He breathed through the lump of grief lodged in his throat and tried to focus on not getting caught. Running into Hunter would be especially problematic.

He hadn't been here since he'd been banished, but he remembered some of the carvings in the walls and the way roots dangled from the earthen ceiling. Back then, there hadn't been nearly as much light. Rooms had been little more than rustic caves, and there had been far fewer of them. Unsure where exactly he should be going, he headed for what had been a crude first-aid station when he'd lived here.

To his relief, the door to the room had a first-aid cross painted on it, as well as a sign that indicated it was now a medical lab.

Good enough.

The door was propped open; beyond it a silver-haired male he didn't recognize was flipping through papers, and a heavily pregnant female was bending over a microscope, her strawberry-blond hair concealing her face. He didn't know her personally, had only seen her from afar, but he'd spoken with MoonBound members who claimed that Nicole had once been the human enemy, an expert in vampire physiology whose family ran a vampire slavery and research empire. Now, as a vampire herself, she was mated to Hunter's second in command, and she was the closest thing the clan had to a real medical doctor.

"Help," he barked as he rushed to the exam table on the far side of the room. "This wolf was shot."

Nicole's pregnancy didn't slow her at all, and she was at Tehya's side in an instant. "Poor thing," she murmured as she pulled on surgical gloves. "What happened? A hunter?"

"Poacher," Lobo spat, practically tasting the acid in his voice. "Wolves are protected." Unnecessarily taking the life of any animal offended everything that made Lobo who he was, right down to his native blood. Nature deserved respect. Reverence. What man did to nature made him heartsick.

The silver-haired male appeared at Nicole's side, his white lab coat speckled with a veritable color wheel of stains. "I'll intubate and start IV fluids. Can you control the bleeding?"

"I don't know." Nicole cursed under her breath and grabbed for a tray of medical equipment on a nearby counter. "What kind of coward kills for the sake of killing?"

Lobo wished he could answer that, but really, the world was full of cowards who killed for fun, and there was no explaining it. He ran his hand over Tehya's rib cage, hating the choppy rise and fall of her chest as each labored breath rattled in her lungs.

So much rage and anguish welled in his throat that he could barely manage a raspy, "Can you save her?"

The expression on the doctor's face made his chest constrict. "Grant and I will do the best we can."

"Do more than your best," Lobo growled.

Nicole's silver gaze flickered up to him. "You seem to be rather invested in this wolf's survival."

Grant nodded in agreement, his own silver eyes snapping up to study Lobo a little too intently for his liking.

Shit. Lobo forced himself to calm down and assume Hunter's haughty arrogance. "She didn't deserve what that human did to her."

That seemed to placate the doctor, and she gave a curt nod as she went to work on Tehya's gunshot wound. Grant's wary gaze made Lobo sweat for another nerve-racking heartbeat, and then the guy turned his attention back to the wolf.

Footsteps out in the hall reminded Lobo that he was on borrowed time. As much as he wanted to stay, he couldn't hold Hunter's image for long—and worse, Hunter himself could show up at any moment.

He had to get out of there. But then what? Eventually either Nicole or Grant would seek out Hunter to update him on the wolf's condition, and the ruse would be exposed. Lobo wasn't worried about himself; he'd deal with the consequences. But what would happen to Tehya? He doubted Hunter would harm her—but then Hunter was his father's son, and his father had been a brutal, vicious leader who wouldn't hesitate to slaughter an animal for no reason other than to punish someone who cared about it. And given Lobo's history with Hunter—

"Hunter?" Nicole snapped her bloody fingers in front of his face. "Hunter!"

"Yeah. Sorry." He was getting sloppy. He raked his hand through his hair, belatedly realizing he was as covered in Tehya's blood as Nicole was. "What is it?"

"Let us handle this." Her voice was commanding yet compassionate, and he relaxed a little. "We'll update you when we can."

Grant taped the breathing tube to Tehya's muzzle, and Lobo's heart clenched. To see such a powerful, brave, loyal creature reduced to this . . . Without thinking, he threaded his fingers through Tehya's thick ruff and bent to press his forehead against hers.

"Be strong," he whispered.

Unable to bear Grant and Nicole's looks of pity, confusion, or suspicion, and even less able to bear watching Tehya die, he got the hell out of there. It was only his rubbery legs, and not his strength of will, that forced him to walk instead of make a mad dash of desperation to the exit.

Empty halls gave him a clear path until, just as he reached the fork that would take him either to the social center of the compound or to the outside world, a female with gray-streaked, spiky black hair rounded the corner.

Su'Neena.

In an instant, icy sweat coated his skin and his ribs ached, as if remembering all the times her foot had cracked them.

He'd come here as an orphan, his parents killed by MoonBound butchers, and Su'Neena had enjoyed using him as her personal whipping boy. So when his chance to take revenge had come, he'd seized it, only to have it backfire. He'd caught her betraying the clan, but she'd lied, and the clan's fear of his abilities had been enough to give her the benefit of the doubt.

He'd been banished, but that hadn't been enough for Su'Neena. She'd called for his execution and had tried twice since then to kill him. Openly. Brazenly. He'd dodged one arrow, but the scar on his thigh would forever remind him that she was serious about wanting him dead.

Tensing, he covertly checked her for weapons, but her hands were empty.

"Hunter." She gave him a respectful nod as she passed, and he blew out a relieved, shaky breath, feeling foolish for worrying she'd recognize him. He was Hunter right now, not Lobo, and he was almost safe. A few more yards . . .

He stepped through the stone doorway and sucked in a huge lungful of fresh evening air. Smelled like victory. He smiled until he remembered why he'd just risked his life.

Holding on to Hunter's form until he could get

safely away, he reached out to Tehya with his mind as he jogged through the twilight toward the safety of his cabin. If she was conscious, he'd feel her.

Nothing. She could be either unconscious or dead; he had no way of knowing.

Anger, sorrow, and frustration boiled in his chest, gathering steam until he felt as though he was going to explode. He needed to do something, but what? He felt so helpless and . . . alone. He hadn't truly realized how much Tehya had enriched his life until now.

Needing to outrun his thoughts, he first slowed down to concentrate on ditching Hunter's skin. As he took a bracing breath to begin the process, a female voice called to him.

Called to *Hunter*.

Son of a bitch. This was the last thing he needed right now. Cursing, he kept going as if he hadn't heard anything, but a moment later a hand gripped his elbow and gently pulled him to a halt.

When he turned around, he nearly groaned at the sight of Hunter's mate, Aylin, standing there in worn jeans, a form-fitting blue tank top, and white running shoes. He'd never met her, but he'd seen her from afar, and he'd gotten bits and pieces of information about her from the MoonBound females he fed from on the nights of the full moon. She seemed to be well liked and smart, and, if the intel was accurate, her influence had mellowed Hunter a lot.

"What are you doing here?" She reached back and fiddled with the leather band holding her long blond ponytail. "I didn't expect you back from your meeting with GraveBorn clan until tomorrow night."

Oh, wasn't that just great. No wonder everyone had been staring at him. Hunter wasn't supposed to be here.

She frowned at his shirt and hands. "And why are you covered in blood?" She sniffed and added, "Wolf blood."

"I found an injured wolf and brought it to Nicole," he said easily, because that, at least, was the truth.

Cocking her head, she studied him for so long that his hands grew clammy and his pulse pounded in his ears. If anyone could see through his disguise, it would be Hunter's mate. Finally she reached out and tugged on his hair.

"This is different. You haven't worn braids in a long time." She frowned. "And I swear it's longer than it was yesterday."

Oh, shit. He hadn't even thought about Hunter's hair when he'd shifted. He'd simply taken his most prominent memory of Hunter and given himself the braids the clan leader sported at formal events . . . such as banishing skinwalkers from the clan.

"I . . ." What had she said about GraveBorn? He was at a meeting? "I thought the meeting with GraveBorn deserved something more formal." He swept the braid back over his shoulder so she'd forget the length, which he couldn't explain.

"Well, you should wear it like that more often. I like it." A sly smile curved her mouth, and his mouth went dry as she eased up to him, pressing her body against his. "Since you're already here, do you have time for me?" Her hand slid from his chest to his abs, and then lower, to his waistband. "We can take a dip in the river. You can wash your clothes and let them dry while we mess around." Her voice went deeper as her blue eyes darkened into tide pools of seduction. "Remember what we did on the riverbank last fall?"

He actually did remember that, because he'd come upon them while out on a run in wolf form. He'd watched, probably for longer than was considered polite, as Hunter made love to his mate with the wilderness surrounding them. Their cries had filled the air with primal sounds of passion but had filled his chest with longing.

"I can't," he croaked, trying to disengage himself from her, but she stayed with him, and now her hand was slipping *under* his waistband.

"Oh," she said saucily, "I know you *can*."

Shit. She was hot and all, but if he thought that impersonating Hunter would get him dead, Lobo knew that messing with Hunter's mate would get him *painfully* dead.

Very gently, as if she were as delicate as a feather, he gripped her wrist and pushed her away. "Later," he said, hoping she didn't notice the slight tremor in his voice. "I still have the GraveBorn meeting. I promise to find you the second I get back."

"Fine." She pouted playfully and dropped her hands to her sides. "I guess I should let you build up your strength for tomorrow anyway."

Tomorrow? Oh, right . . . tomorrow was the new moon, the night when female vampires needed to feed from males.

He hadn't fed a female in months. Tehya's jealousy made it too difficult, so he usually avoided it until around the year mark when the headaches started. He wasn't sure why that happened, and no doubt Nicole could answer that question; but whatever the reason, he always felt better after donating a little vein juice to a hungry female.

"Oh." Aylin reached out and grasped his wrist, and he nearly jumped out of his skin. He wasn't used to being touched, and he certainly didn't know how Hunter would react. "I have to tell you what I did today."

Lobo glanced around, on alert for anyone who might be approaching. Clear so far, but MoonBound was an active clan, and he doubted it would be long before someone came along. "What did you do?"

"I opened a portal to Wallowa Lake, and I held it open for fifteen full minutes."

He whipped his head around and stared. To his horror, he was unable to stop staring. Gaping, really. Surely she wasn't talking about a *portal.* A method of traveling from one location to another distant location in a matter of seconds.

"You . . . wait. *What?*"

"I know!" She bounced on her toes. "That's the longest I've held one open, and it's the farthest away I've been able to get. Well, aside from Samnult's realm, of course. Riker wouldn't let me go through it because he's still on that kick about wanting me to be able to hold a portal open without it flickering before we start using them for long-distance travel, but we're close. Really close."

Sweet Maker, he'd thought the ability to swiftwalk was nothing but legend. Then again, most people thought skinwalkers were fiction as well. But swiftwalking . . . holy shit, with Aylin as his mate, Hunter could rule the damned world. Suddenly the battle among three clans and the humans a few months ago made sense. MoonBound had fought against two large vampire clans and a human army, and had somehow won, while dozens of humans, maybe as many as a couple of hundred, had disappeared off the face of the earth. Had they used one of Aylin's portals to send the humans somewhere? Like, say, to this Samnult's realm she'd mentioned?

"You know," she said in a hushed voice, "if I open a portal for you, you could be at the GraveBorn meeting in seconds, and Riker will never have to know."

Still rattled by the fact that they were casually talking about something he'd thought was impossible, he stammered out a lame, "Ah, thanks, but you know Riker will find out."

In reality, he had no idea if the guy would find out or not. Riker, Hunter's second in command, hadn't been at MoonBound back when Lobo had been a member, and Lobo had only spoken to the guy a handful of times to share information about human movement in the forests.

Aylin sighed. "You're probably right. He's like a drill sergeant in those military movies you make me watch." She went up on her toes and surprised him with a lingering, tender kiss so full of affection that his heart ached. Hunter was one lucky bastard. When she broke it off, he was almost disappointed. "Now get going," she said brightly. "The sooner you take care of business, the sooner you can come back to me."

She gave him a swat on the ass and a naughty smile; as he walked away, he rubbed his chest, but it did nothing to assuage the jealousy and longing that throbbed just under his breastbone.

He'd been alone for so long, with only Tehya as company, and as much as he loved the wolf, snuggling with her by the fire wasn't the same as snuggling with a female of the same species. When Hunter kicked him out of the clan, Lobo had lost everything, including the hope that one of the clan females would become his mate.

Mentally giving himself a kick—feeling sorry for himself wasn't acceptable—he headed back to his cabin to pray to whatever god would listen that Tehya pulled through.

3

Whatever Tehya was sleeping on was soft. At least, it was softer than the cabin floor she was used to when it was too warm to curl up at the foot of Lobo's bed.

Yawning, she lifted her hind leg to scratch her ear . . . but something was wrong with it.

Her gritty eyes stung as she peeled them open, and then she hastily shut them again when bright light nearly blinded her. Did Lobo have *all* the lights on?

She tried again, blinking to focus her blurry vision. As the haze faded, a million colors assaulted her vision, and she realized she wasn't stretched out in front of the fire in Lobo's cabin. She was lying on a pile of blankets on the floor of . . . a hospital? Or laboratory? IV supplies and bandages were scattered around, as if she'd ripped them away in a struggle. Would Lobo have brought her to a veterinarian for some reason? Maybe that would explain why her leg wasn't working right—*oh, Jesus!*

Her leg . . . it wasn't covered in fur. It was the wrong shape. The wrong size. It was a *human* leg.

Panicked, her heart racing and her breath coming in panting puffs, she held her hand in front of her face. Her *hand*, not her paw. Every coherent thought scattered as she scanned her naked body over and over, unable to believe she was looking at herself no matter how many times she counted her fingers and toes.

Could it really be that after twelve winters of living as a wolf, she was human again?

She licked her lips, catching her tongue on sharp fang tips. Right . . . not human.

Vampire.

Her mind spun as she tried to corral the memories that had grown distant over the years. She'd been human once, working as a dental assistant while attending college to become a dentist. And then her mom had died, and she'd been bitten by a vampire. She'd gotten sick, had spent weeks in a haze of nausea and fever as she transitioned into a vampire and then, shockingly, into a wolf.

After that . . . She shook her head, hating how clear her memories were now that she was no longer canine. It was as if someone had remastered an old, staticky black-and-white movie to make it ultra-high-def, with hypervibrant color. There was so much pain in her past, and without the filter of her wolf-brain to tone it down, it was nearly overwhelming.

But she supposed that at the moment her past was the least of her concerns. Right now she was in a strange place, she was naked, and she was freezing her bare butt off.

Shivering, she attempted to wrap one of the blankets around her shoulders. It took three tries and way too much concentration to make her hands behave like hands and not like paws, but she finally managed to cover herself.

But she was still on the floor.

Awkwardly she reached up with one hand to grab the edge of the counter. Her muscles, stiff and unaccustomed to this new form, seized in protest as she hauled herself to her feet. She swayed violently; thank God for the counter, or she'd have keeled over.

She stood there for a moment, sweating and wheezing, allowing herself time to adjust to standing upright and seeing things from twice the height she was used to. What now? She wasn't sure what to do besides run in a blind panic around the room.

Just breathe. You've been through worse.

Yes, she had. And as her mother used to say, "Panic leads to mistakes. Know your surroundings. Get the lay of the land, and always have a plan to escape."

Her mother should know, given that she'd been on the run from the government since the day Tehya was conceived.

Tehya willed herself to calm down and look around. There were rows of counters and tables covered with machines, computers, and lab equipment, but not a single window and only one door. She got the uneasy feeling she was underground. But where?

Tentatively she released her death grip on the counter and took a step toward the door. Then another. And another. Her first steps on two feet in more than a decade.

Her feet padded unsteadily on the hard floor as she shuffled across it. If she could just peek outside the room, maybe she'd get a better handle on her situation. But before she was even halfway across the room, the sound of voices drifted through the closed door.

"I'll tell Riker you're looking for him," a female voice called out. "He's meeting me here in a minute."

The door whispered open.

With a startled yelp, Tehya hit the floor, taking cover behind a cabinet.

"Oh, shit," the newcomer gasped. "The wolf."

Suddenly a strawberry-blond woman came around the corner, stopping short and gasping again when she saw Tehya crouching on the floor. For a few terrifying heartbeats, Tehya stared at the other female, unable to move. More heartbeats. More staring.

"Who . . . who are you?" the other female asked, and that fast, Tehya snapped out of the grip fear had on her.

She leaped to her feet and darted toward the door, but the woman moved like a snake. Her fingers dug into Tehya's shoulder and spun her hard into a wall. Terrified and confused, Tehya went on the attack, sinking her teeth into the other woman's arm and shaking hard. Blood spurted into her mouth, and even as her mind registered disgust, she moaned as the rich, silky nourishment coated her tongue.

The female screamed in pain, and Tehya went into a fresh spin of panic. People were bound to hear this, and then what? What would happen to her?

Who were these people?

Shoving with all her strength, Tehya slammed the female into what looked like an X-ray machine, and then she watched in horror as the woman crumpled to the floor, her mangled arm cradling her swollen belly.

Oh, shit. Pregnant. The female was pregnant.

Torn between wanting to make sure the female was okay and wanting to run, Tehya hesitated. The pounding of feet outside made her decision. She tore out of the room, bounced off a big guy who was heading for the lab at a dead run, and skidded around a corner, belatedly realizing she'd lost the blanket and was as naked as a newborn.

Whatever.

She sped blindly through the maze of hallways, careening off walls and people as she ran. She came to a Y split in the passage and, fighting her instinct to keep running, forced herself to slow down and take a deep breath. A million different scents filtered through her nostrils, from the musky tang of sex and the succulent odor of cooking meat to the crisp, green scent of outside fresh air from the tunnel on the right.

The sound of running footsteps once again spurred her into action. She sprinted down the right tunnel and followed the fresh air until she burst into the welcome sunshine.

She didn't stop. She didn't think she'd ever stop. Accompanied by the chirps of birds high in the trees, she bolted into the forest, easing up only when she caught the scent of smoke and roasting meat and realized she was running toward a human campsite.

Okay, chill out. Think. Get your act together.

Her mother hadn't merely been full of good

advice; she used to make Tehya practice using her brain during an emergency, and as Tehya crouched against a fallen tree she took back every complaint she'd ever uttered during those exercises.

Think. Breathe. List your options.

That last thing was easy, because she had very few options, and only one of them made sense. She had to find Lobo.

But how was he going to react? He knew her only as a wolf. He'd even named her Tehya. She had basically been his pet for twelve years, and now . . . now she was a vampire. A vampire who had been human until only a month before she shifted into a wolf and couldn't shift back. A vampire who was in love with a man who knew her only as a canine.

God, how was she going to explain this?

Her stomach contracted sharply, reminding her that she was truly a vampire, and she needed blood. Desperately. But did she dare risk approaching the human campsite by herself? She didn't know how to hunt or feed. She'd only fed from one human, a sleeping homeless man she'd attacked during the mindless insanity of her transformation. The campers would be healthy, awake, and perhaps even armed.

Worse, something besides hunger was gnawing at her. A need she couldn't quite identify, one that required blood, but also . . . something else. A . . . male?

An instant ache bloomed deep in her chest and in her pelvis at that thought. Of course! If what she'd learned about vampirism was true, it wasn't human blood she would crave during the new moon phase. She automatically looked up at the sky, but the only celestial body hovering overhead was the sun. Still, her instincts were telling her what she needed.

She needed to feed from a male vampire.

Lobo's handsome face filled her vision, his glossy black hair pushed away from his neck so a female could feed from his vein. Possessive anger clawed at her the way it always had when she found him with a female from one of the nearby West Coast clans. Even as a wolf with dulled vampire senses and memories, she'd understood that he needed the blood exchanges to survive . . . but that hadn't meant she'd liked it.

Cursing, she started toward his cabin. This was going to get interesting.

4

*T*wo days spent with GraveBorn clan's chief had given Hunter a powerful need for a shot of whiskey and a few hours in bed with Aylin. Ever since the battle involving humans and multiple vampire clans had shifted the balance of power within the vampire community, the clans had been attempting to set aside their differences and build alliances . . . with Hunter taking on the unofficial role of leader.

But despite the growing call to unite the clans, the process wasn't an easy one. Too many egos, too much distrust and bad blood, and too many different lifestyles made it nearly impossible to put together a coalition to defeat the humans who had enslaved so many of Hunter's people.

At least GraveBorn, like MoonBound, followed the Way of the Crow instead of the Way of the Raven, so ideology hadn't gotten in the way of negotiations. In addition, GraveBorn's leader knew as well as Hunter did that their ideology was false; they were both aware of the truth behind their origins, and both thought it was bullshit that, with the exception of their mates, they couldn't reveal it even to their own clan members.

Really, what had caused the most tension between

MoonBound and GraveBorn was that Hunter had refused to force one of his warriors to wed the other clan chief's daughter. For now, though, GraveBorn would support Hunter's authority and had pledged to fight as part of a united front against humans if—*when*—the time came.

Hunter was pretty sure that the time would come far too soon.

The entrance to MoonBound's headquarters was a welcome sight, especially given the timing. Tonight was the new moon, and even though it marked the time of month when females needed to feed, males felt the need like a vibration in the soul. It was an instinct not only to feed, but to provide. It was an instinct so powerful that the moment he and his contingent of warriors stepped inside the safety of MoonBound's earthen walls, they went their separate ways instead of holding an arrival briefing, with Hunter making a beeline to his quarters to surprise Aylin.

He found her curled up on the sofa reading a book, but she bounded to her feet and threw herself into his arms before he even closed the door.

"Now, *that* is a greeting." He swung her into his arms and spun her as she laughed. Damn, he loved the sweet sound of her voice. He hated being away from her, but until she'd perfected the art of summoning portals, he didn't want her to accompany him on missions that could potentially be dangerous.

"I've missed you," he said as he set her down and bent to nuzzle her neck.

"Not as much as I missed you," she said into

his ear, her voice dripping with unspoken naughty promises. "But you'll be happy to know that when I checked on your wolf earlier this morning, she was still alive."

Frowning, he pulled back and stared down at her. "My . . . wolf?"

"Well, I know it's not *your* wolf, but she's hanging on. For such severe injuries, it's amazing she's survived this long. Nicole hopes—"

"Aylin." He shook his head, utterly lost. "I have no idea what you're talking about."

"The wolf." Her smile faltered a little and her brow came down in confusion. "The one you brought to Nicole yesterday."

"I didn't bring Nicole a wolf. It must have been someone else."

She looked at him as if he were crazy. "I *saw* you with that wolf's blood all over you. We talked about it. Don't you remember?" She reached up and pressed her hand against his forehead as if checking for fever. "Are you okay?"

Was *he* okay? Aylin was the one who should have her temperature checked. "Aylin, honey, I wasn't here yesterday. Maybe you had a really vivid dream?"

Shadows flickered in her eyes as her concern for him grew. She probably saw the same shadows in his eyes. "Maybe we should go talk to Nicole."

"I think that's a good idea." What was wrong with her? Maybe opening portals came with side effects. If so, she was never doing that again.

As they walked toward the lab, Aylin's limp keeping the pace slower than he'd have liked, Hunter watched her warily, and she eyed him with just as much concern. "Aylin, are you sure you saw me yesterday?"

"Not just saw. Touched." She took his hand, and he found more comfort in that small gesture than anything else she could have done. "I know the feel of your lips on mine, Hunter. I felt you."

A knot formed in his belly as his alarm grew like a fast-moving cancer. Something was very, very wrong here. "I swear, it wasn't me."

Aylin, her skin already pale thanks to her mother's Scandinavian heritage, lost even more color in her face. "You're starting to scare me, Hunter. It was you. Ask Nicole. Or Grant. You talked to both of them when you brought in the injured wolf."

Criminy. Had he crossed into an alternate universe somewhere between GraveBorn's territory and here?

"Aylin—" He broke off at the sound of pounding footsteps coming at them and pulled Aylin to a halt as Aiden, one of MoonBound's best archers and senior warriors, rounded the corner at a dead run.

"There's an intruder in the compound." Aiden skidded to a halt and paused to catch his breath as Hunter went on instant alert.

"What happened?"

"It was a female. She attacked Nicole." He cursed, his frustration putting a sharp edge on his words. "We've been searching for the last fifteen minutes, but we haven't turned up anything. I'm sounding the alarm."

Fuck. "Initiate the intruder protocol." Hunter seized Aiden's arm before he could take off. "Where's Nicole? Is she okay?"

Aiden jerked his thumb behind him. "In the lab with Riker."

Hunter and Aylin hurried to the lab, where they found Nicole sitting at her desk holding a cloth soaked in blood against her head. Her other arm, bandaged from wrist to elbow, cradled her belly as Riker held a glass of water to her lips.

Rage bubbled up in Hunter at the idea that someone had assaulted a pregnant female. Right here, inside the clan headquarters, where everyone should be safe. This was his clan, his people, and ultimately his failure. If anything happened to Nicole or the baby, he'd never forgive himself.

Whoever had done this was going to pay in blood.

"Tell me everything," he ground out as he stopped next to Riker and Nicole.

Riker's silver eyes burned like steel shards of murder. "Someone broke into the lab and attacked Nicole when she came inside."

"Aiden said it was a female. Did either of you recognize her?"

"I've never seen her before," Nicole said, her voice laced with pain.

Riker shook his head viciously. "I didn't get a good look at her. The bitch nearly ran over me in the hall." He set down the glass hard enough to splash water all over the counter and floor. "I should have grabbed her. I should have fucking questioned why anyone would be running naked from a lab where there'd been a shit ton of noise and screaming. But all I could hear was Nicole crying for help, and—"

"Hey." Nicole took Riker's hand and brought

it to her cheek, calming him with her touch. "It's okay. This will all heal. The baby and I are fine." She shifted around to talk to Hunter, wincing as she moved, which only made Riker go taut again. "The wolf is missing too. The woman who attacked me might have set it loose in the compound. I'm sorry, Hunter." She smiled weakly, and Hunter cursed silently. She shouldn't be in this position. "But the good news is that if the wolf is running around, it's on the mend."

Okay, so the wolf Aylin had mentioned was real. But he knew damned well that he wasn't the one who'd brought it to MoonBound for help.

"Nicole, this is very important," he said, kneeling so they were at eye level. "Aylin said I brought you the wolf yesterday. Did you actually talk to me?"

"You don't remember?" Nicole looked at him the same way Aylin had, like he was crazy, and frankly, he was starting to feel that way. "You were very insistent that Grant and I save the animal."

For just a moment he considered the possibility that he'd somehow spirit-traveled in his sleep. But seeing how he'd never manifested himself someplace else, not to mention that the ability was considered myth in native and vampire communities, he quickly dismissed the idea.

Which meant that either Nicole, Grant, and Aylin were suffering from a shared delusion, or someone had impersonated him using one hell of a disguise.

"Whoever it was you both talked to yesterday," Hunter growled, "it wasn't me." He straightened, his gaze drawn to a bed of bloodstained towels and blankets on the floor next to a dish of water. Must have been the wolf's bed. "I was with GraveBorn's chief all day. Whoever brought in the wolf tricked you into thinking they were me."

But why? And who was the female who had assaulted Nicole?

"Oh . . . shit." Aylin's fingers trembled as she touched them to her lips. "I . . . kissed him."

Instant, white-hot rage seared his skin. Someone had dared to touch his mate? To kiss her? To—

"What else," he barked. "What else did you do with him?" The blood drained from Aylin's face, and he backed off, kicking himself for being such an ass. But the thought that someone could so easily take advantage of Aylin left him so angry he was shaking with the force of it. "Fuck, I'm sorry, Aylin." He shoved a hand through his hair. "I didn't mean to yell at you. None of this is your fault."

"No," she rasped. "It's not you. I just . . . I was thinking about what I would have done with him if he hadn't been in a hurry to go. I wanted to go down to the river. Where, you know . . ."

Yeah, he knew. The fact that she might have recreated a recent, especially raw, primal lovemaking session with the bastard was tempered by the fact that she hadn't; so instead of blowing a gasket, he drew her against him and held her close.

"Excuse me," Nicole said, "but how is any of this even possible?"

"Magic." Aylin remained plastered against him, her entire body shaking, but her voice was strong and sure. "The mystic-keeper at ShadowSpawn could make you believe that one person had turned into another."

Skepticism flashed in Nicole's expression. Despite all she'd seen since becoming a vampire and joining MoonBound, she still insisted that science could explain everything. "Mystic-keepers often use hallucinogenic herbs to . . ."

The sound of Nicole's voice faded in his ears as Hunter stared at the wolf bed. This was bad. Really bad. The damage someone could do while wearing Hunter's skin could be—

Skin. He sucked in a sharp breath. *Skinwalker.*

Holy shit. Neither magic nor hallucinogenic substances had done this. A vampire shifter had. A vampire shifter he'd banished long ago for impersonating another clan member. *Son of a bitch.*

"This wasn't a result of magic or chemistry," Hunter blurted, interrupting Nicole's lengthy explanation about how hallucinogens worked. "It was a skinwalker. It's possible he's the one who brought in the wolf while disguised as me and who then attacked Nicole in the guise of a female."

Nicole groaned, but not from pain. "Please don't tell me a skinwalker is what I think it is."

Unfortunately, he couldn't do that, and he felt a little bad, because her science-brain wasn't going to handle this well.

"Skinwalkers come from Native American lore that originated with vampires," he explained hastily, anxious to go find the bastard. "They can shapeshift into animals, but usually only their own totem animal."

Aylin pulled back. "But not all of them are limited to shifting into beasts. Before I was born, my father executed a skinwalker who could impersonate humans and other vampires."

"I banished one from MoonBound," Hunter said, his voice bitter to his own ears. "But maybe I should have taken a cue from your father."

Riker frowned. "Are you talking about Lobo?"

"Is that the strange guy who lives in the woods with a wolf?" Aylin asked.

Hunter nodded. "That wolf has to be the one he brought in. It's the only thing that makes sense. He shifted into me so he could get inside."

Nicole considered that. "He must have come back this morning to check on the wolf while disguised as someone else. But why was he naked? And female?"

"Does it matter?" Riker helped Nicole to her feet, keeping one arm protectively around her. "He attacked you. He's going to answer for that."

"He's got a *lot* to answer for," Hunter said.

The door burst open and Aiden's lover, Takis, jogged inside, his dark hair hidden under a Seattle Seahawks cap. "Sir, we've tracked Nicole's assailant into the forest. Should we follow?"

A mental image of Lobo kissing Aylin popped into Hunter's head and triggered his prey drive. "We don't follow." He started toward the armory. "We hunt."

*L*obo had spent the last sixteen hours pacing the length of his tiny cabin. It wouldn't be long before Hunter and a team of his warriors showed up at his door to drag him back to MoonBound, but he wished they'd hurry. He needed to see Tehya, and the only reason he wasn't freaking out right now was that he sensed that the wolf was alive.

The puzzling thing was that she felt different, her energy muted and scattered. It was as if she were half a world away and in no one particular direction.

Beneath his camo pants and T-shirt, his muscles twitched with the desire to do something more than pace around like an idiot. Every time he glanced at the door, scratched up by Tehya's claws, he had to clench his fists to keep from ripping it open and racing to MoonBound. But the coming confrontation with Hunter needed to happen here, in Lobo's own territory.

Oh, having the home field advantage wouldn't help him win a battle—he'd be outnumbered and outweaponed, and he wasn't planning to fight anyway.

Forcing Hunter to come here would make Moon-Bound's chief see Lobo as more than a banished outsider. Hunter would see Tehya's food dishes and toys. He'd see the rug in front of the woodstove where she liked to lie after coming in out of the snow or rain. He'd see how much Lobo loved the wolf and would, Lobo hoped, understand the forbidden lengths he'd gone to in order to save her.

But, damn, the wait was torture. And he knew torture.

He eyed the jar of hooch he'd gotten from a hermit near the Washington-Idaho border last winter, but before he could calculate how much he could drink and still remain civil when Hunter showed up, the sound of a branch breaking just outside froze him in place. A heartbeat later, something scratched at the door.

Tehya.

The scratching noise sounded again, high up on the frame. If it was Tehya, she was up on her hind legs.

Heart pounding, he threw himself at the door, practically tearing it off its rusty hinges in his excitement.

Not Tehya.

Ho-ly shit.

A naked woman stood on the rickety porch boards, her body covered in scratches and scrapes, her long black hair tangled around sticks and leaves. She was a stranger, but he knew her. Holy Maker, he *knew* her.

She was the woman he'd seen so many times in Tehya's mind.

Her slender shoulders rose and fell with each

panting, exhausted breath, and she was shivering, but her amber eyes gleamed with recognition.

"You know me," he said, his voice tight with astonishment and confusion. Where had she come from? Why was she here? How was she connected to Tehya? It was all he could do to keep from blurting out every question at once.

She opened her mouth as if to speak, and he caught a glimpse of fangs. As suspected, she was a vampire. A born vampire as well, or her eyes would be silver.

A blast of hunger hit him in a wave that was almost physical. Desperate need billowed from her, as if she was not only hungry, but chronically starved. She threw herself at him so suddenly he didn't have time to block her. In an instant, she was wrapped around him like a bear cub scaling a tree, and crazily enough, his first instinct wasn't to throw her off him.

His instinct was to hold her tighter and tilt his head to give her better access to his vein.

Lobo held the strange female against him, his body responding like a traitor as she sank her fangs into his throat. Pain and pleasure rippled through him, leaving him so unsteady that he had to brace himself against the wall. Ah, damn, this was good. Bizarre, but good.

Thanks to Tehya's jealousy, he hadn't fed a female in long time, and he had definitely never fed a strange female who showed up at his door naked and scratched all to hell.

But she wasn't a complete stranger, was she? He'd never met her, but he knew her. He'd seen her in Tehya's mind and in his dreams. Hell, she'd even made it into some of his fantasies, the ones that sometimes woke him in the middle of the night and left him drenched in sweat and painfully hard. And how many times had he summoned her image while he stroked himself in the shower?

As if she read his thoughts, she rocked against him, rubbing her bare chest against his, her pelvis against his rapidly hardening erection.

"Hey," he said roughly, tightening his hold in an attempt to calm her, but all that did was bring her even more solidly against him. "It's okay. You can slow down."

If she heard him, she didn't respond. Keeping his grip on her, he sank onto the bed, knowing that at the rate she was feeding, it wouldn't be long before he got light-headed.

She took an extremely hard pull, and a burst of extreme pleasure-pain shot through him. "Jesus," he whispered. "How long has it been since you last fed?"

Her only response was a moan and a slow grind of her hips, which dredged up a moan of his own. Her fingernails dug into his shoulders, creating sizzling pops of pain that heightened all his senses. He became aware of the way her breath tickled his skin. The way her hard nipples pressed into his chest. The way her sex rocked against the bulge beneath his fly. His hands shook as he gripped her waist, but what he really wanted was to slip his fingers between their bodies, release his cock, and drive into her the way he did in his dreams.

She'd let him. Everything that made him the male animal he was demanded he take what she was offering, flip her onto her back and give her his blood and his seed. But even as he shifted to make it happen, he snarled in frustration.

He couldn't do it. She was clearly suffering from feeding deprivation, leaving her vulnerable and too easily swayed. So he gnashed his molars together and kept his hands in neutral territory as she moved against him, feeding with increasing fervor. The scent of her arousal surrounded him, chipping away at his willpower—and the enamel on his teeth.

Heat consumed him as she rode his erection, making little sounds of ecstasy with every back-and-forth sweep across his lap. He could feel her pleasure mounting, could practically taste it as an electric bite in the air.

His heart pounded in anticipation. "Come on," he rasped. "Take what you want."

She rocked faster, the friction and damp heat between them shocking him with its intensity. He could come like this. An orgasm edged closer, boiling in his balls and swelling in his shaft. Nails scored his back, digging deep, and a heartbeat later, she stiffened and clamped down on his throat hard with a husky shout. Her climax shuddered through her, vibrating his body and putting him so close to the tipping point that he felt the cool wetness of precum spread across the tip of his cock.

Then she went limp, the sexual storm fading as she disengaged her fangs. His body still coiled tight with need, he grimaced as he eased them both onto their sides, and for the first time since she'd burst into his cabin, he got a good look at her face. High cheekbones, flushed with color, sloped gracefully to her hairline, and remarkably long lashes framed drowsy, sated yellow eyes that drilled into him not with their intensity, but with their familiarity. He knew those eyes . . . but from more than just the visions. Why?

"I guess maybe I should get your name now," he said, his voice rough with unspent lust.

For some reason, she looked hurt. "I—" She broke off and tried again, but what came out of her mouth sounded more like a whimper than a word. Closing her eyes, she inhaled deeply. "I . . . haven't spoken . . . words . . ." She opened her eyes. ". . . in a long . . . time."

He actually understood that. He'd lived alone for so long that if not for his wolf pals, his voice would be wrapped in dust and cobwebs. But he was impatient for answers, sexually frustrated, and a pint low on blood.

"What the hell is going on?"

She shook her head. "This must . . . be so strange to you."

"What, opening the door to find a naked, starving female who, before now, I've only seen in my head? Nah. Happens all the time."

Wry amusement tipped up the corner of her mouth. "I know it doesn't, because I'm here almost every day."

He propped himself up on one elbow and searched her face. For what, he wasn't sure, but he did know he wanted the truth, and he didn't want to play games to get it. "You can see through Tehya's eyes, can't you? She's your totem animal." He paused, not wanting to ask the question that needed to be asked. Finally, his breath burning in his throat, he spit it out. "Does your being here mean she's dead?"

Instead of answering, she shivered and gestured at his dresser. "Do you mind? You have a flannel shirt that'll fit me. The green and black one you haven't worn for a long time."

"Sure," he said numbly, his mind racing. How much had she seen through Tehya? His cheeks flamed hot as he thought about all the humiliating possibilities. "What else do you know about me?"

She climbed off the bed, giving him a mouth-watering view of her tight, round ass, full hips, and long, graceful thighs. She was perfectly fit, built like a runner with not an ounce of fat on her body. As she pulled the flannel shirt out of one of the drawers, she shot him a sly grin.

"I know everything." The grin faded as she donned the shirt and worked the buttons. "You know everything about me too."

"Look," he said, reaching the limits of his patience, "this isn't a joke. I know nothing about you. At all."

She pointed to Tehya's dishes in the corner. "You know I won't eat anything out of my bowl unless it's clean. You know I like it when you put ice cubes in my water in the summer." She gestured to the fireplace. "You know I like it when you drag my bed in front of the fire in the winter. You know I love to run with you through the river basin because I'm more agile on rocks than you are when you're in wolf form." She met his gaze, and his mouth fell open. Her eyes, holy shit, her eyes. They were familiar . . . because they were *wolf* eyes. "And you know I like to sneak onto your bed and curl up next to you in the middle of the night."

His breath cut out as he sat up straight and stared at her. "Tehya?" At her barely discernible nod, he exhaled on a long, slow curse. "I can't . . . I can't believe it." He shook his head, unable to process this. "I have so many questions, and I don't even know where to start."

For years he'd dreamed of this woman, and all the while she'd been real and right here under his feet. Literally. He'd tripped over her or stepped on her tail dozens of times.

"Start at the beginning, maybe?" she offered.

The beginning. What a novel idea. Maybe that was where *she* should start. "Why didn't you tell me the truth years ago instead of letting me believe you were a wolf?" And how had she maintained her wolf form for so long? As far as he knew, no one had ever held on to a morph for more than two days, and even then, according to the stories, the skinwalker who had made it the full two days had died a week later.

"I couldn't tell you." She lifted her silky mane of hair up out of the shirt and let it cascade over her shoulders. His fingers practically itched to touch it. "I was—" She broke off with a growl so wolflike that if he'd doubted her story before, he believed her now. Her head whipped toward the door. "There are people coming."

That's when he heard it: the alarm yip of a coyote. It was distant but clear, and it came from the south. MoonBound lay to the south.

Hunter was coming.

Damn it! He'd been so wrapped up in everything going on with Tehya that he'd forgotten how much danger he was in. He'd been willing to face the danger, but now that Tehya was safe, he wasn't about to sit around and wait for Hunter's judgment. They needed to get as far away from MoonBound as possible. And, hell, he'd always wanted to see Alaska.

"We gotta go," he said as he leaped off the bed and snagged his loaded weapons belt off the wall.

"Why? What's wrong?"

Oh, not much. He'd only broken into a secure compound, impersonated the clan chief, and kissed his mate. "I violated a few vampire laws when I took Tehya—er, *you* to MoonBound." Still thinking it was crazy that he was having an actual conversation with Tehya, he buckled the belt around his hips and took his favorite hatchet from its hook near the door. "If we aren't out of here in the next five minutes, I'm dead."

And Tehya might be as well.

6

Tehya had never known fear like this. Not even the day she was attacked by a vampire could compare with the sheer terror of knowing that a clan of vampires hell-bent on revenge was only moments away from breaking down the door and possibly slaughtering them.

Lobo shoved his hatchet into a loop on his belt, and the hackles on the back of her neck rose. He never left the cabin without being armed with a few blades, but he didn't take his favorite hatchet unless he was going to practice with it . . . or kill with it. The muscles in his arms and back rippled as he tore weapons from the walls and from the wooden chest near the fireplace. Every movement was brisk and economical, and within moments she swore every inch of his incredible body was armed.

She watched him, fascinated despite the danger they were facing. As a wolf, she'd loved him, but she'd never felt any kind of sexual feelings toward him. Which was a good thing, she supposed. But now . . . now she was a woman again, a female vampire with his blood coursing through her veins and a body that was still liquid from the climax she'd had with him.

She should probably be embarrassed by that, but she'd never been very self-conscious—and he'd seen her using the forest like a big litter box, so she was pretty much over being sensitive about bodily functions.

He swung around to her, his luxurious midnight hair fanning across broad shoulders that blocked the single stream of light coming through a crack in the drawn curtains. His dark gaze raked her from head to toe, and she sucked in an appreciative breath. She'd seen him in warrior mode before, but this was hardcore. He was cool. Detached. And why wouldn't he be? She was a stranger to him.

"You need pants," Lobo said gruffly, turning away to peek through the window.

She looked down at herself. The flannel shirt hung to mid-thigh, but her lower legs, already cut up from the run through the forest earlier, had no protection. Unfortunately, they'd have to stay that way.

"You don't have anything that'll fit me."

"I have a pair of sweatpants—"

"With a broken string." She knew that because she herself had chewed on the cord when she'd been bored one day. "I can't cinch them around my waist." She brushed past him on her way to the door. "Besides, I've spent the last, what—twelve years?—without pants or shoes. I'll be fine."

"You also spent the last twelve years without speaking," he muttered, and she bit back a smile as they slipped outside, moving silently north, in the opposite direction from MoonBound.

Lobo set the pace at a slow run, finding a happy medium that allowed them to move swiftly while

creating the least amount of noise. She followed, resisting the urge to overtake him. For years she'd ranged
ahead or loped at his side, her wolf senses keeping
track of him while remaining alert for signs of danger.

Now she was essentially a month-old vampire
with no experience or understanding of her own
strengths and weaknesses, and the only person she
knew didn't know *her*. He knew Tehya the wolf. He
didn't know Kristen Parker, the once-human dental
assistant, or Kristen Parker, the screwup newbie
vampire who had somehow turned into a wolf and
couldn't turn back.

For twelve years.

A dull crack echoed through the forest, and Lobo
stopped so suddenly that she nearly bumped into
him. "They're at my cabin," he growled. "We need
to run." He shoved her in front of him. "Go! Head
toward the river."

She took off, running as fast as she could on bare
feet, but damn, the sticks and rocks were sharp. Her
wolf paws had been so much tougher. Still, as painful
as the bruises and punctures were, this would have
been much worse if she'd still been human.

They ran for miles, slowing only occasionally to
judge the distance between them and their pursuers.
It seemed to her as if the MoonBound people were
getting closer, but every time she asked Lobo to con-
firm her suspicions, he only told her to run faster.
And once, when a rabbit dashed across their path,
she'd automatically darted after it.

"Damn it, Tehya, get back here!" he yelled.
"Come here! Heel!"

"Hilarious," she muttered, swinging back to run with him. When he smirked, she wanted to both kiss him and bite him.

The rush of the river grew louder ahead, the most welcome sound she'd ever heard.

"Bear left," Lobo called out as they raced along the edge of a meadow populated by wild turkeys that kept wary eyes on them as they passed. "Take the path down the canyon that lands us on the south side of the rapids."

Smart. They could use the water to eliminate tracks, and the noise of the rapids would cover the sounds of their escape.

They leaped the remains of an old split-rail fence and charged up an embankment that ended abruptly on a rocky ledge. Far below, a wide, deep section of the river created a relatively calm spot where animals on the other side came to drink. Even from this distance, she could see deer and elk tracks interspersed with a few canine and big-cat paw prints.

"This way." He started down the narrow, winding trail along the edge of the river ravine. "We'll swim downstream to—" He broke off with a grunt. Stumbling, he wheeled around, and Tehya watched in horror as blood bloomed on his chest around the head of an arrow that had punched through his back.

"*Lobo?*"

His eyes glazed over as his knees buckled. Tehya caught him around the waist before he hit the ground, but his weight knocked her off balance. Her foot caught a root, and he pitched to the side, his momentum tearing him from her grip.

No—oh, God, no!

Her heart stopped, the blood congealing in her veins, as Lobo disappeared over the side of the cliff. A scream lodged in her throat as she scrambled to the edge in time to see his body splash into the river below and disappear beneath the surface.

"Who shot that fucking arrow!" The deep, masculine voice echoed off the surrounding mountains, seeming to come from everywhere at once, making it all the more terrifying. "I wanted him alive!"

They were coming closer, their feet booming like thunder on the forest floor.

Please, please, Lobo. Be alive. Tehya watched the river in desperation, her fingers digging into moss and damp earth as she clung to the edge of the cliff. *Surface, damn you!*

"You!" a male voice, different from the first, called out to her. "To your feet. Turn around slowly."

Fury like she'd never felt before welled up, and she disobeyed both orders, spinning around on all fours with a snarl. She was going to rip out their throats for this. She'd almost certainly die, but not before taking out at least one of the bastards.

A blond male and a dark-skinned female emerged from the forest, both armed with bows, the arrows pointed at her head. Another male, sporting a crossbow, came at her from the side, while yet another male, this one empty-handed, strode toward her with the arrogant confidence of an alpha leader.

Although she didn't know their names, she'd seen all of them from a distance, had once even spent a full day tracking the blond one out of boredom and curiosity. But the guy coming at her didn't need an introduction. He must be MoonBound's chief, Hunter. And she had no doubt that despite his lack of a weapon, he was just as deadly as the others.

"Who are you?" he demanded.

As if she was going to reply to people who had just shot Lobo. Hell, she was shaking so hard she doubted she could speak even if she'd wanted to.

Still growling, she inched backward, until her knees hit the edge of the cliff and her feet dangled over. Dislodged pebbles and crumbling earth bounced off the cliff face, the sound abnormally loud in the hushed, tense silence.

"Get away from the ledge," the guy said, his voice dripping with warning.

Twisting, she peered into the pool below, and her heart stopped when she saw the body floating in the bubbling waters.

She didn't waste another second. Figuring she had nothing left to lose, she shot her pursuers the finger and jumped.

7

*T*he sound of a female voice humming a classic Johnny Cash song was something Lobo had never awakened to. What he *had* awakened to, several times, was intense, throbbing pain. Not often, but enough to know it always meant that something had gone terribly wrong during a fight.

What had he done to deserve it this time?

He peeled open his eyes as his brain tried to crank out an explanation as to why he was wet, in agony, and lying on his back in some sort of . . . room? Shack? What the hell?

"Lobo!" Tehya filled his field of vision as she stood up from a booth covered in cracked, ugly-ass avocado vinyl. "You're awake."

"What . . ." He cleared his raw throat and tried again. "What . . . happened?"

Tucking her damp hair behind her ears, she sank down next to him on what appeared to be an elevated mattress. Mildewed, frayed gingham curtains hung near his head and at his feet, and it took him a few precious seconds to realize they were inside an old camper.

"You were struck by an arrow. I thought you were dead." Very gently, she peeled back a bloody, folded towel from the wound just beneath his left collarbone. "Do you remember being chased?"

Now that she reminded him, he did. They'd reached a cliff on the edge of the river, but he didn't know what had happened after that.

"Yeah," he croaked. "Sort of. But how did we get here?" Wherever "here" was.

"You fell into the water." Her voice faltered with emotion, and he knew exactly how she'd felt. It had torn him apart when he'd seen Tehya suffering from the poacher's gunshot wound. "I went after you. I didn't know if you were alive or dead, but I held your head out of the water and floated us downriver until I was sure those people weren't following."

So she was beautiful *and* smart. The river split into several streams, creating multiple escape routes for their pursuers to have to check out. "Where are we?"

He sucked air as she replaced the dressing on the wound. "Sorry," she murmured, before folding her hands in her lap. "Remember that rusted-out camper we found a couple of years ago?"

It took a second for his brain to kick in, but he finally remembered. They'd been tracking an injured deer that had likely been hit by a car, and they'd found the abandoned camper deep inside state forest lands. If this was that same camper, they were a good ten miles downriver from where he'd gone into the water.

So, yep, he remembered, and he grinned. "I seem to recall that you peed on it."

Her cheeks flamed red, the bright color spreading all the way to her ears. "I had to mark my territory," she said, adding a haughty sniff for emphasis. "Be glad I didn't pee on you." The crimson in her face deepened. "I mean . . . you know, I *was* a wolf. . . ."

He chuckled, but a stab of pain ripped through his chest, turning his laugh into a moan.

"Shouldn't you be healing faster than this?" Her gorgeous eyes darkened with concern. "Vampires are supposed to have super healing powers, right?"

His gaze slid to her mouth and the pearly fangs that peeked between her slightly parted lips, and to his annoyance, his cock stirred.

"You're a vampire too," he pointed out as he casually adjusted his hand to cover the swell in his damp jeans. "You tell me."

Windblown tree branches scraped the top of the camper, something that would have freaked out wolf-Tehya, but vampire-Tehya didn't so much as bat an eye. "I wasn't a vampire for very long before I turned into a wolf."

He blinked in surprise. "How is that possible? You must have been born a vampire. If you were turned, you'd have silver eyes." Plus, she clearly had native blood running through her veins, and because the vampire race had begun in native tribes, most people who were born vampires tended to have at least *some* American Indian blood.

"I don't know why my eyes remained this color after I was turned," she said, "but I assure you, I was born human."

A *human* had been born with eyes the color of golden amber? Eyes that belonged only to wolves . . . or skinwalkers? Huh.

He had a lot of questions for her, but he figured they could start with the basics. "I should have asked this sooner, but what's your name? Probably not Tehya."

"It's Kristen." She looked at him almost shyly. "But I prefer Tehya. What's it mean?"

His face grew so hot he actually looked around for a furnace. "Precious," he said, feeling like a fool. He had few memories of his mother, but he remembered her calling him "*Tehya*," so when the wolf he'd rescued had survived, he'd given her a name he associated with his very best memories.

"Precious." She said it like she was tasting it on her tongue and was pleased with the flavor. "I like it."

Silence fell, made awkward by the fact that they were both in foreign territory. Literally and figuratively. How could he know someone for years and yet not know her at all?

"So what made you turn back after all this time?" he asked, as much to break the silence as to learn more about her. And was it weird that he missed the wolf?

Yes, he knew the wolf and the person were one and the same, but they were also very, very different. He knew the animal, understood her. But the female sitting next to him was a stranger. A beautiful, sexy, long-legged stranger.

"I don't know." She sighed, her full cherry lips parting slightly. "It wasn't like I didn't *try* to turn back. I did. For years. But I didn't know how. I have no idea why it was different this time. I just woke up in that lab, and I was like this." Her gaze met his, and in their jewel-toned depths, he thought he saw a glint of accusation. Or maybe it was his own guilt being reflected back at him. "You said you took me there. Why, if those people hate you?"

Damn, she must have been terrified. Remorse racked him at the thought that she'd awakened in a strange place all alone.

"You'd been shot," he said, his voice rough with emotion. "MoonBound has a doctor. It was your only chance of survival. How did you get out of there?"

"I ran until I found an exit." She looked down at her hands, which were folded in her lap. "But I think I hurt one of their females."

Ah, shit. He was already up to his eyebrows in trouble. This was going to be the final stitch in his death shroud.

"And she was pregnant."

Double shit. A sinking sensation made his gut feel like it had dropped through his spine and was sitting on the mattress beneath him. Tehya was now in nearly as much danger as he was. Had he saved her just so they could both be dumped in the same shallow grave?

Closing his eyes, he tried to work out all possible scenarios for how this could play out, but every one of them ended badly. Worst of all, he couldn't see how they could escape from any of them. Hunter might have given up the search eventually—if one of his clan members hadn't been injured. But now . . .

So. Much. Shit.

"You said I was shot," Tehya said. "How bad? Because I woke up healed."

"It was a critical wound. Probably fatal for any other wolf." He opened his eyes and stared up at the sagging, mold-dappled ceiling. "But shifting can repair most damage, and it's probably what saved you."

Leaning forward abruptly, she gripped his hand in a bruising hold. "Then you need to shift. Your injury—"

"I can't." He interrupted her before she got her hopes up. "In order to sneak you into MoonBound, I had to take the clan leader's form. It takes a lot more effort to do that than it does to shift into an animal, and it temporarily drained my ability to shift into anything."

She took in a startled breath. "You can assume someone else's identity? Can I do that?"

If not for their dire circumstances, he'd have laughed at how eagerly she sat forward, reminding him of her wolfy counterpart. If she'd had a tail, she'd have been wagging it.

"I doubt it," he said, hating the disappointment in her expression. If she'd still been wolfy, he'd have given her a treat and a pat on the head. "The ability is among the rarest of all vampire gifts, and it only manifests in born vampires." At least, that was what he'd been told by the tribal elders in Sedona after he'd made a pilgrimage there half a century ago. "Even if you could do it, it's forbidden."

"Is that why the clan is after you?" She leaped to her feet and peered out a couple of dirt-caked windows, as if speaking aloud about the clan would summon them like demons. He didn't have the heart to tell her that they didn't need to be summoned; they'd be here soon enough all on their own. "Because you shifted to save me?"

The devastation in her voice was like a punch to the heart. He didn't want to lie, but he couldn't let her think this was her fault either.

He settled on a sanitized version of the truth. "Not entirely," he hedged. "There's bad blood between us. This would have happened eventually."

"Why the bad blood?"

Because MoonBound is full of assholes. He contemplated telling her everything, but time was at a premium, so the abbreviated version would have to do.

"MoonBound's old chief led an assault against my clan that wiped it out. His warriors found a wolf cub in the bushes, and they tied it up while they finished raiding my clan's camp. When they came back for the cub, there was a toddler there instead."

"You?"

He nodded. "Me. Some of them thought it must be a trick, but others wanted to slaughter me right then and there." At her uncomprehending expression, he elaborated: "Skinwalkers and people who can speak to animals are considered evil by some."

"That's horrible."

"Yeah, well, some vampires are superstitious fools."

She looked out the windows again. "Obviously they didn't kill you."

No, but there were many times when he'd wished

they had. "They took me back to MoonBound. Named me Lobo and kept me like a dog, even though I didn't shift again. Not until I was an adult." He hadn't known he could. No one had told him about his past. All he knew was that they'd slaughtered his parents and then literally treated him like a dog, keeping him on a chain at night and forcing him to do all the shit work around the clan. It wasn't until a staged battle for position among MoonBound's young males that he'd shifted into his totem animal, a wolf.

"What happened when you shifted? Were you afraid?"

"Of shifting?" He shook his head. "I was more afraid of what they were going to do to me." He closed his eyes, but the memory of being nearly beaten to death played out right there on the back of his eyelids. "It was Bear Roar's son, Hunter, who talked his father out of killing me. Convinced him I'd be useful. Animals could go places vampires couldn't, like into other clans' territories, you know?"

A year later, Hunter had killed his father; and not long after that, Lobo had discovered that he could shift into people and not just animals.

"So what went wrong? Why are you not still with the clan?"

"Because as bad as they think shifting into an animal is, shifting into another vampire is far worse."

"They kicked you out for that?"

"They could have killed me," he said. "Most of the clan members wanted to."

"Those bastards." Brow furrowed with worry,

she hurried back to him, taking his hand once again. God, she was warm. He hadn't felt a female's touch in so long—at least, not a female who wasn't covered in fur. "So what can we do? We can't just wait here for them." Scowling, she nibbled on her lower lip. "Wait. You need blood, right? I remember reading somewhere that vampires heal faster when they drink blood." She flipped her hair away from her slender throat. "Do it."

There was no hesitation, reminding him once again how brave she'd always been. She'd once gotten between him and a cougar, had been ready to defend him to the death. Her loyalty and willingness to sacrifice herself had always humbled him, and nothing about that had changed.

"Please, Lobo, take it."

His mouth watered and his fangs punched down, but even as the primal urge to draw her against him and sink his fangs into her rose up, his brain countered with a depressing dose of reality.

"I can't."

"Of course you can. I've seen you bite plenty of women."

Was it his imagination, or did she sound a little— or a lot—jealous? It shouldn't surprise him, given that, as a wolf, she'd barely tolerated the females he'd met for moon feedings. And if things started to get sexual, as most feedings did, her snarls had put a damper on the situation, fast. She'd been so aggressive that he'd even left her locked in his cabin once while he met with a MoonBound female. Hunter might hate him, but there were more females than males in the clan, so he looked the other way when it came to the bimonthly moon fevers.

Lobo had returned home to destroyed furniture, ripped bedding, and a chewed-up door. And when Tehya had smelled what he'd done with the female, she'd bitten him. Hard.

"I won't take your blood, Tehya. There's no time. You're going to need your strength."

"We'll make time." Reaching up, she yanked on her shirt collar, busting one of the buttons and exposing even more of her long, creamy neck and the shadowy hint of cleavage. "You need to heal."

He inhaled deeply, seeking the same patience he'd always summoned when she gnawed on his shoes or hid his socks, but all he got now was the odor of rusting metal, mildew, and ancient layers of dust and rot. This piece-of-shit trailer smelled like the past, which was probably all he and Tehya had now. Even if Hunter didn't kill him and lock Tehya in a dungeon for harming a pregnant clan member, they couldn't be together. They were skinwalkers, shunned by most clans and banned from mating each other.

Wouldn't want to increase the odds of spawning skinwalker offspring, obviously.

Bitterness soured his mouth. He rarely wasted time dwelling on the unfairness of his situation; he was what he was. But now, with his back up against a wall—or in this case, against a filthy mattress—all he could think about was how he'd been robbed of a future.

Of a pleasant future, anyway.

Damn, that pissed him off. The female of his

dreams, literally, had finally come into his life; but even if he survived Hunter, Tehya still couldn't be his because of some bullshit vampire law.

When have I ever obeyed any law?

True enough. He'd lived on the fringes of vampire society since he was born. Why the fuck should he conform now?

Because I'm about to die, and Tehya's life is in my hands.

Well, there was that.

"Lobo!" Still tugging her collar away from her throat with one hand, she used the other to push down on the towel covering his injury. Not hard, but enough to get his attention. *"Drink."*

"You know," he said lightly, hoping to distract her, "you used to nip me when I ignored you."

She bared her teeth. "I still can." Another button popped as she yanked on the shirt. "But you first."

Fuck, that made him instantly, painfully hard. Every instinct screamed to take advantage of what she was offering, ancient instincts passed down from primitive ancestors whose only pleasures in life came from the acts of filling bellies with food and offspring. But in order to eat and mate, they had to stay alive.

"You got us to safety and bought some time," he said, his gaze lingering on her throat, "but I know Hunter, and he's a hell of a tracker." He snapped his eyes up to hers, hoping she'd feel as much as see the inevitable finality of the situation. "He's going to find us."

"I know." Her voice was grim, determined, and her expression reminded him of how she used to plant her paws and refuse to budge when she wanted something.

"You need to go."

Instead of arguing—or leaving—she yanked on the shirt, destroying another button, and climbed fully onto the mattress. Or, more accurately, she climbed onto him. Oh, she was careful not to hurt him, letting herself lie half on, half off him, one thigh resting on his pelvis, her breasts pressed against the uninjured side of his chest, and her throat only inches from his lips.

"I'm not leaving you." Her hot breath whispered across his ear, and his groin tightened. "I'd rather die with you than die alone."

"Run," he said, his voice rattling as if he'd eaten a load of gravel. "Once they have me, they'll forget about you."

Gently, she used the tips of her fingers to tilt his face even closer to her neck. "I can't survive out here by myself. I don't know how to be a vampire. Please, Lobo," she begged. "You took me in when I was starving all those years ago, and you saved my life again just days ago. Let me do this for you. You might not be able to escape from Hunter, but you can face him with as much strength as I can give you."

Ah, damn. He shouldn't let himself be swayed, but he was a selfish asshole. He wanted to taste her, to have that connection with someone one more time—for what might be the last time. Besides, she was right. She most likely wouldn't survive on her own—and while Hunter might punish her for harming a clan member, he wouldn't kill her, and he wouldn't turn her out to die. MoonBound's clan leader might be a son of a bitch who'd learned to govern from a bigger son of a bitch, but he wasn't a monster.

His hand shook as he threaded his fingers through her hair and pulled her head closer to his. His chest screamed in agony, but he breathed through it, his need to feed distracting him from the pain. Her skin felt like warm satin on his lips, and as he opened his mouth over her jugular, he felt her pulse flutter madly against his tongue.

"Ever been bitten?" He licked at her, tasting the earthy notes of the forest she'd lived in with him for years. "After you became a vampire, I mean."

She arched against him with a breathy, "No," and he shivered in anticipation. "Will it hurt?"

"Does a wolf shit in the woods? Never mind, I know the answer to that." She called him a foul name and nipped his ear, and he grinned before getting serious again. "It'll only hurt for a second, but it's a good hurt you'll want over and over."

This time it was she who shivered. She shifted even closer, draping her body over his until he could feel the burning heat of her bare legs through his jeans and against his hips.

She's not wearing any underwear.

His brain fogged at that thought, and before it stopped running the show, he tapped his tongue against the back of his teeth. Instantly his fangs tingled as the glands behind them released a fluid meant to heighten the pleasure of penetration, and his body hardened in anticipation.

Tehya squirmed with equal eagerness, and he didn't make her wait. Closing his eyes, he sank his fangs into her throat. She gasped and stiffened, but even as he repositioned his mouth and latched on, she relaxed. And when he took his first pull, her silky blood flooding over his tongue, she let out a surprised and husky, "Oh, my."

Oh, my. Her sultry voice fueled his hunger and made him feel as if he was starving. As if he'd missed a dozen moon fever feedings in a row. It wasn't the full moon, but his need for blood was nearly as fierce, his need for companionship far more intense. His body grew hotter with every pull on her vein, until he swore his own blood was on fire.

Tehya clung to him, wrapping her leg around his hips as she ground against him the way she had back at his cabin, her teeth in his throat. She'd come beautifully, her soft cries nearly undoing him as well. So when she reached between their bodies now and tore open his fly, he almost moaned with relief.

Her blood rushed through him, and he could practically feel his flesh knitting back together and the pain fading; but even if he'd been at death's door, he wouldn't have protested when she took his shaft in her fist. Dropping his hand from the nape of her neck to her hip, he slipped his fingers under her shirt to caress the smooth skin of her firm, round ass. She quivered at his touch, spreading her legs even wider as she straddled him so she could rock against his shaft, coating it in her slippery juices.

Sensation lashed at him, the intensity building with the speed and fury of a forest fire during the dry season. If she didn't—*ah, fuck, yeah*. She sank down on his cock in one smooth, hard motion. Impossibly tight, silken heat surrounded him, a powerful combination that made the world around them fade away.

Right now, nothing mattered more than experiencing the best that life had to give.

Tehya pumped her hips to the rhythm of his draws on her vein, connecting them in a circuit of lust and life and warmth he wished could go on forever. No male alive could resist the feel of Tehya sliding up and down on his shaft so furiously that the slap of wet flesh striking wet flesh drowned out everything else, even the sound of his own internal alarms.

What if Hunter and his warriors were, right now, outside the door?

Tehya clenched around him, and, yep, he just hoped Hunter would wait until the trailer stopped rocking before he burst inside.

A harsh cry escaped her, and then she was shuddering, her body spasming as she came. Sloppily he lapped at the punctures he'd made, and flipped her, ignoring the fresh pain in his chest.

Damn, she was beautiful, her hair splayed wildly across the mattress, her skin glistening with perspiration as she shouted at the peak of another orgasm. He drove into her, his body taking over as his climax hovered, close and so hot his skin burned.

He shifted, but his injury gave a big *hey, I'm still here, you dumbass* shout-out that drove his orgasm back behind the imminent line. This was going to be so good—

"Lobo!" The alarm in Tehya's voice froze him on the very razor edge of pleasure. "I hear them."

No, no, no! Her hearing as a wolf had been better than his, and apparently that was still the case. *Fuck.*

Adrenaline punched him like a blast from a cold shower as he rolled to the side and forced his aching cock into his pants. "Whatever you do," he said urgently, "don't tell them anything."

Heart pounding, he leaped off the mattress and wheeled toward the door, keeping Tehya behind him even as she struggled to shove past him. His chest shrieked in agony, and he had to catch himself on the crumbling countertop or he'd have gone down. He must have lost his weapons in the river—not that they'd do him much good at this point. But it would have been nice to have a blade when Hunter tore open the door.

And tear open the door he did—right off its brittle hinges.

"Lobo," Hunter growled, his body filling the doorway. He smiled, but it wasn't a smile of amusement. It was one of victory, the smile of a predator that had cornered its prey.

If Tehya hadn't been there, Lobo would have let rage and unspent lust fuel the first punch. He'd have gone down cursing and fighting. But fighting now would only piss off Hunter more, and there was no way Lobo was going to take risks with Tehya.

So all he said was, "Don't hurt her," and when Hunter's meaty fist came at him, he stood his ground and welcomed the darkness.

8

Whatever you do, don't tell them anything.

Lobo's words kept echoing through Tehya's mind as she was escorted—forcibly—to MoonBound's headquarters. She supposed she was lucky, though; her wrists were bound, but at least Hunter hadn't knocked her out for the journey the way he had done to Lobo. No, she just had to walk through the woods wearing nothing but a flannel shirt with three missing buttons.

She glanced over at Lobo, draped over the shoulder of a dark-haired, leather-clad warrior called Baddon, whose gaze turned smoky every time he got a glimpse of her gaping neckline. She'd have been flattered if it weren't for the fact that he was carrying the man she loved like a slab of meat.

Lobo moaned, and she tensed. *Stay still, Lobo. Don't move.* The last time he'd stirred, he'd gotten another blow of silence from the blond asshole she now knew as Aiden.

Tehya had lost her temper in a big way over that, and Aiden wouldn't soon forget that she could bite. Even now, he rubbed his forearm and slid her silent glares.

The weird thing was that even after she'd attacked

him, there had been no retaliation. She'd expected to be beaten, but the dark-skinned female named Katina had merely pulled Tehya off Aiden, and they'd continued on their way.

Unfortunately, her outburst had triggered a volley of questions that had been nonstop for miles.

"Who are you?"

"How do you know Lobo?"

"How did you get into our headquarters?"

"What clan do you belong to?"

"Are you a skinwalker?"

The only thing she'd told them was her name. The one Lobo had given her when he'd found her, starving and weak, in a snowbank.

"Tehya," Hunter mused from a few feet ahead. "I've heard that word before. Is it Sioux? Zuni?" He eyed her over his shoulder, the leather thong around his head holding his hair away from his face. He had a cruel mouth and hard eyes, but his deep voice was deceptively soothing. When she said nothing, he sighed. "We'll learn the truth about you, you know."

Anxiety spiked. "With torture?"

Aiden raised his bitten arm. "I vote yes."

"Jackass," Katina muttered.

"We're here," Hunter announced, and Tehya was actually relieved that they'd arrived at MoonBound—until she realized that he'd never answered the torture question.

As they traversed the maze of hallways, the earthen walls began to close in on her. People stared, maybe because she looked like a half-wild, half-naked waif with leaves and twigs in her hair, or maybe because she was the enemy. Either way, she felt trapped, and a cage was probably in her very near future.

Her heart pounded against her ribs as if typing out a warning. If it could just type out instructions on how to escape, that would be great.

As they entered a four-way intersection, a blond male came from the brightly lit hall to the right, and her stomach bottomed out. It was the guy she'd slammed into in the hall after she'd run out of the lab. She casually inched sideways, hoping to conceal herself behind Baddon.

"Hunt, did you get him—" He broke off, his gaze skipping over Lobo and landing on her. His silver eyes flashed. *"You."*

Hunter and Katina moved like vipers, putting themselves between Tehya and the crazy-eyed guy. Still, she bared her teeth and crouched, prepared to defend herself the way she had against countless wolves, cougars, and bobcats over the years. Didn't matter that her hands were tied—she had strong legs and sharp teeth, and she knew where all the soft spots were.

"Easy, Riker," Hunter said, slamming his palm into the male's chest. "She's not a threat."

Riker hissed. "Tell that to Nicole."

Oh, God. Nicole must be the pregnant woman, and Riker must be her mate. Taking a ragged breath, she ratcheted the aggression down a few notches, straightened up, and took a tentative step toward him.

"I'm sorry," she said. "She startled me, and I didn't know she was pregnant. Is she okay?"

The guy lost the homicidal glint in his eyes, but

they narrowed, as if he wasn't sure her apology or concern was genuine. "She's fine," he said curtly, "for now." He turned to Hunter. "What's going on?"

Hunter started moving again, and they all fell in behind him, Aiden bringing up the rear directly behind her. But not too close, she noted.

"Call the senior warriors together and meet us in the conference room. Bring Nicole if she's up to it."

Oh, shit. Tehya knew very little about vampire customs, but according to all the government propaganda, vampire clans could be primitive and barbaric. Would Nicole be allowed to exact revenge or determine Tehya's fate? She glanced over at Lobo, who was starting to stir.

Wake up. Please wake up. I can't do this alone.

Riker said something to Hunter that Tehya didn't hear, and then he veered down a tunnel while the rest of them entered a cavernous room filled with an odd collection of artwork and a giant table that could easily seat twenty people. She turned to check on Baddon and Lobo, but they were gone.

A chill ran up her spine. What had they done to him?

She must have looked as panicked as she felt, because as Katina cut the ties around Tehya's wrists and shoved her into a seat at the table, she said, "Don't worry. Your lover is just getting a wake-up call. He'll be here in a minute."

"He's not—" *My lover.* But he was, wasn't he? Before today, they'd been companions. He'd been her pack leader. But now they were . . . what? A mated pair? And was her wolf-brain ever going to convert back to something resembling a human or vampire brain?

"Not your lover?" Katina jammed her fists on her denim-covered hips and gave Tehya a *do you think I'm a dumbass?* look. "Girl, we heard you taking it like a whore in an alley from two hundred yards away. I'm thinking of giving Lobo another look after hearing what he did to you—"

A deep growl vibrated the room, and only after Katina laughed and held up her hands in defense did Tehya realize it had come from her.

"Yeah, not your lover." Katina rolled her eyes and took a seat next to Tehya. "My ass."

Tehya ignored the female and got a quick lay of the land. There were four possible exits, if she went by the currents of free-moving air flowing from beneath the doors, each carrying with it a different scent. Another door must be a closet. There were also several weapons available, from a spear propped in one corner to a selection of ceremonial axes and blades on the walls. Not that she knew how to use any of them.

Over the next few minutes, as she plotted a possible escape plan, a dozen more people filed in. Hunter sat at the head of the table. Then, finally, Lobo stumbled through the doorway, his hair dripping wet and clinging to his bare neck and shoulders. Someone had bandaged his wound, the long, white strips slashing across his hard-cut chest and around his muscular back.

Even though he was clearly in pain, he gave her a reassuring look as Baddon shoved him into a seat across the table from her.

Riker was the last to arrive. He entered with

Nicole, who, to Tehya's surprise, merely glanced at her with curiosity as she waddled in, one arm wrapped in bandages and another bandage taped to her temple. She took a seat kitty-corner from Riker, who sat at the end of the table across from Hunter.

It was like a big, formal dinner, and she and Lobo were the main course.

Once everyone was seated, Hunter folded his hands together on the tabletop and looked at Lobo and Tehya in turn. "Who's going to start?" When neither Tehya nor Lobo spoke up, Hunter gave a resigned nod. "Okay, let's try this again. Lobo, you shifted into my form, broke into our headquarters, and tried to seduce my mate. Tell me why you shouldn't die."

Lobo did what?

Tehya whipped her head around to stare at Lobo, but if he could feel the burn of her glare, he didn't react. His eyes were locked with Hunter's, and she swore the air crackled with electricity. Everyone shifted uncomfortably, and a few of the people sitting around the table actually fingered the daggers at their hips.

A low growl rattled in her chest and her hackles rose as the need to protect Lobo consumed her. As a human, she'd felt like a sheep following the herd; but as a wolf, she'd found her footing and her voice. In her wolf-mind, she and Lobo were a pack, and she'd leap across the table and go for Hunter's throat to protect it.

Tension practically dripped from the walls as Lobo, his hands still bound, rested his forearms on the table and leaned forward. "I only took your form to get help for the wolf," he said, far more calmly than she would have if someone had just asked her to explain why she shouldn't die. "I had no other choice. Without Nicole's aid, she would have died. I was trying to leave when Aylin saw me. *She* kissed *me.* I didn't seduce her, and if she told you that, your mate is a liar."

Baddon whistled under his breath while even more warriors reached for their weapons, but Hunter remained eerily still. The guy's expression was stony, unreadable, and scarier for it.

"She didn't tell me that," Hunter said, "but given your history, it wasn't a stretch to assume." He gestured to Tehya. "What about her? Did she enter the compound with you?"

"She has nothing to do with this." Lobo didn't glance her way, and for some reason that bothered her. It was almost as if he was *avoiding* looking at her. "Drop all charges against her, welcome her into your clan, and I'll tell you anything you want to know."

She gaped at him in astonishment. He wanted her to live with these people? "Lobo, no—"

"LawKeeper," Hunter barked, cutting her off. "What is the punishment for impersonating a clan chief?"

A dark-haired male she'd heard someone call Takis tipped his chair back and pulled a leather-bound book off the shelf behind him. He flipped to a flagged page with more flourish than was probably needed for the situation. He seemed to be enjoying this. They all did.

"For followers of the Raven," he said in a deep,

ominous voice, "death is the acceptable penalty. For followers of the Crow, any punishment is allowed, and no punishment is considered too harsh."

Oh, God. She had no idea what the Raven and Crow stuff was about, but she hoped like hell these people leaned toward the Crow.

Hunter's cool gaze never left Lobo. "And what is the punishment for assaulting a pregnant female?"

Tehya's gut did a slow roll as Takis flipped pages. "That's a little more complicated," he said. "The laws take into account circumstance and whether the crime was committed by a clan member or an outsider. But basically we're talking about anything from imprisonment to lashes to staking atop an anthill."

Tehya felt sick to her stomach. Had Lobo saved her life only for her to be slowly eaten by ants?

Smiling grimly, Hunter gestured to Lobo. "Now, answer my question."

Lobo clenched his teeth and sat back in his seat, regarding Hunter with eyes that glittered with contempt. "Fuck you."

Thunderheads formed in Hunter's eyes, and once again the hairs on the back of Tehya's neck stood up. He nodded at Aiden. "Take him to the dungeon."

"No!" Tehya leaped to her feet. "He's just trying to protect me. All of it—it's all my fault."

"Tehya," Lobo snapped. "Don't say another word."

"Why?" she yelled, fed up with all the rules she couldn't fathom. "I don't understand. They could kill you."

Slamming his palms down on the table, he flashed his fangs at her. "I don't care. I need you to be safe."

"*You don't care?* What about what *I* care about?" she shot back. "I don't want you to die. Did you think about that? You've kept me safe for the last twelve years, and now it's my turn, you stubborn idiot."

"Your turn? You don't think you've kept me safe?" He laughed, but the sound was bitter and hard. "I'm alive because of you, Tehya. After Moon-Bound kicked me out, I had nothing to live for. I was a zombie looking for a bullet to the brain. You gave me purpose. A reason to live."

Tears stung her eyes, but before she could say anything—not that she knew what to say—Hunter stood.

"Enough." He jammed his finger at her. "I know this territory like the back of my hand, and not once in twelve damned years have I, or any of my warriors, laid eyes on you."

"Yes, you have," she said quietly, ignoring Lobo's madly shaking head. "Except I didn't look like this."

Hunter's brows drew down in confusion. In fact, everyone traded bewildered glances, but it was Nicole who turned to Tehya in amazement.

"Oh, my God," Nicole said, her voice tinged with awe. "It's you, isn't it? You're . . . the wolf."

As the room exploded in conversation and questions, Tehya watched Lobo sag into his seat as if drained by disappointment. She couldn't stand the way he was looking at her, as if she'd betrayed them both. How, she wasn't sure. All she knew was that Hunter had been determined to punish him for not talking, and she couldn't allow that to happen.

Hunter held up his hand and called for everyone to shut the fuck up. Once everyone was seated again, he turned to Tehya. "Look, I don't know much about skinwalkers, but I know they can't hold any form but their own indefinitely. So unless you spent most of your time hiding, and then only coming out into the open as a wolf, you're lying."

It hadn't occurred to her that anyone would think she was lying, but with no way to prove that what she was saying was true aside from shifting into a wolf and possibly never shifting back, she knew she had to be convincing. Lobo's life might depend on it.

"It's true, I swear." She told them what she'd told Lobo, that she'd barely been turned into a vampire when she shifted into a wolf and was never able to shift back.

Skepticism wafted through the air, its scent similar to singed hair, and Tehya wondered if her sense of smell would always be so sensitive. It was useful to gauge emotion—but just once, couldn't some emotion smell like chocolate? Or bacon?

"You're saying you were turned into a vampire twelve years ago?" Riker asked, and when she nodded, he added, "How? And why aren't your eyes silver?"

Even though more than a decade had passed, the wounds still felt raw, and she trembled a little as she spoke. "I can't explain my eyes. They've always been this color. As for the rest, I was working as a dental assistant while going to school to be a dentist. Then my mom got cancer. She died six weeks after the diagnosis."

Tehya inhaled deeply, willing herself to not break down. She and her mother, Cherie, had been close, each the only person the other had in her life. A secret had bonded them, and once Cherie was gone, Tehya's life fell apart.

"The pressure and stress got to me, and I made some bad choices." She'd partied too much and hung out with a wild crowd, and one night she'd found herself at an underground blood club on the outskirts of Seattle. Because, hey, all the cool people were illegally feeding and sleeping with vampires.

"I was drunk and stupid, and I let a vampire bite me." She grimaced, hating herself for being so reckless when she'd spent twenty-four years being responsible, the kind of person the government didn't look at too closely. "The really messed-up thing? He didn't even get any blood, because the place got raided by VAST. They collared or killed all the vampires. The one who bit me is probably someone's slave now."

She'd always been disgusted by the vampire slave trade, something humans had legalized long before she was born. Vampires were stronger, faster, and superior in almost every way, but humans overwhelmingly outnumbered them, and free vampires spent their time in hiding, subject to being hunted for bounties or captured for the slave trade.

"Wait." Nicole scowled. "If Vampire Strike Team forces interrupted, how did you exchange blood with the vampire?"

"I didn't."

"You must have," she insisted. "Worldwide mandatory vaccinations against the saliva-borne vampiric infection have been in effect for decades. The failure rate of the vaccine is practically nil. Humans can only turn if they're introduced to the blood-borne version of the virus."

Never let a vampire bite you, sweetheart, and never tell anyone where you're from or that your vaccination document is forged. Never.

Funny how her mother's words, drilled into Tehya since she was three years old, were ringing loud and clear in her ears now, but that night when the vampire was plunging his fangs into her throat, her mom had been as silent as she was dead. And the funniest thing was, none of those warnings mattered now.

"I was never vaccinated." She slid a glance at Lobo, who was watching intently, puzzling her out the way he did a hunter's cruel snare or leg trap before he disarmed and destroyed it. "My mother paid a lot of money to have my immunization record falsified."

"Why?" he asked, but she had a feeling he was already close to the answer. It had never taken him long to figure out a trap either.

"Because the vaccine is fatal to my father's people."

Every eye in the room fell on Nicole, and it was Riker who posed the next question. "Is that possible, Nicole?"

Nicole nodded, almost numbly. She shifted in her seat, fidgeting like a kid in a dentist's chair who was about to have a cavity filled.

"Once worldwide vaccination became mandatory," she said finally, "pockets of anti-vaxxers were rooted out. Most had resisted for ideological reasons, but one group, a native population in Canada, the Kleemut tribe"—she looked over at Tehya almost apologetically—"they resisted out of self-preservation. The vaccine was lethal for them. They would die within twenty-four hours of getting the shot. A lot of the Kleemut went into hiding. They were hunted mercilessly by Canadian and international VAST forces, and those who were caught were never seen again by anyone outside of a Daedalus lab." She gave Tehya that look again, but this time the apologetic expression was steeped in shame, and that was when it clicked. Nicole must have worked for Daedalus, the company that had revolutionized vampire slavery and created the vaccine against the vampire infection. They were the most loved *and* hated company on the planet. "Your father was a Kleemut Indian, wasn't he?"

"I never knew him, but yes." Tehya fixed her gaze on a bear skull hanging on the wall, its surface painted with scenes of ancient Native American bison hunts. "My mom changed her name and fled to Seattle when she found out she was pregnant. They didn't want anyone to ever suspect that I'm part Kleemut. She got one letter from my father, and then she never heard from him again. Apparently, he went *missing*." She turned to Nicole and was surprised to see that the doctor's expression was still tight with guilt. Whatever she'd done in her past was a source of pain for her, and right now it didn't matter that Nicole was supposed to be the enemy. She'd been nothing but kind to Tehya. Offering a tentative smile, Tehya said softly, "Thank you for trying to help me, and I'm sorry I attacked you for it."

Nicole blinked, obviously expecting neither gratitude nor an apology. Even Riker looked a little startled. "It's okay," Nicole said. "You must have been terrified to wake up in a strange place. And with two legs instead of four."

Lobo tugged at the rope around his wrists with his teeth, and she almost laughed. He did *not* know that in order to chew through something—like shoelaces or a drawstring on a pair of sweats—you had to use your back teeth. With a curse, he settled his hands on the table again. "Your mother wasn't a native, was she?"

Not even close. "Except for her name, she was as Scottish as Loch Ness."

Lobo nodded, more to himself than anyone else. "That explains the skinwalker glitch."

"I'm not following," she said, and a murmur of agreement rose up from around the table as everyone turned to Lobo.

He didn't look at anyone else, kept his gaze focused solely on her. "According to lore, most skinwalkers are born vampires, but all of them come from pure Native American blood. You were born neither a vampire nor a purebred native. You shouldn't have this ability at all, so it's not a surprise that you can't control it."

"So why did I shift back in the lab, when I hadn't been able to do it on my own for years?"

Nicole blew out a long breath before speaking up. "I did a little reading up on shape-shifters after Hunter told me about Lobo. If what I read is true,

skinwalkers who are injured while in another body
will revert to their true form when they die. It's
likely that you were so close to death that your body
shifted, and in doing so, you healed." She gave Tehya
a pointed look. "I would recommend that you not
shift into a wolf again."

Good call, Doc. "I don't even know if I can."

"How did it happen before?"

God, this was so embarrassing. How could she
admit that it had been a total accident? "I'm not sure.
I'd turned into a vampire, and I was terrified I'd get
caught. I didn't know what to do, so I drove until
my car ran out of gas." She'd been in the mountains,
hungry, alone, with no idea how to survive. And then
she'd heard it. A wolf howling in the distance. Then
another. And another. They'd seemed to be singing to each other, so in tune that she'd felt the ties
that held the pack together. "There was a family of
wolves that . . . I don't know . . . I heard them, and
they made me want what they had. I had this urge to
join them, and I felt this pull . . . and the next thing I
knew, I had four legs and fur. I tried to switch back,
but I couldn't." She shook her head. "How did I get
this ability in the first place, if it's something so rare,
let alone unheard of in someone like me?"

Lobo cut a sharp look at Hunter. "It seems that
the impossible has become possible lately."

Whatever subtext was at play here struck a nerve,
and Hunter went taut. "What do you mean?"

Lobo shifted his gaze to peg Riker with a mean-
ingful stare. "I know about your son. I always
thought invisibility was a myth."

Tehya tried not to let her mouth fall open. And failed. So she *hadn't* been seeing things that day she and Lobo had been out patrolling the forest and they'd come across a young vampire who had disappeared and reappeared twice before their eyes.

"Bastien is . . . unique," Riker said, a note of pride in his voice.

Hunter sat back in his chair and surveyed everyone. "I think I've heard enough. Lobo, I'll honor your request to keep Tehya safe. We will welcome her as a MoonBound member. I'm sure we can use someone with dental training around here. Vampires are probably a dentist's wet dream. Nicole, unless you want to pursue her attack against you—"

"I don't," Nicole said quickly. She shot Tehya a friendly smile, and Tehya shifted uncomfortably in her seat. She wanted to hate these people, but she was finding that they weren't all the monsters she'd expected them to be.

"Then we'll have quarters prepared for her," Hunter said. "Katina, will you show her around?"

"Wait." Tehya might have conflicting emotions about MoonBound, but she did know that she didn't want to live here. "I don't want this. I'm going home with Lobo."

"That's in violation of vampire law," Aiden said, a little too gleefully. He was definitely one of the ones she didn't like. "Skinwalkers aren't allowed to mate with each other."

"We aren't . . . mated." But, man, her cheeks felt hot, because mating was exactly what they'd done in the trailer. Katina rolled her eyes again. "Not like that."

Lobo didn't meet her gaze, and she realized that, while the mating restrictions might be true, that wasn't what this was about. "You need to go, Tehya."

"No." She crossed her arms over her chest and dug in. "Not until I know what's going to happen to you."

"You'll see him again," Hunter assured her. "You have my word."

She narrowed her eyes at him. "Since I don't know you, your word means nothing to me."

One black eyebrow shot up and his lip quirked in amusement. "I see your point. But given that I'm in charge, you don't have any choice but to trust me."

She hated that he was right.

"Please go, Tehya," Lobo murmured. "Hunter is a dick, but he's a dick who keeps his word."

"Thanks for the endorsement," Hunter said drily.

Reluctantly she rose from her seat and followed Katina out of the room. Only after they were on the other side of the complex did she realize that Hunter had said she'd see Lobo again . . . but he hadn't said he'd be alive.

9

Once the door was closed and Lobo was sure Tehya was out of earshot, he turned to Hunter. "You told her I'd see her again. Before my execution, or after?"

There were a few chuckles from around the table, because, sure, executions were hilarious. He must have forgotten how much he'd laughed at all the people he'd seen die at the command—or hand—of Hunter's father. Bear Roar had been a brutal leader, a strict follower of the Way of the Raven, and a total bastard. Lobo *had* laughed when Hunter killed him.

Hunter gestured at Baddon, who, after giving Hunter an *are you fucking serious?* look, shrugged and sliced through the ropes binding Lobo's wrists. Lobo rubbed the raw skin as circulation flowed back into his hands.

"Leave us." Hunter's tone made it clear that he wouldn't tolerate argument. "You too, Rike."

Riker frowned but, like the good soldier he was, herded everyone out, and mere seconds later, Lobo was alone in the room with MoonBound's chief. The last time they'd been alone, it had been for the same reason and, just like now, his life had been on the line.

The only differences were that this time he wasn't in chains, and there wasn't a horde of people calling for a painful, drawn-out death sentence.

Hunter lounged back in his chair, his fingers steepled as his hands rested on his abs, his cold, hard gaze tracking Lobo as he paced the room.

"I told you that if you ever shifted into another vampire's form again, I'd end you. Do you remember that?"

Lobo laughed, really getting behind the gallows humor thing. "Do you think I get death threats so often that I forget them?"

"You're an asshole, so I'm going to answer that with a yes."

Lobo laughed again as long-held contempt rushed to the surface. "You've been waiting for this, haven't you? I'll bet you couldn't wait for me to screw up so you could put my skull on its own special little shelf in the Cave of the Vanquished."

"We sealed the CV decades ago. And you're the one who broke the law—"

"And you're the one who kicked me out of the clan without listening to my side of the story."

"Your side?" Hunter asked, incredulous. "You were caught seducing Traygen's mate—while wearing his form. You admitted it."

"No," Lobo said wryly, "you asked me if I'd taken his form, I nodded, and then you broke my jaw. I couldn't give you an explanation after that because my face was shattered and half of my teeth were on the damned floor."

To be fair, he hadn't been in shape to speak even

before Hunter's punch. Su'Neena and Traygen had done their best to kill him before other clan members heard the commotion and interrupted.

"You're upset about a few broken bones?" Hunter pushed to his feet and strode over to the liquor cabinet on the far wall. "You're lucky Traygen didn't kill you. If I'd caught you with my mate in my bed, you wouldn't have made it out of the bedroom alive."

"I wasn't—" He started to say that he hadn't been in bed with the female, but the details weren't important. "Listen to me, you pompous ass. I wasn't trying to seduce Su'Neena that night. I was trying to get her to confess."

Hunter took two highball glasses from the cabinet. "Confess to what?"

Well, at least the guy was listening this time. Lobo scrubbed a hand over his face, realizing that this was his one chance to finally set the record straight and maybe get out of this alive.

"I was out on patrol one day, and I saw Su'Neena with ShadowSpawn's leader. The first time it happened, I thought it might be coincidence that they'd come across each other in the forest." Yet something had niggled at him, so the next time she slipped away from MoonBound, he'd followed. "But when I saw her again near Rat Lake, obviously waiting for someone, I knew something was up. A few minutes later, Kars showed up, and they did a lot more than just talk."

"And they didn't see you?" Hunter popped the top off a bottle of whiskey and poured it into the glasses.

"They saw me," he admitted. "As a wolf."

Hunter swung around, offering Lobo one of the drinks. "Did you shift against orders?"

Lobo rolled his eyes. "I tell you that one of your warriors was screwing the enemy, and *that* is what you want to know?" He snatched the glass out of Hunter's hand. Nice of the guy to give him a pre-execution libation. "Su'Neena is a spy, Hunter. I shifted into Traygen's form to confront her about it. Turns out he didn't know about her extracurricular activities. I tried to tell him, but he was too busy trying to impale my liver on his knife to listen." He snorted. "I must have said enough, though. Ever wonder why he was found dead two weeks later, butchered by 'poachers'?"

One dark eyebrow shot up. "You think Su'Neena is responsible for his death?"

"Her . . . or ShadowSpawn."

Lobo downed the alcohol, savoring the smooth, rich burn that was so different from the harshness of the rotgut he was used to drinking. As warmth spread through his insides, he wandered around the room, noting all the changes since the last time he'd been here. Hunter had gotten rid of the enemy scalps his father had kept nailed to the wall. Maybe he really had made some changes around here. Electricity was a nice touch. And who would have guessed Hunter would allow televisions and video game consoles inside the clan? His father had barely tolerated books.

Hunter, still standing near the liquor cabinet, exhaled on a curse. "Why didn't you come to me with this sooner?"

"Seriously?" He slammed his glass down on the table. "I don't owe MoonBound shit. Your father slaughtered my family and then brought me here to survive on whatever scraps people would throw me. I didn't even have a seat at the dinner tables. Maybe you don't remember me begging for someone to drop some food on the floor, only to get kicked in the face when I reached for it, but I do. Maybe you had a bed growing up, but I had a chain and a pile of dirt in a kitchen corner. All of you fierce warriors were so terrified of a boy who might turn into the big bad wolf and eat you. So fuck you, Hunter."

To Lobo's shock, Hunter had the grace to look away. During Lobo's nearly fifty years with the clan, Hunter had never been cruel to him, but he'd never been kind either. As far as Hunter had been concerned, Lobo had been invisible.

Hunter's voice was gruff, tinged with anger. "My father was a monster."

It wasn't an apology, but it was close enough, considering Hunter hadn't been the one whose rule had brought suffering not just to Lobo but to any clan member who didn't measure up to Bear Roar's exacting, brutal standards.

Hunter's gaze snapped back up, his moment of remorse a thing of the past. The position of clan chief suited him. "You still should have come to me."

Lobo snorted. "After you threatened me with death?"

Hunter put the drink to his lips and eyed him over the rim of his glass. "Only if you shifted into another clan member."

"Yeah, well, I did that yesterday, and I was fully aware of the risk I was taking." He flashed fangs, daring Hunter to challenge his decision. "If you're looking for me to beg for my life or apologize for trying to save Tehya's, it ain't gonna happen. I'd do it again in a heartbeat. So if you're going to kill me, get it over with."

Hunter swirled the liquor around in his glass and stared at the deer hide stretched on the wall. For a long time, Lobo didn't know if the guy was going to say anything. He seemed pretty damned content to let Lobo wonder how much longer he had to breathe.

"Is what you said earlier true?" Hunter finally asked. "About having nothing to live for after you were banished from here?"

Lobo let out a deep, shuddering breath. He refused to share his inner pain with Hunter, and he couldn't believe how much he'd already shared—in front of a dozen of Hunter's minions. He hated feeling vulnerable, and right now he might as well be facing Hunter with his rib cage splayed wide open to reveal his beating heart.

"No other clan would accept a skinwalker, and living like a stray dog with other free vampires in Seattle's sewer systems didn't appeal to me. So tell me, oh great clan chief, what I had to live for before I found a half-dead wolf that needed my help?"

If Hunter was annoyed by Lobo's sarcasm, it didn't show. If anything, he seemed genuinely curious, which threw Lobo off balance in a big way. He'd hated Hunter down to his very marrow, but the

Hunter who had kicked him out of the clan didn't seem to exist anymore.

"Did you know she wasn't really a wolf?" Hunter asked.

"I sensed something different about her, but I thought she might be another vampire's spirit animal in physical form." When Hunter cocked a skeptical eyebrow at him, Lobo shrugged. "What? Weirder shit than that happens all the time. Like how Riker's son can go invisible and your mate can summon portals."

The temperature in the room plunged so fast that on Lobo's next exhale, he saw his breath hang in the air.

"The fact that I haven't killed you is proof that this clan has come a long way since the days of my father and my own early rule." Hunter's husky voice was as icy as the room, emerging between lips peeled back from razor fangs. "But when it comes to the safety of my mate, I'm as primitive as it gets. Her ability makes her a kidnapping target for every vampire and human on the planet. So if you tell anyone outside of MoonBound about her gift, I will reopen the Cave of the Vanquished and mount your skull on the wall while you're still breathing. Understood?"

Well, that was graphic. But hey, it sounded like maybe Hunter wasn't going to kill him after all. "Understood."

Hunter eyed him for an uncomfortably long moment, probably trying to determine whether he could trust Lobo's word. Lobo couldn't blame him. He'd stop at nothing to protect Tehya.

Finally, just as Lobo's palms started to sweat,

Hunter crossed to the door and flung it open. He spoke in hushed tones with Baddon, who was standing outside. When he returned, his expression was grim.

"I sent Baddon to find Su'Neena."

"She won't admit to being a spy."

"If she's a spy, we *will* get to the bottom of it." Pivoting on his heel, he moved back to the door. "Come on. You can shower and have a shot of human blood while Nicole looks at that wound."

A wound he had only because one of Hunter's boys had shot him. "I'll be fine."

"It's not a suggestion. I promised your wolf she'd see you again, and I don't want you keeling over in front of her."

"Why? Because it'll be the last time I see her?"

Hunter paused with his hand on the doorknob. "If you're wondering whether I'm going to kill you, I'm not."

Lobo let out a breath he didn't know he'd been holding. "Why not?"

"Because," he said in a voice weighted with gravity Lobo didn't understand, "I'm not my father."

That was something that was becoming more obvious by the minute. "So what comes next?"

Hunter yanked open the door and stepped out into the hallway. "We're going to get to the bottom of your accusation against Su'Neena." He lowered his voice as a group of males walked by, their laughter echoing through the halls, something nearly unheard of during Bear Roar's reign. Hell, even after Hunter had taken over after his father's death, the clan had still been a dark, sobering place. The changes at MoonBound since then were startling. "I don't know why, but my gut tells me to believe you. So until we get this straightened out, you're free to go."

"And Tehya?"

"We'll keep her safe and teach her what she needs to know to survive as a vampire."

Even though it was exactly what Lobo had asked for, his stomach still churned. He'd asked Hunter to take care of Tehya, but that was when the prospect of losing his head had been very real. Now . . . damn. It was for the best. She needed friends. Community. Training. She needed the clan.

He must have looked troubled, because Hunter's hard-ass expression softened. But that was like saying a diamond had softened into an agate. "She won't be a prisoner, Lobo."

"Good. She doesn't like that. You should see what she did to my cabin when I locked her in it once."

No, she didn't take to captivity well at all. But he also knew she didn't take orders well either. Keeping her here wouldn't be easy. He'd have to convince her.

But how could he do that when he wasn't convinced himself?

10

*T*ehya wanted to hate MoonBound and everything about it. But the people were friendly if wary, the compound was clean and warm, and it boasted modern conveniences such as a library and rec center, which she was currently touring. They even had a kitchen and cooks who had made her a venison sandwich she'd scarfed down while she walked around with Katina in borrowed jeans and a fitted green long-sleeved top.

"This isn't anything like I imagined." Tehya stared in awe at a young male and a female with bright orange pigtails as they played some sort of dance-themed video game on a screen nearly as large as one of the rec room walls. "From what Lobo described, I expected dark caves and torches on the walls. This isn't exactly medieval times here."

Katina laughed, her bright white fangs creating a striking contrast with her dark skin. "I would definitely not be here if it was like that. I like my modern comforts." She shuddered, making her sleek black hair, gathered in a low, thick ponytail, brush against her paisley top. "From what I hear, though, Moon-Bound used to be a horror show. I'm sure Lobo wasn't exaggerating. The old guard, mostly the born vampires who follow the Way of the Raven—they're a bunch of primitive, superstitious freaks."

"What's that about? This Crow and Raven thing?"

Katina rolled her pewter-silver eyes. "It's a belief system that supposedly explains vampire origins—if you want to completely discount science and logic. Again, it's pushed by the old guard, mainly as a way to keep everyone in line. Crows are more moderate, and Ravens are just crazy."

Wow, Tehya had so much to learn about being a vampire. As a human, she'd only known what the human powers-that-be wanted her to know about them—mainly that they were dangerous, but they made good slaves when properly trained. Later, as a wolf, she'd learned about vampires by watching Lobo, but he wasn't exactly typical of the species, as she was just beginning to discover.

He must have been so lonely.

"Everything you see is available to you twenty-four seven," Katina said as they walked past an empty pool table. "It's usually busier here, but it's the new moon, so everyone is off feeding and fu—"

"Ah, there you are." Hunter's deep voice boomed through the room, and Tehya spun, heart racing in anticipation of seeing Lobo.

She'd barely laid eyes on him before he was crossing to her in quick, long strides. He'd showered, his damp hair raked back and wildly unruly, and he wore a pair of well-fitting worn jeans made for slim hips and powerful thighs. Fresh bandages crisscrossed his shoulders and disappeared under a black tank top that showed off every ropy muscle. Every female hormone danced in appreciation as he hauled her into his arms.

"You okay?" He buried his face in her neck and held her so tight she couldn't escape if she'd wanted to. Which she didn't.

"I'm fine." She inhaled, taking in the comforting scent of him. God, she loved how he smelled. Like trees and moss, with a subtle hint of musk. "I've been worried about *you*."

He pulled back and glanced over at the doorway, where Hunter was talking with Katina, Riker, and someone Katina referred to as Jaggar. Then, without warning, Lobo took her by the arm and spirited her into the connecting room packed with arcade games and another large-screen TV. Where the hell did they get all of this stuff anyway?

"What are you doing?"

In answer, he pushed her up against the side of the classic Pac-Man game, the long, lean length of his body covering hers. "I don't know what's going to happen after this, but I want you to be happy."

"Then why do you sound so sad?" In his eyes, hooded and shadowed, she saw the reason, and it speared her in the heart. "This sounds like a good-bye. It is, isn't it?"

He dropped his face to hers so their foreheads touched, reminding her of all the times he'd done that when she was a wolf. He'd been so free with his affection, and it seemed that nothing had changed. Which made what he said next all the more awful. "I think it has to be. For now."

What a load of bullshit. "I won't live here without

you," she swore. "You can't make me." She didn't give a crap that she sounded childish. At this point, she'd suck on a pacifier if that's what it took to change his mind.

"It's for the best," he said, spewing more bullshit. But it was bullshit he wasn't going to back down from, and she knew it.

Desperation made her, well, desperate, and she clung to his biceps, clutching him as if doing so would stop this from happening. "I'll turn back into a wolf. Somehow, I'll figure out how. We can be like it was before."

A heartbreaking sound of misery rattled in his throat. "Neither of us wants that, and you know it. You need the kind of life that only MoonBound can give you."

"These are the people who threatened to kill you, Lobo." She cast a furtive glance at Hunter, who was idly bouncing a Ping-Pong ball in his palm as he talked with a growing group of people who were extremely well armed. "They hurt you and then abandoned you. How can you say that I should stay here?"

He stroked his hand over her hair the way he'd petted her fur when he wanted to calm her down. It made her mad that it worked.

"What happened was a long time ago." His voice was calm. Controlled. Too controlled. She could smell the emotion in him. The conflict. "Hunter was different then. The clan was different. Trust me, it's safe for you here. And with everything going on in the human world, belonging to a clan is what you need."

Wrong. He was so wrong. She wasn't a pet to be passed around. "I won't stay here, Lobo. Not without you."

"Damn it, Tehya." Cracks in his tight control made his voice pitch low. "You need to stay."

"I'm not a dog," she ground out.

"If you were, this wouldn't be an issue. You're a vampire. Vampires aren't safe on their own. That's why clans work so well. It doesn't have to be forever. But right now, you need to stay here."

Never. She was about to say as much when Baddon, Takis, Aiden, and a male she didn't recognize rushed into the room, their expressions grim. Baddon looked like he'd been chewing on an electric fence. She'd done that once. Not recommended.

She and Lobo joined the group as Baddon spoke up. "Su'Neena is gone."

"What do you mean, gone?" Hunter stopped bouncing the Ping-Pong ball. "Did you search the compound?"

Baddon gave a curt nod. "I've got people still searching, but I'd bet my left nut the search won't turn up anything. I checked her quarters—looks like she left in a rush."

"She knows." Lobo cursed. "She knows I'm here, and she probably suspects that I've told the truth about her."

"Excuse me," Tehya interrupted, "but who is Su'Neena?"

A muscle in Lobo's jaw twitched with anger. "She's responsible for me getting kicked out of the clan. And she tried to murder me a couple of times."

This time it was Hunter who cursed, his hand closing on the little ball so hard it crumpled. Too bad it wasn't this Su'Neena person's skull.

"Send out a search party," Hunter growled. "Hurry. If she makes it to ShadowSpawn before we catch her, she'll be lost to us."

"But you have a treaty with Kars," Katina said. "You can force him to give her up."

Hunter snorted. "Do you really think he'll give her up so she can admit to being a spy? He'll kill her and blame her death on humans. We won't see her alive again."

Aiden fingered a dagger sheathed at his hip. "Hunter, are you sure Su'Neena is guilty of anything?" He shot Lobo a glare so hateful that Tehya had to hold back a snarl. "We don't know Lobo. This could be a trick. Skinwalkers are deceptive by nature."

Next to her, Lobo went taut, his hand clenching hers in a powerful grip, and she caught the acrid scent of danger rising from him. But she got the impression his anger wasn't about the insult to him—it was about the insult to her. She was a skinwalker too.

"Say that again." Lobo's voice throbbed with menace. "Seriously."

Hunter stepped between them, forcing Aiden back a step. "Back off, Aiden. I might have made a mistake all those years ago, and if I did, and Lobo's right, a lot of the shit we've taken from Shadow-Spawn for decades is my fault. I will fix it—and to do that, we need to find Su'Neena."

"She's a mystic-keeper," Katina pointed out,

easing the tension, if only slightly. "She can evade us, and pretty easily, I might add."

"So . . . what, we're just supposed to sit around and do nothing?" Takis cursed. "No way. I'm heading out."

"Wait." Tehya's face heated as all eyes fell on her. "What's a mystic-keeper?"

Lobo squeezed her hand. "A shaman of sorts. Mystic-keepers can bend nature's energy to their will to hide objects or to create invisible traps, wards, false trails . . . shit like that."

Trails? Tehya was an expert at following those. "Can she mask her scent?"

Baddon shook his head. "But her ability allows her to throw false tracks and to cover up the real ones."

"Then I can track her." When no one reacted, she huffed, "What? Why aren't we moving?"

"You heard what Nicole said." Lobo angled closer to her, a subtle movement that blocked the door, as if he thought she would bolt. "You can't shift into a wolf. You might not be able to turn back."

She wasn't sure she knew how to shift into a wolf again anyway—but the moment the thought formed, she felt an icy pull, a tingle that she instinctively understood was the key to shifting. Not that she was going to do it.

"My sense of smell is powerful." She looked over at Hunter. "I might be able to track her without shifting."

Hunter and Lobo exchanged glances. "It's worth a try," Hunter said, but when Lobo hesitated, she growled in frustration.

"I don't need your permission, Lobo," she said. "If finding this person can clear your name, I'm doing it. End of story."

"Females, huh?" Hunter sighed, and in a surprising move, he clapped Lobo on the back. "Welcome to my world."

Baddon threw back his head and let out what she could only describe as a battle cry, and the wolf in her wanted desperately to howl.

The others joined in, and as the battle cries reached their peaks, Hunter threw open the door. "*Irinami ka'ta uwelet.* May your spear find its mark."

Lobo was pretty sure that every able-bodied member of MoonBound was combing through the forest for the traitor. The woods were crawling with vampires, and he almost felt sorry for any vampire poacher who might be out hunting for an easy target.

It turned out that Tehya was both right and wrong about her sense of smell. She'd been able to track Su'Neena for the first couple of miles, but she lost the scent on the bank of a stream. After that, Hunter and his warriors spread out, while Lobo and Tehya circled the area where she'd lost the scent. She'd refused to leave, determined to pick up the trail again.

Her curses as she moved around amused him, but he knew how frustrated she was. If she were a wolf, she'd be whining and running zigzag patterns with her nose to the ground.

"We've got to do more." She kicked a rotting log, and splinters of soft wood flew everywhere. "This

bitch is responsible for getting you banished from
MoonBound and nearly killed. And—"

"Hey," he said from where he was kneeling next to
a footprint that appeared to be older than what they
were looking for. "It's okay."

"No, it's not." She rounded on him, her expression fierce, her eyes glowing hot, like amber put to
flame. "I know what it's like to have to hide who
you are because some jackass will kill you for it. My
mother was always looking over her shoulder, and
every time someone knocked on our door, she was
sure it was the government looking for me. You lived
that way for decades, an outcast punished because of
what you are, and she needs to pay for that."

Sure, it had sucked to be ostracized because of
what he *might* do with his ability, and he definitely
wanted Su'Neena to answer for any crimes against
MoonBound, but nothing would change the past.
What mattered now was the future. A future he'd
fight for the way Tehya was, right now, fighting for
him.

She needed to learn how to be a vampire, but he
wouldn't give her up. Their relationship might be forbidden by vampire law, but only if they were caught.

Once she'd spent some time with the clan and had
learned more about vampire life than he could teach
her, he could take her somewhere safe. Where no
one knew them.

Alaska was sounding better and better.

"How do you feel about snow?" he asked.

She blinked. "What?" She jammed her hands on
her hips, and he realized he liked her in jeans. Not as

much as he liked her naked or wearing his shirt, but there was a lot to love about the way her curves filled out a pair of pants. "We aren't talking about snow. We're talking about capturing someone who tried to kill you."

He sighed. "You really are a dog with a bone."

She gave him a flat stare. It was the same stare she'd give him when he held a tasty treat out of reach to tease her before tossing it into the air for her to catch.

"What?" he asked, feigning ignorance. "That was funny. You know, because . . . wolf."

Clearly she was not amused, but that was okay, because he cracked himself up enough for both of them. Damn, it felt good to have someone to banter with. To laugh with. There hadn't been enough of that in his life, and he was ready. So ready.

Shaking her head as if he was a lost cause, she went back to searching, disappearing over the top of a shallow rise. He continued scanning the ground for broken twigs, displaced rocks, any physical sign of Su'Neena's passing.

He was about to join Tehya when he heard an excited yip.

A yip he recognized. His heart missed a beat.

Oh, Tehya, you didn't. Tell me you didn't. . . .

He charged up the hill, and his gut slid to his feet at the sight of Tehya in wolf form, wagging her tail. He couldn't utter a word. Couldn't breathe, couldn't move. Not until she put her nose to the ground and took off.

Fuck.

He had no choice but to chase after her. He called out, but why, he had no idea. It wasn't as if she could talk to him, tell him why she'd done such a stupid thing. Besides, he knew why. She'd said it earlier. It was her turn to save him.

Not this way, Tehya. Not this way.

She didn't stop. She was on a mission, and she was going to see it through. This was nothing new. As a wolf, once she'd picked up the trail of a deer or rabbit, she didn't stop until she either caught it or lost it for good.

Sweet Maker, how could he both love and hate her dedication?

His mind was a tormented, tangled mass of anger and sorrow, and even a little reluctant pride that grew with every mile they put behind them. Maybe she could shift back. Maybe Nicole was wrong. *Please* let her be wrong.

Up ahead, Tehya halted, ears pricked, tail high. Then, abruptly, she crouched, hackles raised, and slipped into some thick brush as quietly as a ghost.

On instant alert, he eased behind a fat fir tree and peered in the direction Tehya had gone. Beyond a moss-covered stand of old growth, something moved.

Su'Neena.

What was she doing? He crept closer, trying to figure out why she was hovering over a flat stone, her mouth moving silently. A chant? Was she signaling someone?

Time to get some answers that were long overdue. Fingering the hilt of the borrowed blade in the sheath at his hip, he started toward her, but drew up short before he made it half a dozen steps. Expecting her to chat like an old friend, or even an old enemy, wasn't going to work. She was stubborn and crafty, and she wouldn't give up anything easily. It was even possible that Hunter wouldn't press her unless he had hard evidence that what Lobo claimed was true. Without her confession, Lobo would look like a liar, and his expulsion from the clan would be considered justified.

Fuck that. He was getting a confession, and he'd break every law of man, nature, and vampire to do it.

Inhaling a deep, ragged breath, he summoned an image in his mind of ShadowSpawn's clan chief, Kars, and hoped he was capable of shifting. Tehya's blood and the bag of human blood he'd sucked down after his shower at MoonBound had done a lot to fortify him, but still, taking another form this soon after the last shift would be iffy. Even if he could pull it off, it wouldn't last long. He had to hurry.

He closed his eyes and concentrated, encouraging the burn of the shift, welcoming the pain of it. Every snap of bone and rip of torn nerves could be laid at Su'Neena's feet, and he was going to make her pay.

Finally, agonizing heartbeats later, he was the spitting image of Kars. At least, he hoped so. It wasn't as if he had a mirror to check. He just wished he could shift clothes as well. Kars didn't seem like a jeans-and-tee kind of psychopathic tyrant. He was more of a *my jacket is made from the skin of my enemy* type.

The pain of the shift faded as he circled the

clearing and approached Su'Neena from the front. She looked up from the rock and let out a startled yelp.

"Kars." She swallowed loud enough for him to hear. "I only just sent out the signal. How did you know I'd be here?" She lowered her voice to a near whisper. "Did our . . . mutual friend warn you that I may have been compromised?"

Mutual friend? Did MoonBound have another spy in its ranks?

"Yeah," he said, running with it. "How'd you get out so quickly?"

She looked around, her eyes wild, as if she expected an ambush. "He came to me in my quarters. Said Hunter was questioning the skinwalker. If the skinwalker talks . . ." Her expression twisted into an ugly mask of hate. He knew the feeling. "I told you we should have tried again to kill him."

The way she spoke so casually about killing him made him want to reach out and strangle her. He hoped there'd be time for that later.

"Those were *your* failures," he said, figuring Kars would pin any and all blame for pretty much any failure on someone else. "Contact our mutual friend and have him meet us."

"Yes," she said, bending over the rock again, "of course. He's probably nearby, pretending to search for me—" She broke off with a gasp and stumbled forward, clutching her throat. Blood sprayed from her mouth as she clawed at a crossbow bolt punching out of her neck.

Son of a bitch! Lobo palmed his dagger as Tehya

burst from the brush to put herself between him and a dozen armed ShadowSpawn fighters filing into the small space to surround them. Their leader, Kars, shoved his way forward from the back of the pack, the unholy light of bloodlust glinting in his dark eyes.

"Chain the skinwalker and kill the wolf." Kars gestured to Tehya with his blood-crusted ax. "I want the pelt. Hurry. MoonBound can't be far away."

"No!" A white-hot veil of fury slammed down over Lobo's vision, obliterating everything that made him civilized. He'd spent his entire life protecting himself from vampires who would kill him for what he was. Now it was time to *embrace* what he was, consequences be damned.

He shouted as his body ripped apart, every cell breaking down and reforming, doubling, growing. He heard barked orders, Tehya's snarls. Everything was a blur of rage, fur, claws, and teeth as he charged the nearest vampire. His massive body was faster than he'd expected, his thoughts slower and more primitive. He thought only about killing the ones who threatened Tehya.

His grizzly roar shook the trees as arrows and spears pierced his flesh, but the pain only made him angrier. Bone crunched between his jaws and blood poured down his throat as the stench of death filled the clearing. Dimly, through the throbbing din of fury in his ears, he heard MoonBound join the fray, and the forest filled with the sounds of Tehya's growls, angry shouts, screams of pain.

But he hadn't yet tasted the blood of the one he wanted. All around him, MoonBound and

ShadowSpawn clashed, but Kars was outnumbered. It would be over in moments—

Kars.

The bastard had his arms raised to swing his ax at Tehya. Lobo shot across the clearing and pinned him before the blow landed. Kars slammed into the ground, knocking the air from his lungs in an explosive cough.

Lobo was going to knock more out of him than air. He raised his heavy, claw-tipped paw that was twice the size of Kars's head.

"Lobo!" Hunter's command penetrated the battle haze fogging Lobo's mind. "Ease up there, Smokey. We need Kars alive."

Why? The question came out as a roar that made Hunter take a step back. Something nipped his ear, clearing his mind even more, and he swung his head around to Tehya. She pawed at his shoulder, getting his attention, helping to bring him down. He blinked. Everything was under control. MoonBound's fighters had surrounded and disarmed the surviving ShadowSpawn warriors, and it appeared that Moon-Bound's people had taken only minor injuries.

He probably didn't need to be wearing a half-ton bear suit anymore. Besides, his body was wrecked, pierced by spears and arrows, and he was pretty sure his flank had been flayed open with a hatchet. As if his brain had finally realized how much damage he'd taken, the wounds began to scream.

He clenched his teeth and rode out the agony of the shift, concentrating to keep Kars pinned as the shift bore out. When it was over, his body was healed but weakened; but as he looked down at his scarred, ugly hand, he realized he was in Kars's form.

Even though he hadn't caught his breath, he dipped his head and put his mouth to the male's ear.

"Here's the deal, you bastard. I know you're responsible for killing two yearlings from the Red River wolf pack. If you harm Tehya or any wolf ever again, I'll take you out while wearing the face of the person you love the most. Your daughter, maybe? You'll look into her eyes while you die. Understood?"

Kars's face turned crimson with rage, his eyes bulging from their sockets, but he nodded. With a shove, Lobo pushed away from the asshole and came to his feet, taking grim satisfaction from the way Kars got up a lot more slowly than Lobo had. Having a grizzly bear parked on his rib cage must have been excruciating.

Couldn't have happened to a nicer guy.

Hunter looked Lobo up and down, shaking his head as he took in Kars's double. "You don't learn, do you?"

Lobo shuddered as he let go of the energy required to hold on to Kars's form. The agony of the shift was muted by the sheer relief of finally being back in his own body. He'd never shifted so many times so rapidly, and he didn't want to do that again. His bones felt like rubber, and he wasn't sure how much longer he could stay upright without a little help from a tree.

"I'll gladly take the punishment for this one," Lobo muttered as he knelt to check Tehya for injuries. She licked his face and wagged her tail before hopping out of reach, clearly unharmed and un-happy about being poked and prodded.

Hunter cursed down at Su'Neena's body. "Some-how, Kars, I'm not surprised that you killed your own spy to protect your secret."

"I don't know what you're talking about," Kars shot back, his dark eyes wide with feigned innocence. "I thought she was an enemy."

"He's lying." Lobo might be exhausted, but he had enough piss left in him to beat the truth out of the clan leader. Too bad Hunter stopped him before he could go three steps.

"I know he's lying." Hunter stripped Su'Neena of her weapons. "And he'll pay for it. Someday."

"Arrogant bastard." Kars picked up his ax from where he'd dropped it when bear-Lobo attacked him, and he used it to gesture at Lobo. "I want his head on a stake. He wore my skin, and under Raven law—"

"We don't recognize Raven law." Hunter's voice lowered ominously. "Luckily for you."

Kars sputtered and cursed before getting hold of himself. "Even Crow worshippers can call for the death penalty when someone impersonates a clan chief. This is a major violation of vampire law, Hunter." He practically spit Hunter's name. "When the tribes convene in Sedona—"

"When the tribes convene in Sedona, I will make it very clear that my authority in this instance *is* law." Hunter's black smile reeked of self-satisfaction and the arrogance that came from knowing you held all the cards. "Multiple clans have sworn allegiance to me, and I guarantee that the tribal elders will fall in line. War with the humans is coming, Kars, and without MoonBound and the power we wield, vampires will lose. I *will* have my way in this."

"Dude," Baddon whispered to Lobo, "if I was into males, Hunter's speech would totally have made me hard." He jabbed Takis in the ribs with his elbow. "Right? You hard?"

Takis whacked Baddon upside the head with his palm even as he kept his crossbow aimed at a Shadow-Spawn warrior. "You're an idiot." He shrugged. "And I might be a little hard."

Damn, things at MoonBound had changed. Back when Lobo had belonged, no one would have gotten away with joking like that. Hunter really had chilled out.

Lobo left Takis and Baddon to their banter and joined Hunter, who had just finished telling Kars to fuck off. At least, he assumed those were Hunter's words, spoken in a language Lobo didn't recognize. Kars clearly understood, but even as his face burned scarlet with rage, he turned stiffly and disappeared into the forest with his dead and wounded warriors on the backs of surviving warriors.

"Just so we're clear, you believe Su'Neena was a traitor now, right?" Lobo asked.

Hunter nodded as he shoved his bone-handled blade into the sheath at his hip. "I believed you when you told me. I just had to make sure my clan believed it too."

Well, that would have been good to know. Hunter had changed, but he was still a bit of a dick.

"Before Kars shot her, she talked about a mutual friend." Lobo did a quick distance check to make sure no one was within earshot or listening, but lowered his voice anyway. "Hunter, I think you have another traitor in your ranks."

"I know." Hunter met his gaze, and in the depths of his dark, intelligent eyes, Lobo was stunned to see a spark of respect. "Thank you. Both of you." He bent to pet Tehya, his hand smoothing over her sleek head. "Maybe Nicole or our other mystic-keeper can find a way to turn her back. You're both welcome at MoonBound." He straightened. "Permanently, if you want."

Tehya took off, ears up and tail erect, which meant she was after a rabbit or a squirrel. He smiled, but his heart wept. This wasn't right. How could he have found the female of his dreams—literally—only to have her gone so soon? How could he go back to the way things had been, knowing that the vampire he loved was trapped in another body?

"Yeah," he rasped. "I'll bring Tehya in tomorrow."

Hunter gripped his shoulder and shook him a little. "Hey. Listen . . . Nicole will figure it out. And when Tehya turns back, there will be no repercussions for mating her."

Lobo blinked, unsure he'd just heard that right. "What do you mean?"

"I mean just what I said to Kars. Things are changing, Lobo. The vampire race is evolving, and our laws and customs need to evolve with it."

"Damn," Lobo said under his breath, unable to believe this was the son of one of the most brutal clan leaders in the vampire race's history. "You're not the male I remember."

"Yeah, well, I can't take all the credit." Hunter dragged his hand through his hair and gazed longingly in the direction of home. "I have a mate who has some experience with animal-based abilities, and she sort of led me to some revelations."

Lobo thought of Tehya and nodded slowly. "I know what you mean."

"Come on," Hunter said. "Let's go home."

Lobo's heart turned inside out, because, yes, he had a home. And he had Tehya. But it was no longer the same.

It would never be the same again.

11

*T*ehya woke to the sound of Lobo building a fire. She watched him as she always had, from her rug near the door, but this morning something was different. It was the way he was moving. Instead of his usual brisk, sure movements, he was slow. Mechanical. As if he was going through the motions.

How long had it been now since she'd turned back into a wolf? A couple of weeks, she thought. A couple of weeks of daily treks to MoonBound so she could be poked, prodded, dosed with strange herbs, and subjected to bizarre chants. She was starting to lose her patience with it all, had even snarled at the mystic-keeper a couple of times. But, damn it, she wanted to be a vampire again, and nothing was working. She was frustrated and angry and on the verge of giving up hope.

Maybe Lobo was feeling the same way.

She nudged his arm as he crouched in front of the woodstove, forcing him to acknowledge her. But when he looked at her, the sadness in his eyes broke her heart.

"I know you're in there, Tehya," he said roughly. "I know you can understand me. And I know I shouldn't say this because you can't help it, but I miss you." He took a deep, shuddering breath, and when he spoke again, his voice dripped with pain she felt all the way to her soul. "And you know what I think? I think taking you to MoonBound after you were shot wasn't as much about saving your life as it was about saving mine." He gripped her by her scruff and buried his face in her neck, his big body trembling as he held her.

She whimpered, sensing his distress as if it were her own. Probably because it was.

"Fuck," he whispered. "I can't do this."

Abruptly he was on his feet and out the door, slamming it closed behind him.

And on the floor, in a tiny little puddle, was a single teardrop.

Lobo was hurting, and she couldn't do anything about it. Her presence was probably making it worse. She was a constant reminder of what they could have had.

Sitting down, she howled, letting out her own pain in the only way she could. A few weeks ago she'd been content as a wolf. She hadn't known how to live as a vampire, and she had nothing to go back to in her human life. Not that she *could* go back. Kristen Parker was probably listed as missing or presumed dead, and if she returned as a vampire, she'd either be killed or enslaved. So, yes, she'd been content as a wolf. Happy, even. She hadn't *wanted* to shift back.

But now . . . now she wanted to be a vampire. She wanted Lobo.

Her eyes stung and her vision blurred as tears threatened to spill.

Wolves don't cry.

She froze mid-howl as a warm tingle spread through her body. Both times when she'd turned into a wolf, she'd gotten tingles, but they'd been cold, as if she were being stabbed with millions of icy needles. She still wasn't sure how exactly she'd made the shift happen, but the same pull was tugging at her now. All she had to do was reach out and take it.

Take it.

No!

Panic reached up and seized her by the throat, and it made no sense. She *wanted* to be a vampire. She did. She'd have responsibilities, relationships, love.

And pain. People die.

She didn't want to think about that. Didn't want to admit that maybe part of the reason she'd been content to be a wolf was that she didn't have to deal with the death of her mother, the only family she had. As a wolf, her human/vampire emotions and memories had been dulled, and it had worked for her for a long time. But now she had a family again, and something to run to instead of from.

And she had someone to run *with*.

The thought of Lobo made her heart beat faster, and then she was through with the second-guessing. She surrendered to the pull, surrendered to the pain of the shift, and a few agonizing seconds later she was standing in the middle of the cabin. On two legs.

Naked. Why did she keep losing her clothes? Lobo never lost his when he shifted.

She didn't bother looking for something to wear. She sprinted to the door and threw it open. Fog and drizzle painted the sky and the landscape beyond the porch in somber colors, but as Lobo wheeled around, his hair whipping across the hard planes of his face, the world got a lot brighter.

"Tehya." He stared in astonishment. "What . . . how . . . ?" She threw her arms around him and hugged him so hard he grunted. "Okay," he wheezed. "Doesn't matter."

She peppered his face and neck with kisses. "I figured it out," she said between nuzzles and pecks. God, he tasted good. Smelled even better, as if he'd been chopping wood in the rain.

He eased back and looked down at her, his brows pulled down hard over his eyes. "How?"

"Once I realized *why* I couldn't shift . . . I don't know, it just happened." She slid her hand down to his sternum and measured his heartbeat in her palm. It was beating as fast as hers. "It wasn't a glitch with my breeding or my turning. It was a mental block."

"A mental block?"

"It's so obvious now." She was babbling, but she didn't care. Her body was overflowing with excitement and joy, as if sparkling wine had replaced her blood. "For all of those years, I couldn't turn back because I didn't want to. My life was so messed up, and I'd lost everything. What did I have to go back to, you know? I had nothing left to claim as my own."

He knew. She saw it in his eyes and the way his throat convulsed on a swallow. "But now you have something to come back to? Something to claim?"

"Yeah," she murmured. "This life. You. You're mine."

His grin made her heart soar. "Just promise you

won't pee on me like you do to everything else you consider yours."

She probably turned a dozen shades of red, but she played it cool. "There are other ways to mark my territory," she whispered, stretching upward to kiss him.

She wasn't a wolf anymore, but she still felt the instinctive desire to claim what was hers, and she made that clear by wedging her hand between them to cup his erection.

"Oh, thank the Maker," he breathed. "Finally." In a smooth, blindingly fast motion, he lifted her onto the corner railing so her spine bit into the post and her legs were hooked over the log rails. The position left her wide open and exposed . . . and wildly turned on as she clung to his broad shoulders while he tore open his jeans.

His erection sprang free of its denim prison, and her breath caught in her throat. She'd seen him naked hundreds of times, had even seen him aroused and pleasuring himself. But as a wolf, she hadn't had the same reaction. Not even close.

Now her mouth watered as he closed his hand around his shaft and stroked from the plump head to the thick base. He watched her with hooded eyes, his scent growing thicker and muskier with every stroke.

She gripped his powerful shoulders, her nails scoring his skin hard enough to make him hiss, flashing massive, sexy fangs. He pumped his fist more slowly now, teasing her, letting his fingers caress the heavy sack between his legs before dragging his palm back up to swipe his thumb over the crown, catching the silky drop of precum at the tip.

"You like watching," he said, his voice vibrating through every one of her erogenous zones and stealing her ability to do anything but nod. A cocky smile tilted one corner of his mouth as he released his erection and lifted her hands from his shoulders to pin them over her head, forcing her to grip the post. Before she could ask what he was doing, he dropped to his knees and buried his face between her legs.

She cried out at the first probe of his tongue, and when he licked her slowly, sensually, while looking up at her with those smoky eyes, she arched in ecstasy and damned near fell off the railings. Lightning fast but without stopping what he was doing with his tongue, he gripped her butt, lifting and bracing her against the post.

"Lobo," she moaned. "Yes . . . right . . . there." Throwing her head back, she let herself succumb to the sweet sensations of his mouth on her sex, his lips nibbling at her swollen nub and his tongue spearing her aching flesh. She melted against him, and dear God, she was on fire.

"You taste like honey, Tehya," he murmured against her. "And apples. I fucking love apples."

He eased his finger inside her slick heat and pumped slowly as he kissed her deeply. Intimately. Tremors shook her and a sultry moan rattled her all the way to her core, adding to the amazing sensation whipping her into a frenzy.

Ecstasy spiraled through her, spinning faster and faster as his clever tongue lapped at her. She was close, so close. . . . He captured her clit and sucked, and she screamed as the orgasm crashed over her.

Distantly, she heard the flap of bird wings as the startled creatures flew out of the nearby trees, and then she heard Lobo whispering her name as he came to his feet and stepped between her legs.

"You're so beautiful when you come." His voice was rough, raw, and he was just as rough and raw when he entered her in a single hard thrust.

He didn't give her a chance to adjust to his enormous presence or to catch her breath. He braced his hands on the post and pounded into her, his hips slamming against her thighs. The vortex of pleasure and heat spun up again, and she wrapped her arms around him and clung as if she could get even closer.

"Don't leave me again," he said, lowering his lips to hers. "You're everything to me."

He fused his mouth to hers, capturing her moan of acceptance. She wrapped herself tighter around him, stroking his back, reveling in the flex of the hard muscles under his smooth skin. He ground against her, his shaft hitting just the right place, and she came without warning, a sudden, explosive blast that rocked her all the way to her bones.

She felt Lobo stiffen and jerk reflexively, and a shout tore from his throat as hot jets filled her. His expression . . . ah, damn, she'd never seen anything as amazing as this powerful man locked in the sweet agony of sex. The tendons in his neck strained, the veins next to them pulsed, and her fangs punched down hard.

"Yes," he whispered, sensing her need. "Feed."

She tapped the back of her fangs with her tongue, a sharp instinct guiding her. During her feverish delirium of transforming from a human into a vampire, she'd scoured the SuperWeb, looking for any information she could find about vampires. She vaguely remembered reading something about glands behind the fangs that produced an agent that made penetration more pleasurable.

Glands that were harvested from vampires for use as extreme luxury arousal ointments. She shuddered. Humans were horrible. But they were probably onto something, so she'd have to experiment with using her fangs on more sensitive parts of Lobo's body.

Later.

Right now, the vein in his throat was throbbing in a mesmerizing rhythm that made her mouth water. She struck fast, sinking her fangs deep. His groan vibrated against her teeth as she drank, and then he was moving again, his hips pumping even more furiously than before. Hunger and pleasure swamped her, allowing for only a dim awareness that somehow they'd ended up in his bed, and the hand-carved headboard was banging against the log wall.

They peaked again, this time together. A perfect circuit of sexual energy sizzled through them—she could actually feel what he was feeling, hope, happiness, contentment—and somehow it was all connected inside them both.

Pleasure and warmth flowed over her for so long that she lost track of time and place. She thought she might have lost consciousness too, but eventually the world came into focus again. She and Lobo were tangled together on the bed. At some point he'd stripped, and now they were skin to skin, and he was still inside her.

He blinked drowsily and gave her a lopsided smile.

"Well," he said in a raspy, sexy voice. "You marked me, just like you said you would."

A drop of blood dripped down his throat, and she gasped in horror. "Oh, shit." Shoving up on one rubbery arm, she swiped her tongue over the punctures in his neck to heal the wounds. "I'm sorry. Does it hurt? Will it scar?"

He chuckled, a deep, masculine sound that fired her up all over again. Oh, yes, being a vampire was way better than being a wolf. Well, mostly. There was nothing like running through the forest on four legs and howling into the night.

The beautiful thing was that now she could play in both worlds.

"I wasn't talking about your bite." He pushed up on one elbow and pointed to some angry raised lines just above the scar from the recent arrow wound.

Frowning, she traced the contours of the design with her finger. What the heck was it? A leaf? No . . . a feather. "I don't understand."

He captured her hand, bringing it to his mouth to kiss her knuckles. "It's a mate mark. According to legend, it appears when a match is approved by the gods." He winked. "Or something like that."

She wasn't sure she believed his legend, but she couldn't deny that it sounded wonderful. "What does that mean exactly?"

"It means I'm yours," he said, pulling her on top of him and tucking her head against his chest. "My precious Tehya. You've saved my life in so many ways."

And he'd done the same for her . . . so many times.

12

*A*re you sure about this?"

Lobo grinned at Tehya as they stood, completely naked, at the top of a ridge that overlooked the forest that was their home. Their own personal playground.

Sure, they'd begun to consider MoonBound their home as well, especially now that Tehya worked there a few days a week as the clan's resident dentist and Lobo served on Hunter's advisory committee. He'd been accepted into the fold—not just accepted, but welcomed. There were a few holdouts, older members who eyed Lobo with distrust; but Hunter was sure that a war with the humans was coming, and someone with Lobo's abilities could only be an asset.

Hunter was definitely *not* his father.

But as happy as Lobo was to finally be a real part of a community, he also recognized that at heart he was a loner, content to dedicate the majority of his time to Tehya—and soon, he hoped, their growing family.

"Absolutely," he replied. "I want our children to share our gifts. That is the only way to ensure it happens."

She worried her bottom lip between her teeth for a moment. "And you really think skinwalkers will be accepted in the future?"

"Times are changing, Tehya."

Hell, they were changing faster than he could ever have predicted. The more the clans came together under Hunter's vision, the less important their differences became. The common enemy was the human race, and vampires could no longer afford to fight over ideology, prejudices, or ancient grievances.

"Okay," she said breathily, "let's do it." She shot him a playful wink, and then she was off and running, shifting gracefully as she went.

Son of a bitch. How did she do that? She had far less practice than he had, but she could shift much more quickly, and she could do it on the run without missing a step. Nicole suspected it had something to do with the fact that less of Tehya's energy was spent on the transformation because she could shift only into one species, while he could morph into almost any land mammal of somewhat similar size. A brown bear pushed the very top of his limits, while a large coyote was at the bottom. In her dry, scientific way, Nicole had explained the role of checks and balances in nature, but what it boiled down to was that Tehya always got a head start when they went for their runs.

He'd catch her, though, and this time when he did—

He growled in anticipation as he completed his shift. Throwing his head back, he howled through the last of the pain, sending Tehya a message.

I'm coming.

Pulse pounding, he raced after her, ears flat, his claws digging into the soft earth with every bounding leap. He caught glimpses of her silver fur weaving through the vegetation in the distance, moving fast. She was running full-out, making him work for this.

The effort would only make this better.

For a few minutes he lost sight of her, but her scent was a beacon, thick with need. His body responded, heeding the primal call like the animal he was, and from out of nowhere, he found more speed.

She slowed to slip under a massive fallen log instead of leaping it, which proved to be her fatal mistake. He sailed over it, landing just inches behind her. She yelped and bolted, zigzagging through a maze of ferns and spindly saplings, but she'd lost her momentum, and he hit her flank with a shoulder maneuver that spun her off her feet.

Snarling, she wheeled around and bit him in the hip, tearing out a chunk of fur but not breaking the skin. If he'd been able to, he'd have smiled. She was playing rough, and he liked it.

She lunged again, but he rammed her with his chest and knocked her back. Before she could recover, he crowded her, using his superior height and size to force her backward into a mass of brush and fallen logs, cornering her. Now he would have her.

She growled, arguing with every step. Then, in an impressively quick, agile move, she leaped, twisted, and went over the logs.

Clever girl. But she didn't get far.

He caught her a few yards away, this time bringing

her down beneath him. She rolled onto her back and snapped at him, lips peeled back from sharp teeth. Gently but firmly, he closed his jaws around her throat, demanding her surrender.

Heat rose from her, along with her mating scent, and his loins tightened. They posed there like that in a display of dominance he was going to win. She ruled his life and his heart, and he was putty in her soft, slender hands.

But out here in the forest, with a wolf heart beating in his chest and the call of nature pounding through his blood, he was going to claim his mate. He waited for her signal, knowing she wouldn't drag this out. She wanted this as badly as he did, and moments later he heard the swish of her tail wagging through the twigs and leaves on the forest floor, and she relaxed, submitting.

And yet she still held all the power. The battle had been a test of worthiness for him, not the other way around.

He released her, and she came to her feet, rubbing against him, flirting with him, inviting him. He'd earned the right to take her, and nothing would stop him now. Rearing up, he mounted her, seizing her scruff between his teeth.

They'd mated in the forest before, pretty much daily, but always as vampires, never like this. He was attuned to everything around him, from the whirring of insects to the wind as it rustled through the trees. This was as basic and perfect as life got, and with any luck, they would make a new life today.

Afterward, exhausted, they shifted back, settling

against a tree full of squirrels that had gotten an eyeful. Lobo held Tehya against him, her head on his chest as he stroked her hair.

"If you'd made that easier," he said between panting breaths, "we wouldn't be so tired."

She trailed a finger down his abs, leaving pleasant tingles in its wake. "Just for that, I'll make it harder next time."

His cock stirred, taking the *harder* thing to heart. "You're already thinking about next time?"

"I'm always thinking about next time."

Sweet Maker, he loved this woman. He loved her even more when her hand closed around his rapidly swelling cock. Her fingers were magic as they slid up and down his shaft, nothing serious, just incredibly arousing foreplay.

When she paused, he damned near whimpered. "Okay, I have a question. Making a baby while in a shifted form guarantees a skinwalker offspring, right? I mean, that's why we did this."

"That's what the elders said." They'd also said that when a skinwalker died, he—or she—could manifest as a material spirit to haunt those who had wronged him. Being a skinwalker had some serious perks. Perks he wanted to pass on to his young, knowing that their lives would be considerably better than the lives of skinwalkers before them.

"What if only one parent is a skinwalker?"

He pressed his lips into her hair and inhaled the soft jasmine scent of the shampoo she'd gotten from Aylin. "Then they still have a substantially increased chance of having a kid who can shape-shift." He paused. "But only if the parent who can shift is, ah, in the alternate form when the child is conceived."

She didn't dwell on what that meant, thank goodness, because he didn't want to either.

"Well," Tehya mused, "what if one person can shift only into, say, a cougar, and the other person can shift only into something like an elk?"

This conversation was becoming less sexy and more wrong by the second. "You had to go there, huh?"

Tehya laughed. "Aren't we supposed to share everything? Even disturbing thoughts?" She bounded to her feet. "Come on. I want to run some more. And," she said saucily, "I want you to catch me."

He let her go this time, giving her a head start. He didn't shift until he heard her howl, and when he was done, he answered, sending his voice up into the darkening sky. A dozen voices howled in reply, each one distinct. Then Tehya's call, pure and unique, joined in, calling him to her.

This was life.

And it was perfect.

DARK SWAN

Gena Showalter

*To the amazing Kresley Cole and Larissa Ione.
The fun I had with you guys cannot be expressed
with words—only interpretive dance.*

Good night, sleep tight,
Wake up bright
In the morning light
To do what's right
With all your might.

— A CHILD'S LULLABY, *Author Unknown*

PROLOGUE

*A*ll right, girls. It's time to say good-bye."

Twelve-year-old Lilica Swan longed to tell Dr. Walsh how to die—badly—and when to do it—now. If she succumbed to the urge, and her voice voodoo operated at optimum levels, he would be compelled to obey her, unable to stop himself. But. If she succumbed to the urge, and her voice voodoo *didn't* operate at optimum levels, he would only be compelled to beat her with an old cattle prod. Again. He loved to beat her with a cattle prod.

Decisions, decisions.

Her sister Trinity placed a gentle hand over hers, and Lilica sucked in a breath. Oh! The warmth and softness of another's skin! But even as her body rejoiced, her mind reeled. Why would Trin touch her when the action was forbidden? Taking such a risk . . . well, it could only be a silent request *not* to use her voice voodoo. So. Decision made. Just like that.

Lilica locked her jaw and pressed her lips together. She lived by a single rule: Do anything, anytime, anywhere for her sisters, no matter the consequences.

At the moment, the three of them occupied a small monochrome room. Between Lilica and Trinity was a table piled high with massive tomes meant to raise their IQs. Each girl was supposed to read at least one book from start to finish in their allotted hour together.

Later today they would be tested.

Their other sister, Jade, stood in the far corner, banging her head against the wall. Poor darling. So desperate to escape her pain.

Lilica had to hide a wince when the mirrored wall cracked. If the doctors discovered just how deeply she cared about her siblings . . .

"Trinity," Dr. Walsh snapped.

In a blink, Trinity severed all contact with Lilica. "I'm sorry."

Lilica immediately mourned the loss.

Her voice voodoo and myriad other alien superpowers probably weren't functioning properly anyway. When did they ever? Dr. Strings, her personal tormentor—a.k.a. handler—shot her up every morning with . . . something. It kept her weak. She hate-hate-hated weakness.

And the injection wasn't even her biggest obstacle!

Longing, desperation, and sorrow suddenly flowed through the bond she and the other girls shared, snagging her attention. Trinity's emotions. The urge to hug her proved strong, but somehow Lilica resisted.

"We'd like to stay together." Trinity's voice was as soft as the honeysuckle scent she so often produced. A delicate scent completely at odds with the white-knuckled grip she now had on the table's edge. "Just a bit longer."

Trinity had always been the calm, accepting one, her nature the perfect complement to her angelic beauty. Little Divine, the staff sometimes called her. With her blond ringlets, wide blue eyes, and pale skin, she was exactly what their creators had envisioned.

Lilica was . . . not. But then, she was never supposed to have been born.

The scientists who worked at the Institute of Otherworld Technology—IOT—had hoped to construct a single superbeing. Someone neither human nor alien but the best of both. Then the egg split. Into three.

The girls had often been referred to as the Swans; hideous at first, but expected to grow into incomparable beauties. Not that appearance mattered . . . at first. The triplets had become instant commodities.

Now, however, appearance mattered greatly. And Trinity and Jade *had* grown into beauties. Lilica alone remained the ugly duckling.

Beauties attract. Beasts repel.

The girls created through experiment had also been the *focus* of an experiment. Nature versus nurture.

Trinity, the firstborn, had been awarded the exalted position of the positive. Jade, the second, had been dubbed the control. And Lilica, the last to be born, had been labeled the negative.

Nurture had very clearly won.

Jade mumbled, "Make it stop . . . stop . . . it has to stop." One of her abilities allowed her to see the darkest desires lurking in the mind of anyone nearby . . . to see into the future as well . . . to know when those dark desires would be fulfilled. And despite the drugs that she too was given, the ability never switched off.

Bang, bang, bang. Hair the color of newly fallen snow danced with the movement, the tresses a perfect contrast to her gorgeous green skin—the reason for her name. Although, most of the staff called her Little Delirium. The crazy one.

Better than Lilica's nickname, she supposed. Little Wicked. The evil one.

Dr. Walsh sighed. "Trinity, my dear. I know you merely pretend to read while you and your sisters are together. You stare at Lilica, and she stares at you. It's a waste of valuable time. Especially when you have important work to do."

Anger pricked at Lilica. Anger she knew her sisters experienced through the bond. *Work to do*, he'd said. *People to devastate*, he'd meant.

Trinity could steal superpowers, whether those powers belonged to a human or an alien. On the opposite end of the spectrum, Lilica could amplify superpowers. A curse disguised as a blessing. She had yet to encounter a physical body able to survive the intense surge of energy she unleashed. Within seconds, a person's respiratory and circulatory systems shut down. Within minutes, every other system followed suit.

And . . . Lilica liked that part of her life. She liked being in control. Liked the display of her superior strength. Perhaps the real reason the doctors considered her the evil one.

Trinity pressed her hands together, forming a steeple. "Please. Let me stay with my sisters just a little longer. Afterward, I'll work harder than ever. I promise. Please," she repeated.

—What are you doing?— Lilica mentally screamed at her. When you begged, you revealed a weakness to be used against you.

Here, someone always used your weaknesses against you.

Dr. Walsh offered Trinity an indulgent, adoring smile. "Schedules are important to maintain. You know this, Little Divine." He paused, tilted his head. "I think you're old enough to be called *Lady* Divine now."

The light in Trinity's eyes dimmed as her sense of depression magnified, overshadowing every other emotion arcing across the bond.

Dr. Walsh cupped her shoulder, causing Lilica's stomach to twist. "Besides, separation from your sisters is necessary. What if your ability adversely affects Little—Lady Wicked, or vice versa? What if Lady Delirium adversely affects you both?"

Jade could both steal and magnify, but only at a much lower level.

"I don't want to hurt my sisters," Trinity said, head bowed. *—I'm happy when I'm with you. Without you, I'm not whole.—*

The words were spoken directly into Lilica's mind. The words were spoken directly into Jade's mind as well, despite the mental onslaught she already endured; she wrapped her arms around her middle and stilled at last, the internal conversation distracting her.

Dr. Walsh inhaled sharply. "Why did she finally stop? Are you speaking with her telepathically? Answer me!"

Silence.

Everyone suspected the Swans possessed the ability, but no one had ever been able to prove it.

"We won't hurt each other," Lilica said. She would rather die! "You are a liar, Dr. Walsh, offering flimsy excuses to keep us apart." To keep Trinity all to himself . . .

Lilica's stomach twisted *harder*.

Dr. Walsh shuddered at the sound of her voice.

Despite her anger, every word she uttered contained a musical lilt, as if she were singing a dark, haunting lullaby. He should have been used to the phenomenon by now. Even when she'd cried as an infant, she'd seemed to be singing.

"We are stronger together, and it scares you," she continued. "You fear what we can do." In fact, she was certain the staff would have kept all three girls in different cities if daily contact hadn't been so vital. Without a glance, a smile, or a conversation, the triplets began to shut down.

"One more word out of you," he said through gritted teeth, "and you will be punished."

Never beg, never break. Never back down. "One. More. Word," she said, her eyes spitting hate at him.

Trinity gasped with horror.

—*I want you happy always.*— If Lilica had to deal with a punishment so Trinity and Jade could stay together, she would. To her, no one else mattered. Her sisters were the only people who cared about her well-being, the only people who understood her pain.

Perhaps things would have been different out in

the real world. But besides the staff at IOT, the only other living beings Lilica had ever interacted with were criminals who were being used as lab rats.

A superbeing must hone her most lethal skills *somehow*.

"Very well. You've earned your punishment." Dr. Walsh waved toward the door. "Trinity. Jade. You have five seconds to walk out of this room."

So much for keeping them together.

The girls remained in place, unwilling to leave Lilica to her fate.

"Now you've lost dinner privileges," he snapped. "Continue to defy me, and you'll miss breakfast as well."

He planned to starve her sisters? Lilica's anger sharpened into a nearly uncontrollable rage. She drew in an unsteady breath—*calm, remain calm*—and gazed anywhere but Dr. Walsh's direction. She tried to avoid her reflection, too. An impossible goal. The small room had six mirrored walls, forming a hexagon of two-way glass around her.

Better to observe you with, my dear.

She was a thorn among roses, as dark as her sisters were fair—with a heart to match. Or so she'd been told by the staff.

You *are the true beauty*, both Trinity and Jade had often whispered to her. *We pale in comparison.*

Now Trinity remained fixated on her, ignoring Dr. Walsh, who'd reached into the pocket of his lab coat. No need to guess why. He had a syringe filled with happy juice.

He'd been around since the beginning and

considered himself an expert on all three Swans. He wasn't, not even close, although he *did* recognize the signs of impending doom.

—*Go with him.*— She would survive. —*I'll be fine.*—

"No breakfast," Dr. Walsh announced, his voice lashing like a whip. "Next, you'll receive ten lashes, same as Lilica."

—*Go!*—

A muffled sob escaped Jade, but she stepped away from the wall.

Trinity jumped up, tears welling in her crystalline eyes. "I'll . . . I'll take the lashes for Lilica. Please. Let me. I'd be so grateful to you, Dr. Walsh."

Lilica's heart attempted to burst from her ribs; anything to escape this terrible moment. While her mind couldn't decipher the sudden light in Dr. Walsh's eyes, her heart could. It screamed, *No! Never!*

She would die before she allowed Trinity to be hurt or, worse, indebted to the doctor.

She stood and faced Dr. Walsh fully, a demand for his attention. He gave it . . . and he gulped, his beard bobbing with his Adam's apple. Then he looked away. No one but her sisters had the stones to peer into her black-as-night eyes for longer than a few seconds. Her eyes were a never-ending pit of despair . . . a midnight sky without stars, an orderly had once told her. An expanse so vast that anyone who stared too deeply for too long became lost, never to be found.

"I hate you with every ounce of my being," she said.

He shuddered again. Like all the doctors here, he wore special earplugs whenever he was around her.

An obstacle, but not a dead end. The device was a filter, not a block, able to dilute her voice voodoo but not mute it.

"Your feelings are of no concern to me, and your defiance has earned you another ten lashes." He approached her, lifting the syringe from his pocket.

She clutched his wrist, knowing contact would strengthen her ability, and shouted, "Be still." She pushed every ounce of her power into her vocal cords.

He obeyed instantly.

Excellent! Optimum levels!

Elation joined her rage. But . . . any second, orderlies would burst into the room to grab her. She would be pinned to the ground, Dr. Walsh's needle shoved into her neck. Hours later, she would wake up in her room, bound to her bed, vulnerable to whatever new abuse these people wished to inflict upon her. But she didn't care.

Threaten my sisters and suffer.

"Lilica—" he began. Sweat dotted his brow, and the pungent scent of fear wafted from him.

"Be silent," she commanded, and again he obeyed in an instant.

As his gaze widened with horror, hers slid to the only door, where a pad of lights glowed, indicating someone was punching in the code necessary for entry. "You will not enter this room," she called.

Though voodoo worked best with contact, it still worked without. The lights stopped flashing, and the door remained closed.

Today is my day!

Lifting to her tiptoes, she removed Dr. Walsh's

earplugs. She wrapped her fingers around his neck, and the increased contact delighted her—the warmth, the different textures, the very life that pulsed within another soul.

Disgusted with *herself* now, she gazed deep into his eyes. "If I fail to kill you today, you will kill yourself. You will kill your colleagues too." Always plan ahead.

"Kill," he repeated. "Myself. My colleagues."

Still at optimum levels! With the flip of a mental switch, she created suction between their flesh—a suction he couldn't break without ripping out hunks of his skin. Not that he fought her.

With another mental flip, her power gushed out of her and into him . . . rather than concentrating on his human characteristics, it focused on trace amounts of alien DNA. Well, well. He must have experimented on himself.

His desire for more power would be his downfall. *Her* power met his, charging it like a battery. He shook. He seized. Sun-weathered skin turned red, and blood trickled from his eyes and nose, his body unable to contain so much excess so swiftly.

She felt no pity, offered him no mercy. Little Wicked? Yes, oh yes. She was the coldhearted monster he'd trained her to be. She *owed* him pain.

Suddenly the door opened. No, no, no. The orderlies must have summoned others, those she hadn't compelled to stay out. Smart. Next time she would have to make sure to cover *every* base. They surged into the room, pulled at her, hit and kicked her, but they failed to separate her from Dr. Walsh.

"Leave her alone!" Trinity shouted.

"Don't you dare touch her!" Jade screamed.

The girls fought with all their might to reach her, determined to protect her from further injury. The orderlies turned their aggression on her sisters, striking with fists and steel-toed boots.

"Stop. You will stop." Argh! No more voodoo. She'd used too much power on Dr. Walsh.

Speaking of, his knees buckled. He tumbled to the floor, taking her with him. Only then did the suction loosen.

One of the orderlies pounced, shoving the syringe into her neck. A sharp sting. A stream of warmth in her veins . . . Darkness shrouded her mind.

As she fought to remain awake, she laughed. "If he lives, he's going to kill you all. . . ."

Someone punched her in the stomach. Air exploded from her lungs.

—*Lilica!*— A cry from both her sisters.

She didn't have the strength to respond.

No matter. Things at IOT would never be the same. Either Dr. Walsh's colleagues would kill him, fearing what he would do if he lived, or he would do exactly as she'd commanded. He might be able to resist her voodoo for weeks, months, even years, but one day, he *would* obey her. The compulsion had taken root; she'd seen it in his eyes.

These orderlies were doomed. One day, she and her sisters would be able to escape. One day, they would finally have a chance to *live*.

As the darkness beckoned her deeper into the abyss, she smiled.

1

*H*elp me."

The feminine whisper drifted through the hall. Dallas Gutierrez finished tying his boot and glanced up. No one had entered the small corridor. He straightened. As the sound of muted gunshots and squealing tires rang out, he solved his first case of the day. The TV was on.

Clearly I'm the greatest Alien Investigation and Removal agent ever to live.

But then, Dallas Gutierrez did his job the same way he did everything else, even bragging: with style.

He was certain the one-night stand he'd left sleeping in bed would agree. Not that he would ever ask her. He shuddered. Waking her would defeat the purpose of tiptoeing into the hall to dress.

And yeah, okay, leaving without saying goodbye was a total douche move—even when done with style—but both he and . . . Cori? Cadi? They'd agreed their time together would revolve around pleasure, not permanence.

Dude. I even suck in style.

To be honest, he deserved a participant ribbon for last night's performance, not a gold medal. Picking a companion for the evening had become a chore, kind of like deciding which STD he preferred. And sex . . . sex had become a duty rather than a desire.

"Help me."

As the second plea drifted into his awareness, he was forced to reopen the case file. The voice couldn't have come from the TV. He *recognized* it.

Shock and fury combined as Dallas reached for the pyre-gun holstered at his side. He inched forward. Maybe he should have invited his date to his place, where he controlled security, but only three people were ever allowed inside: Dallas himself, his friend Devyn, and, when he felt like being tortured, his boss, Mia. No one else ranked high enough on the DG scale of excellence to receive such a—dare he say it—amazing privilege.

Yeah. He dared. Truth was truth.

Footsteps soft, he rounded the corner, and the living room came into view. There were eight pieces of furniture: a floral-print couch, two matching chairs, a side table/serving cart, a coffee table, a TV, and two barstools. The only thing missing? The speaker.

"Help me."

He stiffened as she crawled around the couch and, strength abandoning her, collapsed on the floor. Long blond hair tangled around an emaciated face, pale skin sagging over a delicate bone structure. Even her eyes sagged; they were bloodshot and framed by open sores rather than lashes.

Trinity, queen of the Schön, would probably scare the boogeyman right now. Not that it mattered.

The beautiful monster—now just a monster—had the power to emit a potent pheromone that lured unsuspecting men into her arms, no matter how ugly she happened to be, addicting the poor bastards to her taste. Those men would then find themselves infected with the Schön disease, faced with a gruesome choice: have sex with others to spread the disease, keeping it from feeding on their own bodies, or rot from the inside out, ultimately succumbing to the desire to eat human flesh.

Yep. The bitch created sex-zombies.

AIR had been on her trail for months, but she'd always managed to evade capture. Then she'd been sucked into a parallel universe by—no joke—Father Time, and Dallas had thought he'd seen the last of her. Three cheers!

But now, here she was, back in his life. Three boos and a hiss.

How had she found him?

To his knowledge, she wasn't able to teleport to specific people. And why the hell was she here, anyway? To seduce him, infect him, and place him under her command? She'd tried before and failed royally.

As her gaze met his, she stretched a trembling arm in his direction. A sizzle of lust burned through him, disgusted him, and he stumbled backward, increasing the distance between them. At least the lust wasn't genuine, and he wouldn't have to scrub his hormones clean with bleach.

"Your pheromones don't work on me," he reminded her.

"Help. . . ."

"You say *help*, but all I hear is *please put me out of my misery*." He crouched to withdraw a second gun.

The SS—also known as the Schön slayer. A special weapon created exclusively for her and her victims. A single shot may or may not kill her; it was designed to trap the disease inside her, providing time to figure out what to do next.

The Schön disease was a separate alien life-form, according to the researchers at AIR. If the host died and that life-form wasn't trapped, it would search out a brand-new sparkly host. A.k.a. the person in closest proximity.

"You shouldn't have come here," he told Trinity. Once, she'd killed nearly an entire contingent of AIR agents. His coworkers. The only family he'd ever really had, and he wanted her to pay for it. And pay hard. "I'm enemy number one."

"Help . . . pleeease. . . ."

Such desperation. How delightful! "Poor Trinity. Did you get yourself into a pickle and now hope to pull my heartstrings to convince me that you've— what? Changed? Atoned for your sins?" Too late. "I'll tell you a secret. I don't actually have a heart." On the streets, he was known as the Heartless Foe.

Resolve and relief swirled in the depths of her ocean blues, even as tears spilled down her cheeks.

His brows knitted together. Why relief?

Did it really matter? Today he stopped her.

He canted his head to tap his ear against his shoulder and turn on the internal cell phone he'd recently had installed.

"Yo," Mia said a few seconds later, her voice so clear she could have been standing beside him. "This better be important, Agent Gutierrez."

Mia Snow liked to act as tough as nails, but underneath her bark-that-was-just-as-bad-as-her-bite, she was actually a marshmallow—if the marshmallow was made with poison.

"I'm in the presence of a Schön. *The* Schön, actually. She's injured, even docile."

Her shock crackled over the line. "You're kidding. If you're kidding, I'm going to deep-fry your testicles for my afternoon snack."

"No need to break out the blowtorch."

"Bless you! Is it contained?"

It. How accurate. "Yes. *It* is. And I'd like permission to use it as target practice."

A pause. A heavy sigh. "Denied. Sorry, my friend, but hold your position without firing. Why take risks if we don't have to? I'm dispatching a unit for pickup. Expect arrival in four minutes, thirty-eight seconds."

There was no need to rattle off his location. He knew the cell had been tracked the moment it had activated. "You spoil all my fun."

"I know! Because that's how I have *my* fun."

He disconnected the call with another tap of his ear. While he sheathed the pyre-gun, he kept the other one, the SS, trained on his target. "We've got ourselves a good news/bad news situation here. Which do you want to hear first?"

"Help. . . ."

"The good news, then. You're going to be locked up, probably studied like a lab rat. Bad news is you're going to live. Wait. Did I fail to mention that the good and bad were meant for me?"

Her relief completely overshadowed her resolve, which made exactly zero sense. "If live . . . they . . . live . . . die . . . they die."

They. Meaning the people she'd infected? Were the Schön forever tied to their queen, what happened to her happening to all? Well, well. Hello, beautiful loophole. "Why didn't you say so sooner?" If he could neutralize all her people at once . . .

Screw permission. This woman had already triggered one epidemic, with hundreds of lives lost. Why give her a chance to cause an actual pandemic, with thousands, maybe even millions, of casualties? If Trinity were stopped here and now, the others stopped with her, AIR wouldn't have to hunt for her victims, the disease spreading all the while.

"Enjoy your taste of karma, Trinity. I'd like to say it's been a pleasure, but I never lie." He squeezed the trigger.

A soft *whoosh* sounded as a beam of liquefied fire blazed between them. Contact!

Her entire body seized before going lax, smoke wafting from the new hole in her torso, the edges already cauterized. The light in her eyes dulled as she cried in pain.

Unlike his coworkers, he wasn't burdened by remorse when it came to harming a target. Especially one that posed a threat to innocents.

Harsh? Maybe. He didn't exactly care.

Harried, panicked, his date rushed around the corner. She trembled as she tied the belt of her robe. "What's going—what the crap? You shot my couch! You shot my freaking couch!"

"Stay back," he snapped, wondering what he'd seen in her. Sure, she was everything he'd thought he needed to start enjoying the world of dating again. The supposed ideal standard of modern beauty: a short, curvy blonde with blue eyes. Basically a replica of Trinity, before the disease had ravaged her appearance. But come on. Would a little calm have been amiss? "Return to the bedroom."

She did the opposite, stopping at his side because he'd outstretched his arm to block her from going farther. "You have two seconds to tell me why you shot my couch, or I'm calling the police. And who were you talking to?"

Who else? "The woman on the floor. And I *am* the police, honey."

She scanned the small living room, a frown pulling at the corners of her mouth. "What woman?"

Was she serious? "That—" He pointed, but Trinity's image wavered . . . disappeared altogether.

She'd been a *hallucination*?

Cursing, he stomped to the spot where she'd lain. *Excuse me, where I* thought *she'd lain.* He swiped his gun through the air, encountered no resistance, and pressed his free hand against the hole he'd blasted in the couch. The fibers were hot but dry. Had the beam gone through a physical body before hitting the furniture, the fibers would have been ice-cold. A safety measure meant to prevent wildfires.

Yep. Trinity had been a hallucination. And not his first this week. Not even his first this month!

He straightened with another curse. What was *wrong* with him?

"I'll buy you a new couch," he said through gritted teeth.

"Damn right you will." Capri? Cara? She scrubbed a hand down her face. "Look. Why don't you just go? I'll call you a cab."

A few hours ago, this woman had begged him to stick around for a second marathon of bliss—her words, not his. Now she couldn't wait to get rid of him, all because of a little gunplay.

He'd told himself personality never mattered with a one-night stand. From now on? Personality came first. "Forget the cab. I'll walk." Which was exactly what he did—straight out of the apartment.

When he reached the sidewalk outside, he fired up his cell phone. First he canceled the AIR unit. Mia had questions, and threats, but he faked static and hung up on her. Then he phoned his closest friend, Devyn. An alien. An outlaw alien. A *royal* outlaw alien. The man was king of the Targons, a race with the power to control other races, including humans.

Dallas had been born a human, but after pyre-fire blasted a hole in his chest, nearly killing him, Mia's husband, Kyrin, had fed him Arcadian blood to save him; he was now considered a hybrid with benefits. He could move faster than any eye could track, heal from nearly any injury in a matter of minutes, and dream visions of the future.

A thought occurred to him. One he'd had before. What if the hallucinations were a new type of waking vision?

The first one had featured a strange woman reclining in his favorite chair—naked—while sipping a glass of his favorite single malt. Though her face had been shrouded by thick, impenetrable shadows, the rest of her had been bathed in light and utterly magnificent.

Her hair had been a glorious waterfall of jet-black silk. Her skin had been dark, flawless, and covered in sweeping, scrolling tattoos that were a few shades darker. Elegant symbols he'd never before seen, the edges seemingly dusted with glitter. Her breasts had been plump, her waist small, and her hips heart-shaped. A perfect hourglass—and a perfect comparison. He'd counted every second in her presence, praying time never ran out.

He'd seen her over and over again. Perhaps the reason he hadn't been able to purge her from his mind. She haunted him now. The beauty he never would have chosen in a dating lineup but now couldn't forget . . . and hadn't stopped craving.

She was the real reason he'd found romance so tedious lately. No other woman compared to her.

"Look how pretty," she'd said, and a bolt of sizzling lust had struck him. She'd cupped her mouthwatering breasts. "We can pretend. You like to pretend, yes? You are a man, and I am a woman. Nothing more, nothing less."

The first time he'd experienced the hallucination—possible vision—he'd shoved his gun in her face and demanded answers. How had she gotten past his security?

The barrel had whisked through her, hitting the back of the chair. A second later, her image had vanished.

"You think you're hallucinating," Devyn said in lieu of a greeting, drawing him back to the present. "Or perhaps even having visions of the future."

The guy always knew everything about everything, and being surprised would have been a waste of Dallas's valuable time.

"Yes. Exactly." Sunlight glared over box-shaped buildings made of materials capable of surviving a second human-alien war, if necessary. A myriad of people had opted to walk to work, congesting every direction. Gazes were glued to smartphones or hidden behind smart lenses, lives lived online rather than in person.

Welcome to New Chicago.

"What I don't know is why," he added.

"Then get your ass over here," Devyn said. "We'll talk."

"Way ahead of you, king douche. I'm on my way now."

"If that's true, why are you ignoring my driver?"

Dallas skidded to a halt and scanned the cars on the road. A black limo was parked at the curb, a human waving at Dallas with one hand and holding open the back door with the other.

Okay. He was officially surprised.

He stalked across the distance and slid inside. Devyn reclined in the seat across from him. The cocky bastard wore a pin-striped suit that fit him so well it could only have been woven by magical sex fairies. Surely the only reason the guy laid more pipe than a plumber. Or rather, he *used* to lay more pipe than a plumber. Then he'd gotten married.

Sucker!

The door shut. The driver settled up front and a few seconds later, the car motored forward. Devyn offered Dallas a glass of *viski*. A single malt mixed with some kind of Targon sugar. He accepted with a muttered "Thanks" and drained the contents, the overpowering sweetness appealing to his Arcadian side.

"By the way. Your scowl is harshing my mellow." Devyn claimed the empty glass and set it aside. "You know I like to start my day with a smile."

"You like to start your day with the murder of an enemy."

Devyn beamed at him. "You know me too well."

"And I'm scowling because my plate was already overflowing with excrement. I seriously did not need a second helping with these visions."

"First, you know I hate when you use big words. Second, you have no reason to complain. I pay my people to clean your plate for you."

A laugh broke free, which was another surprise. No one, not even Devyn, should have been able to amuse him right now.

"Anyone ever tell you that you should be a life coach?" Dallas asked him.

"Yes. Unfortunately, I'm too busy being a melon felon." The Targon wiggled his brows, earning another laugh from Dallas. "But you're right, you know. You *are* having visions of the future."

He rubbed the back of his neck. "How do you know?"

"Because I'm a master—"

"Bator," he interjected. "Yeah. I'm aware. What does that have to do with the Schön?"

Devyn snorted. "With me, humor is a man's most expensive defense. Payment is always collected with my fists."

As if. No one had ever been more loyal than Devyn. The blessed few he loved, he *loved*. Nothing held back. There was no line he wouldn't cross to protect and defend. In fact, he'd taken a bullet for Dallas—and Dallas had no doubt the Targon would do it again if ever he felt it necessary.

"How do you know?" he repeated, as serious as the weapon he'd fired at Trinity.

"As I was saying, I'm a master *strategist*."

He waited for Devyn to say more, but silence reigned. "Um. That's great. Wonderful. But you've actually told me nothing."

A heavy sigh filled the space between them. "I'd heard rumors of Trinity's return, so I found someone who was once very close to her and . . . asked a few questions."

"You mean you kidnapped and tortured someone who was once very close to her and demanded answers."

Devyn waved a dismissive hand. "The torture sessions have been so minor it's hardly worth mentioning."

"I'm sure." Dallas loved the Targon like a brother, but even he had to admit the guy had a cruel streak a mile wide.

There was a slight chance Dallas maybe possibly might have possessed a cruel streak as well. During

Devyn's first—and only—official mission for AIR, they'd bonded as their target screamed in pain.

Dallas had continued to work with the Targon off the books, and his admiration had only grown. *Gets the job done, no matter the cost.*

Devyn changed the subject, asking about Dallas's newest "date."

As the car bumped along the road, Dallas complained about being tossed out of the apartment like garbage. "I'm not just a piece of meat, you know."

"My wife would disagree. She says I've convinced her that we males are only as good as the—and I quote—*peen* between our legs."

Dallas deadpanned, "I love how she loves you."

"I know." Devyn flattened a hand over his heart. "I'm *adored.*"

They were still snickering about the mighty *peen* when the limo finally stopped. Dallas glanced out the window. A history-rich area on the edge of town, located by what had once been a beautiful hidden lake. Devyn's home.

The king smiled with relish. "Come. I'll introduce you to my informant."

"Male? Female?"

"Female." The door opened, sunlight spilling into the vehicle. Devyn emerged, and Dallas followed.

They stood before a château-inspired mansion, its impressive stone walls rising to four stories. He sniffed and frowned, suddenly overcome by the odd—and far too pleasing—scent of freshly cut roses and aged wood set ablaze in a campfire, though there were no gardens nearby. No plant life of any kind, really. No campfires or fire pits.

Another sniff. The scents seemed to come from the detached garage.

"How long have you had the woman locked away?" he asked.

"Only a few weeks."

Only. "What's her connection to Trinity?"

"My wife has begun to remember bits of her past. Not just life in the vampire underground, but her first months topside. Those memories led me to a mostly abandoned shadow lab—the Institute of Otherworld Technology. I broke in and, while there, found information about the Schön disease. I also discovered two females who were living there, a green-skinned otherworlder who escaped, and the woman you're soon to meet. Her name is Lilica Swan."

Lilica Swan. A delicate name. Practically a song . . . a lullaby.

"Were the two females part of the staff or were they patients?"

"Lilica hasn't confirmed or denied either option. No matter my . . . persuasions, she's remained mute on the subject."

"Has she told you *anything*?"

"Not nearly enough. Let's question her together, shall we?"

2

*L*ilica Swan sat in the center of her cage. She'd remained like this for weeks . . . or mere days? Though the barred walls were so tall she could stand to her full five-foot-nine-inch height, she preferred this position. She could observe the happenings around her without drawing unwanted attention. A predator's trick of the trade.

To her right, four armed guards played holocards. They discussed recent conquests in detail and elbowed each other in the ribs. To her left loomed "the table." Knives of every shape and size were scattered over the surface. The Targon who'd captured her liked to stroke one or six while speaking with her.

Once he'd used the serrated blade on her. He'd held her motionless with a stream of energy and cut shallow lines into her neck, arms, and legs. A painful and humiliating process. Other times, he'd stabbed her outright.

She'd healed, of course, but as weak and malnourished as she was, she'd healed slower than usual. The last wound he'd inflicted had yet to fade.

Memories of her torment sparked flames of rage deep in her chest. *Can't use my powers on him. Not yet, not yet.*

When the time came, well, she would ensure he got his.

Though she still couldn't amph another person's life force without skin-to-skin contact, her abilities had only grown stronger over the years, her skills more honed. She could amph—and kill—within seconds. The biggest obstacle, currently—she couldn't amph effectively *and* use voice voodoo at maximum capacity in the same day. For the best results, she had to choose one or the other and follow through; no changing her mind midway.

"—ordered not to go near her?"

Her ears twitched as the guards brought her into their conversation. Doing her best to appear bored—*listen in? what? who? me?*—she attended to their next words.

"Why else? Because she's his sex slave."

"The greedy bastard doesn't like to share."

"Who does?"

"Especially a woman like her."

Silence fell over the group as all four males studied her with renewed interest. One gaze burned with malevolence while another crackled with lust. Both expressions were familiar to her. Two of the men regarded her with . . . compassion?

She couldn't be sure, considering she'd so rarely encountered it.

The Targon had commanded the foursome to wait outside every time he'd visited; they had no idea what he actually did to her. She'd assumed he'd wanted no witnesses to his crimes, but now she wondered. . . .

Did he suspect the two with *maybe, maybe not* compassion in their eyes would try to help her?

"If she keeps her mouth shut, he'll never know he's shared her," Malevolent said.

"Oh, he'll know," Lustful replied with a shudder. "He always knows."

"Believe me when I say you don't go against the orders of Devyn Targon and live to tell the tale. Just . . . don't go near her."

She dubbed him Smart.

He shifted in his seat, clearly uncomfortable. "Okay? All right?"

She smiled her coldest smile at Malevolent. *Come near me . . . dare you.*

He snapped his teeth at her, but he also slid his gaze away from her. The latter was a usual occurrence with almost everyone, and one she should have been used to.

Lustful finished off his beer, banged his chest, and belched. "No man is ever as bad as his own legend," he said, acting brave.

"You're right. Devyn is worse."

I'll call him Smarter.

"The Targon won't ever know he has reason to strike at me." Malevolent stroked his chin, thoughtful. "I don't think the girl even knows how to speak. Or how to move."

Now a slow grin lifted the corners of Lustful's mouth. "I bet *I* could get her to move."

Crude laughter echoed from the walls.

Suddenly the only set of usable doors opened, light spilling into the building . . . garage? . . . to illuminate the dust motes dancing through the air. The guards leaped to their feet, Lilica forgotten, the pungent odor of lust quickly replaced by the tang of motor oil, fear, and—she sniffed—the surprisingly floral scent she would forever associate with Devyn. Today, there was another scent mixed into the mélange. Something new and incredibly sweet.

Hinges squeaked as the door slammed shut. The light vanished, and from the shadows stepped two imposing males figures. The king and a companion.

While the Targon was as beautiful as ever, her gaze simply grazed over him, snared by the other man. Finally!

She'd found the blue-eyed man Jade had warned her about. The one her sister had claimed she would meet through the Targon. The very reason Lilica had allowed herself to be "abducted" in the first place.

He was the key to finding Trinity.

His dark hair could have used a trim, and yet it provided the perfect frame for his face—a face both rough and gorgeous.

He's a warrior and *a seducer.* To her surprise, he took her breath away.

Bronzed skin spoke of a Spanish heritage, but ethereal eyes of arctic blue hinted at alien ancestors. No, not just hinted. Screamed. He was an Arcadian. A strong one, judging by the buzz of power even now reaching out to stroke her, which meant he had to come from one of the more prominent families. But the only other Arcadians she'd encountered possessed fair hair and skin.

Was he, perhaps, a hybrid like her?

She scrutinized the rest of him, and any air she'd managed to return to her lungs was snatched all over again. His body was a masterpiece of muscle and sinew. Strength radiated from him, so much a part of him it was like a second layer of skin.

Her mouth watered, her own body suddenly hungry . . . starved.

Her brow furrowed with confusion. Hungry for what? Him?

His gaze pursued her languidly before lifting and colliding with hers. She gasped as a zing of electricity arced between them.

He missed a step.

Unlike most people, he didn't look away or stare at her as if she were a circus freak. He eyed her with . . . appreciation?

"Leave us," the Targon commanded in his smooth voice.

In seconds, the guards beat feet outside.

In front of her cage, the Targon smiled with his customary smugness. "How's my favorite prisoner?"

Until she knew exactly what these two men could and couldn't do, and what they did and didn't plan for her, she had no desire to use voice voodoo, revealing her ace and demolishing her best defense. So she batted her lashes at him and said, "Why don't you come in here and find out, handsome?"

Arctic Eyes jerked as if he'd been punched. Liked the timbre of her voice, did he? He wasn't the first, and he wouldn't be the last.

The Targon had never reacted to it, and today was no exception. He clenched a fist over his heart, as if wounded. "I know a death threat when I hear one, beauty, and yours might as well have been a dagger through the heart. However shall I recover?"

He called her "beauty" only as a taunt.

The other man said nothing. And never removed his gaze from her. Seconds passed in silence, adrenaline and something else, something she couldn't name, scorching her veins.

In the whole of her life, she'd had almost nil interaction with anyone other than her sisters, the old farts who'd raised her, and the aliens they'd brought to the lab with orders to boost or kill; she had no idea how to react to the physical sensations this man evoked.

"A dagger through your heart," she finally said, her gaze returning to Devyn. She sighed wishfully. "A girl can dream."

"Yes, she can." He stalked to the table and stroked the hilt of a blade. "But should she?"

How predictable. What he didn't know? There was nothing he could do to her that she hadn't already endured. And a thousand times worse!

For a moment she wondered what would have happened if he'd brought her here and pampered her. If he'd simply asked his questions rather than demanded answers. If he'd treated her with kindness.

He would have thrown her for a loop, that was certain. She might have cooperated fully. Perhaps they could have worked together.

When he'd sneaked into the lab, she'd hidden with Jade. Intimately acquainted with every hidden nook and cranny of the building, they couldn't be found if they didn't want to be found. But Jade had seen into his mind . . . had caught glimpses of Trinity and her interactions with the arctic-eyed man. . . .

At that point, Lilica would have tied herself up and presented herself to Devyn on a silver platter. Instead, she'd moved to a hiding place he could easily unearth and pretended to be shocked and dismayed when he'd discovered her.

He grinned at his friend. "Did I mention my prisoner is a sasshole?"

Arctic Eyes shook his head, the action clipped.

Well. She'd been called much, much worse. "Don't leave me in suspense, Targon. I'm metaphorically *dying* of curiosity. What's your friend's name?" *Act casual.* "Does he get to play with me too?"

Finally the male in question spoke up. "I'm Dallas."

The coarse resonance of his voice caused her nerve endings to heat. She frowned. People reacted to *her*; she didn't react to people. "Like the city in New Texas?"

Silence.

"Like the old TV show," Devyn answered for him, clearly amused with himself.

"Well, whatever you want to know about me," she said, "I won't tell you willingly. You'll have to beat it out of me." No more waiting, she decided. Once she got Devyn inside the cell, she would finally amph him, causing his own ability to control her motions to kill him. Then she could deal with Arctic Eyes.

"Beating you." The Targon tapped a finger against his chin. "Isn't that what I've been doing?"

"You've been love-tapping me." Was goading him

a too-obvious tell? Maybe, maybe not. But she had no other recourse at her disposal. "I hate to break it to you, big boy, but acting like a pussy is the leading cause of uterine cancer in men."

His amber eyes narrowed, while Arctic Eyes barked out a laugh.

That laugh . . . her nerve endings *boiled*.

"Oh, don't you worry, beauty. I won't be a pussy. I'll be a complete dick, you have my word." Devyn picked up the serrated blade, the silver metal glinting in the light cast by the single bulb hanging over her cage.

"You'd do that for me? My hero!"

Contrary to his boast, he said, "We'll start today's Q and A with something easy. You spent time with the Schön queen, but you aren't infected with her disease."

His friend stiffened. Why? When their gazes met a second time, his expression revealed nothing.

She faked a yawn. "I didn't hear a question."

Devyn exchanged the serrated blade for one with a hook. "This morning Dallas had a five-star vision of shooting her, and I'd like to do my part, ensuring that vision comes true. So. You're going to tell us whether you're immune to the disease, and if so, how you're immune, how you know Trinity, if she's contacted you recently, and anyplace you think she might go to hide."

A barbed lump grew in Lilica's throat. Seeing into the future was an Arcadian ability. The same ability Jade possessed. If Dallas had had a vision of shooting Trinity . . . most likely killing her . . .

If he *hoped* to kill her . . .

He would do so.

No. No! Lilica would die first. *He* would die first.

Her hands curled into fists.

Metal banged against her cage, making her gasp.

Devyn stood in front of the door, she realized.

"Do I have your undivided attention, beauty?"

He wasn't inside the cage, but he *was* within reach. If she could get her hands on him before he gained control of her motions . . .

How would Dallas respond? With violence?

Worth the risk.

He hadn't moved from his spot, and his expression remained blank, as if he'd completely removed himself from the situation. Except . . . the pulse at the base of his neck beat swiftly, and like hers, his hands had curled into fists, his knuckles white.

"You have my undivided attention," she said. "Let's see if I can get yours."

She dove toward Devyn—

Contact! Her fingers curled around his wrists, her flesh instantly adhering to his.

"Aw. You wanted to hold my hand?" Devyn smiled. "How adorable."

Silent, she pushed a charge through their link. The charge returned to her. He had defenses she'd never before encountered; they were almost like firewalls in a computer. No matter. She sent another charge, and another, until those firewalls thinned . . . vanished. He didn't fight her, because she wasn't hurting him—she was helping him. Or so it seemed. . . .

She sent another charge, this one strong enough to make his body quake.

His eyes widened, and his indulgent smile disappeared. He tried to yank his hand from hers, realized they were stuck together, and yanked harder. Again he proved unsuccessful, allowing her to hit him with yet another bolt of power.

Scowling, he yanked with every bit of power she'd just fed him and finally broke the suction. Agonizing pain ripped through her, and she bellowed, stumbling backward. The scent of old pennies filled the air, and she peered at her hand. She'd removed hunks of his skin, the mutilated tissue dripping crimson onto the cement floor.

Devyn gave her a faux pout, seemingly impervious to his own wounds. "I hate to add more bloodstains to your clothing, beauty, but you're going to bleed buckets before I'm finished with you."

Dallas stepped in front of him, as if to have a go at her himself. But . . . he just stood there. Intending to stop his friend before he hurt her?

Wishful thinking. No doubt he wanted a front-row seat to her downfall. And she *would* fall. At least for a little while. Devyn's words were more than a scare tactic; they were a vow.

Never let them see your pain. "You call what I'm wearing *clothing*?" She tsked and smiled at him. The glow-in-the-dark jumpsuit was a staple of IOT and all she'd ever worn. "You are too kind. And haven't you heard? Blood is the new black."

Both men peered at her, silent. Baffled by her boldness?

They shared a look, but still didn't speak a word, and she wondered if they could communicate telepathically the way she and Jade did. A link she'd struggled to maintain since her capture. Because of the distance between the garage and the institute, she had to use more power than she could spare, which was why she'd only checked in once a day as proof of life.

Devyn tapped a bloody finger to his chin, leaving a smear of crimson. A smear that should have been obscene; on him it was right at home. "Either you're afraid of what Trinity will do to you if she finds out you betrayed her, which means you fear the wrong person. I will do much, much worse than she could ever dream. Or you like her, maybe even consider her a friend. Otherwise you'd help us. So tell me. Which is it?"

Panic threatened to overtake her. The more they knew about Lilica's connection to Trinity, the less her chances of success. *Reveal nothing.* "You're the world's worst host." *Blithe smile.* "Why would I want to help you with *anything*?"

He arched a brow. "Do you think she's going to swoop in and save you? She won't, I assure you. I've never met a more self-serving individual—and I meet myself every day." He shrugged. "I told you the day I found you I wouldn't hurt you if you told me everything you know about Trinity. The deal still stands."

"Why should I believe you?" She ran a finger along her neck, where he'd last sliced her. "What makes you think I know anything?"

"Perhaps my Spidey senses are tingling."

She didn't understand the reference, but she would never tell him the truth or even attempt to weave a lie. The scientists had lied to her always, about everything and nothing. A beating was preferable to emulating the ones she despised.

Devyn's head tilted to the side, his examination of her intensifying. "What's your endgame?"

Easy. Once Lilica had dealt with Dallas, the newest threat to Trinity's life, then found and cleansed her eldest sister of the Schön—somehow, some way—the Swans would leave New Chicago for good and start over.

Start over? Please. They'd finally *start*. Live for the first time, do normal things like grocery shop and date. Move into a normal house. Drive a car. Host a cocktail party. Celebrate the holidays like a real family. The way she'd seen families celebrate through Jade's visions. Maybe Lilica would even fall in love with a tall, dark, and handsome man, get married, and have children.

A dull pang of longing struck her.

Could she have children? Should she? She was part of an experiment gone wrong, not human and not alien, but the worst of both. If ever another research lab or government agency learned of her abilities, she would be hunted to the ends of the earth, and so would her kids. Their lives would end up as terrible as hers. No, thanks.

"Tell him," Dallas said, those arctic blues no longer cold but hot on her. "Please."

Her eyes widened. His voice! The epitome of sex. And his plea! Why? Why would he beg, willingly revealing a weakness?

"I . . ." Want to obey him. She sucked in a shocked

breath. Did he possess his own version of voice voo-doo? *Resist!* "No. I won't."

"Very well. If blood is the new black," Devyn said, "you'll be *very* pleased with what happens next." In a single fluid motion, he withdrew a gun from the holster at his side, aimed at her, and squeezed the trigger.

No time to react. A whoosh of air, a sharp sting in her neck where a dart embedded in her vein . . . A rush of warmth tugged her toward a never-ending pit of darkness. . . .

Son of a scientist! He'd drugged her while his friend distracted her. She fought to retain her lucid-ity, but her knees were too weak to hold her weight and soon crumpled. "Both . . . will . . . pay. . . ."

"That's right," Devyn said. "You will pay. Nighty-night now, beauty. You'll discover your punishment as soon as you wake."

Wake . . . wake . . . she had to stay awake. . . .

Her mind raced back to another time she'd ended up like this: drugged with predators around her. The time she'd attempted to kill Dr. Walsh. He'd survived, but his coworkers had feared for their lives, as she'd suspected they would, and locked him away, ensuring he remained comatose. She'd wondered why they hadn't just killed him themselves, but they'd known something she hadn't. Not until eight years later, when Walsh woke up and slit his own throat—and then, because her compulsion was so strong, he had risen from the grave to pick off his coworkers one by one. Even those who no longer worked at IOT.

A horror movie come to life.

She had no idea where he was now or what he was doing. She'd lost track of him.

And because the lab was top-secret, independent of any other affiliation, and operating completely in the black zone with zero paper trails, no one had shown up asking questions or demanding answers.

Walsh's actions had marked the end of her torturous existence and the beginning of her fresh start.

Suddenly the lab had been devoid of employees, and with no one there to drug Lilica and Jade, they'd soon begun to operate at full capacity. For the first time in their lives, they'd had complete access to the computers and recordings . . . and antidotes. . . .

The antidote to sedation! Hidden in the sole of her shoe as a "just in case."

She tried to reach it, but her arm was far too heavy. And so were her eyelids. They closed so tightly she couldn't pry them open. All too soon, darkness swallowed her whole.

3

*D*allas reeled as a thousand and one thoughts rolled through his head. This woman . . . she was the one he'd seen in his first waking vision. The naked intruder who'd reclined in his chair, drunk his single malt, and asked oh, so seductively to play a game of pretend.

She wasn't even close to his type, but . . . he wanted her in his bed at his earliest convenience. Or now. Yes, now would do.

She was tall and slender with a glorious ebony mane, the silken strands curling like ribbons. At her temples were braids that had been twined with a string of blood-red rubies. A perfect match for her lips. Blood-red, heart-shaped. Provocative and provoking. Her eyes possessed the catlike slant of a Teran. Her irises were deep . . . an endless span of ocean crowned by the darkest night.

Every time she'd looked at him, he'd been set adrift in that ocean, lost and drowning. The worst part? He'd had no desire to be saved.

He took in the rest of her. She had pointy ears and sharp, prominent cheekbones. Too prominent to be human. In contrast, she had a delicate nose.

When she'd attacked Devyn, Dallas had seen what looked to be butterfly wings etched into the corners of her eyes and a strand of ivy etched across her fore-head, as if she were wearing a mask. The markings weren't tattoos, exactly. They couldn't be. At certain angles, they appeared iridescent and jewel-toned. Which had to mean they were a natural, if unusual, pigmentation in her flesh. Something he'd only ever seen once before . . . on . . . what race? He couldn't remember the name, could only remember the people had been experimented on before total extinction.

The extinction had happened before his time. But when he was a plucky AIR trainee, he'd spent most of his free time studying different human-alien battles, as well as the strengths and weakness of the creatures who'd lived and died so that he could better defeat the ones still in existence.

A feminine moan pulled him out of his head and into a haze of lust he struggled to control.

The prisoner moaned, nothing more, and he shot hard as a rock?

Not exactly the greatest start to their relationship. And they *would* have a relationship. His visions had never lied.

The rest of her skin glittered as if it had been dipped in diamond dust, an effect he'd only ever seen on Targons. But she wasn't a Targon. Devyn recognized his own, and he would have pegged her at moment one.

Those sharp cheekbones and pointy ears some-how lent a shocking wildness to her serene beauty. Even better, she had a voice like sex. A voice that *was* sex. The raspy pitch had stroked over him, making him think of a feather at the end of a flogger.

The scent of roses and a campfire ablaze with aged wood was stronger here, and most assuredly wafted from her. It only made him want her more. *Must taste. . . .*

She wasn't a sweetheart with a ready smile, the kind of woman a lawman like him *should* want. This girl had a mouth on her. *Hold me back!* Her mouth. Over and over again his attention had returned to it. So lush and red . . . decadence made flesh.

She was exotic, unique, and that had to be the draw. But honestly, he thought he would have wanted her even if he were blindfolded. That scent . . . that *screw me and screw me hard* voice . . .

He motioned to the cage with a jerk of his chin. "Open it."

Devyn sighed. "If you tell me your conscience is bothering you . . ."

He simply lifted a brow.

With another sigh, Devyn opened the cage. Dallas stalked inside, crouched beside the exotic beauty, and gently rolled her to her back. Despite the blood, dirt, and grime caked on her, the dusky hue of her skin revealed an even greater shimmer at close range.

A suspicion about her had danced at the periphery of his mind since the moment he'd laid eyes on her, and now solidified. "She's related to Trinity."

"Hell, no." Devyn crouched beside him. "I would have noticed a resemblance."

"They have the same bone structure. Same oval face. Same prominent cheekbones that gracefully taper to a strong chin."

"'Gracefully taper'? Did you acquire a degree in

hideous poetry in the past hour?" His friend's tone was as dry as the air in No Man's Land. Then he cursed. "My boy, I think you're right."

Perhaps the two females were cousins. Maybe even half sisters. Either way, he could use Lilica to draw Trinity out of hiding.

"But she's not diseased, right?" he asked, seeking reassurance even though his friend had already provided the answer.

"She's definitely clean. I had tests done before I brought her here."

She wasn't Schön, then. But what was she? The power she radiated . . . he felt as if he'd been hit by shrapnel, with too many bits and pieces to identify a single source. His Arcadian side had reacted oddly to it, buzzing with a need to escape her *and* to draw her closer. He thought he understood the latter, though. Once, when she'd glanced in his direction, his Arcadian side had hinted at a very dark future—she planned to kill him.

Keep your friends close and your enemies closer. . . .

Devyn had mentioned Dallas's pop-a-cap vision. Was that the reason Lilica now wanted him dead?

Whatever the reason, she would fail.

But he would not. He would use her as bait. Which meant, he would have to spend time with her. Could he resist her potent allure, or would he willingly risk his life in an attempt to seduce her?

Her in his chair, drinking his whiskey . . .

Yeah. He'd risk it.

Desire wasn't always a weakness; sometimes it could be a weapon.

"I may not survive my association with her," he admitted. But what a way to go.

Devyn stiffened. "Well, then. She dies today."

To the Targon, all threats to Dallas were to be eliminated immediately, no questions asked. No investigation.

"Your bromantic gestures always warm my heart, but I'm asking you to stand down just this once." Dallas traced a fingertip along Lilica's jaw. Softer than silk. "I'm taking her with me."

"Like hell. She's not diseased—she's worse. My people once warred with hers. The Falle."

Falle. Yes! The exterminated—well, the *nearly* exterminated race. Predators to the core. Wily, even deceitful, with off-the-charts possessive instincts.

"For the first time in my reign, we almost lost a battle." Devyn held up his arm, revealing the five finger-long wounds that hadn't yet regenerated. "This one amplifies."

"And that's bad because . . . ?"

"With a single touch, she can make you stronger. Too strong."

Again he said, "And that's bad because . . . ?"

"Think of it this way. Right now you are able to run faster than the human eye can track. But after contact with her, you would be able to break the sound barrier, and you wouldn't be able to stop yourself. You would run until you died. *If* your body could contain that kind of power for any real length of time."

Was that her plan, then? Kill him with his own alien abilities? "You have a way to neutralize her, I'm assuming."

"Of course," Devyn replied without missing a beat. "I'll cut off her hands."

Of course. "There's no other less . . . damaging way?"

His friend pursed his lips. "You're losing your edge, and it's embarrassing."

"Just tell me what you know."

"Fine. My people have indeed developed a poison that neutralizes the abilities of otherworlders, but the effects wear off quickly, lasting no longer than twenty-four hours. And the drug can be easily counteracted by a shot of doctored adrenaline."

"I'll keep her away from extreme sports," Dallas replied drily.

"I said *doctored* adrenaline. There's a difference."

"Give me two weeks' worth of doses for her." Surely he could spread the word of her capture and draw Trinity out of hiding within that time frame.

Let's do this. He straightened to his full six-foot-three height. "Also, I'm going to need a few hours to get my shit together. Do not—I repeat, *do not*—hurt her while I'm gone. You do, and I will be highly displeased."

There were cuts and bruises on her neck, arms, and legs, and probably more under her clothes. Dallas wasn't against the use of torture whenever warranted—he believed in equal opportunity and all that garbage. But he didn't like the thought of Lilica's lovely face twisted with pain or her voice screaming with torment rather than moaning with pleasure.

The protective instincts could be linked to his desire for her, but the intensity of that desire baffled him—until he remembered the pheromone Trinity released. He'd assumed it came from the Schön, but perhaps it came from a shared familial line.

Devyn scowled at him. "What the hell is this?"

"What the hell is what?"

"This look." A finger zigzagged in front of his face. "Are you fantasizing about our bait?"

Bait. The guy had already deduced Dallas's plan. Shocker. "Now *you're* the one being ridiculous. She isn't my type." The absolute truth. And yet . . .

She tried to amph and kill my friend, and I got a hard-on for her.

Well, *another* hard-on for her.

Devyn's scowl only deepened. "Do yourself a favor and remain detached with her."

Something in his tone hinted at a deeper meaning. "You're going to use her to amplify your powers, aren't you?" Dallas demanded. "You think you're going to stop her before she goes too far."

"*Think* is incorrect. I *will* use her, and I *will* stop her before she goes too far."

Power-hungry Devyn. Nothing new there.

"There was another girl at the institute," Devyn added. "I sensed her but couldn't find her. I've had an agent watching the place since I left with Lilica."

"Which agent?"

"John No Last Name."

John, who'd been little more than a feral animal the last time Dallas had seen him. Poor guy had only recently been found and freed after months of torture— his skin flayed from his body over and over again.

"Perhaps the other girl will help convince Lilica I'm the lesser of two evils," Devyn concluded.

Dallas couldn't come up with a valid reason to argue over the matter. Lilica meant nothing to him. Proof: the slight prick of irritation in his chest stemmed from a sense of urgency to find Trinity, *not* a desire to protect Lilica.

"I meant what I said. Don't touch her while I'm gone, or you and me, we're going to have a problem. The only contact she's to have is with the needle you use to dose her."

Devyn studied him for a long, silent moment. Understandable. Dallas had never spoken to his friend so harshly. To everyone but his enemies, Dallas was a happy-go-lucky bachelor without a care. In this, he blamed Lilica and her mystical appeal.

"All right," Devyn said with a nod. "Consider it done. I just hope you know what you're doing."

"I don't, but that's not going to stop me."

Bang, bang.

Lilica dreamed of taking over IOT . . . of the day she finally uncovered the truth about herself and her sisters. Turned out they were a mix of twenty-three alien races, plus the human race, and each girl exhibited different dominant qualities found within the different species.

Jade took after the Maleahdolla, a warrior race feared throughout the galaxies. Their ability to read the minds of others gave them an edge in combat, technological advances, medicine, and even relationships.

Lilica took after the Falle, a corrupt race AIR had tried to exterminate during the human-alien war. And

AIR wasn't the first to try! Centuries ago, the Falle had nearly been obliterated by the Maleahdolla. The survivors were enslaved and used to amph their masters. But the Falle—insidious creatures who strengthened themselves by killing others—had bonded their lives to the lives of their captors, ensuring one race could not survive without the other.

Her voice voodoo came from the vampires. A specific vampire, actually, someone identified only as "the bride."

Trinity took after the Forførn, a seductive race lovely beyond compare, with saliva as addictive as any drug. They'd once been hunted and used as sex slaves, but were now nearing extinction.

Something else they'd learned? Three years ago, the staff at IOT had decided to use Trinity's beauty and abilities to their advantage by sending her on a dangerous mission. Of course, they'd threatened to kill her sisters if she failed to return. Her objective: Find the king of the Schön and, through any means necessary, obtain a sample of his DNA.

She'd obtained a sample of his DNA, all right. Inside her veins! She'd absorbed his alien life force—a parasite—and in the ensuing weeks, the infection had spread through both her mind and her body, completely taking over.

Telepathic conversations with her had ceased, their bond to their eldest sister broken. Sweet, shy Trinity had then seduced her way out of the lab, infecting several doctors and guards. Doctors and guards who'd soon sickened. They were contained, studied, and eventually rotted to death inside their cells.

Once Lilica and Jade gained their own freedom, they'd left the lab for the first time in their lives, hoping to find and save their sister. But the crowds had been more than Jade could withstand, the onslaught of thoughts and possible futures . . . of evil . . . making her crazed. For Lilica, the stares had been disconcerting. In a world filled with humans and otherworlders of every kind, she and Jade were still freaks. Dejected and ill prepared, they'd returned to the lab.

Bang! Bang!

Lilica awoke with a jolt and jerked upright. A flood of dizziness sent her crashing back onto the mattress. A soft mattress, not like her hard cot at the institute, or the cold concrete floor in her new cell.

The cell . . .

Memories swamped her, and anger sparked. Devyn . . . Dallas. That stupid dart.

When the dizziness subsided, she sat up slowly, gingerly, and catalogued her surroundings. A spacious room with four white walls and a closed metal door. The only piece of furniture was the mattress she rested upon. A stack of clothes and a basket of toiletries perched at its foot.

There was no sign of her captors.

Nausea churned in her stomach as she stood to shaky legs. Deep breath in . . . out . . . Cool air kissed her bare skin. Bare? Heart hammering, she looked down. Her filthy scrubs had been removed, but her plain white bra and panties were still firmly in place.

Which man had stripped her?

Did it really matter? When cameras recorded every aspect of your life from birth to adulthood, a panel of men and women watching from the other side of a two-way mirror, you never developed a sense of modesty.

Her balance steadied as she searched the basket. No razor, only soaps and lotions. Great for beautification, useless for defense.

Bang, bang, bang.

Once again, she jumped. The sound came from beyond the door.

She ignored the clothes. Countless times, her jumpsuits at the institute had been washed with chemicals meant to alter her state of mind. She quietly padded across the room and tested the doorknob. Unlocked. The Targon and the Arcadian were suspicious bastards; they wouldn't trust her with a button, much less give her free rein here, wherever here was.

If they'd wanted the door locked, it would have been locked. Neither was the type to make such a critical mistake. So. This had to be a trap of some sort.

She used a stream of power she couldn't afford to lose to force a thought out of her head and into Jade's.

—I've been transferred to a new location. Don't know where I am, or what's planned, but I've found the arctic-eyed man.—

Unlike every time before, the power fizzled before leaving her, and she frowned. She tried again . . . with the same results. She waited one minute . . . two . . . breathing deeply, hoping for a reply, but only silence greeted her. Her hands curled into fists. What had Dallas and Devyn done to her?

She couldn't risk trying again, or she'd have no protection against her captors.

As she sneaked into the hallway, the anger she'd

lived with most of her life blazed with new heat. The males planned to kill Trinity. They had to die . . . but not until after they'd helped her *find* Trinity.

No. Can't risk it.

Never wait to slay. Missed opportunities only led to regrets.

Her captors needed to die, so they *would* die.

The smell of warm syrup and—Lilica sniffed—raspberry jam saturated the air, but there was an even sweeter scent . . . the one she'd encountered in the cell, when Dallas arrived.

He was here.

A sense of eagerness and excitement overtook her—angering her further. She moved forward at a brisker pace, noting details along the way. The walls were as bare as the walls in the lab that had been both a hell and a home to her. The only home she'd ever really known. Around the corner was a living room with only two folding chairs, which had been nailed down.

The banging continued. Pots and pans, she realized. At the entrance of the kitchen, she paused. A tall, muscled man had his back to her. He wore a tight black tee and jeans. His hair was dark and rumpled, his skin bronzed. Arcadian power stroked over her, making the blood in her veins warm . . . catch fire.

He was here, and he was right in front of her. He was here, and he planned to kill Trinity. There was no better time to strike.

Should she go with her amph ability or voice voodoo?

If she made the wrong choice, she would have to

rely on her physical strength, punching and kicking like a champ, hopefully getting her hands on a blade.

He stopped slicing . . . whatever it was, and placed a knife on the counter beside him. Scratch *hopefully*. Add *definitely*.

Without making a sound, she prowled toward him—and leaped on his back, winding one arm around his head, the other around his neck, and her legs around his waist. While applying enough pressure to choke him out, she sent a blast of power through—nope, no power. The blast remained trapped inside her.

He didn't judder with surprise or panic but reached over his shoulder, grabbed her by the nape, and flipped her over his head. As she fell, she managed to grab the knife. Impact emptied her lungs, but she ignored the pain to pop to her feet and face him, holding the blade between them.

Meeting his arctic gaze threw fuel on the already blistering fire in her veins. "You will stay still," she told him, deciding to give voice voodoo a try, since amphing had failed. "You won't move."

He moved, crossing his arms over his chest.

Argh! *None* of her abilities were working.

"Well, well. Sleeping Beauty awoke at last."

His tone lacked the taunt Devyn always used. Dallas might actually . . . consider her a beauty?

No, another trick, surely.

He looked her over, and for a moment, only a moment, she forgot all her troubles, the air between them crackling with hotter heat and sizzling electricity. Goose bumps broke out over her arms, along her spine.

One corner of his mouth twitched. "Is that any

way to greet the Prince Charming who oh, so carefully undressed you?"

By mentioning her state of undress, he hoped to disconcert her, didn't he? Well, it would take a lot more than that.

"No, it's not," she said, and finally he juddered, his pupils spilling over his irises. He was turned on? By *what*? "I should have greeted you like this." She faked left and stabbed at his right side.

He managed to block—somewhat. The blade sliced through the center of his palm and came out the other side. Blood dripped, and he hissed. He latched onto her wrist with his uninjured hand and twisted until she released the weapon.

He clasped the hilt and wrenched out the blade, causing more blood to drip to the floor. The sweet scent of honeyed champagne intensified. Yes! That was what she'd been smelling . . . it reminded her of the bottle of bubbly she'd stolen during her trip outside IOT. Her head swam.

She acted anyway, making a play for the weapon.

He spun out of reach, saying casually, "I wondered how hard you'd come at me. Now I know."

So. This *had* been a test.

As she stalked around him, he spun with her, his gaze remaining on . . . her puckered nipples, peeking through her bra.

"What did you do to me?" And he *had* done something. Otherwise he would have bound her.

He didn't pretend to misunderstand. "Don't worry, sweetness. You'll regain full use of your power . . . one day."

He'd drugged her with more than a sedative, hadn't he? Just like the doctors at the lab.

Well. She just happened to have the antidote to power negation too. "Where are my shoes?"

"In the trash, where they belong."

"I want my boots! They're my favorite pair."

"I'd venture to guess they are your only pair."

True. "I want my boots," she repeated.

"Why? So that you can kick me in the balls with them?"

She smiled with saccharine sugariness. "Your friend devoted countless hours to my torture, and I just woke up in a strange place, wearing only a bra and panties. *Of course* I'm going to continue attacking you. What else am I supposed to do? Thank you?"

"Yes!" He rubbed his lower back. "You're heavier than you appear. I injured myself carrying you up a thousand flights of stairs."

How dare he! "I'm not heavier than I appear. *You* are *weaker* than you appear."

For a moment, he looked like he wanted to grin.

Deep breath in, deep breath out. All right. Anger, sarcasm, and demands had failed. Light flirting? Worth a shot. "If I *do* kick you, so what? You're so strong . . . so powerful. Surely you'll overcome me."

"You just called me weak."

Argh! She tried a different path. "Think of the perks. If you block my kick, you prove your skill. If you don't and my boot makes contact, your manhood will swell, and you can finally tell your girlfriends you're hung like a champ—and mean it!"

His lips twitched at the corners. "Let's circle back to

the boots and my swelling manhood. First, I want to know if you have a familial connection to Trinity, the queen of the Schön." He pressed a towel to his wound.

She sucked in a breath. He knew about the familial connection. How? Like Devyn, he should have assumed Lilica and Trinity had both been prisoners or employees at IOT.

"I supposed cousins, but didn't rule out sisters," he said. "Now I'm certain. Sisters, it is."

"You're planning to kill her." An accusation, not a question.

He answered anyway, not missing a beat. "Yes."

How easily he spoke of murder! Her hands once again curled into fists, her nails cutting into her palms, drawing blood. "In that case, my kicks aren't the only thing you should fear. I'm going to be on you every chance I get."

"Is that a threat . . . or an attempt at seduction?"

She mimicked Malevolent and snapped her teeth at him.

"Don't get me wrong," he said. "I'm totally open to seduction."

Bastard! "Good luck surviving until *one day*."

He heaved a sigh. "If you're going to start a 'taming of the shrew' role-play, you've got to set the scene for me first. Am I so afraid of you that I run away and you give chase so you can capture me and give me the tongue-lashing I so richly deserve? Or am I supposed to put up a well-intentioned but hopeless fight?" He air-quoted the word *fight*.

Frustrating bastard. Did nothing faze him?

And he wasn't even done. "Also, I should probably

have a safe word." Leaning toward her, he placed a hand at the corner of his mouth and whispered, "It's 'Beetlejuice.'"

For a woman who'd only ever dealt with scientists and orderlies who'd viewed her as a commodity—or worse, a thing—being a desirable, sexual object was new . . . and wasn't entirely unpleasant. Her heart slammed against her ribs. "Stop talking about sex. We're enemies."

"Please. We're frenemies at worst, and we're going to live together in harmony."

"Me? Live with you?" She laughed, a sound both husky and purring. "Never."

He lost his air of superiority, his eyelids growing heavy. "Your voice . . ."

The sensuality of his reaction affected *her*, making her shiver.

Keeping his gaze hot on hers, he reached toward the stove and picked up a fork already loaded with pancake. "I know you want to find Trinity as badly as I do."

"More badly." Her mouth watered as he chewed and swallowed, and she licked her lips. She didn't even care that she'd abused the English language.

He speared another forkful and, his hand trembling slightly—had she weakened him? Or had his desire done the job for her?—offered it to her. She wanted to protest. *I'll accept nothing from you!* But her stomach twisted with hunger. Devyn hadn't fed her much, preferring to keep her feeble.

Unable to resist the goodness, she snatched the utensil, devoured the bite, then went ahead and snatched the plate to polish off what remained of the pancakes.

"Was the taste to your satisfaction?" he asked, clearly trying not to grin.

Irritated with her show of fragility, she forced a casual shrug. "I've had better." *In my dreams.*

He laughed . . . and then he began a slow stalk toward her, closing what little distance there'd been between them. For the first time in her existence, she found herself backing away from an opponent, unsure how to proceed but knowing she needed space if she wanted to think clearly.

All too soon, her back hit the edge of the counter, stopping her retreat. He paused only long enough to pick up the knife she'd dropped.

She lifted her chin. "Go ahead. Cut me."

"Why? Do you crave pain?"

After everything she'd already endured in her short life? "Never."

"Then why would I cut you?"

"To torture me, of course." Why else?

"With you—with us—torture will never be on the table."

"There isn't an *us.*" She glanced at the only bay window in the kitchen, where a small, round table had been centered. "And there is *nothing* on the table."

He chuckled softly, pricking at her ire. "How about I put *you* on the table? You ate my breakfast, so you owe me another one."

As she gaped at him, he stepped closer to her; his strength enveloped her. His complete lack of fear— well, it did something to her. Amplified *her*, her blood sizzling, boiling. Bone-deep tingles raced through her before rising to caress her skin and collect within the lines of her *tätoveerimine*. The dark, glittery markings she'd had since birth. They stretched over her forehead, around her eyes, and along her sides, also around her waist and down her legs.

She gasped. This was the first time she'd ever *felt* them, which was why she'd always thought they were purely decorative. Now she wondered . . . was some alien part of her reacting to the alien part of him?

"Exquisite," he rasped, as if entranced.

Tremors caused her to sway. "What are you doing to me?"

"Hopefully the same thing you're doing to me."

She wanted so badly to lean against him. To *rub* against him. *Resist!*

"I'm ready to bargain with you, Lilica."

Her name on his lips . . . She shivered, heated another thousand degrees, but forced herself to say, "You have nothing I want." Her sister's well-being mattered more than *anything*. Always had, always would.

His smile bloomed, slow and deliberate. "I may not have something you want, sweetness, but I have something you need."

4

*F*rom the moment Dallas had sensed Lilica in the
kitchen, he'd been fighting dark, animal impulses.
He'd *never* desired a woman the way he desired her,
so the sensations couldn't be natural.

But. Oh, how he hated that stupid word. These
few minutes with her, teasing her, had proved more
entertaining than . . . absolutely anything. And far
more arousing. At one point, the designs in her skin
had glowed with soft amber light and he'd nearly
come in his pants then and there, the urge to touch
her—to get inside her—nearly irresistible.

Everything about her screamed SEX. Seductive.
Erotic. X-rated. From her voice to her scent to the
way she moved, as if she'd been created for pleasure
and no other purpose. As if she'd been created for
Dallas alone.

It was a concept his mind wholeheartedly rejected.

"What do you think I need?" she asked, with a
breathless quality added to her already raspy voice.

Every word fueled the inferno inside him.

*Do not reach down to adjust your newest erection. Do.
Not.* Her effect on him . . . had to be the power still
swirling inside her. Despite the drug Devyn had
used on her, waves of electricity rolled beneath the

surface of her skin. Dallas should probably give her a second dose, just to be safe. Her intentions toward him were malicious, no doubt about it.

But so were his intentions toward her.

He tossed the blade she'd used across the room, the tip embedding in the wall. Then he braced his hands at Lilica's sides, his fingers curving over the kitchen counter. "I can think of three things you need right off the top of my head," he said.

"Well. Let's hear them."

"A spanking, a hug, and a good hard fuck."

Her eyes—those dark, endless eyes—widened.

While she'd slept, he'd decided that the guy who didn't like to lie would put the bulk of his efforts into convincing her that he would help save Trinity. Lilica would then do one of two things: lead Dallas to Trinity, or convince Trinity to come to him. Either way, he wouldn't hesitate to shoot the Schön queen at first sight. His waking vision come to life.

Should I pat myself on the back now or later?

She trembled as she flattened her palms on his chest. He expected a push. Instead, she curled her fingers into the fabric of his shirt and asked, "You want to hug me?"

That's the one she'd focused on? Well, hell. Why not? The urge had shocked him too. Comforting wasn't in his wheelhouse. Casual sex? Absolutely. A great time? Baby, get ready. He gave more than he received. But there was something haunting—and haunted—about this particular woman. Her eyes weren't just endless, they were windows to the wounds that festered inside her. Wounds she couldn't hide. Not from him.

His Arcadian side saw far more than his human side appreciated.

What had caused those wounds? What kind of childhood had she had? As a relative of Trinity, she must have been a patient at IOT, not a staff member.

He smiled, hoping to turn up the charm. "I want to give you a *naked* hug."

Longing sparkled in her eyes, only inciting his unprecedented lust. She wanted him too. She wanted him just as intensely. The chemistry was there—and explosive.

"A naked spanking too?" she asked, even more breathless.

"Of course."

"So . . . really you think I need a fuck, a fuck, and another fuck."

Dirty words on those porn-star lips . . .

Should be illegal. "Exactly," he said.

A tremor rocked her against him—against his throbbing erection—and she licked her lips.

He swallowed a groan.

"You're thinking about sleeping with me," she said, "but you know nothing about me."

"I don't have to know you to want you."

The longing began to fizzle. "If you don't know me, you don't want *me*. Not the real me. You just want my body."

His gaze slid over her. "Can you blame me? It's a beautiful body."

Fizzle, fizzle. "Beauty fades. So do feelings."

All right. Charm wouldn't work on her. Noted. "I watched you with Devyn. In a way, I *do* know you.

You're determined, capable, lethal. You don't bow to fear, but conquer it."

A-a-a-and the longing began to intensify, making him feel as if he'd conquered the world. But quick as a snap, it fizzled again. "You plan to hurt Trinity, so I can promise you only one thing: You won't like what you learn about me."

The perfect lead-in for his plan. Time to get to work. "What would you do if I promised not to hurt her?" A promise he *could* truthfully make and actually keep. He didn't have to hurt the woman to kill her. When AIR found a way to dispose of her properly, that is.

Surprise softened Lilica's ethereal features, but she maintained her rigid stance. "I wouldn't believe you."

"Something you'll learn about me. I never lie. Weaving truth and lie is too complicated for my poor masculine brain." Exactly what he was doing right now?

"I believe *that* is the first honest thing you've said. Your poor brain." She patted the top of his head, adding, "While I admire truthfulness with every fiber of my being, I'm not blinded by it. Even liars claim they are telling the truth. The only way to stop you from hurting Trinity is to kill you, so that is what I will do."

Her admission stunned him. Why reveal her intentions? Why not try to take him by surprise?

Why was his erection now *harder*?

"She means that much to you?" he asked. "Even though she's diseased, and willingly spreads her disease to others? To innocents?"

Her gaze held his for a second longer, only to slide away . . . to hide the quick flash of guilt and remorse he'd glimpsed? "You don't know how she became diseased."

"And you do?"

In lieu of an answer, she lifted her chin.

I'll take that as a "Hell, yes." "I'm an officer of the law. An agent at AIR. Some would call me a superagent."

"By *some*, do you mean *only yourself*?"

He continued as if she hadn't spoken. "Attacking me will get you labeled a predatory alien and sign your death warrant. But hey, if you want to risk it, you should know I'm most vulnerable after sex. The stronger my orgasm, the weaker I'll be."

Her gaze whipped back to his face. She studied his lips, then his eyes, then his lips again. She gulped, the air between them thickening, crackling with awareness. Always crackling. The sweetness of her scent intensified, a delicious waft he suspected he would follow to the ends of the earth.

Already addicted . . .

"Forget Trinity," he said, his molars gnashing. Before she could protest, he added, "Just for the next few minutes." He remembered the vision he'd had of her and decided to use her own words against her. "Right now, I'm just a man, and you're just a woman."

"But you're not just a man, and I'm not just a woman."

"We're pretending." He brushed the tip of his nose against hers.

She closed her eyes, her lashes casting shadows over her cheeks, and leaned toward him, as if seeking another touch. When he gave it to her, she rewarded him with a sexy purr as arousing as a caress.

"I don't know how to pretend." Her eyelids fluttered open, revealing pools of yearning and confusion. "I don't even know why we'd want to do it."

A pang in his chest. Did she truly not know? "We pretend because it's fun . . . and we want to do it because we desire each other and we're desperate for an excuse to touch."

Her gaze returned to his lips and lingered. "I don't want you . . . shouldn't want you . . . but I *do* want to know what it's like to be kissed." She whispered the last, reverent.

She'd never been kissed? No. Hell, no. She was playing him. She had to be playing him. But he would pretend he believed her. He would do anything to learn the taste of her.

"Let me teach you how." He lowered his head, driven by an insatiable hunger he could no longer override. "If you bite me . . ."

"I won't."

"I'll probably like it," he finished. Right now, she could do no wrong.

Her breath caught, but just before his lips met hers, she placed a finger on his chin, holding him just out of reach. "This doesn't mean anything. Afterward, I *will* kill you."

"May I suggest you kill me with pleasure?" he whispered, and her finger fell away.

"Yes. Pleasure." She sounded drunk.

He pressed his mouth against hers. She opened for him eagerly, welcoming him inside, gifting him with his first taste of heaven on earth. In that moment, stroking his tongue over hers was as much about survival as pleasure. The woman *devastated* his senses, lust for her consuming him.

She leaned closer, but remained tentative, again seeking more contact with him. The action, small as it was, only inflamed him more, animal need threatening to fell him.

Slow and steady wins the race.

He gently bit her bottom lip, running the delicious little plum through his teeth. Her gasp of surprise slowed him down further, and in a moment of startling clarity, he realized she hadn't been kissing him back, had merely accepted his possession.

A stray thought jolted him. *What if she'd told the truth? What if this really is her first kiss, and she doesn't know what to do?*

No, no. Impossible. There was no way a beauty like her had gone her entire life without the attentions of a man. But his suspicions lingered. . . .

And a lance of possessiveness nearly cleaved him in two. One side would kill to keep her while the other would keep her to kill her.

Too much too fast! And yet he only wanted more. "Going to kiss you harder now." A warning.

A warning she failed to heed. "Yes . . . harder . . ."

He ate at her, and this time she responded in kind, her tongue rolling against his, her teeth biting at his lower lip, her mouth sucking on his. No finesse between them, only white-hot need, and he didn't just like it; he loved it.

"That's the way." He anchored his hands on the back of her thighs and lifted her up. "Getting me so hot."

He set her on the counter, and she moaned, her

arms and legs winding around him, her breasts smashing into his chest. Her nipples were hard little buds of arousal, creating the perfect friction every time she inhaled.

"More," she all but growled.

"Greedy girl." He tangled his fingers in her hair, and she tangled her fingers in his. She bit down on his lip with a little more force, a bead of his blood welling.

Her next moan tapered into an animalistic snarl, and the power inside her—just—exploded.

No warning. Just *whoosh!*

A second later, he was flung across the room, though he never hit the wall or even the floor, instead hovering as if suspended by invisible chains. The apartment he'd rented just for Lilica faded, and a midnight sky took shape around him—around *them*. She floated a few feet away, her eyes and strands of her hair aglow, as if the northern lights had just been made flesh. Stars fell around her, leaving rainbow-colored streaks in their wake. A clap of thunder boomed.

"What's happening?" he shouted.

"I don't know!" She cried out, her back bowing, her head thrown back.

"Lilica!" Her powers . . . she had her powers as if she'd been shot full of adrenaline . . . or intense sexual arousal—

What the hell had he done?

The rainbow lights shot out of her to coil around him; they burned and scalded him . . . before drawing him closer and closer to her . . . until they were only a whisper away from each other—then completely flush against each other. Though he fought with every bit of his considerable might, he couldn't sever the connection.

~

I'm being touched. . . . I'm touching someone else . . . touching a man.

Lilica was overcome by astonishment and joy, awe and lust. So much lust. But at the forefront of each emotion was an instinct she'd never learned, never honed, and now couldn't control. An instinct to possess. To master, to brand . . . to own.

It had started with the kiss, when Dallas had backed her into the counter and caged her in, his scent blending with hers, his gaze hot on hers, his body as hard and intractable as steel while hers softened against him, as if melting.

She'd thought, *Killing him is a must, and I will strike—later. What would it hurt to indulge my curiosity for a few seconds . . . perhaps a few minutes, to pretend just as he asked? To be touched. To touch in return.*

He was a beautiful man, the sexuality he exuded raw and in-your-face. She was drawn to it—drawn to him—and utterly captivated by his words, expressions, and thought process, desperate to experience everything he had to offer. He'd been right about that. Any excuse . . .

And she couldn't regret it. Her first kiss had come from a master. His tongue had expertly caressed hers, his body heat wrapping around her, hugging her. Her first hug too. A previously untapped and untamed ferocity had consumed her then, and she'd needed more, needed to give and to take. That's when she'd remembered something she'd read about her ancestors. How they'd bonded with their captors to save themselves.

She'd thought, *If I bond with Dallas, perhaps I can save Trinity.*

The urge to bite him had struck, so she'd bitten him. Hadn't even considered resisting. His blood—

Oh, his blood! She'd never hungered for blood before, but she thought she would now forever crave his. The power that had come with a single drop . . .

At her first taste, the drug he'd used on her had disintegrated. Just, boom, gone. She'd amphed his alien abilities without even trying and, because he'd been a part of her, she'd amphed herself in the process. They'd ended up in this strange, endless night where they were seemingly being knit together with light.

Knit together . . . bonded?

Would they now share pleasure and pain? Life and death?

No, no. Impossible. Instinct and blood couldn't bond two people . . . right?

Of course not! Especially because nothing and no one mattered more to Lilica than her sisters. They were bonded to her too, though not like this. Not this intensely.

The girls had been her only source of joy for so long—for all the days of her life, really. They loved her, and she loved them. Dallas was simply a blip, here today, gone and forgotten tomorrow.

But even as she tried to convince herself that he meant nothing, that *this* meant nothing, a deluge of memories she'd never lived began to pour inside her head. A drug-addicted mother . . . the many boy-friends the woman had entertained . . . her screams as she was beaten . . . living on the street . . . dead, she was dead . . . the little orphan boy no one wanted . . .

Fat tears rolled down Lilica's cheeks. Had she just gotten a glimpse of Dallas's childhood?

Dallas caught the tears, rubbing the moisture between his fingers. "So rarely touched . . ."

He knew. How did he know?

He must have seen into her past as well. The knowledge unsettled her. *All* of this unsettled her.

He let his arm fall to his side, and she whimpered. Anger replaced his tenderness. "Make it stop, Lilica."

"I can't. Trying . . ." However, the stars ceased to fall at last. The rainbow lights faded, but so did the darkness—until she and Dallas were once again inside the kitchen.

Now they were both sprawled on the floor.

Up, up! For one bright moment, she would be the taller of the two. She would have the position of power. Unable to catch her breath, she lumbered to her feet.

The moment ended in a snap. Dallas jumped up, a tower of menace and rage.

He closed in on her, aggression in every step. "Whatever you did to me, undo it. *Now.*"

She opened her mouth to tell him to back off, but her mind beat her to it. —*Back off!*—

"What the hell?" He ground his fists into his temples. "You spoke inside my head. How did you do that?"

What! Telepathic communication? With him? No! No, no, no. She absolutely refused. If he had access to whatever thoughts she had while they were open to each other, she would be unable to keep secrets from him, and she *had* to keep her secrets. All the secrets.

But . . . on the flip side, he would be unable to keep his secrets from her.

"You're going to tell me everything you did to me, Lilica, and exactly how to undo it."

"No, you're going to back off and ask nicely, or you're not getting *anything* from me." With her power no longer under siege, she was able to gather a powerful bolt of energy. She reached for him, ready to unleash as soon as they touched—but the power shot out of her *before* they made contact, the invisible stream launching him across the room.

He slammed into the counter, smacked into the floor, and grunted. *She* grunted too, pain suddenly ricocheting through her as if *she'd* been the one to experience impact. But even with the pain, she wasn't weakened, her power used up. No, on the contrary. She was strengthened. She'd once again amphed herself by amphing him.

They *were* bound.

Dread unfurled as the truth—and the consequences—slapped on spiked boots and danced through her head.

Dallas rolled his shoulders, shook his head. He spoke one word, only one, but it burned with enough rage to torch the entire world. "Nicely."

Well. She had to admire his unwillingness to

back down, even when circumstances continued to worsen. He was—

A deluge of information shoved its way to the forefront of her mind, claiming her focus. He was a love-'em-and-leave-'em guy. One and done. Dick it and quit it. Hit and run. Many women had accused him of having no sticking power. Many of his victims had called him the Heartless Foe, lamenting his willingness to kill for cases, pouting about his lack of concern for the people he hurt.

The knowledge boiled in her mind, as real to her as he was . . . as real as the memories she hadn't lived.

She didn't have to see into the future to know what would happen next. He would attempt to break the bond, realize he could use her to complete his mission, then actually use her. Once her sister had been defeated, he would attempt to sever the bond again, through any means necessary.

Rational of him. Can't fault him.

When he failed, and he would, he would forever resent her. Resentment she would feel through the bond.

If he killed Trinity, Lilica would resent *him*. She would kill him, even if she had to die too.

If he allowed Trinity to live, his resentment for Lilica would only grow.

Always unwanted . . .

I don't want him either. I don't! "I don't know a lot about the Falle," she said, treading carefully. "I was raised in the lab."

He blinked, shook his head again, as if surprised by his thoughts. "You weren't just raised there. You were *created* there."

How had he—

Never mind. The same way she'd known about him. "I was an experiment."

"You and your sisters."

"Yes." A spasm in her chest, a cramp in her stomach. "According to everything I've read, the Falle are able to establish bonds with others, but there's a special bond we can establish with only one person— the one we select as a mate," she added softly. She looked away, unable to meet his gaze.

Is that what I did? Selected him as my one and only?

"Mate," he grated. "Sweetness, there's no way but brutal honesty to break this to you, but I am not your mate. Not now, not ever."

"I know that," she snapped, fighting past a wave of hurt. *I don't want him either, remember?* "But it happened. It's done, and I don't know how to undo it." She threw her arms into the air. "So congratulations. You're now married to me. *Husband.*"

"Like hell. Consider yourself divorced, effective immediately."

She blew him a kiss using a single finger. The middle one. "Yes, because that's exactly how it works."

Fury blazed in those arctic eyes. "How does it work, then?"

"I told you I don't know." She drew in a heavy breath, held . . . held . . . certain of only one thing. "Unless one of us dies. Then the other will follow."

Wait. Wait! An exception to the rule teased the back of her mind—but though she concentrated, that exception remained hidden in the shadows of Dallas's deluge.

He bared his teeth in a scowl, and suddenly all she wanted to do was rip away his clothes, one passion exchanged for another. She wanted to claim his mouth in another savage kiss, wanted to bite and suck on his tongue, his lips . . . wanted to grind on him and crawl all over him. To take and take and take some more. To be the bad girl—the evil one—the doctors had always considered her.

Lady Wicked wants her man.

Maybe Dallas desired something similar. His hands clenched and unclenched at his sides, his chest rising and falling quickly but shallowly, his nostrils flared.

"Why would you do this to me?" he demanded.

"Like I had a choice," she snapped. *Did I?* Then she repeated, "It happened. Get over it, move on."

"Move on? Please, enlighten me. How am I supposed to do that while details I never learned bombard me?"

"What kinds of details?" she asked, though she already knew the answer.

"When the Falle mate, the heart of the male and the heart of the female click together like puzzle pieces, their lives forever entwined. If the two fail to consummate their unison in a timely manner, they will devolve into a monstrous state until they think of nothing but copulation, until they will do anything to screw each other—until they will slay anyone who tries to stop them."

Yes. She'd read those things in the files at the lab. And for the first time, she worried she might turn on her sisters. Just to get naked with him!

No. No! She would have sex with Dallas, and soon, so her head would remain clear. Then, despite the bond, she would figure out a way to save Trinity from him.

So. Okay. All right. She had a new mission. Seduce the prick.

He scowled and tapped his ear on his shoulder. "What?"

She bristled. "You did *not* just speak to me like—"

He held up a finger, looking preoccupied, indicating he needed a second. "Jade," he said—but not to her, she now realized. "What's her connection— never mind. The answer just came to me."

"Jade? What about her?" Lilica rushed over, fisted his shirt, and shook him. "Tell me!" But there was no need. The information filled her head. Walsh had attacked IOT. Jade was injured. An agent named John had saved her.

The front door of the apartment slammed open, jolting them both. Without hesitation, Dallas shoved her behind him and grabbed a pyre-gun from somewhere underneath the kitchen counter.

Protecting and shielding me?

Shock and pleasure battled for supremacy.

Concentrate! The apartment had an open concept, allowing anyone standing in the living room to see directly into the kitchen, and vice versa. Horror slashed at her forced calm when she spotted Dr. Walsh. He was a monster. His once sun-drenched skin was now gray and oozed pus. His thick cap of hair had fallen out, half his scalp hanging down one side of his face.

Here to kill me?

"Don't move," she shouted, using compulsion as she stalked forward.

He moved, baring crimson-stained teeth in a parody of a smile. He lifted a skinny arm to point a gnarled finger in her direction. "Mine." Even his voice had changed. It was deeper than before, harder, as if it had been forged in the bowels of hell.

Dallas gripped her bare wrist and yanked her back into place, as if he didn't want another man to see her in her bra and panties. "She's *mine.*" He aimed the gun and fired off a shot, a beam of blue light nailing Walsh in the chest. The former doctor—former human!—merely stumbled back a few steps, the new gaping wound sizzling and steaming.

I'm his? "I just need to touch him," she told Dallas. "I'll tell him to die, and our problem will be solved." Except that Walsh no longer had a life force. He was *already* dead. Would compulsion *ever* work on him again?

"You're not touching him." In a single heartbeat, Dallas shot a circle around her. The floorboards, support beams, and insulation burned, ash swiftly rising up to choke her.

His thoughts were now blocked. "What are you—" The floor gave and with a scream, she dropped with it.

She landed inside another apartment, air gusting from her lungs, her knees buckling. She rolled out of the way, expecting Dallas to jump down and join her.

He didn't. But he did open his mind again, probably unwittingly, allowing his plan to crackle through the bond. He would stay behind, fight Walsh, find a way to free himself from Lilica, then kill Trinity.

Well, good luck with that. Lilica leaped to her feet.

The owner of the apartment raced around the corner, took one look at the damage to her home, and shrieked.

Part of Lilica shouted: *Dress, return to Dallas, help him.* The other part demanded she leave now, now, now, while he couldn't do anything to stop her. She would find Jade and make sure her sister was okay.

Yes. That one. Lilica rushed past the woman. She entered the first bedroom she came across and grabbed two pieces of clothing from a dresser. Then, dressing along the way, she sprinted into the hall, down the stairs, out of the building, and into the evening darkness.

5

*M*onster-man pawed a bare foot over the floor, preparing to attack.

Dallas had two options: stay and fight him, now that Lilica was out of the danger zone, or chase Lilica before she managed to drop off the grid.

The problem? If Dallas found her, Monster-man could find her. So, no contest, really. Dallas would fight.

"Mine," the bastard repeated.

The name *Walsh* drifted through Dallas's mind, startling him. Another of Lilica's memories?

With a roar, the creature rushed him. No, not him. Monster-man had his gaze locked on the hole in the floor. He intended to follow Lilica through, didn't he?

Rage surged through Dallas. He dove at Walsh, shoving him in the opposite direction. They slammed into a counter, pieces of rotted flesh falling from the bastard and adhering to Dallas. Disgusting!

Maintaining his grip on his gun, he stood and kicked Walsh in the stomach.

"What's going on?" Devyn demanded through the internal cell phone.

The Targon had called to tell him about the other sister, Jade. Although Devyn didn't yet know Jade was fruit from the same tree. Dallas wasn't sure how, exactly, he himself knew. Or how he also knew that Monster-man used to be a doctor at IOT, responsible for the care and feeding of the eldest Swan triplet. Trinity, Lilica's full-blood sister.

No wonder she hoped to save the diseased girl.

"Dallas. An answer, if you please."

Right. "I'm dealing with John's problem. Give me a minute."

As Dallas pistol-whipped and kicked, more facts swam through his mind. Lilica had once commanded Walsh to kill himself and his colleagues, and the compulsion to obey had been so strong, he'd risen from his grave.

I'm actually fighting the living dead. At least the creature wasn't contagious like Trinity.

"Why are you after Lilica?" Pistol-whip. "She isn't your colleague." Kick.

Good old-fashioned vengeance? Or had his rotting brain gotten stuck on the kill setting?

Walsh swung a meaty fist at Dallas. He didn't even try to dodge, using the opportunity to shove the barrel of his gun into the bastard's mouth. With a jerk of his thumb, he dialed the weapon to his favorite setting: play and spray. Then he squeezed the trigger.

Whoosh!

The back of Walsh's skull popped off, splattering pieces of bone and bits of tissue across the kitchen.

Unfazed, Walsh threw a punch. For a moment, Dallas saw stars.

"So? Who's winning?" Devyn asked, and it sounded like he was eating an apple.

"Shut up." Pain exploded through Dallas's head as he took a blow to the cheek. "Tell me how to kill a zombie."

"Which do you prefer? Shut up or tell you? You can't have both."

"Devyn!"

"Fine. You have to eat his brains. Wait. Abort mission! That's what you do if *you're* a zombie."

"Funny." He worked his legs up, flattened his booted feet on Walsh's chest, and kicked. "Any other suggestions?"

"You have to decapitate him."

Walsh collided into the kitchen counter again, but quickly jumped to his feet and tried to dive through the hole in the floor.

"The zombie is my favorite sexual position, you know." Ice clinked in a glass as Devyn paused to take a sip. "I just lie back and let myself get eaten."

Dallas fisted the back of Walsh's shirt, stopping him. Barely. "Can the jokes wait? I'm fighting for my life here."

"But I wasn't joking."

He tried to tug Walsh backward, but the shirt tore, and Walsh fell through the hole at last, crash-landing in the apartment below.

Without a moment's hesitation, Dallas followed him through.

Monster-man was crouched on all fours by the time Dallas smashed into him. Walsh thumped against the floor while impact did nothing but shake Dallas's knees. Apparently zombies made excellent cushions.

A human female screamed obscenities at them,

her fear and distress only intensifying as Dallas pressed the barrel of his gun against Walsh's shoulder and, in less than a second, fired off three consecutive blasts. The male's arm detached.

Walsh bucked him off and bolted to his feet. He swung around to throw another punch. But without his dominant arm, his body merely jerked. Frowning, he kicked Dallas in the face. Brain and skull went head-to-head, and skull won.

Pounding footsteps echoed as Walsh raced to the door—and burst through it.

Wonderful. Dallas pursued, the only person in history ever to run *at* a zombie. He caught up at the bank of elevators and jumped on Walsh's back, taking him to the ground. He kept his arm extended, shooting at Walsh's ankle as they fell. Upon landing, the foot detached.

"Are you done yet?" Devyn yawned.

"No! Why don't you make yourself useful and hack into—"

"Like I haven't done so. I'm watching you through security cameras right now. You need to shower, by the way. In bleach."

Walsh lumbered to his feet—foot—and hobbled to the stairwell door to sniff. Did he smell roses and aged firewood?

Dallas hopped up and threw himself into Monsterman yet again. They smashed into the door and ricocheted backward. This time, the gun fell from Dallas's grip. Oh, well. Both hands now free, he gripped Walsh by the shoulders and rolled, slinging him overhead.

Ding.

The elevator doors slid open. The people inside caught sight of the pus-covered agent and his one-armed, one-footed victim and gasped with horror. Most smashed themselves against the far wall. One pressed all the buttons on the panel in an attempt to escape.

Walsh leaped up and stomped on Dallas as he returned to the stairwell. But Dallas clasped his ankle, tripping him, and scrambled to his feet. He performed the only move available to him and kicked Walsh between the legs; slippery with pus and bodily fluids, the creature slipped forward. Another kick, this one stronger, and Walsh slid across the floor until his head and shoulders were inside the still-open elevator, the rest of him outside of it.

Dallas didn't have to issue a command to Devyn. His friend knew him well, and had already guessed what he wanted. *Click, click, click.* The sounds of fingers tapping against a keyboard to override security settings filled his head.

The elevator doors shut before Walsh was able to stand and, with the sensors now turned off, sliced him in two.

Click, click, click.

Ding.

The door opened again, revealing Monster-man's severed head . . . and the screaming people inside in the cart.

"Clean up on aisle five," he muttered, kicking the motionless body out of the way.

"I already called your boss," Devyn replied. "She should be there any—"

The door to the stairwell swung open, Mia Snow soaring into the hall, a pyre-gun aimed and ready. Her black hair was pulled back in a ponytail, nothing hiding her lovely features and the determination painted all over them.

"Thanks for nothing," he told her as he held up Walsh's severed head. The small patch of hair couldn't carry the weight, the follicles ripping free. The head fell to the floor.

Walsh's mouth continued to move, the word "mine" leaving him again and again.

He still lived?

"I told you. *Mine*." Dallas stomped on the creature's face. Rotted bones caved easily, leaving only fetid pulp. "What's the old saying? Bad enough to gag a maggot."

"A-a-a-nd this is where I say good-bye." The call with Devyn ended.

As field agents got to work, calming the humans, cleaning up the mess, Mia looked Dallas over. Her eyes—as blue as Dallas's own, as *Arcadian* as Dallas's own—twinkled merrily. "I've always wanted to say this and mean it, and now I can. You disgust me."

"I disgust myself. I definitely need to be decontaminated." He swiped up his pyre-gun. Every instinct he possessed screamed, *Go after Lilica. Now!* But he resisted. He could find her any day, anytime, he realized, her current location like a beacon in his mind. She was headed to IOT, hoping to check on Jade.

There was no place she could hide from him. And the fault was hers. She'd bonded them, becoming the author of her own downfall.

The bond! That was how he'd known so much about Walsh, Trinity, and Jade.

Well, well. The bond wasn't such a hardship, after all. At least for now.

Go get your woman!

No. Not yet. First, he was going to shower. In bleach, as Devyn had recommended. Then he was going to do more research on the Falle. Then and only then would he track down his supposed wife. What he'd do to her when he reached her—well, only time would tell.

The night's shadows concealed Lilica as she made her way to the institute. The farther she was from Dallas, the more intensely her body ached, as if every cell already missed him. Which was pure craziness! But even worse was the pain that had just exploded through her cheek and jaw, as if she'd run into a wall. Not the pain itself, but the tormented thoughts that had accompanied it.

Had she just experienced *Dallas's* pain? Was he all right?

Determined, she ignored the sensations and thoughts and increased her speed. Unlike her previous foray into this unknown world, no one stopped to point or laugh at her. But only because they couldn't see her.

A few minutes ago she'd reached out to Jade, and this time her telepathic power had worked. But her sister had yet to reply.

Fear bombarded her. If Walsh had slain sweet, tormented Jade . . .

I will burn this world to the ground.

She increased her pace yet again. IOT was head-quartered at the far edge of No Man's Land, where the air was so acidic humans couldn't visit without wearing masks and bodysuits. Some alien races thrived there and lived within the surrounding build-ings, but none of the otherworlders dared approach the institute. They'd heard the rumors. Go inside, never come out.

On the outside, her home looked to be an aban-doned warehouse with walls made of beat-to-hell metal. On the inside, everything was state-of-the-art, the interior walls made of an alien metal stronger than titanium. Nothing passed through the doors without permission, not even a slight breeze. Well, except Devyn. And Walsh. And someone named John, apparently.

Lilica could withstand the acidic air, but not for long. Right now, too much of her flesh was exposed. She wore two short-sleeved T-shirts. One as in-tended, while the other was tied around her waist, pretending to be a skirt. Next time she needed cloth-ing, she'd do a better job stealing.

By the time she completed the palm-print ID, the front door sliding open to welcome her inside the purification sector of the building, her eyes, nose, and throat were raw and bleeding.

The pain lessened as a cool, scentless mist sprayed every inch of her.

"Purification complete," an automated voice an-nounced.

Another door opened, this one leading deeper inside. Ah, home sweet home.

There were only three floors. Trinity had been kept up top, Jade in the middle, and Lilica at the bottom. Their bedrooms had differed greatly. Trinity had enjoyed a luxurious suite fit for a princess. Jade had a bedroom with minimal comforts, while Lilica had a closet without windows. Her only furnishings were a cot and a bucket.

The difference in bedrooms had been one of a million tests. Would living conditions influence a person's personality?

The doctors had concluded: yes.

The bottom floor also contained the main laboratory and multiple cages, used for any other test subjects who had been brought in. A.k.a the otherworlders the triplets had used to hone their superpowers.

Simply more tests, Lilica now knew.

The middle floor held the viewing rooms, where most testing had been done. The top floor had been reserved for bedrooms. Some employees had lived here while others had stayed for extended periods.

"Jade," Lilica called.

No response.

She flew down the halls, searching every room. No sign of her sister.

With a scream of frustration, she banged her fist into the wall. The action unleashed memories that had been stored in the back of her mind. *Dallas's* memories. No! Not here, not now. She had to focus on finding Jade.

She rubbed her fists into her eyes and pulled at hanks of her hair, but the memories remained front and center, demanding her attention.

A little boy with dark hair and dark eyes kicked his way out of a locked cupboard to crouch over his mother's bleeding and broken body. He sobbed as he pulled a blanket around her, his tears splashing over her swollen face. Earlier a man had pounded at their door, insisting rent be paid. She'd forced the boy inside the cupboard and told him to be still and quiet or he would be in big trouble. Then she'd let the man inside their home.

She'd begged for more time, and the man had agreed . . . and then he'd told her to take off her clothes. The sounds that had followed confused and upset the boy, but he hadn't attempted to free himself until his mother had cried, "No," and the man had laughed again.

Fast-forward. The little boy was being kicked and punched by a drunken older man. Blood trickled from his mouth, his head throbbing, but tears never welled in his eyes. He accepted the abuse as his due. This was his life now. If he hadn't called the ambulance the night his mother had been beaten by their landlord, if he hadn't told the police what he'd overheard, if he'd just taken care of his mom himself—taken care of the *landlord* himself—they would have been living at home rather than fighting to survive on the streets.

Fast-forward. The little boy had a new home now. An orphanage. A group of older boys circled him, calling him mean names while throwing bits of food at him. Still he didn't cry. He didn't deserve the sweet release tears would offer. He held up his chin instead, once again accepting the abuse as his due. His mother—a back-alley whore, the boys called her—had been found dead only a few weeks ago. The scene backtracked.

I have more boyfriends than other women, she'd once told him, her eyes darkening with pain, shame, and remorse. *That's all.*

When she hadn't returned home for dinner, he'd gone looking for her. He'd come across a crowd of people blocked by a police banner, and he'd known. Momma was dead. After the cops had questioned him, he'd overheard them talking to a homeless man who'd witnessed everything. A john hadn't wanted to pay her after having sex, so he'd killed her instead.

Fast-forward. The little boy was an adult now. Agent Dallas Gutierrez. He lay dying in a pool of his own blood. He'd taken pyre-fire meant for his partner. A woman he loved like the sister he'd never had but had always wanted. He was rushed to the hospital, but no one could help him. He'd reached the end of his life, and he knew it.

The partner, Mia Snow, never allowed herself to cry either. Not until that moment. A tear had slid down her cheek. She hadn't realized the king of the Arcadians watched her, a witness to her despair; it had touched both men deeply, irrevocably. When finally she left the hospital room, the Arcadian had fed Dallas blood straight from his vein. *Royal* blood. Powerful.

Dallas had gasped, his eyelids popping open—eyes changed from brown to arctic blue, he'd realized the first time he peered into a mirror.

Emotions flooded Lilica, sorrow quickly claiming the lead. The pain Dallas had endured throughout his life . . . the guilt he still carried and hid behind a charming smile . . .

Like her, he'd known isolation and disappointment time and time again. She wanted so badly to hug him, to comfort him as she'd never been hugged or comforted.

Can't worry about him right now. Must find Jade.

She increased security and turned on every alarm. Devyn would not be sneaking in again. And if Dallas managed to find her . . .

Still not going to worry about him.

Throughout the night, she sent countless telepathic messages to her sister. All went unheeded. In the morning, exhausted and despondent, she showered and dressed in a clean shirt and pants, hiding weapons in select places. She ate as much breakfast as she could stomach, knowing she needed to keep up her strength.

—Jade, come on! Where are you?—

Again, there was only silence.

At least she knew beyond a doubt that Dallas had survived Walsh's attack. Otherwise she would have died with him. Had he gone to work, Lilica written off as a nuisance? Probably. The bastard! Otherwise he would have found her and attempted to break in.

Well, he wouldn't be able to forget her for long. The bond would compel him to spend time with her, to want her, as surely as her voice had once compelled Walsh.

What would he think of her home?

She hated the fact that he'd probably already seen it, reliving her memories as if they were his own, the same way she'd relived his. Her stomach churned. Did he now pity her?

She scaled the stairs to the top floor, deciding she'd pack a bag and head out. *She* would go to *him*. He could put her in touch with John, who could tell her about Jade. Yes. Perfect plan. If he happened to make a pass at her—

She turned the corner and came face-to-face with Dallas. He wore a clean black T-shirt and black pants, his strength on perfect display. Shock jolted her.

He arched a brow at her, smug and beautiful, and her heart raced as if she'd just been injected with adrenaline. "Hello, Lilica."

Just. Like. That. Her panties were soaked, desire for him a triple jab—one to the chest and two to her still-churning stomach. Tremors nearly rocked her off her feet. "How did you get in here?"

"Apparently there are times I know everything you know. I simply disabled the alarms."

But . . . but . . .

"Are you going to collapse with joy? You look like you're going to collapse."

His smugness snapped her out of her daze. "Yes, I'm going to collapse. Catch me?" The moment he was within reach, she'd strike!

"Now, now. Plotting my harm is low, even for you. Wouldn't you agree . . . wife?"

6

The woman reduced him to a state of desperation. She'd showered, damp hair hanging in silken waves, the ends curling at her waist. Her black-as-night irises were still lit up like the northern lights, as if she'd brought the illuminations with her. As if she'd become part of the universe—or the very heart of his.

The glittery marks in her ebony skin began to glow again. Muted, but noticeable.

He wanted to lick those marks.

There was a bruise on her left cheek and another on the right side of her jaw. Usually she healed quickly—he knew through memories of her life. Memories he shouldn't possess. Usually *he* healed quickly, but he bore the same bruises on *his* cheek and jaw.

What happened to him would now happen to her, he realized. On the flip side, what happened to her would now happen to him. Their bond should have complemented their individual abilities but had somehow tempered them.

Anger now sparked. He lived a dangerous life, which meant *she* now lived a dangerous life. No matter where she was or what she did.

Another complication arose. To save her sister

from his murderous clutches, she could easily kill him by killing herself.

Would she try?

No, highly doubtful. He knew her better now. Those memories he'd never lived had invaded his head all night. He'd managed to suppress most of them, but a few had weaseled past his defenses.

When her creators had punished her, strapping her to a bed and hitting her with a cattle prod, she hadn't responded with despair. She'd responded with determination.

She'd thought: *I will survive. I will not be defeated.*

He'd been filled with awe—such strength!—and with rage. If Walsh hadn't already killed the staff, Dallas would have added their severed heads to his collection, mounting them on his wall.

But . . . he tried to read her now and came up empty.

She lifted her chin, a captivating mix of longing and rebellion. "I'm not your wife."

"I would have sworn you told me our divorce hadn't yet gone through."

"We'll find a way to negate the bond. Isn't that what *you* said?"

He offered a clipped nod. It was indeed what he'd said, and what he still wanted. Which was one of the reasons he'd fought her memories so diligently. The more he knew about her, the harder a separation would be. Already he wished he could fuse her to his side and protect her from any—every—hurt.

"Where were you going in such a hurry?" he asked.

"You mean you don't know?"

"I can't read you right now." He'd done his research. Extreme emotion slowed the flow of information that passed between them. Extreme arousal too. If he wanted to keep his secrets, he would need to keep her aroused.

Such a dirty job.

Secrets could also be buried. After the initial exchange of memories, only the information they specifically pondered while in each other's presence would flow through the bond.

"Where were you going?" he asked again.

"To find you."

Truth or lie? He would have liked to know *that* through the bond.

She wrung her hands. "I haven't been able to reach Jade. Do you know where she is?"

"Yes. She's somewhere else."

She closed the distance to fist his shirt and shake him. "Tell me, Dallas."

His name on those two-thousand-dollar-an-hour lips . . . better than a stream of dirty words. He was hard as a rock in seconds . . . and she was close enough to rub against. So close he could feel the heat pulsing off her lithe body.

"Jade is injured but recovering in a secret location, where she's being guarded."

"*Still* injured? Tell me *everything*!"

The worry on her face softened the worst of his anger. "I don't know the specifics of her wound, and the guard is a black ops agent called John No Last Name."

She lifted her chin. "Is Jade to be bait for Trinity too?"

So. She'd picked up on his plan to lure Trinity out of hiding and end her reign of terror without hurting her. *Lost my edge.*

He changed the subject, gritting out, "You left me behind to deal with Walsh on my own."

"Uh, yeah. I'm evil. That's what I do." She chewed on her bottom lip. "But thank you."

The rest of his anger faded. Evil. The doctors had called her Little Wicked as a child and Lady Wicked as an adult. All part of an experiment. By calling her evil and making her believe it, they postulated whether they could predict how she would react to certain situations. She knew what they'd done, and why, but mental knowledge wasn't the same as heart acceptance.

"You aren't evil, Lilica."

"Yes, I am." The lights in her eyes brightened, swirling with the gale force of wind he couldn't feel. "I kill without remorse."

"So do I."

"Yes, but you do it to protect humans. I do it *just because.*"

He cursed. She knew every aspect of his past, didn't she? She'd seen his memories the way he'd seen hers. "Did you kill anyone on your way here?"

Offended, she practically spit at him. "No."

"Then you don't kill *just because.* You *used to* kill, when you were told to do so or suffer the consequences. You had a reason. You hoped to protect yourself and your sisters."

She opened her mouth, closed it with a snap. He knew she wanted to refute him, to call him a liar, but she couldn't. The bond . . .

"You're welcome by the way," he said. "Walsh is dead. Again."

"How do you know he won't—never mind. You chopped off his head with an elevator."

Had he sent the image into her mind?

She backed away from him, and he nearly shouted a command for her return. "I won't let you end Trinity," she said.

"She's diseased. A predator." He wouldn't lie to her about that. Not because she would sense the truth, but because he respected her. Warrior to warrior, he tried to make her understand. "She purposely infects innocents, and there's no cure for her or for them."

Desperation darkened her features. "I'll keep her locked up. I won't let her hurt—"

"That's not an option. You don't have the resources to deal with her. If she isn't allowed to purge, the disease will strengthen inside her and kill her." AIR had locked up a handful of her victims and learned that truth at a high cost. "Then it will escape her and find a new host. She must be contained *the right way* until we find a way to destroy the disease. By taking her in, I'll be doing the world a favor. And when the time comes to kill her, I will do so humanely."

Her shoulders rolled in, and she whispered, "My sisters are all I have."

Her look, her tone . . . everything about her caused his heart to crack straight down the center. Part of him longed to tell her: *You have me now.*

He ran his tongue over his teeth. *Not going there.*

Her eyes widened. "Not going where?"

"Nothing. And I'm sorry you're going to suffer when she dies, sweetheart, but I won't change course. I can't. There's no other way."

Lilica drew in a deep breath, held it, then slowly released it. Dallas was somehow more beautiful to her right now, and it actually hurt to look at him. But it hurt to look away from him too. Like, her ovaries were seriously considering exploding.

The worst part? Desire for him no longer felt like a want but a need, as he'd once tried to tell her.

She had to save her sister. Through any means necessary.

Not all means have to be foul. . . .

She peered deep into his eyes, trying not to lose herself in his rugged masculinity. "You will not hurt my sisters," she said, using what remained of her power to compel him.

He simply arched a brow in a way she now despised. "So. You're able to compel."

Ugh! He was one hundred percent immune, most likely because of the bond.

There had to be another way to get what she wanted from him.

Sex? What about sex?

Her ovaries decided, yes, they would go ahead and explode.

"Vow to convince AIR to let Trinity live," she said, "and I'll give myself to you." *Gladly.*

He hungered for her the way she hungered for him; she knew he did. Others might see a freak when looking at her, but he saw a sex kitten ready to be stroked.

The knowledge flummoxed her . . . thrilled and delighted her.

His eyes narrowed to tiny slits. "As much as I want you, and I do want you, I'm going to decline. The moment we have sex, the bond will solidify."

He'd just . . . rejected her?

The realization stung in ways she'd never imagined possible. Which was odd. She'd been rejected the whole of her life. By the institute's employees, but also by the people she'd met upon her escape. This was just more of the same.

So why did it feel so different? So personal?

Wait. The bond hadn't yet solidified? "There's a way to break the bond?" He shouldn't know more about her race than she did.

He offered one of those clipped nods. "Over the next few weeks, we're going to become little more than animals who need to rut, but only with each other. If we can resist, the bond will fade and eventually disintegrate completely."

He wanted the bond to disintegrate. And so did she. Really. Truly. But . . .

Deep down, she also wanted to keep the man she'd chosen. Whether or not she'd chosen him wittingly or unwittingly. How was she supposed to give him up?

Um, quite easily! He was Trinity's future killer.

"You think you can resist me while you're in an

animal state?" she asked, her gaze stroking over him. He had a hard-on.

"I don't think. I know."

His plan drifted through her mind: *lock Lilica away until Trinity is dead.*

The coldhearted intention fueled her rage. No. Hell, no. She pounded her fists into his chest. She would never be locked away again. She would fight to the death to maintain her freedom.

He caught her by the wrists. "This. This is why I want nothing to do with your bond. I have no secrets."

"Your secrets are so unoriginal, I could have guessed!"

A stream of curses. The connection between them had gone quiet, no new information flowing.

Once upon a time, alone in her closet of a bedroom, she'd dreamed of sharing her life and her secrets with a man. He would love her and be loved by her. He would touch her *all the time* and welcome her hands on him. They would always be together, never alone.

But Dallas craved his solitude. And if he ever *did* decide to settle down and start a family, it would be with a short, curvy blonde. Someone sweet, with an easy smile. The kind of woman he wanted to want but didn't, not really.

Well, that short, curvy blonde didn't have a sister to save. If Lilica could get him to solidify the bond with her, he would never want to hurt her, mentally, physically, or emotionally, because hurting her would hurt him.

Her rage subsided. His must have as well. They

peered at each other. She began to pant. He began to sweat. She licked her lips, and his gaze followed her tongue. Then he sucked in a sharp breath.

"You've got a picture of another man in your mind." He barked the words. "Who is he?"

Her eyes widened. He was jealous of her dream man?

"I'm not jealous," he grated.

He was. He really, really was.

I've so got this.

Any means necessary . . .

Though Lilica had never seduced anyone, Dallas had often been seduced. Through a new flood of memories, she detected a common thread. Nakedness. Not just the act of being naked, but the act of *getting* naked.

This is going to be as easy as taking candy from . . . anyone.

Peering into that gorgeous arctic gaze, she hooked her fingers on the hem of her shirt and lifted.

He stopped breathing altogether. "What are you doing?"

"What does it look like I'm doing? Getting more comfortable." She unfastened her bra, tossed the material aside, and shimmied out of her pants so that only her panties remained.

As she straightened to her full height, shoulders back to properly display her breasts, he took a step toward her. Stopped. Took another step forward.

At war with his desires? Desires now clouding the bond. Once again, she couldn't read him.

"Do you want to touch me?" she asked, cupping her breasts. Her thumbs traced over her puckered nipples. Like the *tätoveerimine*, they possessed a glittery sheen, and they throbbed oh, so deliciously. "Perhaps I'll even let you taste me."

Agony tightened his features. "Don't you dare . . . put your clothes back on."

Feminine power flooded her—remade her. This man—this beautiful, perfect man—couldn't get enough of her.

Not you, the bond.

Whatever. She rested her hands at the waist of her underwear. "What about these? Should I take them off?"

"Yes," he croaked. "Off. Now."

Candy. Anyone.

But beneath her confidence was a yearning she couldn't deny, and she trembled as she drew the material down her legs. She kicked, the panties soaring. He caught them in a single fluid motion, his gaze never leaving her, but roving over her, as languid as a caress. Where he looked, she tingled and ached worse.

She traced her fingertips down her stomach, circled her navel, and delved between her legs, a moan parting her lips. A groan parted his. He closed the rest of the distance in seconds, invading her personal space.

"I was your first kiss." His voice was part pride, part demand. "I will be your first lover. Your only."

The words shook her to the core.

A handful of orderlies had attempted to start something with her, but she'd never known what was an experiment and what wasn't, and she'd never wanted to be filmed during an intimate moment.

And she would have been. Here, the cameras had never ceased to record.

"But I won't be *your* first." She cringed when she heard the pout in her tone. But how could she *not* pout? Other women had put their hands and mouths on her property.

He's my property now?

Only doing this for Trinity, remember?

Scowling, Dallas cupped her shoulders, the skin-to-skin contact electrifying her, desire vibrating inside her veins. He spun her, placing her back against his chest, and said, "Even though you're only using me, I'm sorry."

Heat spread across her cheeks. Both sets. "You don't need to apologize for having past lovers. You were living your life."

"Not sorry that I was with other women. One day, you'll even thank me for the things I learned. I'm sorry about *this*." He pinched her nose and held her mouth closed with one hand while restraining her with the other. "I'd use another sedative on you, but I'm not sure how *I'll* react to it."

What . . . why . . . bastard!

She fought him, cursing how easily he'd kept his actions hidden from the bond, but no matter how hard she bucked and clawed, he maintained his hold. A hold he should have softened as he experienced her emotions—or if he'd felt any remorse or guilt. But the only thing he projected at her was cold, hard determination.

Hope you pass out too, she mentally screamed at him. Then darkness descended, and she knew nothing more.

7

*L*ilica." Her sister's voice called to her from the abyss. "Lilica."

Lilica blinked open her eyes to find a thick white mist surrounded her. She frowned, confused and a little light-headed, and realized she wore a T-shirt, bra, and pair of panties. More than she'd had on before she'd passed out.

Passed out . . .

Dallas! The callous bastard had knocked her out.

Then, through the tendrils of mist, she spotted Jade.

"Jade!" Already on her feet, she glided forward. "Are you hurt?"

Jade pulled at the collar of her shirt, revealing bruises around her neck. "Walsh tried to choke me out, but I'm healing."

As children they'd learned not to touch each other. And even after gaining their freedom, when the rules had no longer applied, they'd kept each other at a distance. But in that moment, Lilica couldn't stop herself from wrapping the stunning beauty with skin the color of a fern and hair as white as snow in her arms. The sweet scent of sugarplums helped anchor her. Jade's scent.

"Where are we?" she asked.

"This is the spirit world in existence around the natural world. I found you and pulled your spirit from your body."

Spirit world? Frowning, Lilica eased back, though she maintained a tight hold on her sister lest the girl float away. "We're dead?"

"Not even close. I've learned a lot these past few days. A person—whether human or otherworlder—is first and foremost a spirit. A spirit has a soul and lives in a body. Your spirit is your battery, or power source. Your soul is your mind, will, and emotions. And your body is the house that moors you to the natural world. With a little help, your spirit can leave its house for a short period of time. It's called spirit walking."

Fascinating. No telling what Lilica would have done if she'd known about this . . . if she'd been able to move between the realms of the living and the dead, the daydream and the nightmare . . . when the doctors had lived.

"How did you acquire the ability to spirit-walk?"

Jade fluffed her hair. "I borrowed the ability from my *protector*." Like Trinity, she could steal a life force, even a specific ability. Unlike Trinity, she couldn't steal a life force or ability in its entirety. She always left pieces behind, and whatever she took always returned to its owner a day or two later. "His name is John. He's a Rakan."

Rakans. Golden ones, they were called, once hunted like the Forførn. Their pelts were made of malleable gold, the purest form this world had ever seen. "If he's harmed you . . ."

"No. He's actually been quite . . . gentle with me. When he can actually bring himself to touch me." Bitterness seeped from her sister's voice. "Contact with me literally makes him vomit."

Because he considered her a freak? Anger bloomed. "I will *murder* him."

"No. No." Jade shook her head, white tresses dancing over her shoulders. "He's built so many internal defenses, I can't read his thoughts or his future. For the first time in my life, I'm experiencing peace and quiet. I'll endure *anything* to stay with him."

Well. That, Lilica understood. The way Dallas affected her . . . she hated it, but she kind of loved it too.

"I'm here because I had to know you're all right." Jade squeezed her hands. "John told me Walsh found you."

"I'm fine, and Walsh is dead."

"Truly?"

She nodded, a sense of pride welling inside her. "Dallas—*my* protector—killed him." *My protector . . . and my tormentor.*

Next time she wouldn't give him an opportunity to strike at her. She would not allow him near her until he would do anything, sacrifice anything, to get inside her.

Dallas . . . inside me . . .

She shivered, excitement waking up every nerve ending in her body, making her ache from head to toe.

"I tried to reach out to you," she said, doing her best to maintain a neutral expression, "but I was drugged and failed. When the drugs wore off, I tried again but failed again."

"I wonder if John is somehow stopping *all* tele-pathic communications." Jade pursed her lips. "We'll worry about that later. Right now, there's something I have to tell you."

Just then, Lilica was certain she was seeing the Maleahdolla part of her sister's DNA. Unwavering determination peered at her through eyes of emerald green. "What is it?"

"I found Trinity. This spirit world . . . I can *see* the ties between us, tattered though they are, and I fol-lowed the one I still have to her."

What! After three years without a word from their eldest sister, Jade had found her? Just like that? "Why do you sound upset? This is wonderful news."

"No. It's terrible. She's not the girl we remember, Lil. She's changed. She's . . . darker." Jade shuddered.

"I don't care. She's still our Trinity." The girl who'd offered to take a beating for her. Someone as starved for affection as they were. Tormented by a past they couldn't change. A by-product of the hor-rendous things they'd all been forced to do. "We can help her." They *had* to help her.

"She doesn't want to be helped."

"You've talked to her?"

Tears welled in Jade's eyes, spilled down her cheeks, and the sight hurt Lilica on a cellular level. "I pulled her spirit into this place"—she motioned to the mist—"before I pulled yours."

Feeling as if she'd just been dipped in acid, Lilica croaked, "Her disease." *Can't lose them both.*

Can't lose either one!

"You can be around her without becoming infected.

The disease isn't airborne or even passed through casual contact."

"You're sure?"

A confident nod. "I read her mind."

Lilica chewed on her bottom lip, a habit she'd only recently developed. "She didn't want to stay here? Didn't want to see me?" How needy she sounded. But she didn't care. Lilica had missed Trinity as intensely as she would miss a limb, had been fighting to save her life, and her eldest sis couldn't be bothered to say hello?

Jade's shoulders hunched. "I'm sorry."

Another rejection. This one almost drilled her to her knees. She had to curb the urge to scream up at the skies, to shake her fists in the air. *Why does no one want me?*

"Pull her spirit again," she said. Maybe . . . maybe the disease had affected Trinity's mind. Maybe it had spoken for her. Maybe she just needed a reminder of Lilica's love. "Yes? But don't tell me where you find her." She could inadvertently reveal the location to Dallas.

Jade hesitated, clearly uneasy, but ultimately she nodded. "All right. Wait here." She closed her eyes— and vanished.

Both eager and overcome by nerves, Lilica paced. If Trinity rejected her to her face, fine. Whatever. She would deal. But she wouldn't abandon her sister. *Nope. Not me.* She would continue to fight to give Trinity a better life. Or any life at all. And somehow, some way, she would find a way to cleanse Trinity of the Schön.

The records at IOT claimed the Schön king had died the instant Trinity stole his life force. Because he had been dependent on the parasite, or because of a reason she couldn't yet comprehend?

If the parasite remained separate from Trinity, simply living off her, its dark influence could be cleaved; it could be removed and killed without killing Trinity. In theory. The doctors had left notes in their files and had hypothesized the same. But they hadn't known how to remove or kill it.

Had Trinity stuck around the lab, the doctors had planned to force Jade to steal as much of the Schön as possible, and use her as a guinea pig, testing different possible cures on her. If Jade had died when the Schön had died, well, they would have still had Trinity, the star pupil.

Thanks to Walsh, the doctors had gotten what they'd deserved!

Jade finally reappeared in the center of the mist, with Trinity at her side.

Lilica stopped, her knees nearly buckling, her heart swelling with a sudden burst of love. She wanted to rush over, hug and shake her eldest sister . . . but she planted her feet firmly in place.

Shouldn't overwhelm her.

She studied the piece of her heart she hadn't seen for so long. The fact that all three girls had sprung from the same egg was even less apparent now that they were adults. They differed in every area. Hair and eye color. Skin and height. Even body type.

Trinity wore a lacy bra and panty set, revealing lush curves meant for seduction. With her blond ringlets, thickly lashed sapphire eyes, and pretty pink cheeks, she was more gorgeous than ever.

No one would ever look at her and think, *Gross! She's a walking STD!*

The only real difference was her scent. She no longer smelled like honeysuckle. She smelled like . . . nothing. As if the girl Lilica had known no longer existed.

No! She existed. She could be saved.

Topping out at five three, Trinity was the kind of woman Dallas considered state-of-the-art. Not just the kind he should want, but the one he *had* wanted—and perhaps still wanted.

Just as Lilica knew more about his past than he'd ever told her, she knew how desperately he'd desired Trinity the few times the two had interacted.

A turbulent storm suddenly rained acid inside Lilica. This wasn't jealousy she felt. It wasn't! Probably wasn't even anger. Surely. Because, if Dallas still desired Trinity, Lilica would have an easier time convincing him to forgo lethal force.

What Lilica felt . . . was it self-pity? If she slept with him, solidifying their bond, and managed to cleanse Trinity as she hoped, she would be forever bound to a man who preferred her sister. Every minute of every day, she would feel his hunger for Trinity like a thorn in her heart.

Doesn't matter. Do what's best for Trin. "How are you?" Lilica asked, cutting through the silence that hung so thick between them.

"Not well," Jade answered. "She was in bed with another human. The second one tonight."

"What? There's nothing wrong with enjoying a bag of mixed nuts." Trinity wrenched free of Jade's hold, all the while watching Lilica. "I can feel you judging me with your gaze."

"I would *never* judge you." Lilica flattened a hand between her breasts. "I know why you do what you do. I love you. I've missed you. And I want to help you."

Trinity flinched, her shoulders rolling in. "You can't help me."

"I can. I will." *I must.*

"You don't think I've tried to help myself?"

"We're stronger together," she said, and it was true.

"You don't understand." Trinity's irises appeared as hard as diamonds. "I don't need you anymore. For months I was trapped inside a realm without time or people. I was alone, and I nearly died. To get home, I had to endure horrors beyond your wildest imaginings. But I'm glad I did. I learned to rely on myself. To stop wishing you'd rush to the rescue."

"Whether you want my help or not, you're going to get it. I will do whatever proves necessary to find a cure and cleanse you."

"Maybe we shouldn't," Jade said. "Maybe the agents are right. While we are struggling to save her, she's going to be turning her lovers into killers."

Trinity lifted her chin. "Your point?"

Such disdain for the ones she harmed. *This* isn't *the girl I used to know.*

Dallas was right, Lilica realized: there was a huge difference between defending yourself and slaying an innocent. That wasn't judgment but fact.

"There has to be another way to save you," Jade insisted.

"There isn't." The corner of Trinity's mouth lifted in a sneer. "I tried other ways, and I paid dearly for it."

Very gently, Lilica said, "Right now, you're trapped

in the middle of a great and terrible storm. But one day, the rain will stop. It must. A garden will grow."

"When did Lady Wicked become such a romantic fool?" Trinity turned her scowl to Jade. "Take me back. Now."

"No. Not yet." This wasn't even close to the happy reunion Lilica had imagined, but she wasn't giving up. Would *never* give up. "Why did you stay away from us after you escaped the institute?" The question had been part of her for so long—years!—that it slipped out without permission, her voice drenched in despair. "Why didn't you come back for us? Why didn't you communicate with us?"

Trinity blanched, only to buck up a second later. "You should cry your thanks rather than issuing complaints. I kept you safe."

"We were trapped inside IOT." Jade rubbed the spot over her heart. "Trust me. We weren't safe."

All attitude and zero finesse, Trinity snapped, "If the doctors had gotten hold of me, *you* would have suffered." She turned away. "I'd planned to come for you. Eventually. First I had things to do. I still have things to do."

"What things?" Lilica asked. "Maybe I can help."

"You can't." Spine rigid, Trinity added, "You should have left me alone. You should have waited for me to come to you. I don't want to be with you right now. I don't want to see you."

Being whipped, the skin flayed from her back, would have been easier than hearing those words. And yet, Lilica detected a thread of vulnerability in Trinity's tone, and it gave her hope. *My sister is still in there.*

"Talk to me. Tell me why don't you want to see us. We're your family."

A pause. A heavy exhalation of breath. "No, Lilica. We haven't been family for a long time. I'm not sure we ever were."

A barbed lump grew in her throat. "No. No!" She stomped her foot. "I don't believe that, and neither do you. The disease is speaking for you."

Trinity pointed a finger in her face. "You don't know me. You say you want to help me. To cleanse me. But I don't want to be cleansed. Not anymore! What you call disease, I call power."

What! "You're either joking or fooling yourself. You aren't empowered. You're subjugated. Dependent on the harm you do to others."

Hatred gleamed in her eyes, crackling amid flames of rage. "Perhaps I am. But I *control* my people."

Understanding suddenly dawned, chasing away the shadows of confusion. As children, the triplets had had little control over their own lives. Actually, they'd had zero control. Of anything! The lack had warped them, and the doctors had known it.

Those doctors had even predicted that Trinity, Jade, and Lilica would one day do *anything* to control *everything*.

They'd just been proven right, at least in Trinity's case, and it galled.

"AIR is actively seeking your assassination," Lilica said. "I'm doing my best to—"

Trinity held up her hand for silence. "They've actively sought my assassination for a long time. They will never succeed."

"Well, they've now got their best agent on the case." The pride had returned to her voice. "Dallas Gutierrez will stop at nothing—"

"Dallas?" Trinity smiled slowly . . . evilly. "Worry not. One day, he'll belong to me."

Well, well. Lady Divine had invaded Lady Wicked's turf. In more ways than one!

"I'm bound to him," Lilica said with more force than she'd intended. "He belongs to *me*, and I will *never* allow you to infect him."

Trinity's fury returned in a snap. "Break your bond with the man trying to kill me, sister. Today!"

Lilica stood rooted, stupefied. "I won't. I can't."

A brute of a man suddenly stalked through the mist. A brute, yes, but a beautiful one. His curling hair was the color of spun gold, just like his eyes and skin. He had the face of an angel but the scowl of a demon.

"Woman, I told you what would happen if you stole from me."

"John," Jade said on a wispy catch of breath. Her cheeks flushed, and she trembled.

With fear . . . or desire?

Whichever, Lilica jumped in front of her, ready to fight and defend.

Trinity stepped in front of them both. "Who do we have here?"

John ground to a halt. Scowl deepening, he stretched out his hand. "Jade. Come to me. Now."

Jade trembled harder, but remained in place.

"Don't worry, warrior," Trinity said, her voice a carnal rasp. "I have no plans to harm her. You, on the other hand . . ."

"Go," Jade whispered in Lilica's ear. "Return to your body while she's distracted."

As if. "I don't know how. Besides, I'm not leaving you with him." She spoke the last with enough volume for John to hear. "I don't know what he plans for you."

He clenched and unclenched his fist. "I'm her shield. Nothing more, nothing less." If his possessive tone meant anything, he wanted to be *more*. "And you're preventing me from doing my job."

"What job is that?" she demanded. "Protecting Jade or killing Trinity?"

"Just . . . leave the circle of mist." Jade gave her a little push. "Your spirit will do the rest."

She dug in her heels.

"Do you plan to kill me, John?" Trinity took a step closer to him. "Perhaps we can negotiate a truce instead."

Fear radiated from Jade. Obviously she cared for John. And not just because he provided peace and quiet.

Lilica made a split-second decision. She couldn't allow Trinity to hurt him, so she dove on her eldest sister, flinging them both outside of the mist. Before they landed, invisible chains yanked them apart. Those chains pulled Lilica on a roller-coaster ride . . . until she slammed into a brick wall. No, not a wall. Her body!

With a gasp, she jolted upright.

8

Dallas had been pacing inside his bedroom for hours. The entire time, Lilica had slept on his bed. His own personal Sleeping Beauty.

At the lab, when she'd gone limp in his arms, he'd almost passed out himself. Somehow he'd found the strength to stay awake and dress her in her bra, panties, and the shirt off his back. He'd had other options. Like her own clothing. But he'd wanted her perfect body draped in *his* clothing, her skin touched by his scent. A possessive instinct he hadn't been able to override.

He'd driven her here, because he'd *needed* her here. He'd needed his woman surrounded by his things. As soon as he'd tucked her into bed, a sense of contentment had sprouted, and it had only grown.

What was he going to do with her?

His resistance to her—to a future with her—was crumbling fast and would soon be nothing but a pile of ruin. When she'd stripped for him, he'd basically had a near-death experience. Ecstasy overdose. Her nipples had glittered like pink diamonds, and the scrolls etched on her flesh had glowed softly, like a thousand rose-scented candles meant to set the mood.

Moth to flame? Yeah, he finally understood the phrase. He would do anything to follow those marks with his tongue, no matter the end result. Hunger clawed at him, leaving him raw and aching, nothing but exposed nerve endings and raging testosterone.

Why had he knocked her out? Why had he turned her down? How stupid could he be! She was everything he'd never known he needed.

If Lilica wanted him to attempt to save Trinity after the disease died, he would attempt to save her.

What's wrong with me?

With a gasp, Lilica sat upright. Her wild gaze scanned her new surroundings.

Incapable of staying away, he strode to the side of the bed and eased beside her. *Moth. Flame. Going to get burned.* Didn't matter. He had to touch her.

No, no. Not without permission. Only a few hours ago, he'd knocked her out to save himself from temptation. Because he'd wanted her, and she'd only wanted to control him.

His body cried: *Want me the way I want you.*

She would be frightened of him, or determined to hurt him back. He had to tread carefully.

"Where am I?" she demanded.

He hardened instantly. Her voice had always made him think of sex, lots and lots of dirty sex, and the forced nap had only made it worse.

"You're in my apartment."

He tried to look at the bedroom through her eyes. Everything screamed *bachelor*. The bare walls he'd never cared about decorating. The king-size bed with a light-brown comforter. The nightstand filled with condoms. The minifridge in the corner, currently stocked with beer.

Her northern lights gaze roved over him, softened . . . and then sharpened. Her leg shot out from under the covers to kick him off the mattress. "Bastard!" She stood, fury pulsing from her.

He thumped on the floor and, glaring, jumped to his feet. "I'm a bastard, yes, but you're worse. You were using me to save your sister."

Wait. Was he seriously complaining about her reason for seducing him?

"That's right. I was trying to save the sister I love . . . and the woman you wish you could screw before you kill!" As she stood before him, chest heaving, dark hair tumbling to her waist, he waited for her thoughts to fill him. . . .

Silence.

Irritation darkened his mood. He needed help with the conversation—or rather, the mountain studded with land mines—but because their emotions were high, he wasn't going to get it.

What he said next would either whisk him to the safety zone or throw him behind enemy lines.

Tread carefully.

For the case. Of course.

"You told me yesterday I couldn't want you because I didn't know you. I've never known Trinity and have no interest in learning. You, I'm learning, and I only want to know more." The words were truth, the whole truth, and nothing but the truth.

She'd been created in a lab, an experiment gone wrong—or incredibly right. Even now, despite everything, it gutted him to remember the loneliness she'd lived with her entire life. Her strength humbled him.

Scowling, she lifted her chin. A stubborn gesture he was coming to loathe. "The bond is speaking for you."

"Maybe, maybe not." Was it the bond feeding his curiosity about her? The bond causing every cell in his body to crave information as much as sex? "Before you say anything else . . . don't. We're not thinking clearly right now, and we won't . . . until we come."

Breath snagged in her throat, the pulse at the base of her neck suddenly hammering. "The bond will—"

"Solidify. I know. *If* we have sex. But we won't. We can make each other come in other ways. With our hands and mouths."

She licked her lips with slow deliberation before shaking her head. "I don't trust you."

"I won't knock you out again. You have my word."

Her eyes narrowed to tiny slits. "Perhaps I like the idea of leaving you like this. Hungry for me. Desperate."

His erection jerked beneath his fly. "Trust me, sweet. I won't be staying in this condition. If I must, I'll take care of it on my own."

Her eyes widened as he kicked off his boots and unfastened his pants, then made a big production of sliding the denim down his legs and kicking the garment a few feet away, the many weapons hidden in panels of material thumping as they crash-landed on the floor.

Trembling, she reached for him, caught herself, and let her arms fall to her sides. "The rest," she rasped. "Remove the rest."

"Is someone else hungry?" His erection stretched past the waist of his underwear, revealing a bead of moisture that welled at the tip. He rubbed a hand up and down. "Desperate."

She watched his hand, and her breathing quickened.

"I'll make you regret this," she grated, then gripped the hem of her shirt to slowly . . . so slowly . . . work the material overhead, revealing the exquisite femininity no other woman could ever match.

Satisfaction hit him like a bolt of lightning.

On a rack—or hell, even on someone else—the bra and panties would have been nothing special. On Lilica, they were a treasure and belonged in a museum.

Her body formed the perfect hourglass, flaring at the hips. Her breasts were more than a handful, high and pert, her legs long and lean . . . providing the perfect path to dessert.

"Your panties," he said. "Remove them."

Dark hair danced over delicate shoulders as she shook her head in negation. "You first."

"Mine are called underwear, sweetness, not panties." He smiled, even though the moment of levity failed to lessen the tension between them.

He hooked his fingertips in the elastic waistband and pushed.

Her gaze locked on his steel-hard length, and her

hand fluttered to her throat. "You are so big . . . so beautiful."

"So ready for you." Cupping his sac, he repeated, "Your panties."

Her tremors worsened as she shimmied out of the fabric.

Need clawed at him. *She's going to be the death of me.*

Without being asked, she freed the front clasp of her bra. The material parted, revealing the pink-diamond nipples that would forever haunt his dreams.

He closed the distance and twined his fingers with hers to lead her into the bathroom. He wanted to run or, barring that, to pick her up and carry her, but he forced himself to remain unhurried.

With the press of a few buttons, water sprayed from the shower spout rather than enzyme mist, as the rest of the world used. Thick steam filled the air, drawing a delighted gasp from Lilica and a smile from him.

"Water?" she squeaked. "I've heard about it, read about it, but never actually seen it."

After the human-alien war, when three-fourths of the planet had lain in ruins, plant and animal life destroyed, the oceans and lakes poisoned, new methods of sustainability had had to be found. Fast. Now people lived on synthetic everything.

He stepped into the stall, drew her beside him, and closed the door. "Feel free to drink the water. I'll be drinking you."

Her cheeks flushed. She chose to stand directly under the waterfall, the heat of the spray deepening the pink hue of her skin, her hair curling down her back. Her eyes closed, a purr rising from her.

"This is amazing."

"*You* are amazing. Beautiful beyond compare."

Frowning, she faced him, water droplets catching in her lashes. "You truly think I'm beautiful."

"That surprises you?"

She leaned toward him, the tip of her tongue emerging to snatch a water droplet from his chin. "Do you want me more than you've ever wanted anyone else?" she asked in lieu of an answer.

He scowled, his body *aching*.

She grinned slowly. "You do."

"Enough talk. Come here." He drew her closer while lowering his head. His lips pressed into hers, claiming a deep, wet kiss.

This time, she kissed him back right from the start, their tongues thrusting together. He wasn't gentle, but then, neither was she. The need blazing between them was too great, driving them both into a madden frenzy.

He cupped and kneaded her ass, the harder pucker of her nipples abrading his chest, creating a dizzying friction.

"More . . . give more." She bit at him, as if she wanted to devour him. Her nails dug into his shoulders to keep him in place as she grinded against him, her hips moving forward and back in a too-fast rhythm.

Attempting to sate her need?

He gripped her hips to still her and lifted his head to stare down at her. Her eyelids were hooded and heavy, her lips blood-red and already kiss-swollen. "Will this be your first orgasm?"

She fought his hold, doing her best to rub her core against his throbbing erection. "Gave myself one or two . . . I think."

"If you *think* you had one, the answer is, yes, this will be your first."

She nipped at his chin. "Then make sure I enjoy it."

"Oh, sweetheart, I most definitely will, but you have to let me set the pace." He brushed his thumbs over the rise of her cheeks. "I promise I'm up for the challenge."

Another nip. "Is that a reference to your penis?"

The word *penis* said in that carnal rasp should be considered a weapon of manly destruction. "Just so you know, ninety percent of the things I say are a reference to my penis."

She twirled a lock of his hair around her finger. "I'm curious about it . . . your penis."

Well, hell. *Those* words were a weapon of *Dallas* destruction. "I think it's time for an introduction, then." He guided her hand to the base, hissing with sublime satisfaction as she wrapped her fingers around it.

"Just like that," he told her as she squeezed him.

She angled his length as she arched her back, rubbing the tip between her legs. Just the way she'd wanted.

"My Lily is determined to have her orgasm. Very well. I'll help." He kicked her ankles apart, spreading her legs, and slid his fingers through all her succulent heat and wet to spear one deep inside her.

"Dallas!"

"Tell me when I hit the right—"

"Yes! There!"

"—spot." He moved the finger in and out of her, her inner walls clenching on him. The feel of her . . . better than he'd imagined.

"Don't stop." A growled command. Her free hand landed on his shoulder, her nails not just digging but also cutting into his flesh.

In. "Dying would be preferable to stopping, sweetheart." Out. He kissed her jawline, then her neck, and sucked her hammering pulse. Maybe it was the bond. Maybe it was her alone. But no woman had ever been so sweet, a drug he couldn't live without.

"I don't understand how I can want you so much . . . how you can want me . . . too soon, too intense." She licked his neck, sucked on his pulse as he'd done to hers.

Sharp teeth grazed his flesh, and he shuddered with rapture.

"This wanting is only beginning, Lily." He speared her with a second finger, stretching her. Preparing her for his invasion.

No, no. *Hands and mouth, nothing more.*

But she was so deliciously tight, as if she'd been made for him alone. A gift he would never deserve.

"Dallas . . . I need . . . give me . . ." She writhed against him, trying to force him to go deeper. She had no finesse, no rhythm, operating solely on need, and he loved it.

"You are silk inside." He ran the lobe of her ear between his teeth. "My new favorite playground."

Her nails cut deeper into his shoulder and even

into his shaft, the sting as much a pleasure as a pain. She dove in for another kiss, working his tongue hard and fast before rearing back to gaze down at his shaft . . . at the beads of blood she'd drawn there. As if in a trance, she licked her lips, a look of absolute hunger consuming her expression.

His Lily was part vampire. Noted.

He throbbed as he ran a finger over his length to collect the beads. Beads he then smeared over her mouth. Her tongue darted out, pink and pretty, to lap them up.

"More." The word was a rough command.

Yes, oh yes. "You can have more. From here"—he pointed to his mouth—"or here." He pointed to his erection. "Your choice."

A loud beep suddenly erupted from his phone. Hell, no. Not now. *Take her!* But the beep continued, and Lilica stepped away from him, the spell broken. A good thing. The beep was not a call but a warning. Security had just been breached.

He cursed as he hopped from the stall, the urge to murder the intruder strong. A quick scan of the screen revealed an open front door. He pressed a few buttons, rewinding the camera feed, and discovered Devyn.

Send him away. Return to Lilica.

She flattened her palms against the clear glass wall, her gaze hot on him. "You promised me more."

Yes—no. Their first time wouldn't be rushed or witnessed. She was going to scream. He was going to make sure of it.

Planning to do more than give them both an orgasm now?

Yes. No. Hell. Maybe. He was screwed—just not the way he wanted. "We have a visitor."

The lights in her eyes slowly faded, and *he* almost screamed. "Danger?"

"No. Friend."

She scowled. "Let me guess. Devyn."

He offered a stiff nod. "I won't allow him to harm you."

"*I* won't allow him to harm me." She cupped her breasts. "For today's meeting, I'll be staying in here."

"Good idea." He pinched the hard crests of her nipples . . . then pressed another finger into the paradise between her legs. "Do not bring yourself to orgasm." The honor would be his, and his alone. "Wait for me."

She unveiled another smile, this one pure challenge. "If I *do* bring myself to orgasm?"

He liked that smile. Naughty and nice, innocent and wicked all at once. "I'll forget we have an audience and have you on your back in two seconds flat."

9

Trembling, alone in the bathroom, Lilica slid to the floor of the shower. She should dress, march out of the bedroom, and teach the Targon king the error of his ways. *Mess with me, die horribly.* But she ached, and as the hot water continued to rain over her, a thousand little caresses from head to toe, she contemplated bringing herself to orgasm despite what Dallas had said. Or maybe *because* of what he'd said. Exploring her body was something she'd only ever done after taking over IOT, but she'd never felt like *this*. As if she were burning alive, and glad of it.

She should have told Dallas no, should have let him sink deeper into an animal state, but she'd been stinging from her encounter with Trinity. And then he'd taken off his shirt, all those delicious muscles on display. And his tattoos! He had three. A tree of life along both sides of his rib cage; a pair of eyes, one on top of each foot, and her absolute favorite, a group of musical notes over his heart.

The heat inside her disintegrated her restraint.

Screw waiting for Dallas, and screw his consequences. She brought herself to a swift orgasm, but oh, it wasn't as satisfying as she'd hoped, leaving her confused once again about whether she'd actually had one.

Dallas would tell her she hadn't. And maybe he'd be right. She still ached. Still *needed*.

Legs unsteady, she emerged from the shower at last. As cool air kissed her wet skin, she rifled through Dallas's closet, then dressed in a T-shirt, a pair of boxers, and pair of sweatpants.

If he complained about sharing his clothes, she'd probably claw his face off. *If you want to keep me, be prepared to provide for me!*

Should probably provide for . . . myself?

Whatever. She braided her hair and, wanting to assassinate *something*, ripped up another of Dallas's shirts to use as a tie.

A quick search for weapons proved unfruitful, not that she was surprised. No matter. She still had her wits and her powers. Dallas hadn't dosed her. Had he forgotten, or had he decided to trust her?

He wasn't the type to forget anything. He also wasn't the type to trust anyone but his elite circle of friends. Did he not mind that she could hear what he was saying to Devyn through the bond?

But then, there was a third option, she realized. Negating her powers would have negated his own. So, one point Lilica. The bond had been a good idea after all.

"Lilica!" Dallas's bellow echoed through the bedroom, and oh, wow, he'd never sounded more enraged.

What had she done this time?

And why did she already miss the nickname he'd given her? Lily.

"Lilica! Get out here." He was closer now, probably stomping this way.

—Ask nicely, Arcadian. Shouting demands will get you nowhere fast.—

A pause.

—Stop speaking inside my head.—

—Why don't you come in here and make me.—

Wait. She didn't want him storming in here and dragging her out, so she decided that, just this once, shouting demands would get him somewhere . . . slowly.

—Never mind. I'm on my way.—

Head high, she exited the bedroom at the pace of a hundred-year-old woman with a walker and a bum hip.

He wasn't storming after all, but standing a few feet away, his body radiating tension, his muscles bunched.

"What?" she snapped.

His gaze spewed fire at her. "You met with Trinity," he snapped back.

Right. He hadn't known about that. Her little visit with Trinity hadn't been on her mind while they'd been . . . otherwise occupied.

Not yet ready to discuss her interaction with her sister—and her subsequent rejection—she studied his apartment. In the living room, the furnishings were just as masculine as those in the bedroom; the couch, two recliners, coffee table, and two side tables were dark and well used.

Devyn saluted her with a mocking grin. He sat in one of the recliners, which looked to be made of real leather. Leather was just as expensive as water. He held a glass of amber liquid the same color as his eyes and as he sipped, ice cubes clinked together.

Actual ice cubes, made from water, not just frozen blocks of H2Syn.

——*We're rich!*——

"*I'm* rich." Dallas pinched the bridge of his nose. "Devyn invested my money. Without my consent. One night I went to bed with only a few thousand bucks to my name, and the next morning I woke up with millions."

"I'm still waiting for my thanks," Devyn muttered.

She ignored him, saying to Dallas, "Well. As soon as our bond is broken, I'm taking half your stuff."

"What bond?" Devyn asked.

Again she ignored him. She gave Dallas a pitying look. "Alimony is going to suck, but what can you do?"

He scowled at her, and gritted out only one word. "Trinity."

"How did you find—never mind," she said. "I can guess. John called Devyn."

"*You* should have told me," he said, pointing at her.

She anchored her hands on her hips. "I think that's the dumbest thing you've ever said. Think about it. You plan to harm her. Why would I *ever* tell you anything about her?"

"She could have infected you, and you could have infected me."

"She didn't, and I didn't. But she *does* want to infect you." The admission escaped before she could weigh the pros and cons of telling him. "And before you go charging after her guns blazing, know that I'm going to change her mind." Lilica had to believe that the sister she loved was buried underneath the anger, the sense of rejection, and the thirst for power.

Dallas's features softened as he closed the distance to frame Lilica's face with his big, calloused hands. "I'm sorry she hurt you, sweetheart."

Her stomach dropped, and though she longed to lean into his touch, she stepped back, severing contact. *Can't let myself need him.* "I'll never give up on her. If you knew her like I did . . ." Her eyes widened. He *could* know her.

She dug through her memories, focusing on the ones involving Trinity at her sweetest and pushing them across the bond, into Dallas's mind.

"Stop that." He shook his head. "Just stop."

Devyn unfolded from the chair, rising to his feet. "What are you doing to him?"

Dallas pointed a finger at his friend. "Don't even think about hurting her. She's under my protection."

The Targon blinked in surprise before holding up his hands, all innocence. "I was only thinking about making her hurt *herself.* Big difference. Huge."

Don't read too much into Dallas's words, she told herself. *By protecting me, he merely protects himself.*

Catching her thought, he scowled at her.

"Did I hear you correctly? Devyn hurt a female?" A beautiful woman soared through the front door, kicking it shut behind her as she glared at the Targon. She held a tray of hors d'oeuvres. "Apologize to her. Now!"

"For you, love? Anything." Devyn blew the woman a kiss. To Lilica, he said, "I'm sorry you forced me to take action against you. I mean that from the bottom of my heart."

The woman bared her teeth, revealing sharp white

fangs. She was a vampire. One of the first alien races to make themselves known to earthlings. The blood-drinkers now lived underground and very rarely surfaced.

Excitement bubbled up. Considering that Lilica had vampire in her DNA, she would love to talk shop.

Devyn smiled his most devastating smile at the vampire. "You knew about my bad-boy reputation before you married me, pet."

Married?

"Lilica, meet Bride McKells. Devyn's wife," Dallas said. "Bride, meet Lilica, my—"

"Prisoner of war," Lilica interjected before he could call her something worse.

Dallas stiffened.

"Her name is Bride Targon," Devyn corrected.

"Just Bride," the woman in question said. "It's lovely to meet you, Lilica."

The scents of roses, sugarplums, and honey-suckle wafted from her, and as Lilica drew in a deep breath—scents had always been her thing—a strong sense of familiarity struck her, as if she were peering at one of her sisters; she studied Bride more intently. The vampire had jet-black hair, so like Lilica's own, and eyes the color of emeralds. Just like Jade's. Her pale skin had a pink-roses glow of health . . . like Trinity's. Her lips were scarlet, like Lilica's.

The scientists at IOT couldn't have used this woman's DNA . . . could they? What were the odds?

But . . . peel back the layers of coincidence and it made a strange sort of sense. Because vampires so rarely surfaced—and no one at the institute had been brave enough to venture below—the scientists would have snagged the first one they'd come across.

Dallas stiffened as he looked from Lilica to Bride, then back again. Cursing, he scrubbed a hand down his face. He'd read Lilica's thoughts—but more than that, he believed her suspicions.

"At IOT, scientists used DNA from captives to create Lilica," he said to Devyn. "You yourself told me Bride was locked there for months."

Devyn laughed, and yet he appeared far from amused. "What you're suggesting is ridiculous."

"Is it?" Dallas massaged the back of his neck. "You found the lab because of Bride's memories."

The color drained from Bride's cheeks as she focused on Lilica. "You're really from the lab?"

"Born there," she said softly. "Along with my sisters, Jade . . . and Trinity."

Dallas cursed again, and this time Devyn joined him.

"I was a child. No more than eight years old. I can't be what you're . . . I mean, that would make me your mother, and I—" Bride looked helplessly at her husband. "Right?"

He sprang into action, taking the tray from her trembling grip and placing it on the coffee table before drawing her into his arms, protective, possessive, and gentle all at once. For the first time in their acquaintance, Lilica could guess how the cruel brute had won the heart of the vampire.

Lilica swallowed. "If . . . if it's true, you would be one of twenty-eight parents. Twenty-three other-worlders and five humans."

"When I was at the lab," Devyn said, "I found no paperwork, no computer files."

"We hid them." She rattled off the coordinates to where he needed to look. No reason to keep the data secret, even though she would have enjoyed torturing *him*; she'd never be able to hide the information from Dallas.

Devyn nodded in what might have been thanks. "I'll have answers by morning, pet."

Needing a distraction, Lilica grabbed a handful of the hors d'oeuvres.

The bite-size cakes smelled like . . . she couldn't identify the scent, only knew she liked it, her mouth watering.

"Crab," Dallas muttered.

She scoured her mind, but came up blank. "I'm unfamiliar with the term."

"Seafood."

Her brow furrowed with confusion. "Sea animals were killed during the war, when the oceans were contaminated." She might not have lived in the world, but she *had* studied its turbulent history.

"Some people," Dallas said, hiking his thumb at Devyn, "have private stashes."

Lilica nibbled on the edge of a cake and moaned with delight. Amazing! "I've decided I'm keeping your friends when we divorce."

Dallas stole one of her cakes, popping it into his mouth before she could kill him. *Mine!* She watched his mouth as he chewed, suddenly mesmerized. When he swallowed, their gazes met and locked, awareness crackling between them. The air thickened, making it harder for her to breathe. Which was probably a good thing. His scent had blended with hers, creating a fragrance so potent, so arousing, she nearly leaped into his arms to rip at his clothes.

If she didn't put her hands on him soon . . . if he didn't put *his* hands on *her* . . . his fingers *inside* her . . .

I'll die.

His fingers were so different from hers. Thicker, and rougher. When they brought her to orgasm, she would know it beyond a doubt.

"Yes. You will." His pupils flared, black spilling over those arctic irises, as if he wanted to throw her down, strip her, and penetrate her with a single stroke, just as he'd promised in the bathroom. As if he wanted to fill her up, possess her, brand her. Own her. As if he wanted to take and take and take, but only after she'd begged would he give and give and give.

"I'll never beg for you," she whispered.

"Oh, sweetheart. I think we'll both beg."

Her tremors returned. To hear this man beg for her . . .

The soothing balm to every rejection she'd ever faced.

No. No! She would not surrender to her desires, would not give in to her animal urges. Not again. She'd thought sex with him was the answer to her problems. Bound forever, he would choose to save Trinity. But there had to be another way. A way she would actually survive.

As a muscle jumped under his eye, he backed away from her.

As cold reality chilled her desire, one of his thoughts filled her head. —*Such a naughty girl, my Lily.*—

His Lily. His.

Her heart sped into a dangerous rhythm.

"Wow. Anyone else hot?" Bride asked with a shaky little laugh. "I feel like I just watched a live and in-person porno."

Dallas ignored her, grating to Lilica, "You can have all the crab cakes you want . . . if you tell us where to find Trinity."

Anger flickered deep inside her chest. Every interaction always came back to her sister, didn't it. "I don't know where she is, and that's the truth. And if John tries to force Jade to find her again, I'll—"

"John wouldn't. He doesn't want Jade near Trinity again, and he won't let us near Jade."

Well. —*Some protectors know how to do their job right.*—

Dallas glared at her.

She glared right back. What a nightmare this had become! She had to keep AIR away from Trinity, but doing so would prevent Lilica from digging past her sister's uncaring facade to reach her heart.

"She's a parasite." Disgust dripped from his voice. "She isn't the girl you knew."

Trinity had said the same. "She is still my sister." She pushed the memory of Trinity willing to take a beating for her through the bond.

He stiffened, then pried the remaining crab cakes from her hand and picked up the tray. "There are lobster and salmon cakes on here too, and they're better than crab."

"I've never had lobster or salmon." But her mouth watered for them. *Must have!* "Give them to me. Now."

"Sorry. You'll have to put them on your bucket list." He stomped into the kitchen and dumped the contents of the tray into the garbage can.

He . . . no! He was worse than Devyn.

"Fine. You win. I'll help you find her, but not because of your stupid cakes. You can stuff those up your ass! I plan on saving her before you can *contain* her."

"Too bad, sweetheart. I plan on containing her before you can save her."

Of course he did.

She batted her lashes at him, all sugary sweetness, so angry for wanting a man who was so determined to hurt her flesh and blood. A man who was unwilling to give her a chance. Just one chance.

"Then we'll have to wait and see who wins," she told him. "Won't we?"

10

$\mathcal{D}$allas tossed and turned on the couch.

He'd actually made up the couch for *Lilica*. No reason to be a gentleman for his mission's competition.

Meanwhile, Lilica had made herself right at home in his bed, crawling under his covers and eating a bag of chips while she watched him work through the open door. She'd looked so comfortable, so adorable . . . so sexy with her dark hair spread over his pillows. He hadn't had the balls to eject her. Or the desire. She'd had few comforts in her young life. How could he take one away?

Now he couldn't sleep. Hunger for her plagued him. Again and again he'd contemplated sliding in beside her and picking up where they'd left off in the shower. But he knew better now. If he touched her, he wouldn't stop touching her until he got inside her. Screw good intentions—the solidification of the bond wouldn't matter to him.

He considered slaking his sexual need with another woman . . . but the idea left a foul taste in his mouth. He'd never been a cheater.

I'm not committed to Lilica. Not really.

Wasn't he?

He pinched the bridge of his nose. Committed or not, his body craved hers, only hers. She'd become an addiction, his drug of choice, and everyone else paled in comparison.

He banged his fists into the cushions. Lilica was now as determined to resist him as he was determined to resist her. Foolish woman! Did she not realize her attitude only made him want to change her mind, seducing her until she begged for his touch?

I'm so messed up.

He forced his mind to blank and at last drifted to sleep . . . only to be plagued by dreams of Lilica pleasuring herself in the shower, not quite satisfying herself, because she wanted—needed—him.

By the time morning arrived, he was wide-awake and hardwired for aggression. He stomped into the bedroom, not even trying to be quiet, and grabbed clothes from the closet. He slammed the bathroom door as he felt her prick at the edge of his subconscious. Trying to deduce his new plan for her sister?

—*Good luck, sweetheart.*—

He showered, purposely replaying his dream of her on a loop.

—*Bastard!*— Her sensual voice filled his head.

As he toweled off and dressed in a white button-down and a pair of black slacks—standard AIR attire—he smiled.

He focused on an image of Lilica on her knees, sucking him off as he hid his pyre-guns under a jacket and the Schön Slayer in his boot. Her curses echoed from the bedroom.

In the back of his mind, he heard whispering female

voices and frowned. He concentrated, doing his best to discern their words, but a soft vibration in his temples signaled a call was coming in, and it distracted him. With a sigh, he tapped his ear against his shoulder.

"What?"

"Wow. Is that any way to greet your boss?" Mia asked.

"Sorry. Let me try again." As he exited the bathroom, he said, "Hello, Madame Terror. What the hell do you want?"

Her soft laughter crackled over the line. "Better. So. Based on the description Jade gave John and John gave Devyn and Devyn gave me—try saying *that* three times fast—we've found Trinity's latest victim. We've got him in custody at our facility in No Man's Land. We don't want him around civilians."

His bedroom was empty, his sheets wrinkled, the covers askew. Lilica's scent—freshly cut roses and aged wood—saturated the air, revving his engine all over again. When would this wanting end?

"—listening to me?" Mia said.

"Not really. But I'll meet you in No Man's Land."

"Fine. What about your girl?"

Your girl. The words were kindling on his arousal. "I'll . . ." What? He refused to bring Lilica with him, wouldn't put her in danger of infection.

But she would be in danger regardless, because *he* would be in danger.

Still. He also didn't want her around other AIR agents. If anyone threatened her, he would willingly leap off the deep end, no doubt about it. He would probably lose a boatload of friends too.

Yesterday he'd had to fight an overwhelming urge to kill Devyn, a man he loved like a brother, just because the guy had simply *thought* about restraining her. A thought Devyn had entertained because he'd suspected Lilica planned to harm Dallas.

"Don't worry about her," he finally said. "She's my responsibility."

"Dallas—"

He tapped his ear, disconnecting the call, and strode into the living room, spotting Lilica in the kitchen. She sat on a barstool, her dark hair piled in a sloppy knot on the crown of her head; she leaned across the counter to snag another bag of chips. A clean T-shirt covered her. One of the shirts Devyn had given him. It read "Targon: Tastes So Good."

Dallas had always loved that shirt. Man crush! Today, he hated it. On Lilica, the hem reached mid-thigh, revealing mile-long legs he would give anything to have wrapped around his waist . . . or his head.

Anything? His hands fisted.

She drained a can of soda. "This stuff is amazing!"

She was amazing.

She gasped. Glaring at him, she crunched the can and tossed it at him. "Don't you dare compliment me!"

The metal pinged against his chest and fell to the floor. "I'll compliment you if I want, and you can't stop me."

"Well. I've said it before, but I'll say it again. You, Agent Gutierrez, are a bastard."

"In every sense of the word." His beloved mother had never married his father because she'd never known which of her johns had shared his baby batter. "But you only think so because you find me harder to resist when I'm charming."

As she floundered for a response, Dallas swiped the chips from her grip and stuffed the bag in the trash. "You need to start eating nutritious foods. I'm watching my girlish figure, and I don't want your fat grams clogging my arteries through the bond."

"Are crab cakes nutritious?" she asked with narrowed eyes.

Still pissed about that, was she? "Maybe," he said, "but you're only getting vegetables until you start cooperating with me."

"You're the one who bought all this junk food, and I'm willing to bet you don't own a single vegetable." Leaning over the counter, giving him a peek at her panties—making him groan—she swiped up a prepackaged brownie, ripped into it, and stuffed the entire thing in her mouth.

As she chewed, crumbs falling out, he fought a laugh.

When finally she swallowed, she growled, "Enjoy your saddlebags, bitch!"

This time, he barked like a freaking robodog.

Robodog . . .

The word sparked one of Lilica's memories. The doctors at IOT had run different experiments on her, but the time they'd given her a robodog was the worst. For weeks, she'd played with, loved on, and laughed with the adorable hunk of metal. Then, when she'd formed an attachment to the faux animal, it was taken away from her—and smashed in front of her.

She'd been ripped apart inside, but not by word or deed had she betrayed her sorrow. She'd refused to give the doctors the satisfaction.

Suddenly *Dallas* felt ripped apart inside. He wanted to soothe the brave, strong girl she'd been, but needed to comfort the prickly, determined woman she'd become. When she'd permitted a bond to grow with him, she'd had to override every protective instinct she'd ever honed.

Why? Why had she done it?

And why did he want to bang his chest? Why were his shoulders rolling back with pride?

She picked me!

Now she feared losing the ones she loved . . . the very reason she was so determined to save Trinity, despite the hopelessness of the situation.

Night sky eyes beseeched him. —*Help me save her, Dallas.*—

He shook his head to dislodge her voice. He had to get out of here. "I'm going to work."

"Yeah, yeah. You've got one of Trinity's victims to interrogate."

"An innocent man your sister sentenced to death."

She bristled. "How do you know he's innocent? Perhaps she chose a criminal."

"His record—"

"Means nothing, even if it's clean. People aren't always what they seem, and you know it."

Gaze dead serious, he said, "Yes, but people can change. The sweet kid you knew has grown into a violent adult."

She flipped him off.

He blew her a kiss. Why had he ever tried to convince himself that sweet women with sweet smiles were right for him? Fact was, those sweet women with sweet smiles had never fully satisfied him. He'd never wanted one for more than a single night, because none had ever meant anything to him. But this woman with her carnal smile and quick wit utterly fascinated him.

He couldn't get enough of her.

A blush stained her cheeks, and he reached out, desperate to know just how hot her skin burned, but he dropped his arm to his side just before contact, his hand fisting.

She gulped, and rasped out, "You had better be careful while you're out there. Not because I care about you, of course, but because I care about myself."

Not even close to the truth. He *felt* her concern for him, and it eased some of the tension he'd battled all night. "I'd like you to stay here and—"

"No way! I spoke with Jade a few minutes ago. We're meeting at ten."

He crossed his arms over his chest. "When did you speak with Jade? *How* did you speak with Jade?" Wait. He already knew the answer. The conversation he'd heard/not heard in the shower.

"We've always had the ability to communicate telepathically," she said. "Except the day you drugged me. After your best friend tortured me. If we were in a movie, you and Devyn would be cast as villains. You know that, right?"

The day he'd drugged her . . . only two days ago, he realized. Kind of felt like years. "Our introduction is what's called a meet cute. And I would be cast as the antihero. There's a difference."

"I, of course, would be the star everyone roots for." Pure elegance and grace, she stood.

He reached out a second time, moving without thought, wrapping his fingers around her wrists. The silk of her skin derailed whatever good intentions he'd had. He yanked her against him, hard, and she gasped.

He lowered his head for a kiss—*must taste*—but caught himself just in time. He jumped back, severing contact as if she were toxic waste. In a way, she was.

I will not be a slave to my desires.

Her irritation slithered around him, nearly choking him as he said, "Don't kill anyone today."

"I won't. Dad."

"If you do, you'll be labeled predatory. I'll have to lock you away. Forever. I'll even throw away the key for good measure."

"Like that would be a hardship for you."

It would. It so would, and that was part of the reason he needed to escape her for a few hours.

He stalked to the bag of goodies Devyn had brought with him yesterday. A cell phone, a packet of sedatives disguised as peanut butter candies, and—Dallas refused to let himself think about the third and final item, lest he alert Lilica to his nefarious intentions.

"My number is already programmed into the phone. Call me every hour, on the hour." He tossed the device in her direction, his aim perfect, but she watched it sail over her shoulder without even trying to catch it. He gnashed his teeth, picked it up, and slapped it into her palm. "I mean it. If you fail to call me, I'll come gunning for you."

"Tsk, tsk. Threatening your wife?"

"You are my temporary inconvenience."

"Tears. Sadness." She ran a fingertip down her cheek. "I have a sinking suspicion you are going to be a permanent ass pain."

Can't smile.

Stop stalling. He struck, shoving a syringe into her bicep and emptying the contents.

She didn't flinch or hiss, as he'd expected and dreaded; she simply frowned up at him. His stomach knotted as the reason for her lack of reaction crystallized. She'd been poked and prodded since birth, needles a part of her daily life.

The urge to hug her returned, stronger than before.

"Power negator?" she asked, calm. Too calm.

"No. An isotope tracker." Now, even when they were apart, he would be able to monitor her every move with a few clicks of a computer keyboard. He wouldn't have to rely on the bond.

"Congrats. You've mastered hiding your actions from me. Now it's my turn." With no more warning than that, she slammed her knee between his legs.

He hunched over, gasping for breath, stars winking through his vision.

She smiled at him. "Sorry there's not a tracker to help you find your balls."

~

Dallas hobbled into the AIR warehouse located in No Man's Land. Once he'd been sprayed with

decontamination mist, he removed the full-body protective suit that had shielded him from the acidic air.

Mia, who'd beaten him there, snickered at him.
"Your problems with your little bit o' honey are fun.
For me!"

Apparently, after Lilica had unmanned and taunted
him, he'd shouted in pain—pain she'd then experienced for herself, her bellows blending with his—
his cell phone had activated on its own. A safety
setting. He'd only managed to grunt an explanation
to Mia, but she'd gotten the gist and had called him a
dozen times during the half-hour drive out here, just
to laugh at him.

He was mad as hell, but only at himself. He'd
treated Lilica just like the doctors at IOT had treated
her. As if she were property. As if she were evil and
couldn't be trusted. As if her feelings and free will
meant nothing to him.

He should have *asked* her to check in with him
rather than forced her. She was many things—sexy,
frustrating, easily provoked—but she wasn't a liar.

"Let's just get this over with," he muttered.

"My sweet Dallas." Mia patted his shoulder.
"Does your vagina need to be iced?"

He glared at her. "Kyrin should seriously consider
taking up BDSM."

"Why? He hates when I tie him up and whip him."

Now Dallas rolled his eyes. Women!

He followed Mia through the warehouse completely emptied of agents. Cameras monitored Trinity's newest victim: a Teran male in his early thirties
with multicolored hair, the strands varying from the

palest flax to the darkest ebony. His eyes had a slight
uptilt at the corners; his teeth were sharp, especially
his canines; and every move he made contained the
feline grace inherent in his race.

He was confined inside an invisible cage, lasers
acting as walls. The Schön disease usually had a slow
incubation and progression rate, but though this
man had only slept with Trinity yesterday—to AIR's
knowledge—he already had several oozing sores.

Mia stalked around the edge of the cage, all business. Dallas remained behind her, the SS clutched
in his hands. Despite his unhurried gait, he suddenly couldn't catch his breath. His heart hammered
against his ribs, and sweat trickled down his neck.

A sense of unease pervaded. Was Lilica running?
Or being chased?

"You're going to tell me everything that happened
to you yesterday," Mia said. "From the time you
woke up to the time we stormed into your home."

The male stared at her with a disturbing mix of
lust and desperation. "I bet you taste good."

"Every time you ignore my demands or veer off
topic, I'm going to make sure you regret it." She
stopped in front of a control panel and pressed a
series of buttons.

Volts of electricity shot from the floor through
the Teran's entire body, causing his muscles to lock
onto bone. With another press of the buttons, the
electricity shut off.

"I'm sorry." The man's shoulders rolled in and
tears spilled from his eyes. "I don't know what's
wrong with me."

"I do. And believe it or not, I'm trying to help you. So talk to me. Tell me what I want to know."

His gaze found her again, and he licked his lips. Then he shook his head and frowned. "The woman I slept with . . . she told me to tell you I'm the first of many, and that I would be part of her army."

The word *army* echoed in Dallas's head, a land mine set to explode. Left unchecked, Trinity could infect the world. And Lilica wanted her kept alive?

A sharp pain lanced through his hand, drawing his gaze to his palm . . . a wound stretched across the center, blood welling and trickling.

Lilica must have been cut, the bond ensuring he experienced the same injury. For a moment, fear nearly paralyzed him. How had she gotten hurt? Was she all right? Though he tried, he couldn't get inside her head.

"We have to go," he told Mia. *"Now."* He didn't wait for a reply but raced for the door, switching on his cell phone and dialing Lilica's.

11

Lilica spit on the motionless body at her feet. She stood in the middle of a dirty alley. Her hand throbbed as she swiped up the blade that had nearly sliced her heart in two. If not for her quick reflexes . . .

I'd be dead.

Those quick reflexes allowed her to raise her hand and block. The sharp metal had slicked in one side and come out the other.

She hadn't slain the man who'd attacked her, or even cut him in turn. No, she'd overruled her kill-at-all-costs instincts and amphed his alien life force only enough to make him pass out. She hadn't known he was fully Schön.

He should have had *two* life forces: the Schön as well as Teran. He had multicolored hair, uptilted eyes, and skin with faint tawny undertones, the hallmarks of the Teran race. But there'd been no Teran power inside him, as if it had been stolen from him. It probably *had* been stolen. By Trinity.

Her phone rang, and she didn't have to wonder who waited on the other end. With a sigh of resignation, she pressed a button to answer.

"Lilica." Dallas breathed her name, the relief in his voice disconcerting her. "Tell me you're okay."

"I'm fine. I'll be fine." Would she? Despair began to beat at her. "No need to worry about your precious life."

He hissed. "I'm worried about *yours*."

He truly cared? The realization shocked the truth out of her. "A Schön attacked me soon after I left your apartment. I won. I think . . . I think Trinity sent him." Hadn't she bragged about controlling her people?

"I'm sorry," Dallas said, and he sounded sincere.

Betrayal had left a wound far deeper than the one in Lilica's hand. She wanted to save Trinity, but Trinity hoped to end her. And she'd almost succeeded!

After Dallas had taken off, Lilica had sifted through the memories of him stored in the back of her mind, determined to locate a weapon he'd hidden so that, when she was out in the world, she could properly defend herself if the need arose. Instead, she'd seen two of his missions. Dallas being attacked by a gang of otherworlders. Dallas refusing to take a bribe to let a predatory otherworlder go free.

Underneath his charm and unwillingness to make a commitment, he was loyal. Honorable. And his strength . . .

He could carry her through any storm.

No! If Lilica wasn't strong enough to walk through a storm, she would crawl. At the end of the day, she could only ever rely on herself. She couldn't even rely on Jade, not really. She loved her middle sister with every fiber of her being and she would fight to the death to protect her, but the two of them . . . they'd been raised in different ways. One with encouragement, one without. They didn't always understand each other.

Dallas's memories had continued to play through Lilica's mind and, in an effort to stop them, she'd made her way out of the apartment, into the morning light . . . trading one torment for another. People had whispered as she passed and children had pointed at her, but she'd walked down the busy sidewalk with her head high and, she'd thought, her instincts on high alert. Trinity's assassin had attacked as soon as she'd reached a dark alley, nearly succeeding because she hadn't even realized she was being followed.

"I need to know everything," Dallas said. "Every detail."

"The Schön is currently alive but unconscious. None of his blood was spilled."

"Does he have open sores?"

"Um. Yes." Could the disease spread through contact with one? She'd avoided touching the scabs but . . . "Am I going to sicken?"

"No." But still Dallas cursed. "Stay there. I'm sending a crew to pick him up, secure the area, and check you out. They'll beat me there."

In other words, more people to poke and prod her. Wonderful.

"Lilica—"

"Good-bye, Dallas." She hung up on him because—just because!

A team of twelve AIR agents arrived soon after, all wearing full bodysuits. As promised, they carted the Teran away, blocked off the alley, and checked her out while she sat in the back of a van.

When the tech gave her a clean bill of health without ever breaking her skin or testing her blood, another suit-clad figure walked over. A familiar face smiled at her through the mask.

"I'll see to her wound care," Bride McKells-Targon said.

The tech nodded and strode away.

"A bandage really isn't necessary," Lilica said. "I'm already healing." A welcome surprise. Since her bond with Dallas, the ability to self-heal had slowed.

"Humor me. It's protocol," Bride replied, already cleaning what remained of the injury.

"I didn't know you worked for AIR."

"I don't, exactly. I work for a special task force Devyn oversees. A few months ago, I mentioned wanting to get a job. Since my skill set includes breaking and entering, dirty street fighting, and evading the law, there weren't many legit positions for me, but the next thing I knew, Devyn had joined forces with a black-ops team that's not so black-ops anymore, and my particular skill set was suddenly in high demand."

"Your husband doesn't strike me as the type to sit back and cheer while you place yourself in the line of danger." And . . . was that a pang of envy in her chest?

"Oh, he's not." Bride's smile only grew. "He complains regularly. He even commands me to quit—but you see, he would rather make me happy than anything else." She stowed the medical supplies in the van. "Devyn ordered me to take you to AIR headquarters. It's what Dallas wants. But . . ."

Lilica arched a brow, mimicking Dallas at his most annoying. "But?"

"I'd rather go with you to meet Jade."

So. She'd accepted the fact that they might be related by blood. "I'd like that," Lilica said, and it was the truth. "Jade will too."

"Good." Almost defiantly, Bride stripped out of her bodysuit. "First thing we're doing is buying you clothes that actually fit."

"Um. Slight problem. I have no money."

"Well, I have the solution. Devyn owes you, and it will be his pleasure to purchase you anything and everything your heart desires."

I like this woman.

They left the crime scene arm in arm, and no one dared protest the actions of the boss's wife. This time, as Lilica made her way down the sidewalk, she didn't have to pretend to ignore the stares and whispers she generated. She ignored them for real, wrapped up in the experience of spending time with one of her many moms/sisters/whatever.

Buildings stretched as far as the eye could see. Some were box-shaped while others knifed through the skyline, disappearing in the clouds. No matter the size or shape of the building, however, each connected to its neighbors through shared walls or concrete tunnels. A postwar precaution. That way, if one building was bombed, the people inside it could race into another without having to go outside, where there might be gunfire.

"In here." Bride drew her into one of the boxier shops, Mulier in Gloria, a boutique for women.

A bell tinkled overhead, and a salesgirl rushed over to greet them. She missed a step when she realized the new customers were otherworlders, but quickly pasted a smile on her face; a sale was a sale, Lilica supposed.

To her surprise, she remained in a state of euphoria as she tried on dresses, faux-leather pants, shirts, belts, hats, jewelry, gloves, lingerie, and a thousand pairs of high heels. Her first shopping extravaganza would go down in her personal history books as one of the greatest days of her life.

She bought everything she tried on, even things that didn't fit, because *screw Devyn*. She even picked presents for Jade . . . and one for Trinity.

Maybe I can buy her love?

I'm pathetic.

What would she wear out of the store? Oh! That one. Lilica dressed in a white spaghetti-strap top, skintight black leggings, and ankle boots with white lace around the edges.

"Nice," Bride said with a nod of approval.

Lilica smacked herself on the butt. "I don't always wear sassy pants, but when I do, I wear 'em classy and smartassy."

The vampire snorted. She paid extra to have everything but the gifts for Jade delivered to Dallas's apartment. As she signed the receipt, she said, "I love a girl who speaks in meme."

What would Dallas do when he got a look at her new clothes? Yank her into his arms as he'd done this morning? Would he actually kiss her this time, or spring away from her again?

Kiss! Need shivered over her, her markings tingling.

Can't think about him. She'd only sink deeper into a state of desire for him.

—*I'm working. Knock it off. And my balls haven't forgiven you.*—

Her eyes widened. She must have sent an image of them making out through the bond. But the most surprising part? He'd been able to push his voice into her head while she was so turned on.

The bond was . . . strengthening?

"Oh, wow." Bride leaned in and sniffed her nape. "What perfume are you wearing?"

"Uh, I'm not."

"You sure? Because whatever it is, it's making me want to find Devyn and destroy a bed." The vampire wiggled her brows.

The salesgirl sniffed the air and shrugged. "I don't smell anything."

Well, she was human, while Bride was a vampire with heightened senses . . . who'd probably detected Lilica's arousal for Dallas.

"Let's get out of here," she muttered, her cheeks burning.

Outside, the clouds had evaporated. Bright rays of sunlight stroked her markings, only making her tingling intensify.

Bride pulled a tiny stick from her pocket, and with the press of a button, that stick grew and grew until it provided an umbrella of shade.

"I can tolerate sunlight," Bride said, "but not for long. And just so you know, the scent you're producing hasn't lessened." She pulled at the collar of her shirt, a pretty flush spreading over her cheeks, her pupils expanding. "Is it hot out here or just you?"

She wasn't the only one to react that way. Every otherworlder Lilica passed stopped to stare at her, and not with distaste. Not anymore.

"I produce a special scent for Devyn," Bride admitted. "It drives him crazy."

The bond with Dallas . . . Lilica wondered if she was unwittingly sending out smoke signals, for lack of a better phrase, to draw him to her side. "Yes, well, I'm sure I'll be able to produce this scent for *many* men."

"Good luck with that." Bride bumped shoulders with her. "Speaking of unbridled passion, you'll be happy to know I'm withholding sex until Devyn *properly* apologizes for his poor behavior."

Oh, to be a fly on the wall of the Targon's bedroom. "I liked you before, but now I think I love you."

They reached the diner where Lilica was to meet Jade, and Bride breathed a sigh of relief as cool air-conditioning chased away her flush.

While there were multiple waitresses and two cooks at a griddle, the only patrons were Jade and John, and both wore strained expressions.

Had John *politely* asked everyone else to leave?

The pair sat at the farthest table, their backs against the wall. As Lilica and Bride joined them, John's nose twitched and his shoulders straightened, but he revealed no other hint of unease.

Jade looked Lilica over and gasped. "Wow! You are so beautiful."

"I know, right?" She fluffed her hair. "But, uh, you look like crap." Her sister had a scratch on one cheek and a bruise on her chin. She'd lopped off her snow-white tresses, the uneven strands now swaying just over her shoulders. "Do I need to punish anyone in particular?" she asked, casting John a pointed glance.

"Nope. I did this to myself."

She frowned. "Why?"

Rather than answer, Jade said, "John actually saved my life."

Well. "Thank you," Lilica told him.

He nodded curtly.

She handed Jade a bag filled with accessories and feminine tops, and her sister thrilled over every gift, warming her heart.

Jade's attention finally moved to Bride. "Who's she?"

"I think she's one of our . . . donors."

Emerald eyes widened with interest. "Really?"

"Really," Bride responded.

As the two girls fell into an easy back-and-forth, getting to know each other, Lilica studied John. Such an odd male. Anytime Jade moved, even the tiniest bit, he moved with her, ensuring that the same distance remained between their bodies, yet he couldn't hide the longing he projected, as if he desperately wanted to touch her.

He was clearly an alpha used to getting his way. So why didn't he simply take what he wanted, damn the consequences? That's what the doctors at IOT had done—what they wanted, when they wanted.

After a waitress had logged in their order, Jade noticed the bandage on Lilica's hand.

"What happened? Do *I* need to punish anyone in particular?"

"Already done." She told her sister what she'd told Dallas. About the Schön, about her suspicions considering Trinity. Tears burned in her eyes, but she blinked them away just as she had throughout her childhood. Tears revealed weakness. Weaknesses were exploited.

"I can't believe . . . how could she . . ." Jade patted her uninjured hand. "We know it's the disease, not her, but more and more I'm having trouble distinguishing between the two. I just . . . I'm so sorry, Lilica. I really am."

"Thank you. But I'm not giving up on her. I can't." It would be like giving up on herself.

"I was able to find her through the spirit realm. I could, in theory, find her again and lead AIR straight to her door. So why didn't she try to kill *me*?"

An excellent question. Clearly she considered Lilica the bigger threat. But why?

"I won't sit idly by while she plots your murder," Jade said.

The fierceness of her tone struck a chord within Lilica. *I'm a priority to her. Higher on the totem than Trinity.*

The knowledge astonished her . . . secretly pleased her. *I'm a horrible person.* "Everything will change when she's cleansed of the disease."

Bride traced a fingertip over the edge of the table. "I hate to ask, but what makes you think Trinity can be cleansed?" Her tone was gentle and without a single hint of malice.

"Hope," Lilica replied honestly.

"But what if you're wrong . . . ?" Still using that gentle tone. "How many will die while she roams free?"

"Maybe I could lock her up in a secret location." A difficult suggestion to make. Captivity would be hell on earth for her sister, reminding her of her childhood, but at least it would buy her time and save others. "Just until we find a cure."

"We've locked up the Schön before." Bride smiled sadly. "The doctors became infected."

"Because they did their doctor thing and worked with infected fluids," John said. "On the other hand, when the hosts died, the disease was able to bypass security barriers to infect those who hadn't handled the fluids."

Jade's brow furrowed. "How can a cure be found if doctors can't work with infected fluids?"

Death couldn't be the only answer. It just couldn't.

"I've told Jade you are both in a position of power," John said, speaking up for the first time. "You have something AIR wants. Bargain."

"Good idea, except we're missing the key ingredient to a successful bargain," Lilica said. "Trust." Although, if she were to bargain with Dallas, she could unearth his every move and countermove, just as he could unearth hers.

Problem one: What was there to bargain over if Trinity couldn't be tested or treated?

Problem two: AIR could plan something despicable without altering Dallas.

Problem three: What if he managed to hide his intentions from her?

Gaze on Jade, she said, "Find me in the spirit realm tonight. We'll talk to Trinity. Her response will dictate our next actions."

The tiny hairs on the back of Lilica's neck suddenly stood up, and a nervous sensation twisted her stomach. Nervous? Why?

The answer stomped into the diner, a little bell over the door tinkling.

Rage pulsed from Dallas as he neared her. She jumped to her feet, her heart thundering against her ribs. When Bride and Jade attempted to stand with her, she held out her arm, a silent demand for the pair to remain seated.

Dallas's gaze locked with hers in challenge before it swept over her new clothes. He missed a step, the intensity of his rage . . . changing. A bolt of desire slammed into her with so much force, she stumbled back.

He stopped a whisper away from her, cupping the back of her neck and hauling her closer—never close enough—bending his head to sniff her.

"That scent . . . it was like a summoning finger. I didn't need to check the tracker."

As he lifted, her attention dipped to his mouth, his beautiful, sensual mouth, and she couldn't look away. Couldn't catch her breath. Couldn't think of anything but kissing him.

"Yes. Kiss." A growl rose from him. A second later, his lips were pressed against hers.

12

Every possessive instinct Dallas possessed continued to scream. Take Lilica here and now. Here. Now. The audience didn't matter. He would strip her out of her new clothes—*Will be careful not to rip, look so good on her, want her to wear them again . . . so I can strip her out of them again*. He would let the world know she belonged to him—and he to her.

Here. He wound his arms around her and cupped her ass, lifting her as he continued to eat at her mouth. Now. She wound her legs around his waist, clinging to him, her breasts smashed against his chest. Her taste . . . as rich and decadent as she smelled, reminding him of everything he'd loved in the past, everything he loved right now, and everything he would love in the future. She was sex, victory, and a high like no other.

No more waiting, he decided. He needed her, and she needed him. He would have her. Here and now. He would give her that orgasm she's been wanting.

Good plan. He bent down to lay her on the table.

A hard shackle suddenly clamped around his bicep and wrenched him backward, forcing him to sever contact with Lilica. He roared with fury. No one kept him from Lilica!

"Enough!" John No Last Name entered his awareness. "This is a public place, Dallas."

Like he cared. He palmed a gun and aimed at the Rakan. In the back of his mind, he heard a woman shout, "No!"

He heard Bride order, "You will not fire. You will put the gun down. Now."

Compulsion. She'd used it on him before, and he'd been unable to stop his body from obeying her. This time he was able to override the compulsion, his finger twitching on the trigger.

"Dallas," Lilica said, her voice trembling. "Put down the gun."

He . . . obeyed. Not because he had to, but because he *wanted* to please her. He sheathed the gun, the fog of desire beginning to clear inside his head.

He *was* in a public place, with windows, and he'd almost taken Lilica on a table. He'd aimed a pyre-gun at a fellow lawman, and he would have shot to kill.

"I'm so sorry," he said, voice ragged. That damn bond! He had to shatter it or accept it, because he clearly couldn't go on like this much longer.

"Trust me. I understand." John cast a side glance at the green-skinned beauty now standing beside Lilica.

Jade. Lady Delirium. The knowledge filled him. Jade had the power to read the thoughts of those around her, as well as amph and borrow alien abilities, but only for a day or two.

"I've got myself under control," Dallas said, and after a slight hesitation, John stepped out of the way. His gaze found Lilica of its own volition. She was panting and wringing her hands as she spoke with Bride about . . . his ears twitched . . . compulsion.

"—the ability myself," she was saying. "I call it voice voodoo and—"

"I call it voice voodoo too!"

You've got to be kidding me. Dallas had just kissed her, had just threatened a fellow agent as well as his best friend's wife, and Lilica was taking a moment to connect with the female.

The two even shared a small smile.

"It requires all my strength, and after I use it," Lilica said, "I'm completely drained for the rest of the day."

"You just need practice," Bride replied. "I mean, think of it this way. If you started lifting weights, you'd have to work with the lighter ones before you could move on to the big ones. The more you lift, the stronger your muscles grow." She lowered her voice. "But be careful where you practice and who you practice on. Among humans, voice voodoo is one of the most feared alien abilities, and where there's fear, there's violence. Oh, and voodoo rarely works on family, and that includes non–blood related family. Intimate ties create an immunity of sorts."

Like the bond he had with Lilica.

"Thank you." She embraced the vampire, actually clinging to her, holding on far longer than could be deemed polite, but Bride didn't seem to mind, was clinging right back. Together, the two reached for Jade, who clung just as tightly.

How little affection the sisters had received throughout their lives.

He rubbed the pang in his chest. Lilica would love to hug Trinity like this. How much would she hate Dallas for destroying the girl?

First lesson he taught would-be agents: Never allow your emotions to supersede logic. Or a job. Or doing what's right.

"Tonight Jade and Lilica are going to use my ability to spirit-walk." John spoke to Dallas but directed the words to Jade as she broke from the embrace. "Before you protest, don't. I'll be with them. They're going to meet with Trinity."

His first instinct? Like hell! "Why?"

"To help decide their next move. They're beginning to accept the need for Trinity's incarceration."

That was something, at least. Far from mollified, however, Dallas stalked to Lilica's side and held out his hand. "Let's go home."

She batted his hand away. "Dream on. My food hasn't arrived."

"Forget the food. It's crap. I'll have crab cakes delivered."

Her midnight eyes widened, and she licked her lips. "Today?"

"So suspicious." He tsk-tsked. "Yes, today."

"Lobster cakes too. And salmon. And you can't toss them in the garbage."

"Deal."

He offered his hand again, and this time, she accepted. Satisfaction bloomed even as the contact nearly sent him into another uncontrollable spiral of lust. He bit his tongue until he tasted blood. *Calm. Steady.*

"What are these cakes?" Jade asked.

"The devil's candy," John muttered, somehow nudging her away from the group without actually touching her.

Through Devyn, Dallas knew a little about the guy's sitch. As an otherworlder foster child, John had endured some of the worst abuse ever recorded. Only a few months ago, he'd been captured while on an off-the-books mission, his skin peeled from his body. And as soon as his "pelt" had grown back, he'd been skinned alive again.

Upon his rescue, Devyn had to lock him up for his own safety. He'd been little more than an animal, snarling and attacking anyone who neared him. The difference in him was astounding, and Dallas wondered whether Jade had anything to do with it.

If she was anything like Lilica, she'd stripped John to the studs and rebuilt him into a stronger, better version of himself.

"You," he said to Bride. "Devyn is looking for you and mumbling about finally giving you the spanking you so richly deserve."

Merriment danced in her emerald eyes. "Ah, yes. A spanking. A one-handed round of applause for my magnificent ass."

Lilica nodded enthusiastically.

"You are a bad influence on my girl," he said, and led Lilica to the door.

"Your girl?" she whispered, her grip tightening on his hand.

Silent, he shouldered his way outside. Releasing her—and swallowing a curse—he scanned the sidewalks. No suspicious activity or—

His gaze returned to the short, curvy blonde across the street. Her back was to him. She peered into a shop window—a shop for power tools. She wore a dark jacket, a hood hiding her hair, but several strands had escaped, pale ribbons whisking in the breeze.

A prickle of awareness crawled down the ridges of his spine.

Lilica gave him a little shove. "Regretting your promise of cakes already?"

Dallas turned to the side, keeping the shop window in his periphery. He could just make out the girl's reflection of health, vitality, and seduction. No doubt about it, he was looking at Trinity Swan, queen of the Schön.

Acting casual, he led Lilica down the street. Trinity followed them. Excellent. He could lead her straight into a trap.

Lilica gasped. "Are you sure it's her?"

Accursed bond! She could spoil everything, alert her sister and send the girl running. "Don't look back. Please. She'll realize we know she's here."

Lilica wound her arm around his, squeezing with more force than necessary, and smiled up at him, as if she were about to tell him a naughty secret. "All right. I concede. I won't wait to speak with her. Just promise me you'll lock her away and let Jade and me try to cleanse her. We'll be the only ones ever at risk."

He blinked in surprise. She'd offered more than he'd ever expected from her. "Lilica—"

"I'm willing to help you, Dallas, but we both need

to get something out of the deal. So let's bargain. And despite everything, let's trust each other to do as promised."

"Your bargain is too open-ended. If you and Jade can't cleanse her after a month . . . five months . . . a year? What then? The longer she's locked away, the higher the probability she'll rot and die or even escape."

He knew he was getting through to her, but he also felt the despair picking at her insides like carrion birds who'd finally found a meal.

"A year, then. Give us a year."

"Judging by her newest victims, she might rot within weeks."

"Just . . . give us a month. Please," she grated.

Shock hit him. Because of the bond, he knew she had sworn never to plead with anyone for anything. "Why are you so concerned with saving her? She tried to kill you."

"And you're clearly an only child or you wouldn't have to ask. The *disease* tried to kill me."

"Sweetheart, she *is* the disease."

She shook her head with violent determination. "The Schön disease was forced on her, and while I couldn't save her then, I *can* do everything in my power to save her now. I must. For years we wove rescue fantasies; they were our only real life raft. The only reason we survived. Now I'm free, but she isn't. She's still locked in a prison of the institute's making."

Comprehension suddenly dawned. She loved her sister, yes, but more than that, she wanted to right what she perceived as a terrible wrong. She tortured herself with thoughts that if she'd just been stronger, she could have helped Trinity before all this started; she refused to accept the fact that she'd been a child herself, with no way to save herself much less her sister.

How could he refuse her?

"Let's see if I can convince Mia." He tapped his ear, turning on his cell phone and dialing his boss's number with only a thought.

As soon as she answered, he explained the situation and the offered deal. He expected her to curse and refuse, and he wasn't disappointed. "This is the best deal you're going to get. Turn it down, and we may not capture Trinity at all. Say yes, and you get two new assets along with a prisoner. Lilica and Jade have abilities like none you've ever seen. You want them. Trust me."

"You sound like Devyn and John," she grumbled. "Both called earlier today."

Laying the groundwork before Dallas accepted what had once seemed like the unacceptable. Nice. "I need your decision. I've got a lock on the Schön right now."

She sucked in a breath. "Yes, you mangy mutt. Yes, I agree."

"Thanks." *Click.*

For once—twice, thrice, whatever—he stopped cursing the bond and enjoyed the benefits. He didn't have to explain the conversation to Lilica. "Let's get Trinity into an alley. Without innocents in the way, I'll be able to shoot her with a gun created just for her and—"

A tendril of betrayal drifted through him.

"—and," he continued through gritted teeth, annoyed by her immediate distrust of his intentions, "prevent her from running away. It'll be a flesh wound; she'll recover while you search for a cure. You'll keep anyone from entering the alley. There's a pyre-gun at my side. It has a stun setting and should work on everyone. If it doesn't, press the small black button on the handle and a blade will pop out."

"Thank you for understanding." She rested her head on his shoulder and wound an arm around his waist, letting her hand slide under his jacket. Her fingers curled around the weapon's handle. "And thank you."

Feels so good against me.

Concentrate. He turned them into the first alley he came across. A massage parlor on one side and a gourmet dessert shop on the other. Immediately they broke apart, Dallas standing in the center, aiming his gun while Lilica shooed away the handful of homeless men and women living in makeshift boxes, shepherding them toward the opposite end of the alley. When she finished, she pressed her back against a brick wall, the weapon steady in her hand.

One minute passed, two . . . five. People continued to meander along the sidewalk, but none were a short, curvy blonde with a hood pulled up. Where was she?

He waited another minute . . . another five . . . ten, but still no sign of her.

"She must have realized we'd pegged her," Lilica said, a slight tremor in her voice.

"Did you tell her?" He lowered his arm, shaking with fury. "Did you have a telepathic conversation with her?"

"No! She blocked me years ago. But even if she hadn't, and I'd tried, *you* would have heard every word."

True. He owed her an apology. "Failure made me cranky. Sorry."

"Whatever."

"Does she have any abilities I don't know about? Teleporting? Invisibility?" Could she be here even now, listening to their conversation?

"No." Her eyes widened. "Unless . . . she stole someone else's abilities. The Teran I fought today. He'd been drained of that particular life force."

The number of problems tripled. Terans were known for stealth, the ability to camouflage themselves, and an aptitude for climbing the unclimbable.

On instinct, he glanced up—and met Trinity's gaze.

13

$\mathcal{H}$er sister had scaled a building to watch Lilica interact with Dallas. But as soon as Dallas had spotted her, she'd hurried away, disappearing over the roof. Dallas had called for reinforcements, and a helicopter had arrived shortly thereafter, but Trinity had already vanished by then.

Infecting men to steal their abilities. Creating an army of soldiers who would do anything she demanded, the need to please her more important than survival. Trying to harm her youngest sister. And that had been her goal, hadn't it? Not to kill Dallas, not even to kill Lilica through Dallas, but to straight-up destroy Lilica in the worst possible way.

Sadness blended with devastation. What would Trinity do next?

Dallas rushed Lilica to his apartment, stationing AIR agents throughout the entire building. He also used special equipment to bar every door and window. AIR issued a statewide alert for all humans and otherworlders to be on the lookout for Trinity Swan. They posted a photo of her beautiful face with the words: *If seen, do not approach. Do not engage. Do not injure. Call AIR.*

Bad move, AIR. Bad. Lilica knew people. Had

hacked into camera feeds throughout the city to watch and observe crowds in the isolated comfort of IOT. If Trinity was spotted, she would be mobbed. Her disease would spread.

My fault. I should have captured her when I had the chance.

In an effort to keep her mind busy, Lilica unpacked the garments and accessories she'd bought during her shopping extravaganza. But she couldn't dredge up any excitement for any of the items. Light-years seemed to have passed, the girl she'd been no longer the girl she was now.

The doorbell sounded. Dallas answered, a gun in hand. A man she'd never met handed him a bag and left without saying a word.

Dallas offered the bag to her. Inside she found every kind of cake he'd promised, plus an array of dessert cakes, but she couldn't bring herself to eat a single one. Her stomach hurt.

She sat on the couch, and he paced in front of her.

"I want you to know I watched video feed of the fight. And before and after the fight. There were cameras everywhere," he said. "You have skill. I was impressed."

"Thank you. But cameras are illegal." She made no mention of the ones she'd hacked. "Over the years, too many people used advanced software to manipulate what others would see."

He ignored her, saying, "You think people stare at you because they considered you a freak. You're wrong. People stare and children point because you are the most exquisite woman on the planet. And because you glow as if you are life itself—as if you are *my* life."

Her eyes widened, her breath catching in her throat. *His* life?

And could he be right? She detected no lie through the bond.

He ran a hand down his face. "Okay. I'm getting delightfully poetic, and that's not good for either one of us. I can't trust myself around you. The things I want to do to you . . ." He stepped toward her, only to stop himself with a curse. "Once I'm inside you, I have a feeling nothing and no one will be able to drag me out. Not duty. Not responsibility. Not all of AIR. And my need is only growing . . . better."

Every word he spoke lit a new fire inside her. No, not true. She always burned for him. His words merely threw accelerant on the flames.

"I'm going to lock myself in the bedroom before I do something stupid," he muttered, and stomped away. The door slammed shut, and the lock engaged.

She stared after him, her heart pounding. She paced, but her desire never cooled.

As one hour passed . . . two . . . she began to hate her body. The aches were worse than ever. Her nipples were hard little points. Her core was drenched and ready. Her limbs trembled. Her skin . . . was too sensitive for her clothing.

She stripped to her brand-new lingerie. Chilled air kissed her, but even that was a stimulant.

Finally she could take it no more. She knocked on the bedroom door. —*Dallas! We're making out, and that's an order. We'll stop before going all the way.*—

Desire was strong, stronger than ever, but this time, not even it could stop the flow of the bond.

—*Said the seductress to the helpless victim. No!*—

—*I'll straddle your waist and grind against your erection. We'll both climax and*—

—*You are* killing *me.*—

—*I'm killing* myself.—

A tension-laden pause stretched between them. —*Screw this. Yes. Hell yes.*— The lock turned—only to turn again a second later. A fist banged into the door, rattling the frame, and this time he shouted his denial. "No!"

—*Don't think you can control yourself?*— She *clawed* at the door, her nails sharp enough to slice little slits into the metal. —*Have a little faith in your strength.*—

—*I know I can't control myself with you!*—

Another hour passed, the most torturous hour she'd ever endured. He'd finally stomped out of his room to demand satisfaction, but she'd been unable to forget his valiant fight and hadn't wanted him to lose, so she'd denied him. The push-pull maddened her!

And she seriously regretted her act of mercy.

When she could fight her arousal no longer, she got down and dirty, trying to bring herself to climax, letting Dallas see, hear, and feel her through the bond. But nothing worked. Satisfaction remained a pipe dream.

Dallas opened the door with frenzied lust in his eyes, took one look at her splayed on the couch, legs open, and slammed the door without touching her. And she needed him to touch her! She was nothing but a husk for hormones and lust.

Finally—blessedly!—the madness began to fade.

"Distract me," she croaked. No more speaking inside his head unless absolutely necessary. Too intimate.

"How? I can't think about anything but your beautiful . . . hot . . . wet . . . delicious body."

Deep breath in . . . out . . . good. "Tonight Jade is going to pull Trinity and me into the spirit world. How is AIR going to capture her?"

"While you're in the spirit realm, you'll use our bond to tell me where Trinity's physical body is located. We'll swoop in and contain it while she is unable to fight back. By the time her spirit returns to it, she'll already be in prison."

A sound plan, and yet Lilica's nerves threw a fit. Surely Trinity would prepare for such an eventuality. "What if she leaves her physical body in some kind of trap?"

"It's a chance we have to take. I'll be careful, though, and so will you. Understand? If you're hurt . . . or worse . . ."

His concern thrilled her, easing an underlay of strain she hadn't known she still carried.

When his internal cell phone rang a few seconds later, they both breathed a sigh of relief. Another distraction! But their relief evaporated in an instant. Devyn delivered devastating news. Bride was missing. No one had seen her since she'd left the diner. Her husband was enraged, frantic, and beyond worried.

If Trinity had taken her . . . harmed her . . .

Motions jerky, Lilica dressed in a black leather vest and a pair of black leather pants.

"It's time." Dallas emerged from the bedroom. His dark hair stuck out in spikes, and his clothes were torn, as if he'd ripped them off and put them back on a hundred times. His tortured expression gutted her.

"If Bride is with Trinity, I'll bring her back," Lilica told him. "No matter what I have to do."

"There's been a change of plans. You stay. Jade goes alone."

"What? Why?" she demanded.

"Trinity is out for blood. You're not going to do anything but anger her." He cared more about Lilica's welfare than Trinity's demise? When had *that* happened?

"I'm going, and that's that. I have to do this." She closed the distance and hugged him tight before returning to the couch. In a tug-of-war, only one side could win. She'd tried to work both sides. Trinity, then Dallas . . . Dallas, then Trinity. Well, no more.

A thousand and one things could go wrong tonight, but she finally had a clear goal: the safety and wellness of the world and the innocents who populated it. She would start with the safety and wellness of Bride.

She blinked, and suddenly she was standing in the center of a thick white fog with Jade at her side.

—*Dallas?*—

—*Yes?*— His voice drifted through her mind, fainter than ever before.

—*I'm with Jade.*—

A pause. —*Be careful, sweetheart. If anything goes wrong . . .*—

—*I know. Save everyone, then run like hell.*—

—No. Hell, no. Save yourself.—

"Is John here?" she asked Jade, forcing thoughts of Dallas to the back of her mind.

"Yes. He's hidden deep in the mist, where he'll remain unless something goes wrong." Her voice grew louder on the last few words, directed not just at Lilica but at John, wherever he was.

"So, what do we do now?"

"Now I take us to Trinity. I've been practicing with John. I can find her while also anchoring you to this realm, allowing you to exit the mist without returning to your body. Come." She linked their fingers and led Lilica forward. Though they moved step by step, the apartment and then the outside world whizzed past at a dizzying speed, leaving Lilica unable to track the path they took.

By the time they stopped, they were in an underground tunnel, dark and damp. Rats—among the only animals to survive the war—scurried along the edges, toward a wall of cages. Fifteen people were trapped inside, all otherworlders.

Trinity's captives provided another hated blow to the memory of the sister Lilica had cherished. Her gaze landed on the dark-haired beauty crouched in the back of the middle cage, and acid filled her stomach. Bride.

I'm doing the right thing. Trinity cannot be allowed to roam free.

Waves of fury and fear pulsed along the bond. *—I found Bride. Trinity has her, and a handful of others. No one looks to be infected, and there's no taint of the Schön disease in the air.—*

—Thank God.—

—I think . . . I think Trinity stole their abilities, though.— Why else would she have taken them and not infected them?

But. If she had taken Bride's voice voodoo . . .

Did she know the ability wouldn't work on Lilica or Jade?

—Thanks to John, we've got a lock on your location.— Dallas's voice again. *—Devyn and AIR are already on the move.—*"

"Our sister is a grade-A bitch," Jade said, her hands fisted.

"Shhh."

"Why? No one can hear or see us."

—What the—Lilica, the Schön have invaded my building.— Dallas's voice filled her head once again, fainter than before, barely audible. *—You have to . . .—*

Silence.

Panic turned her blood to icy sludge and her skin to smoldering coal.

"What's wrong?" Jade demanded.

Her throat was as dry as the air in No Man's Land. "Trinity sent the Schön to Dallas."

Her sister paled. "Did she send her people to John? Without his spirit, he's—"

"I don't know, but he can handle himself." And so could Dallas. There was no need to worry. He'd probably slipped into silence because the bond was weakening. They'd made it through the worst of the animal hunger without having sex.

Sorrow joined her fear. *Going to lose him.*

"They've trained for situations worse than this," Lilica added.

"But John is vulnerable. A body cannot move or fight without a spirit."

"He knows it. He would have taken measures to protect you both."

Jade rallied quickly. "You're right. Of course you're right."

"Now, where's our infamous sister?" Lilica walked toward the cages, amazed by Trinity's capacity for evil. She'd taken men, women, even children. The children were scared and sobbing, the women doing their best to remain strong and unaffected, calming influences. The men—those who weren't cowering in back— were murmuring about ways to escape.

Two half-naked men—guards?—strode from behind a series of boulders. Those boulders were a block to another room in the cavern, she realized. The two men carried a naked male between them, who didn't have the strength to hold himself up, his legs dragging behind him. The scent of the Schön accompanied all three, a mix of sweet, salty, and rot. Each of the three sported at least one open, oozing wound.

"I hate this," Jade said, a tremor in the words. "I hate the woman Trinity has become."

"I know."

The trio stopped at the last cage, the only empty one, and placed the man inside. The guards turned their attention to the cage with the most women, licking their lips as if they were starved.

Brave Bride marched to the forefront and smiled a cold, hard smile. "I'm going to enjoy killing you."

"We're already dead." The guard reached through

the bars to pinch a lock of her hair. "Soon you'll join us."

She yanked the strands from his grip. "How sad for you. You just guaranteed you're going to lose your hand."

"Quiet." Trinity strode out from around the boulders, tightening the belt at her waist to cinch her robe in place. Her pale hair was tousled, her skin pink with health, her eyes glittering with far more power than yesterday.

Lilica pressed her heels into the ground, stifling the urge to leap across the cavern and smack her sister silly.

Trinity stopped before the cages. Searching the masses for her next victim? Then her shoulders squared, her spine as straight as steel. Slowly, so slowly, she turned, her gaze roving here . . . there . . . everywhere. Had she sensed her invisible audience?

"Welcome, sisters. I'm so glad you've arrived." She smiled just as slowly, though her gaze never locked on Lilica or Jade. "I expected you earlier. No matter. Let me tell you how this is going to work."

Oh, yes. She'd sensed her audience.

"Jade, you're going to pull me into the spirit realm. If you fail to return me within five minutes—and trust me, my men will be counting down—everyone in the cages will be decapitated. If I return and my prisoners are gone, I will infect the entire city. I've found a way. . . ."

No. A lie! If she'd found a way, she would have done it already.

—Dallas, you there? Trinity is threatening to infect the city if we don't do what she wants.—

No response. As if the bond was already gone.

Her gut tightened in fear, and her fingers curled into fists. For the first time, she knew she could kill her sister.

She had to try one more time. *—Dallas?—*

Again, silence.

"What should I do?" Jade asked her.

Split-second decision. "Exactly what Trinity demanded. Pull her into the spirit realm."

Jade closed her eyes before nodding. She approached Trinity . . . reached through the girl's body and yanked out her spirit. Suddenly there were two versions of her: the body and the spirit. One unmoving, the other gloating.

"How can you be so cruel?" Jade took a step back.

Trinity flicked her long mane over her shoulder. "I told you. I've learned I can only ever rely on myself. You would do well to learn the lesson yourself. Now. You're going to give me your abilities, strengthening my own. And you," she said to Lilica. "You'll do the same."

Voice voodoo. *Bride's* voice voodoo. No, Trinity didn't know her blood relations were immune.

Trinity had done many terrible things, but this might be the worst. Planning to steal her sisters' powers, leaving them helpless in an unforgiving world.

Jade played along, holding out her hands, as if complying helplessly with Trinity's command. Trinity linked their fingers, initiating skin-to-skin contact.

Sensing what Jade wanted her to do, Lilica clasped her forearm. A second later, Jade whisked the three of them to a new location, preventing Trinity from reentering her body.

A thicker cloud of mist surrounded them, nothing else visible.

With a screech of fury, Trinity ripped free of Jade's hold. "Take me back. Take me back, or you will suffer in ways you can't even imagine."

"Lilica?" Jade asked, unsure now.

"No," she said. To Trinity, she added, "You should have done your homework. Compulsion doesn't work on family."

"You aren't my family!"

The words cut at her. "I suppose we aren't. Not anymore."

Trinity wasn't done. "This is your fault! You should have used your gifts to free us from the institute rather than sentencing Walsh to death. After that day, they kept us so drugged we couldn't even think straight. If I'd been free, I never would've had a worse doctor see to my care. I never would've been forced to absorb the Schön. I never would've done any of this."

So much resentment . . . *Am I truly at fault?* "Is that why you wanted me dead?" Lilica whispered.

"Wanted?" Trinity laughed without humor. "I *want* you dead, and I want to see it happen."

Cutting deeper, making her bleed inside. "Surely you don't hate me so violently because of something I did as a child."

Trinity hissed, "You're the ugly one. The one they

didn't want. And yet here you are, the one bonded to Dallas. The object of his fascination. But he's mine. I have plans for him."

Her sister was . . . jealous? Trinity wanted Dallas to be *her* man.

Rage . . . "Your plans just got canceled." Her sense of possession flared. "He's *mine*, and I'm keeping him."

With a screech, Trinity launched at Lilica and knocked her to the ground. A bundle of fury, Trinity punched, scratched, and kicked her, and Lilica let her do it, accepting the abuse as her due. Punishment for her sins. Trinity was right. At least in one regard. Lilica should have worked on escape rather than retribution.

But the next thing she knew, Jade was there, pulling Trinity off her and . . . not letting go.

Trinity began to tremble. "No. No! Stop." A scream parted her lips. "Noooo!"

"You don't get to hurt my sister." Jade finally released her, and Trinity went limp.

"No," Lilica said, shaking her head. "Jade! Tell me you didn't—"

"I did." The green-skinned beauty eyed her with a devastating mix of determination and remorse before grabbing her hand and yanking her to her feet. "I stole the Schön life force. Took what I could, anyway. She's weakened, and we . . . we have to act fast."

14

*L*ilica woke up crying, and it broke something inside Dallas. Resistance, maybe. Or a link to a past he would rather forget, where a little boy feared losing the people he loved and did his best to remain detached.

This beautiful, strong woman should only ever laugh . . . or moan with pleasure.

When more than twenty Schön had swarmed the apartment building, Dallas had remained by Lilica's side. He and the agents positioned nearby had put their SS guns to good use, bagging and tagging every soldier. Trinity had planned ahead, but so had he. No one had reached Lilica's vulnerable body. He would have died first.

Now he gathered her in his arms, needing contact the way he needed air. She buried her face in the hollow of his neck and wrapped her arms around him, clinging to him as she sobbed, her hot tears trickling over his skin.

He combed his fingers through her hair. "Trinity's men had orders to hide her body the moment her spirit left it. AIR was able to free her prisoners, but not capture her. Not at first. John followed her and was able to lead us straight to her. She's now in custody and on her way to a holding cell."

"Good. I'm glad. But Jade . . ." Shudders racked Lilica. "She stole a portion of the disease, as well as a portion of the otherworld abilities Trinity acquired."

Silence. Such oppressive silence.

"She's going to be all right," she said. "Yes? She's never kept what she's stolen. Ever. She's never been strong enough. The abilities have always returned to their owners."

"I don't know. Nothing like this has ever happened before."

"I want to see her. I *need* to see her."

"She'll have to be locked away. For her own good," he added before she could protest. "For yours too. For everyone in New Chicago."

Her nails dug into his shoulders. "I don't care. I love her, and I have to know she's being treated well."

"Yeah. I thought you'd say that."

He made some calls before driving her to the facility in No Man's Land, where AIR had also locked away the rest of Trinity's victims. Lilica stared out the window, her features blank. The worst part? He couldn't feel her emotions through the bond.

Why couldn't he feel her emotions?

As soon as he was parked in front of the warehouse, he gave her a mask and gloves to cover every area of exposed skin. The filters in the nostril holes would prevent her from breathing in the acidic air.

"I used to live out here, you know," she said, her voice soft and yet heavy. "The institute is only a few miles away. From one prison to the other."

Wind whistled as it swept over the car, and sand

pelted the doors. *Ping, ping, ping.* An eerie soundtrack. The only one audible within the thirty-mile stretch of desolation and ruin. This was no place for a child.

"Your life is better now," he said, squeezing her hand.

"Is it, though? Both of my sisters are suffering."

The words haunted him as they raced inside the building. Armed guards were hidden throughout the terrain, and the number of ID scans had tripled. After decontamination, Dallas and Lilica stripped off the extra gear. He took her hand, holding on tight. Too tight. But he couldn't help himself. He felt as if he would lose her. As if he was *already* losing her.

Mia was there, staring into Trinity's cell. "I can't believe we have her."

Trinity huddled on the floor, despite the cot in the corner. Her pale hair was tangled, her skin smeared with dirt, but she bore no sores.

Dallas said nothing, following Lilica.

"Lilica," Trinity called. "Lilica!"

Lilica paid her eldest sister no heed, moving past her cell to stop in front of Jade's. John was there, silent but not stoic as he watched her pace from one side to the other. Fury pulsed from him.

Lilica trembled as she flattened her hand on the glass. The room had all the comforts of home. A soft bed with even softer covers. A toilet hidden by a privacy screen. A minifridge. Even a holoscreen TV.

Jade noticed her and rushed over, pressing her palm against Lilica's. Unlike Trinity, she was covered with open sores. Her once silky hair was now limp and dull.

"Why did you do it?" Lilica demanded.

Tears welled in Jade's red-rimmed eyes. "It was the only way."

"It wasn't. The disease is going to return to her, but part of it may stay inside you, your own personal infection. You might have done it for nothing. Nothing!"

The hurt Lilica projected, the pain . . . as if she'd finally been crushed. The doctors who'd raised and tortured her hadn't been able to break her, but her sisters had managed to do so. Tears burned the backs of *Dallas's* eyes, and he had to blink them away.

—Everything could work out for the best. Let's not give up hope.—

He pushed the thought into her mind, but seconds passed . . . a minute . . . and there was no response. Could she not hear him anymore?

Frowning, he dug through her memories, the ones the bond had stored in hidden corners of his mind. Determined to find the reason, and the solution. To his consternation, many of the memories were no longer as clear, as if the corners they'd been stored in had been flooded, the boxes ruined. Even so, he found the answer he sought.

He and Lilica hadn't had sex, and the bond was fading. Soon he would have no tie to her at all.

Every cell in his body shouted a denial. He wasn't sure when he'd stopped resenting the bond, or when he'd come to rely on it, expect and need it, but he had. It had happened, and he didn't want to go a single day without a tie to her. She meant something to him. More than he'd ever thought possible.

But . . . did she mean enough for him to make things permanent?

How did she feel about him?

"What are we going to do if you remain sick?" Lilica whispered.

Jade offered her a sad smile. "We're going to say good-bye. The Schön will die one way or another—because you're going to kill it."

"Kill *you*, you mean." Lilica slammed her fist into the wall. The glass was bullet-, pyre-, and shatter-proof, and she hissed, her knuckles crunching, her skin splitting.

A wound he didn't acquire. He bit the inside of his cheek.

She glared at her sister. "You would leave me on my own? To endure this terrible world without you?"

She would never again be on her own. She would always have Dallas.

The thought jolted him, because suddenly he knew. Yes. She meant enough to him to make things permanent. She meant *everything* to him, and right now she was breaking what was left of his heart.

"I'm sorry," Jade said, her tears continuing to rain. "I'm so sorry. But now you have a chance to help Trinity. The one you wanted."

"I don't want it anymore." A screech from the depths of her soul.

Jade bowed her head. "I'm sorry," she repeated.

Dallas wound an arm around Lilica's waist. "We won't know if the disease is going to return to Trinity until tomorrow morning, or how Jade will be affected afterward. Let's go home and wait there."

Her shoulders rolled in, and she allowed him to lead her away from the cell without protest . . . down the hall, where she once again ignored Trinity.

"Lilica! Please," Trinity called. "I'm sorry too. I never meant—"

Lilica missed a footstep. "Begging," she whispered. "But it's too little too late."

As they entered the decontamination room, she swallowed what looked to be a sob. Together they reapplied the safety masks and gloves, and Dallas ached for her all the while. For the girl she'd been and the woman she was.

Lilica remained silent the entire drive home. He reached for her hand, but she drew back, and he didn't need the bond to tell him why. She was preparing herself for their separation, arming herself against him.

He gnashed his teeth, but kept silent. She was hurting right now, and he wouldn't add to her problems.

He hustled her inside the apartment; as soon as the door was locked, a laser bar engaged, and he kissed her temple and said, "Wait here." He strode to his bedroom, where he dug inside his dresser.

If he was going to do this, he was going to do it right.

He held the small gold ring to the light. Worth more in sentiment than cash, but all the best things were.

It had first belonged to his grandmother. A thousand times over, his mother could have sold it. She *should have* sold it. They'd desperately needed every penny for food. Instead, she'd saved it, as if her parents' love and affection were the only ray of hope in the doom and gloom of her life.

Lilica had missed out on so many human experiences, but no more. Not on his watch. More than that, she needed as many ties to him as he could give her. Hell, *he* needed those ties.

He needed a bond . . . in body and in soul. Marriage could protect her—the sister of a predatory otherworlder—in ways humans would respect.

He strode out of the bedroom, but skidded to a stop when he spotted Lilica. She sat in the recliner, gloriously naked and partially hidden by shadows. One hand held a glass of iced whiskey while the other clutched the arm of the chair.

"Look how pretty," she said, and a bolt of sizzling lust struck him. Just like in the vision. She cupped her mouthwatering breasts. "We can pretend. You like to pretend, yes? You are a man, and I am a woman. Nothing more, nothing less."

This. This was the vision coming to life.

He shot hard as a rock. "Sex?"

"No. It'll be like before." She set the glass on the side table and stood, the light falling over her, revealing small but pert breasts, nipples like diamonds, the scrolls etched into her skin glowing. "In the shower."

Her delectable scent hit him, arousal in its purest form, and he nearly fell to his knees. "I want more," he croaked. "I want sex."

She frowned at him. "But . . . the bond."

"I know. I want the bond too."

Her eyes widened, the pulse at the base of her neck fluttering wildly.

"I want the bond. And I want marriage, want us *legally* bound in front of witnesses. I want you to become my permanent inconvenience."

"Marriage?" she gasped out, as if the notion were preposterous. "Permanence?"

He didn't back down. He couldn't. Somehow, she'd become the most important part of his life. It had happened too quickly. Fine. Whatever. But the simple fact was, it had happened. He could have lost her today. He wasn't prepared to lose her.

"I want you, all of you. I want everything you have to give." He closed the distance and held out the ring. "I want you to bear my name. I want to be your partner. A *legal* pain in your ass. I want you with me, always and forever."

Her hand fluttered over her mouth. "Dallas . . . I don't . . . I can't believe . . ."

"We'll never be alone again. No matter what happens, we'll have each other."

"But . . . *why* do you want me? I'll never be your type, and my situation is—"

"You are my type," he interjected. "You are my *only* type. And we'll deal with your situation the way we'll deal with all our problems. Together."

She trembled as he slid the ring on her finger. She looked at the band, then at Dallas, then at the band again.

"I know it's not much. I'll get you something better. Just say yes."

"Why would I want something better? There is

nothing better. This is absolutely *exquisite*," she whispered as she pet it.

With a groan, she leaped into his arms, smashing her lips against his.

He opened for her, their tongues thrusting together, rolling and dancing. A mating dance. Her sweet taste sparked a passion-fever inside his veins, her titillating scent enveloping them both, creating a cocoon. No one and nothing else existed outside this moment.

She tugged at his clothing, ripping the material. "Get naked. Get naked now."

Need consumed Lilica. As soon as Dallas was bare, she forced herself to slow. He was her man. Willingly. Happily. She wanted to know more about him. *All* about him. Wanted to save him.

She caressed the musical notes etched into his pec. "Tell me," she beseeched.

His pupils flared. "For you? Anything." He kissed her temple. "My mother was an Onadyn user, and during the rare moments she was lucid and cheerful, she would sing to me."

Onadyn. A drug some otherworlders needed to survive Earth's atmosphere. Humans used it to get high, even though it destroyed portions of their brains.

Her fingertips stroked a path of fire to his rib cage, where the tree of life bloomed.

"A reminder every time I look into the mirror," he said. "Every word and every action is a seed.

One day something *will* grow from it. Whether good or bad. Just depends on the kind of seed I planted."

"That is beautiful." *He* was beautiful. She bent down to flick her tongue over one of his nipples, then the other. "And the eyes on your feet?"

One corner of his mouth quirked up. "A reminder that someone is always watching." He dragged his fingertips along the *tätoveerimine* marking her shoulders. "The first time I noticed these, I wanted to lick them. I still want to lick them."

"Me first." She pushed him into the chair, and he stared at her, utterly transfixed, as she dropped to her knees. "I'm going to be much nicer to these from now on." She kissed one testicle, then the other. "I promise."

He chuckled, and she loved the sound. As charming as he was, as carefree as he sometimes seemed, very few people could make him laugh with genuine amusement.

I am one of the few. I'm special!

She curled her fingers around the base of his erection. "As you may or may not know, I'm fascinated with this part of you." Out flicked her tongue. She traced the outer edge, then the slit in the center. A bead of desire welled, and she lapped it up.

He sucked in a breath—and she sucked him to the back of her throat, soon growing used to the way he stretched her jaw.

"I've wanted you too badly for too long," he rasped. "You keep that up, and I'm going to blow in your mouth. I'd rather blow inside you."

Inside her . . . yes. Her first time. *Their* first time. She stood and straddled his lap, the long, hard length of him bobbing between them. "I will finish you in my mouth next time."

"And you won't hear any complaints from me. Maybe a few commands for you to work me harder and faster, but that will depend on your skill level. We'll evaluate and discuss."

"Funny man." She wrapped her hand around his shaft. "Are you sure you want to tease me when I have control of your precious?"

"Yes. Teasing you is my new favorite hobby." He kneaded her breasts, his thumbs brushing over the puckered crests. "Such a perfect view."

As he leaned forward to run his tongue over the scrolls etched on her shoulders, sensation shot straight to her core, where she ached with molten desire. This man . . . oh, this man . . .

He was every dream she'd ever had, every dream she'd never known she'd had, and every dream she would *ever* have. And he wanted her too. Wanted her fiercely, madly, deeply, as if she were a prize.

"You *are* a prize," he said, and tortured her nipple with a glorious suck.

The bond had begun to strengthen again! For a moment she could even see herself through his eyes. An exotic creature with skin of ebony silk, extraordinary markings to explore, hair a mane of jet-black satin, and eyes as mysterious as a midnight sky filled with countless stars glittering with abandon. Her curves were an irresistible smorgasbord. An all-you-can-eat buffet.

He smiled at her slowly, wickedly, before fitting his teeth over her other nipple. He did something with his tongue . . . something strange and wondrous, as if his Arcadian powers stroked her too. Stroked *deeper.*

She cried out in bliss, her hands moving to his scalp, her nails digging in deep to hold him in place. He caressed down . . . down the ridges of her spine before cupping her ass to yank her closer. Her core rubbed against his shaft, the pleasure too much but not enough.

"It's as if you were created just for me," he said, the awe in his tone undoing her. "As if I gave the lab a list, and they made my perfect woman."

The warmth of her breath fanned the shell of his ear before she bit the lobe . . . kissed the stubble along his jaw . . . finally reaching his lips. As their tongues thrust together, he reached underneath her to slide a finger deep, deep inside her, making her gasp.

"So hot," he praised. "So wet."

"More." Her voice was so thick with arousal, she sounded drunk.

"I'll give you whatever you need. Always." He fed her another finger, stretching her, moving the two in and out of her, mimicking the motions of their tongues. They weren't just having sex with their mouths and his fingers, they were making love.

"Don't stop. Please, don't stop. Please . . . give me more. All."

I'm willing to beg?

As a child, she'd refused to beg Walsh for mercy. Refused to beg for treats or scraps of affection. She'd feared revealing a weakness, a vulnerability. Had only broken to help her sister. Nothing else had ever tempted her. Until this man. Yes, she would beg. Wanting him was a very real part of her being. The fabric from which a new, stronger Lilica had been made.

"Would rather die than stop." —*Can't get enough of her. Will never get enough.*—

His thoughts drifted through her mind, as rapturous as his touch. Need for him grew into a frenzied rush. She bit his tongue and sucked on the wound, savoring the taste of his blood. Her head fogged, making her ravenous for more. The same hunger consumed *him*. His hips jerked up, his rigid length sliding more firmly between her legs, creating a friction that sparked a thousand new fires in her veins.

She flattened her hand on his chest, just above his heart. The muscle was as hard as the rest of him, the organ itself pounding swift and erratic. Pushing herself up so that her breasts hovered just out of reach, she peered into his eyes.

"Your other women—"

He scowled, interjecting, "No other women. Can't remember them."

Tenderness swamped her, but she continued as if he hadn't interrupted. "—they didn't know you, because you wouldn't let them. I know you, and I want to see you as you fill me."

"Yes. I'm going to fill you up, brand you, make you mine in body as well as soul." With his fingers anchored on her hips, holding her tight enough to bruise, he guided her to the tip of his erection.

She reveled in his strength.

"I don't want anything between us," he rasped. "Do you?"

She hadn't even considered using protection, had been more concerned with the present than the future. But, like him, she wanted nothing between them. Not this first time.

"I just want you. And don't worry. I won't get pregnant. The birth control I was given hasn't yet worn off." She pressed down, taking an inch of him . . . tried to take more but couldn't. He was so big, so wide, and she needed a moment to adjust. Panting, she said, "No . . . going back . . . after this."

"Don't want to go back." Sweat trickled down his temples, falling to his shoulders, rolling down his chest. All the while, their gazes held. His pupils were blown, arctic irises hidden by a pool of black. And . . . she gasped. Amidst the black were pinpricks of light, like the ones found within *her* eyes.

They were becoming . . . one?

The knowledge electrified her, aroused her to the point of madness. With a desperate cry, she slammed down on his erection, burying his length inside her. A sharp lance of pain quickly vanished beneath an onslaught of undiluted pleasure; she was fully seated on him.

"Okay? All right?" he panted.

"Good, so good."

He levered himself to his feet, still inside her, his hands on her ass to keep her balanced as he walked forward, every step wringing a moan from her. Sliding him in and out. In the bedroom, he eased her onto the edge of the mattress while he remained standing.

She lay before him, a feast for the taking . . . and take he did.

He pulled out of her slowly . . . only to slam back into her swiftly. The pleasure—oh! For a moment, she was almost blind with it. "Dallas."

"My Lily." He slid out, slammed in again, and hissed a curse.

"Yes!" Enjoying the ferocity of the ride, she arched her back and reached overhead to fist the covers.

His—control—snapped.

He hammered into her again and again, completely unrestrained. She loved it. Her head thrashed, and her hips rose to meet him. Without slowing his thrusts, he leaned down, taking one of her legs with him. Her thigh pressed against the mattress, making her more open to him, more vulnerable.

He kissed her then, his taste as drugging as his sex. Pressure built inside her. Pressure and pleasure, pleasure and pressure, until the two were the same. A heady combination. She bit at him, sucked on his lip, demanded more . . . more . . . oh, he gave her more!

She gasped his name until she was no longer coherent, until all she could do was moan and groan. He reached between them, his fingers finding the heart of her, where she throbbed. With a single press, he sent her hurtling over the edge, screaming her release.

As her inner walls clenched and unclenched around him, he thrust into her a final time, threw back his head, and roared.

15

*D*allas stood under a spray of hot water, his mind in turmoil. He'd left Lilica sleeping in bed. His woman. The girl who'd gifted him with her virginity. He'd been her first, and he would be her only. Just as she'd been *his* first. The first to work her way past his defenses and reach the man inside.

As they'd cuddled, enjoying the afterglow, he couldn't help but tease her. "*That* was an orgasm."

She'd slapped his chest. "Figured that out on my own, thanks."

"Just so you know, I'm the only man in the entire world who can give you one. Sure, your friends will try to tell you any man can do it, but they are lying."

She'd snickered, and he'd cherished the sound of her amusement.

Just as wondrous, she'd trusted him enough to fall asleep in his arms.

Though he'd wanted to wake her and shower with her, he'd known just how badly she needed rest. She'd gotten none the night before, and he doubted she'd get much in the coming days. Plus, she had to be sore.

Soon, her sisters had to be dealt with.

A few minutes ago, he'd been as high as a kite,

ready to conquer the world. He and Lilica were bonded for good. She'd agreed to marry him. His body had never been so completely sated. Then he'd gotten a call from Mia. Trinity was sick again . . . and Jade hadn't healed.

Mia now thought the only way to contain the Schön once and for all was to burn the hosts with a full-body SS. Maybe the alien hosts would die, maybe not. Maybe they'd heal and need to be burned again, maybe not. But even trapped inside a dead host, the Schön could live on, perhaps dormant. If ever some-one opened up the bodies, all bets were off.

If AIR performed such a deed, Lilica would rage. And rightly so. It was cruel. Beyond cruel. And it might not work.

And what if she blamed Dallas for it? Would she ever be able to forgive him?

He wasn't sure *he* would be able to forgive *himself*. But AIR couldn't let Lilica's sisters go free. Trin-ity would continue to spread the disease. Maybe Jade would resist the need to spread it, maybe she wouldn't . . . if measures weren't taken, she would die and the disease would spread anyway, finding a new host—maybe even if she were shot with the SS. Right now, there were too many unknown variables and zero room for mistakes.

This was a lose-lose situation all the way around.

He needed to speak with Lilica. And whatever she wanted him to do, he would do.

Determined, he shut off the water, towel dried, and dressed in the white button-down, slacks, and boots required for the job.

Hinges squeaked as he stepped out of the steam-filled bathroom. He moved toward the bed—and drew up short.

Lilica lay on the floor, fully dressed despite the fact that she'd been naked when he'd left her. Her eyes stared out at nothing, the stars no longer inside them, no longer twinkling, blood smeared at the corners. Blood smeared the corners of her mouth too.

Horror drilled him to his knees. How had she . . . what could have . . . no. *No.* He crawled toward her, his mind locked on a single thought. No! She couldn't be dead. The bond—

The bond!

"Dallas?"

Her voice! He whipped around, seeing a very much alive and well Lilica standing in the doorway. Her bloodied image had already vanished from the floor.

Another waking vision, he realized. Relief chased away the horror as he dove on her, wrapping his arms around her, locking her against him, taking comfort in the beat of her heart.

"I thought you were—"

"I know." She clung to him just as tightly. "I saw it too. And I know about my sisters. I heard your thoughts."

"I'm so sorry, sweetheart."

"I think . . . I think what I'm planning to do is what caused—causes—my death."

"What are you planning?" He lifted his head, his hands on her shoulders, holding her in place. "I won't let you put yourself in danger."

"I must. I have to try to save Jade."

"She wouldn't want you to endanger yourself."

"You're right, but I can't make my decisions based on the wants of others. I can only do what's right."

"This isn't right." He gave her a hard shake. "Dying isn't right. Leaving me isn't right." *He* would rather die than live without her. Not that he would go on living. They were bonded. What happened to one would happen to the other. "You'll be putting *me* in danger."

"Just as you'll be putting me in danger every time you leave to do your job. But I'm not going to stop you. Your job is part of who you are." She placed a soft kiss on his lips. "I would rather die knowing I tried than live knowing I did nothing. And now that we know a possible result, we can take measures to prevent it from happening. We can have medics on standby. That *is* why you have visions, isn't it? So you can change the outcome of what you see?"

"Maybe. Or maybe I'm being warned about what will happen no matter what."

Another kiss. "Then we're screwed either way, so why not go out fighting?"

Dallas led Lilica through the warehouse in No Man's Land, his footsteps heavy, his heart and stomach contemplating switching places.

Devyn waited in the hallway entry that led to the cages, his expression wiped of its usual smirk. He ignored Dallas in favor of hugging Lilica. "Thank you. Thank you for saving Bride. I will be forever in your debt."

"Yes, you will," she said, and Dallas smiled. His first since Mia had called him, but it didn't last long. "I'm going to expect regular payments."

"And you'll receive them."

"All right," Dallas said. "The chitchat can wait." A sense of urgency beleaguered him. If they didn't put Lilica's plan into motion soon, he was going to knock her out, carry her away, and deal with the fallout later.

He clasped Lilica's hand and drew her toward Mia, who stood in front of Trinity's cage. The disease had most definitely returned. Her hair now hung in limp tangles around her emaciated face. Her pale skin sagged, and sores circled her bloodshot eyes.

Because she hadn't been allowed to share the taint with others, the toxins had built up inside her. They were *feeding* on her.

Trinity spotted Dallas and stretched out her hand. "Help me." Her voice was weak, frayed at the edges. "Help me."

This. This was his vision. If only he could shoot her, ending the whole debacle here and now.

"Help me."

The vision hadn't changed the future, he realized, but had led him straight to it. Same with the one he'd had of Lilica in his chair. The third waking vision would happen. He knew it with every cell of his body.

"Help . . . please."

"You can't do this," he told Lilica. "You just can't. We'll find another way."

"There isn't time to find another way. You know that."

"If . . . live . . . they . . . live . . . die . . . they die," Trinity said between panting breaths.

A suspicion arose. What if she wasn't talking about her people but about her sisters?

He swallowed bile as a horrifying thought dawned. If he'd killed her at any point in the past, he wouldn't have met Lilica.

Mia pressed a button, and a door between the two cages opened, allowing Jade to step inside the cell with Trinity. In the corridor, John, who'd stood sentry all night, moved with Jade, stopping beside Mia.

Trinity disregarded her sister, remaining focused on Dallas.

Jade had continued to deteriorate, her once vibrant skin now littered with sores.

Dallas's hand twitched on the handle of the SS, which was sheathed at his side.

John spotted the action and growled at him.

"Lilica, please," Dallas said, willing to beg.

As she turned to meet his gaze, he grabbed hold of her and kissed the air out of her lungs.

When they pulled away, she lifted her chin and squared her shoulders, and he knew. He knew she wouldn't back down.

"I love you," she told him. "I love you with all my heart."

World. Rocked. He'd felt her feelings, but hearing the words . . .

She wasn't done. "I love you just as I love those girls. Trust me when I say I will not lose the ones I love. I'll fight. I'll *never* give up. And I'll survive." Then she nodded to Mia, who pressed another button.

The front door opened, and Lilica stepped inside the cell. Dallas followed her and the door closed behind him, preventing either infected girl from racing out. Not that they had any interest in leaving.

"We do this together," he snapped. "And I love you too."

Both Trinity and Jade peered at him as if he were the last slice of beef at a free buffet. The disease, and the need to spread it, was taking over their minds.

Trinity even found the strength to stand. She licked her lips and smiled, the sweet fragrance of her pheromones intensifying in an effort to send him into a fit of lust.

Both women prowled around him, sharks that had scented blood.

"I'm going to make all your dreams come true," Trinity said.

As she spoke, her image changed. For a moment he saw her. Not her sickness but her beauty. A trick, nothing more. A means of her survival. "The only way to do that is to keep your mouth shut."

Lilica grabbed Jade's hand, and the girl blinked at her rapidly, as if coming out of a trance.

Moaning, Jade said, "You can't touch me, Lil."

"It's fine. I'm fine. Now, take Trinity's hand. Please."

Jade frowned, but did as commanded. Trinity tried to rip free, but Jade held on with every bit of strength she had left. The three formed a circle.

Again Trinity tried to pull free, but Lilica stopped her by creating a suction the infected girl couldn't break. The parasite . . . it threw itself against the connection, doing everything in its power to get inside Lilica too. But she kept a stream of power at the edges, creating a barrier.

"Jade, I want you to steal as much of the Schön as you can from Trinity. Just like before. The more equally distributed it is between you, the better the likelihood of saving you both."

Trinity began to buck.

"Done," Jade said through clenched teeth, as if speaking had become a chore.

Dallas braced himself for what came next.

Wasting no time, Lilica closed her eyes. He knew she'd just sent a bolt of power to each girl, strengthening the Schön part of their beings. Too much power too fast would, they hoped, cause the parasite to shut down and die—like pumping a heart full of adrenaline until it basically exploded—while leaving the girls alive.

Jade cried out, and Trinity screamed. A tear streamed down Lilica's cheek, followed by a bead of blood, but she sent another bolt of power. This time, her sisters began to convulse.

Dallas wanted to stop the proceedings but shouted through the bond instead. —*Do it! Give them everything you've got! Starting slow isn't doing anyone any good*—

Bolt, bolt, bolt. All three girls quaked. Blood poured from Lilica's nose and the corners of her mouth.

Dallas took a step toward her, intending to rip her from the circle, but the minutest bit of power traveled through the bond and zapped his Arcadian side. He felt as if he were suddenly hooked to a generator, his nerve endings on fire. Every hair on his body stood on end, his back bowing, his head thrown back. He was lifted off the floor, where he levitated, unable to move.

More crying from Jade. More screaming from Trinity. No, not true. All three girls were now screaming. *He* was shouting curses. Lilica was beginning to wilt. She was draining herself, giving every ounce of her power away, leaving nothing for herself.

She needed an amph, but there wasn't another—

Yes. There was! Him. Through their bond. When she'd first bonded to him, she'd amphed him, and he'd amphed her. Concentrating, he sent his own bolt of power rushing along the bond. A second later, he eased back to the ground, the strain leaving him.

But Lilica screamed, and he feared he'd done more harm than good. He started to withdraw the power—but she lifted her head, her spine straightening. She was strengthening! He sent another bolt, and another, allowing her to send an even stronger bolt of power to her sisters.

Just like that, all three girls toppled to the floor, the suction and the circle broken.

Lilica's mind went black—a blackness trying to close around Dallas's mind as well. He fought it. Trinity was on the ground, reaching for Lilica, her face bloodied.

Maybe she was still infected, maybe not. He wasn't taking any chances. Dallas unsheathed his gun, set it to stun, and shot her. Then he too gave in to the dark and passed out.

"Lilica. Wake up for me, sweetheart."

Beep, beep, beep.

Lilica blinked open her eyes. Dallas hovered over her, dark hair shagging over his forehead.

Beep, beep, beep.

"There you are." He smiled at her—the devastating smile that rendered her useless. He caressed her jawline. "Tsk, tsk. Sleeping on the job. I might not have asked you to marry me if I'd known you were so lazy."

Beep, beep, beep.

"Please. You can't get enough of me. But . . . where am I?" She scanned her surroundings and frowned. A hospital room. Tubes extended from her arms and connected to machines. "What happened?"

"You did it. You killed the Schön."

Her eyes widened. "And my sisters?"

"They're alive and well. You should probably get used to hearing this, because I have a feeling I'm going to be saying it a lot in the coming years, but . . . you were right. About the vision. About the amph."

"I was right. I was right, and you were wrong!" A sob of relief escaped her. She jolted upright, throwing her arms around him. "Thank you. Thank you for trusting me and helping me. I would have died without you. They would have died and . . . and . . ." More sobs.

"Jade is in a room with John, who won't let anyone near her. I think we may be attending a wedding in the future. Or maybe not. He refuses to touch her, and she keeps yelling obscenities at him." He leaned back to gently wipe away her tears. "Trinity is being treated in lockup. Where she'll stay until she's sentenced or exonerated of all the charges against her."

"Trinity," she said, and sighed. "It really was the disease driving all her decisions and actions. Even Jade came after you when she was infected. I have to forgive her, don't I?"

"Sweetheart, we both know you *want* to forgive her."

"That's fair. I do. I've missed her so much."

"You'll be a family again."

"But if she makes a pass at you—"

"Don't worry. I'll shoot her dead this time."

"We'll shoot her. Together," she said.

He nodded. "Together."

Her own grin finally began to bloom. "Because you love me?"

"Because I love you," he said with a laugh. "You're going to take advantage of that fact for the rest of your life, aren't you?"

"Oh, most certainly. Lady Wicked wins her man—and keeps him in line." She patted his chest. "Remember the time you negated my powers and the time you made me pass out?"

He pressed his forehead against hers and groaned.

"I'll feel better about our past as soon as you go get me some crab cakes. And a soda. Maybe a brownie. I'll let you decide about the fat grams we consume. And I want a robodog. We're a family now, and we should have—"

"Woof."

The noise came from behind and below him. Her eyes widened, and she gasped. She looked past him to see a metal dog bouncing on the floor, panting up at her with adoring eyes and wagging a tail. Tears spilled down her cheeks.

"You already got me a dog," she whispered.

"His name is Beetlejuice."

"Mine!" She pushed Dallas out of the way to get to her new dog, cuddling the creature to her chest.

"Remember the time I bought you the robodog of your dreams?" he asked.

"No. Now, make yourself useful and go get me those crab cakes."

He laughed. "I knew you'd say that."

She smiled her widest smile at him. "Because you know me and you love me anyway."

He blew her a kiss and headed for the door, saying over his shoulder, "Sweetheart, knowing you *is* loving you."